The
Astronaut
and the
Star

JEN COMFORT

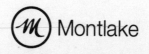

Published by Montlake, Seattle

www.apub.com

Amazon, the Amazon logo, and Montlake are trademarks of Amazon.com, Inc., or its affiliates.

ISBN-13: 9781542032605
ISBN-10: 1542032601

Cover design by Hang Le

Printed in the United States of America

To PopPop:
Thank you for passing the writing genes on to me.
In your honor, I'll try to get rich and famous.

CHAPTER 1

Wes's off-key rendition of Europe's "The Final Countdown" crackled over her headset.

Reggie took a long, deep breath. Her exhale misted the visor of her helmet before dissipating so she could see the drab instrument panel she was working on. If she looked up and out into space, her entire field of vision would be swallowed by the vivid blues and greens of Earth, and she'd have to deal with the dizzying but false sensation of falling back down to the surface.

"Wes, how you doing on timeline?" she asked. They'd been allocated six and a half hours for this run-through, but yesterday two of her colleagues had completed the exercise in a record-breaking six hours and three minutes. Reggie could beat that.

After all, astronaut Regina "Reggie" Hayes had done everything else she'd set her mind to do. Before the age of thirty-five, Reggie had graduated with honors from MIT, deployed twice as a combat naval aviator, finished a master's degree in planetary geology, accumulated over two thousand hours of flight time as a test pilot, and—after being selected for NASA's astronaut program on her first try—already completed a coveted mission aboard the International Space Station.

Aside from one small incident six months ago, Reggie was—as they liked to say—the best of the best. Above all, she was a *Hayes*, and the Hayeses didn't sully their unblemished reputation for excellence by accepting second place. Ever.

If only Wes would cooperate.

His humming cut off. In his languorous southern drawl he replied, "Running a little long, but nothing to worry about."

Of course he was. Irritation swelled in the back of her throat, but she compartmentalized it before it spilled out. Emotions were an unnecessary distraction in space, where even the smallest screwup could be fatal. More importantly, she couldn't afford to lose her cool—not with the board narrowing down their Artemis III lunar mission short list this week.

If all went according to plan and Reggie was selected to join the crew, she'd have the opportunity to win the coveted title of "First Woman on the Moon."

It was a goal she'd been striving toward with single-minded purpose for well over a decade.

A legendary, awe-inspiring accomplishment worthy of history books.

Hell, her mother might even deign to have her secretary send a congratulatory card! Now *that* would make not murdering Wes during this training exercise worth it. No matter how much he deserved it.

Reggie held up her left arm until the checklist attached to the wrist of her spacesuit was visible. She was on her last task. "I'm almost done over here. Why don't I head on over?"

"I got this, Hayes."

Do you, though? Reggie stifled the retort. "Good to hear," she said instead. Maybe she'd sounded a tad sarcastic—so hard to tell with all the static.

Okay, so she didn't exactly play well with others, but she'd managed to get this far without winning popularity contests, hadn't she? Her temperament had only gotten her into trouble one time. That had been an outlier, one she'd continue to overcome by being so damn good at her job that nothing else mattered.

"How about a song request instead? You said no country, right? Wait, I think I've got just the song for you . . ." She could almost hear Wes's grin through the comms.

Reggie ignored him. "Houston, what's our time?"

A veteran astronaut, Nadine, was playing the role of ground control for their exercise today. "Five hours, twenty-eight minutes. You're right on target."

"Copy."

Reggie tried to refocus on the task before her, but all she could think about was Wes, somewhere out of sight on the aft end of the station, taking his sweet time. Wes didn't seem to care about beating yesterday's record; he was one of those guys who'd be genuinely excited to receive a participation trophy. He'd even signed up for the one assignment no astronaut in their right mind wanted—he was going off-site for a whole month to train some Hollywood actor for a movie role instead of getting to do actual science and mission-prep work. Worse, he'd be filmed the entire time, essentially filling the role of on-camera babysitter for some sort of *How to Pretend to Be an Astronaut* promo special. Who the hell volunteered for that kind of thing?

Wes started up again. He was desecrating Garbage this time. The teenage misanthrope inside her howled at the travesty, and she wasn't sure if she should be insulted that Wes thought this song would appeal to her or pleased that she'd branded her public image so well. After all, applying heavy eyeliner in zero-gravity took a great deal of effort, but ever since she'd been labeled "NASA's resident goth astronaut" on a popular podcast years ago, Reggie had decided to really lean into the persona.

It stopped people from expecting too much charisma.

She wrapped up her task and carefully stored her tools so they wouldn't float away. Loose objects tended to be dangerous when careening through space at 17,500 miles per hour—the same speed at which the Space Station orbited the earth. And of even greater concern: a mistake like that would cost her points.

"Houston, can I get a time check?"

"Five hours, thirty-nine minutes." If Nadine was irritated at being asked again, her tone didn't reveal it.

Reggie checked in with Wes.

"Almost done," he replied.

If his assessment was accurate, there was still a chance they'd finish in under six hours. Not bad. The tiniest thrill of victory zipped through her.

Reggie rotated herself parallel to the handrails bolted to the station and began maneuvering herself toward the airlock. It was a slow process, made slower by her exhaustion. Her pressurized gloves made gripping things hard, and her hands were almost numb from the strain.

Wes had switched to caterwauling through Bon Jovi's greatest hits. If anything, this was the worst auditory torture of all, because she secretly *adored* Bon Jovi, and she'd never live it down if her colleagues found out she listened to such optimistic music.

She concentrated on placing one hand over the other. The airlock was thirty feet away. Then twenty. Fifteen.

"Shit."

She stilled, stomach plummeting. They weren't supposed to swear on the comms because on a real space walk everything was aired live on NASA TV, but that wasn't what alarmed her. It was that Wes rarely lost his cool. And that meant he'd screwed up.

Wes grunted. "Looks like one of the vent valves is jammed."

"I'm heading over," Reggie told him. She knew those valves inside and out; she'd spent four hours repairing them on a real EVA during her six-month mission aboard the ISS. Wes was all the way on the other end of the truss, but if she started now, there was still the slimmest chance they could match yesterday's time.

"That'll take too long, and the sun's about to set. I can handle it."

4

Reggie almost laughed in disbelief. *Now* he was concerned about the speed? "If you can't close it on your own, I'll have to come out there anyway."

"Hayes, hold position." He sounded annoyed. Was he concerned with how this exercise would reflect on him? If so, he should have taken it seriously from the start.

Reggie clambered over the truss. Her breathing was coming hard, her visor fogging and then clearing over and over.

Nadine's voice came back on. "Reggie, I'm getting some elevated vital readings from you. Everything okay?"

"Fine." Reggie forced strength into the word. "What's my time?"

A pause. "Reggie, this isn't a timed exercise."

"I know."

This training exercise's official objective was to complete the assigned tasks and return safely. But *unofficially*, tests like these were being used to vet astronauts for the lunar mission, using metrics that weren't explicitly disclosed. Reggie wanted to prove she could exceed expectations, whatever they might be.

She was not going to let Wes and his abysmal singing voice hold her back.

At that moment, the sun's last rays winked out of view, and her world was plunged into darkness. It would be forty-five minutes before it rose again, and until then she only had the lights on her suit to guide her. The utter blackness of night was disorienting at first, but Reggie had experienced this phenomenon in real life—and in simulation— enough times that she could adjust within seconds.

For her, the space walk was the easy part. It was dealing with someone else's incompetence that put Reggie on edge.

Finally, Nadine said, "Five hours, fifty minutes."

Reggie redoubled her efforts. Her heartbeat throbbed against her temple, but she ignored the physical discomfort. She was trained to push her body to its limit. They all were.

Her hands closed over the handrails. When she reached Wes, she'd send him back to the airlock and fix the vent flap on her own. She didn't need him. He'd only slow her down.

Wes finally came into view when she cleared the solar arrays. He was upside down relative to her position and on the opposite side of the station node. To get to him, she needed to switch to a perpendicular handrail and rotate her entire body by swinging her back legs until they hooked onto the new rail.

She was halfway through the maneuver when she slipped.

The hand that should have closed around the target handrail lost its grip, numb fingers failing for the first time. In gravity, this wouldn't have been a problem. But in a near vacuum, her momentum carried her forward until something stopped her. In this case, that something was her helmet slamming into the side of the station with an ugly crack.

The jolt rocked her. The muscles in her neck tensed reflexively, and a painful twinge arced through her right shoulder. Alarms blared.

"Hayes, you okay?" Wes asked.

Reggie bit off a curse. "I slipped. Visor is showing damage."

"How bad?"

Bad. But not in the way Wes meant. Their helmets were constructed of a bulletproof-like polycarbonate material. A fracture that went all the way through was extremely unlikely, and even if she did start losing oxygen, real decompression was far slower and less dramatic than in Hollywood movies.

It was bad because this entire test was a failure. Forget beating the time record and accomplishing mission objectives; now they'd have to walk through accident protocol. She had done nearly six hours of flawless work, and none of it mattered anymore because Reggie had made one sloppy mistake.

She'd let her emotions cause her to do something stupid. *Again.*

"It's over, Wes."

The alarm blared. She fumbled at the buttons on her torso until she found the one that shut it off.

Nadine did not sound pleased. "Reggie, begin recovery actions."

Reggie started to comply, then stopped, patience depleted. They'd woken up at four in the morning to prepare for this, just like they would have done for a real space walk, and she hadn't eaten since breakfast. What was the point of seeing this through? Her mistake had just obliterated a perfect run-through and probably tanked her chances of making it onto the Artemis III mission. None of this was worth it if she couldn't have the moon.

"Reggie," Nadine prompted. "Take a second. Breathe. Don't let frustration take over."

Too late.

Better to quit on her own terms. Salvage what little pride she could before going home, tearing into a sandwich, and licking her wounds in private.

She slapped her hands on both sides of her helmet and twisted until the locking mechanism released. Her ears popped as air hissed out, and Nadine's voice went muffled. The helmet was heavy. She struggled to lift it off her shoulders, and finally the lab techs came to her aid, whisking it away—and with it, the virtual view of the International Space Station. In its place was a far less spectacular view of the Virtual Reality Lab with its black walls, linoleum flooring, and spacesuits rigged to heavy-duty cables.

The fluorescent overheads were blinding after the nearly total darkness of space, and Reggie squinted down at her gloves as she fumbled at the place where they attached to her suit. Even though she'd only been gripping virtual objects simulated by dozens of wired sensors, the gloves were fully pressurized to simulate a full space walk, and her grip strength was abysmal after wearing them for so long.

Another tech rushed over, his face pinched with concern. "Let us do it. Please."

"Get me out of here," she snapped.

Three feet to her right, Wes struggled with his own helmet. When it was off, he angled his head to frown at her. Sweat plastered his dark hair against his forehead. "What's going on? Everything all right?"

It would have been easier to blame Wes if he were a jerk, but despite being a hotshot pilot who never seemed to take anything seriously, he was unfailingly *nice*. It was one of the many reasons she hadn't slept with Wes like she had with several of her other single colleagues.

The nice ones were prone to hurt feelings, and hurt feelings often led to tears, and Reggie had been raised by a bloodthirsty Navy admiral father whose favorite saying was *Crying is for cowards* and a brilliant scientist mother who could flash freeze Lex Luthor's tear ducts with a concisely scathing performance review. As she was the sole product of that unholy union, it was highly likely a misplaced teardrop would cause Reggie's flesh to ignite, and she refused to spontaneously combust before she'd secured a premium spot in the history books. Better to spend her free time with rocks instead; a chunk of lunar granite didn't ask more of you than you had the capacity to give.

Her gloves came free with a rush of cold air. She flexed her fingers, wincing at the pins-and-needles sensation as blood flow returned. "We failed."

"We still have to finish—"

"No. I'm done. We failed." Reggie wriggled down, maneuvering herself in the mock spacesuit until she could slither out the impossibly small hole in the back. It wasn't easy, and her right shoulder screamed in protest.

When she was finally free, she stripped out of the cooling base suit and down to her bike shorts and sports bra, then marched over to her duffel bag. Nadine came over as Reggie was dressing, her green eyes communicating concern and sympathy. She wore the standard astronaut-casual uniform—a NASA-logoed polo and khakis—which looked fantastic on her curvy frame, as always. But it was her doctorate in orbital mechanics and the way she waxed poetic about lateral thrust that had once attracted Reggie most.

Speaking of ex-hookups who turned out to have too many feelings . . .

"Everything okay, Reggie?"

Reggie stabbed her legs into her old MIT sweatpants. "I'm fine. I screwed up, and I don't want to talk about it."

Maybe she could sneak out the back hallway before anyone noticed she was gone.

"If you change your mind, I'm here for you. As a friend, or—"

"Noted. Anything else?" She was a human iceberg. Dead inside, nothing to offer—*beware all ye softhearted souls who dare pass betwixt these thighs, for this beast is the product of a Cold and Lonely Childhood™ and has no warmth to spare.* She'd always been up front about that; it wasn't her fault if people didn't take her seriously.

Nadine's face hardened. "Right. Guess I'll just fuck off then. Oh, by the way, Deb wants to see you."

Ruh-roh. Guess word had spread fast, and now she was in trouble.

Reggie stuffed a sweatshirt over her head, using the brief delay to steel herself. When her head popped out, she knew she looked calm. "In her office?"

Nadine nodded. Reggie swung her bag onto her shoulder and left without another word.

Deb Whitford glanced up from her dual monitor screens as Reggie entered her office. She raised a brow but didn't say anything.

Great—Deb was pissed off.

The chief astronaut's office was not glamorous. Like everything else at the budget-strapped Johnson Space Center—with its ubiquitous scuffed linoleum and fluorescent overheads—the room showed its age and had a distinct air of *it's not pretty, but it works.* But chief astronaut was the most senior leadership position an active astronaut could hold, so Deb's office did have a window.

It was a second-story window, but Reggie thought she might have a good chance of making the drop down to the parking lot if she climbed out, and then she wouldn't have to explain herself to Deb. Reggie had never run away from anything before, but still . . . it was awfully tempting.

Though Deb had taken Reggie under her wing and served as her informal mentor for six years, the woman was still intimidating as all hell. Like many of NASA's senior astronauts, Deb was former military, so she wore her graying brown hair short and buzzed at the sides, her posture was impeccable, and she'd long since perfected the squadron commander's art of separating an individual's soul from their body with a single withering glare. If looks alone weren't enough to inspire abject fealty, Deb's accent hinted at her Queens-based upbringing, and she kept a two-foot-tall replica of a Klingon Bird-of-Prey warship on her desk; Deb's true destiny (as Reggie liked to imagine it) was to be the first person to punch someone who deserved it—in space. She was also the first Black woman to hold this office, and the fact that she hadn't earned it easily was evident in the exacting standards she held her astronauts—and herself—to.

"You wanted to see me?"

"Go ahead and have a seat." Deb waited until Reggie did so; then she got up and closed the door. This was both a sign they could speak informally and also a red flag—whatever Deb had to say, she didn't want anyone else overhearing.

Reggie took a deep breath. "Ending the training exercise early was unprofessional of me. I was frustrated with my own mistake, and I made an emotional decision. It won't happen again."

Deb sat behind her desk and clasped her hands atop it. "Spare me the bull, Hayes."

"Fine. Wes was treating the simulation like a dress rehearsal for a community theater musical. I wanted to beat yesterday's time, and he was slowing me down."

"If you want something done right, you have to do it yourself," Deb translated.

"Exactly—"

"No, *not* exactly," Deb snapped. "I put my ass on the line to convince the higher-ups that you're not a hotheaded liability, and you go and pull this stunt today?"

Reggie's face heated. *Will I ever live down that disastrous interview?* "I didn't know it was on record—" She saw Deb's expression and stopped. There was no point in rehashing what had happened six months ago. Her record was otherwise impeccable. "If I'd done that training exercise alone, I'd have completed it in record time. I am the best astronaut in my class, and we both know it."

"So?" Deb threw up her hands. "You want a medal, Hayes?"

No, I want to be the first woman on the moon. I want to matter. I want to do something so legendary that no one cares that I'm not likable. I want to know that the last fifteen years of obsessive work, dedication, and loneliness weren't a waste of fucking time.

Reggie bit back the words before they escaped in a projectile vomit of emotion—along with all the other feelings she'd crammed into the back of her skull for later disposal. The problem with superlative compartmentalizing was that she was starting to run out of space in her metaphorical closet, and boxes occasionally fell and exploded at inconvenient times.

She sat back hard in her chair. "I apologize. It's been a long day."

"I know." Fortunately, Deb knew better than to offer pity. "I'd throw in a cute speech about how I see something of myself in you, which is why I continue believing in your ability to succeed, but I won't waste your time. The real reason I wanted to see you is because I got an email from the Astronaut Selection Board this morning with the short list for the Artemis III mission."

If it were good news, Deb wouldn't have let her off so easy about the simulation. Her voice hollow, Reggie said it aloud. "I'm not on it."

"No, you are not."

"Okay. Thank you." Part of her wanted to ask why, but deep down, she knew the answer: *not the right fit.* (Subtext: *arrogant, stubborn, and—if we're being entirely honest—kind of a bitch.*)

She stood to leave.

Then she sat back down. "I don't accept that."

"I'm shocked." Deb did not look remotely shocked. She had to have known Reggie wouldn't calmly surrender her lifelong dream without a fight—hell, Reggie didn't surrender *anything* without a fight.

"How many astronauts are locked in? The mission commander? Probably. Medical? Maybe. But until their first-choice selections formally accept the mission and the roster is announced to the public in February, I still have a chance."

Deb raised both brows and sat back. "And? What compelling evidence do you plan to provide the board to convince them you're a supportive, patient *team* player with whom your fellow astronauts would be thrilled to spend six weeks in a cramped lunar habitat? And that's not even addressing your disdain for all media- and social media–related activities, which this mission will require in abundance."

"I don't disdain social media. I updated my NASA Instagram last week."

Deb clicked something on her computer screen and swiveled the monitor to show Reggie the post in question. A slightly blurry photo of a lumpy, pockmarked sample of lunar basalt. The caption read: *Lunar basalt.* It had five likes, and one of them was from user @KVolkov. Roscosmos—Reggie's best friend.

Only friend, really.

Reggie slid her eyes away from the screen and muttered, "Not my fault if people can't appreciate the beauty of rocks."

"Don't break your heart over this, Reggie. There will be other missions."

Not like this one. Not the chance to be the *first*. The *best*.

Reggie's right hand strayed into her pocket, feeling for the lump of rock in it. It wasn't real moon rock, but the jagged anorthite was as close as you could get from an earthborn mineral. This kind of volcanic rock was a rare find because of how easily it weathered under wind and water, but on the atmosphere-bereft moon . . . it was everywhere. She kept it with her as a reminder that there were other worlds out there where the rules were different, but the only way to get to those brave new frontiers was to try really, really fucking hard. Not exactly poetry, but it motivated her well enough; she was a geologist, not a playwright.

The thought dinged an adjacent idea. Before she could think about it too much and muster the appropriate revulsion, she blurted, "Give me the movie-actor-training thing."

"Wes already volunteered for that project."

"Only because no one else wanted to do it," Reggie argued. "I'll talk to him." She'd talk him out of it, more like; Wes was so damn polite that he'd fold under the slightest pressure.

As if Deb could read her mind, she pursed her lips. "Do you have any idea what you're signing up for? The movie's director has a reputation for going to extreme lengths to film his movies. He originally reached out to our public affairs office about actually training his lead actor to be an astronaut *on* the Space Station."

"What? That's impossible."

"You'll be surprised what money can buy," Deb said dryly. "He didn't even blink at the price we quoted him, and the only reason we're conducting this training at our Artemis analog base instead is due to time constraints on his end." NASA had built the analog base last year in a remote part of the Arizona desert that was meant to simulate the desolate, isolated lunar landscape. The habitat was designed to be nearly identical to Gateway, the actual habitat the Artemis III crew would be building on the moon—not the worst place Reggie could think to visit, given her goals. How bad could this thing be?

Deb continued, "He wanted it to be a truly 'immersive experience,' so you'll be isolated at the base with only the actor and a two-member filming crew for the whole month of December, aside from, I believe, a short break for the holiday weekend. And you know they'll be filming your entire training experience to make a promotional behind-the-scenes special, right?"

She'd rather bathe in molten lava, but she forced a cheery "Sure, that sounds fine."

"You'll also be representing NASA to the media, which means we expect you to uphold our public relations standards at all times, and frankly, given your checkered history in that arena, I'm highly skeptical that you're up to the job."

You and me both. "Which is exactly why I need to do it. It'll prove to the board that I'm media friendly and team oriented."

Deb gave Reggie a look. "You'd be more convincing if you didn't sound like you were dying inside every time you say the word *team*."

Reggie pasted on the biggest, brightest smile she could muster. "Team," she chirped. "Better?"

"Worse."

"Who's the actor?" Reggie wasn't sure why she bothered to ask. She hadn't been to the movies in years.

"Jon Leo." She must have seen Reggie's blank expression because Deb added, "The guy from *Space Dude*? It's very popular with the 'cool teens,' according to my in-house expert. Google his name. He's not bad on the eyes, I'll tell you that, and he's reportedly very easy to work with. Kurt from media relations chatted with him on the phone and said he's a nice guy."

Nice guy. Her nose wrinkled. Was she cursed? Would nice people infiltrate her entire life, forever haunting her like ghosts who hadn't died right? Reggie intentionally ignored the part about his looks (which had never mattered)—along with the doubt creeping its way to the surface. "That's the dumbest movie name I've ever heard," was all she could think to say.

"I'll inform Hollywood to call for your opinion next time, since I certainly didn't ask for it." Deb shook her head. "See? This is what I'm worried about. I want to believe in you, Reggie, but you can't cop an attitude like this on camera. If you can't even hold your tongue for the span of five minutes, how do you think you'll last a month?"

"I filmed a dozen educational videos on the ISS without issue. It was only that *one* time that I slipped, and I think you'll agree the circumstances were very different," Reggie argued, even though she knew she was merely scraping the bottom of the barrel in desperation. Deb was going to say no. She could feel it. And when backed into a corner, Reggie had a bad habit of lashing out. "Buzz Aldrin punched a guy's lights out for saying the moon landing was faked, and everyone called him a badass. I just told that sorry excuse for a reporter—"

"Buzz Aldrin walked on the moon. You haven't. And if you can't learn to control your temper and get along with people, you never will." Deb rose and marched over to the door, stopping short of opening it.

In that moment, Reggie saw clearly that everything she'd spent her life working for was drowning in a toilet bowl and her own finger hovered over the flusher.

"Give me a chance. Let me prove I can do this. *Please.*" She never begged. But today, she'd beg. After begging, there was only one weapon left in her arsenal, but she really didn't want to use it. *Don't make me have to.*

Deb didn't open the door. But she didn't take her hand off the knob either. "I've made up my mind. Wes is a better choice for this project."

Reggie closed her eyes, choked down her pride, and gritted her teeth against the humiliation to come. She'd never, ever wanted to sink this low, but as they said . . . desperate times.

"My mother will be so disappointed in me," Reggie said in a quiet voice.

It wasn't a lie. Not exactly, anyway. It was just that Dr. Hayes was *always* disappointed in her only offspring. Not that Reggie cared, because she was a grown adult who'd moved past the instinctual need to be seen as worthy in her parents' eyes. Going to the moon was what Reggie wanted; it had nothing to do with satisfying her mother's impossible standards.

The important thing was that Deb worshipped Reggie's mother, who'd served as Deb's academic adviser at MIT for her quantum engineering master's program. Even the formidable Deborah Whitman quavered at the possibility of disappointing the Nobel Prize–winning Dr. Victoria Hayes, the world's foremost expert in both nuclear fusion and making everyone else feel hopelessly inferior. This was the first—and the last—time Reggie would ever play the mother card.

Deb let out a defeated sigh. "I swear, if I didn't owe my career to that woman . . ."

"I will be on my best behavior from this point forward. Every single aspect of this training will be flawless. No mistakes. No PR gaffes. No complaints from anyone on the film crew." As she spoke, the confidence she was faking became real. Maybe she really *could* do this. "I'll even update my social media regularly!"

For the first time in memory, Deb appeared startled. "You will?"

"Absolutely. I'll even . . ." Reggie searched for the appropriate lingo. "Hashtag NASA in them."

Deb's hand fell away from the door. *Victory!* "Fine. If you can convince Wes to step back, I'll talk to media relations. Don't make me regret this. If there's a lick of trouble—"

"There won't be," Reggie assured her.

"A single complaint—"

"Not a one, ma'am."

Deb slowly returned to her desk and sat back in her chair, looking a bit like she'd just signed away her fortune to a mysterious man in a trench coat and was quite certain she'd never see it again. "Then good luck, Astronaut Hayes, and Godspeed . . . you'll need it."

CHAPTER 2

Jon Leo had been staring at the same script page for fifteen minutes, and he still had no idea what it said. In retrospect, he should have known better than to try and learn his lines on a plane. Even a luxurious plane like this one, with its plush carpeting and leather bucket seats, was loud when nearly everyone aboard was talking over each other.

He desperately envied the film crew's sound guy sitting across from him, who'd put on noise-canceling headphones the minute he'd fastened his seat belt straps. He was now riveted by whatever he had pulled up on his e-reader. Jon could see the screen reflected in the sound guy's glasses, the words scrolling by at an impressive speed. He didn't seem to be fazed at all by everything going on around him.

Jon had never been able to tune the world out like that.

Near the front of the cabin, the director was holding an expletive-laden conversation on his cell phone with someone from his production company. If Jon had overheard that many f-bombs in such a short time span from anyone else, it might have been cause for concern, but this was *Rudy Ruffino*, the man who held the dubious record of delivering an Oscar acceptance speech so curse laden and inflammatory that the Catholic Church had purchased a one-page ad in the *New York Times* to publicly disavow him. While other visionary yet temperamental directors might toe the line of social acceptability, Rudy actively warred against the line's very existence. But as far as Hollywood's best visionary yet temperamental directors went, Rudy was one of the better ones. After all, he reliably produced masterfully thought-provoking, award-winning films (and more importantly, he hadn't yet fallen prey to a sex scandal).

Seated to Jon's left was his publicist, Jacqueline Shaw, who was engaged in a spirited discussion of astrology with the director of photography, or DP, as the role was often referred to on set (she'd introduced herself, but Jon had forgotten what she'd said already, because he was really bad at remembering names). Though the DP looked to be in her early forties, she wore a yellow beanie over long, pigtailed brown braids and had asked Jon to autograph her Converse sneakers when she'd first met him.

Beneath the layers of conversation and the blare of the television were the persistent hum of the engines, the clink of ice shifting around in glasses of soda, the clatter of Jacqui's nails on her laptop, and the grating electronic music that someone had inexplicably turned on in the background. It was all so . . . *much*.

He closed his eyes, as if he could read better through his eyelids. At least things were a little more peaceful in the dark.

"You've been staring at that page for a while. Must be good." Jacqui's voice startled him out of his brief respite.

"Uh." Jon blinked at her, then smiled reflexively. "Yeah. I'm digging it so far."

Jacqui smiled right back, both because they were in front of other people and because there was no such thing as an unfiltered exchange in her world. She was always *on*. She turned back to the DP (he really needed to find out what her name was), waving a graceful hand in Jon's direction. Her gold bracelets made a pleasant tinkling sound. "Jon's a Sagittarius," she said, as if she were explaining something.

The other woman laughed. "No shit? My sister's a Sadge too. Always off in another world. Must be an actor thing."

Jacqui nodded like some wise sage. "There are a lot of fire signs in Hollywood, especially on the talent side. That's why they need people like us water and air signs to keep it in check. See this spreadsheet? This is pure Virgo energy."

Jon couldn't deny her claim—he had a copy of that same spreadsheet in his pocket, and he wasn't sure what he'd do without it. Jacqui kept a list of everyone they were working with, their names, contact info, and any pertinent information that he might need to know. When he got to his hotel tonight, he'd pore over the list until the information sank in. Hopefully she'd added the names of everyone else on this plane besides Rudy. He didn't want to be one of those actors who treated the support crew like interchangeable peons, and Jacqui knew that. She was the best. He owed his career to her.

Eight years ago, he'd been waiting tables by night and auditioning by day, desperate for the smallest shred of hope from callbacks that never came. Now, he was sitting in a luxury jet on the way to the Johnson Space Center to meet an actual astronaut, because he was filming a movie that had "serious Oscar potential" with legendary, award-winning director Rudy fucking Ruffino. He wanted to punch himself to see if he was dreaming. The urge to bounce around in glee like a deranged weirdo was in the back of his head *all the time*.

Jon had no illusions about how he'd gotten to this place in his career. He was a good actor, but there were a lot of good actors in LA who weren't getting work. No matter how talented he might be, he knew he wouldn't be sitting in this million-dollar sky limo if it weren't for his pretty face, his famous dad, and—above all—the fact that Jacqui and his agent had devoted themselves to painstakingly crafting his image and career path.

He was like a prize show pony: all he had to do was show up, follow instructions, and not do anything wrong.

Which was why he didn't want to admit he hadn't memorized a single thing beyond the movie's title: *Escape Velocity*. He'd promised

Jacqui he'd have his lines down cold by the first table read in two weeks, and he wasn't anywhere close.

In fact, he hadn't even *read* the entire script through—not even once—which he probably should have done before signing on to the project in the first place, but he'd been so enraptured by the words *Oscar potential* and Rudy's renown that he'd skipped right ahead to signing the contract. He *did* have a bad habit of making impulsive decisions, but he'd looked it up, and this sort of thing happened all the time in the upper echelons of Hollywood. Tom Hardy hadn't read Bane's lines before signing on to do *The Dark Knight Rises*, but he'd trusted Christopher Nolan, and it had been fine, hadn't it?

I'm grateful, I'm lucky, and I'm living my dream, he repeated for the billionth time since landing this role. Now he needed to get his shit together and read.

He hunched over the script and started at the top of the page again. *Focus. Focus. Foc—*

"Script's fuckin' dynamo, isn't it?"

Jon started. Rudy was standing over him, one hand braced against the ceiling and the other on his hip.

Jon gave the director an easy grin and thanked his lucky stars no one could hear his heart pounding. "I love it. This is exactly the kind of role I can sink my teeth into."

Jacqui, ever attuned to everything going on around her, came to his rescue. "Jon's kind of a space buff, right, Jon?" She didn't wait for his answer. "Everyone thinks of him as a comedic talent because he got his break on a sitcom, but this script for *Escape Velocity* is going to give him a chance to show the world he's got the chops to handle something meaty. Wait till the table read, Rudy; you're going to lose your mind over what a perfect fit this is."

Jon continued to grin and nod like an animated mannequin, letting Jacqui work her magic, though anxiety still balled tight in his stomach. Rudy was notoriously mercurial, and he'd been known to make

---

sweeping production changes on a whim. It was rumored he'd once had a supporting actress's role written out of the script because she'd refused to agree with his vehement assertion that the movie *Charlie and the Chocolate Factory* was an avant-garde allegory for cannibalism (although according to a gossip-savvy production assistant on Jon's last film, the edit was more likely a result of said actress sleeping with Rudy's now-ex-wife).

What if the table read was a disaster and Rudy regretted casting Jon? It still seemed unreal to be at a point in his career where he wouldn't always have to formally audition for a role.

Jon slid the script off the "fancy plane" version of a tray table in front of him and into his lap. His damp fingers stuck to the pages. Though he was trying to pay attention to what Jacqui was saying, his worried thoughts kept interrupting, swirling around in his head like conversations of their own. All he could do was look happy and feign paying attention, and that seemed to be enough—for now.

He was saved by the pilot announcing over the loudspeaker: "Buckle your seat belts and prepare for landing."

When Rudy returned to his seat, Jacqui's catlike gaze turned on Jon. Her brown eyes swept up and down, like a human barcode scanner. "I like the longer hair. I wasn't sure if it was going to work on you, but it does." Her voice was quiet enough to keep the conversation subtly private. She reached into the pocket of her white blazer and pulled out a hair tie. "Pull it back so that when you get out of the plane it doesn't blow into your face. And the beard is good, but I don't want it to get longer than this. We're going for sexy gravitas, not unkempt scruff. Did you bring trimmers? If not, I can get some sent to the hotel."

"I have some." Jon fought back the self-consciousness. He should be used to this by now.

"Good. Did Kahlil email you the workout and diet plan?"

Jon grimaced at the mention of his personal trainer. "You mean the thing that lists five hundred squats as the daily *warm-up*? Yeah, I got it.

He's a very bad man, and I think he hates me." In reality, Kahlil was a complete teddy bear and a clutch teammate for fighting space pirates in their online *No Man's Sky* game.

"Make sure you forward that to me." Jacqui's eyes narrowed. Jon had no doubt about whose side she was on. She'd promised to make him into an A-list actor, and A-list actors had cyborg bodies constructed from the deepest depths of misery and starvation. In Kahlil's world, every day was leg day.

Jon dutifully pulled out his phone and forwarded Jacqui the email. If he didn't do it now, he'd forget to do it later.

Her eyes raked over him again, but this time she looked below the surface. "You feeling good?"

"Yeah." Beneath his tray table, his hands closed over the script, folding it into a thick tube. Jacqui would see right through a lie, so he went for something akin to truth. "Honestly, I'm a little nervous. I feel like I'm meeting Captain Marvel or something."

Jacqui rolled her eyes, but in a good-natured way. "Nerd."

"These guys are heroes! Didn't you want to be an astronaut when you were a kid?"

"Not particularly. I wanted to be Halle Berry." Jacqui shrugged. "Anyway, did you have a chance to familiarize yourself with your astronaut trainer's profile I forwarded last week?"

He nodded. Boy, had he.

At first, he'd checked out the info because as a kid he'd dreamed of being an astronaut, and he couldn't wait to learn more about the super cool space hero he'd be training with. Then he'd seen the picture of Reggie Hayes—and watched her infamous interview—and he'd been interested for wholly different reasons.

Really interested.

"Yeah, she's been somewhat off the radar ever since that 'goth astronaut' segment that went viral a few months ago, but Kurt assured me Regina is eager to create a more positive media image, so we'll see how it goes. She'll be joining us for the tour of the facility, as well as dinner tonight, so it'll be a great opportunity to confirm you two have good on-screen chemistry. Oh, and NASA is looking to generate some positive press for the moon base thing they're doing next year, so I added that to the notes for your social media updates. I'll make sure your posts have the appropriate tags, but they'll want to make sure you mention it verbally too."

Jon nodded and tried to appear respectful and engaged as Jacqui continued talking about audience reach and crossover appeal and a bunch of other things that were probably important but impossible for him to stay focused on. Gratefulness washed over him when she reached into her boat-size handbag and handed him a binder. "Everything you need is in here," she said with a knowing look.

"Uh, will you also—"

"It's already in your inbox. But please try not to lose the hard copy on day one."

He promised he wouldn't misplace yet another binder, then treated himself to a look out the window. As the plane descended, he could see the Johnson Space Center spread out below them in a cluster of generic gray rooftops, like some glorified office complex.

He couldn't see the landing strip below, but somewhere down there was Regina Hayes, the intimidating, brilliant woman he was about to spend a month with. After exhausting the background file Jacqui had sent him and then deep-diving into the internet to do his own research—for educational purposes!—he'd been determined to impress her on their first meeting, and thus he'd spent a good deal of time memorizing space facts he could casually slip into conversation. While he usually had no problem winning people over, something about Reggie made his gut twist whenever he thought about her. Not only because as a kid he'd kept an Action Man Space Explorer doll on the same shelf as his superhero toys—for lots of other reasons too.

For one, she was a stone-cold smoldering babe. Could one be both cold and smoldering at the same time? Like dry ice? Yeah, Reggie was a dry ice kind of babe, which was exactly Jon's type—he'd imprinted early on comic book villainesses, with their black lipstick and cunning brains, and never quite grown out of it.

Two, she was scarily accomplished and intelligent, and he was absolutely neither of those things, and he wasn't sure how long he could hide his mediocrity before she figured it out.

But most important, he really needed her help, so making a good impression was extra essential. If Reggie could somehow teach him how to act like an astronaut, he might stand a chance of proving to the world that he was more than a pretty face with good comedic timing and a famous dad. If he was nominated for an Oscar from this role, he'd have . . . what had Jacqui called it?

Gravitas.

And actors with gravitas were taken seriously. They got to pick their projects, rather than smile their way through movies called *Space Dude* while their dignity shriveled up and winked out of existence.

This movie was his big break—a chance to be more than a show pony. He just needed to get through the next month without screwing anything up.

☆ 🌠 ☆

Kurt from media relations had decided Reggie should be at the space center's landing strip to greet the film crew when they arrived, so two weeks after her disastrous space walk simulation, she stood on the weathered gray tarmac watching the Gulfstream G650's pilot execute a very average landing.

From the corner of her eye, Reggie spied movement and turned to see Yekaterina Volkov—Katya, to her colleagues—approaching with a deceptively casual stride.

"I thought you were training with the new rover today," Reggie said, loud enough to be heard over the noise of the taxiing aircraft.

"I am finished early. Very convenient."

"Convenient, my ass."

Katya was a Russian cosmonaut training here in Houston for a year as part of NASA's collaboration with Roscosmos, the Russian space agency. They'd been friends ever since they'd had to survive Siberian wilderness training together for their joint mission to the Space Station three years ago, and while Katya had no official reason for being here on the tarmac, her superiors were currently asleep on the other side of the world, which meant Katya could technically do whatever the hell she wanted.

Katya gave the barest of smiles—the equivalent of a full grin on anyone else—and sipped from her coffee thermos, her glossy fawn-brown ponytail whipping in the wind and her green eyes hidden behind mirrored shades. It was a rare clear day in December, and her lenses reflected the crystalline blue sky.

"I am here for support. And also, I am told this Jon Leo is very handsome."

Reggie turned back to watch the aircraft come to a stop in front of them, eyes narrowed. "Go away, Katya."

"Perhaps you will be married. He will fall in love with your friendly smile."

Reggie gritted her teeth.

"I look forward to this wedding. I have not met a Hollywood actor before. Perhaps my true love, Zendaya, will be at this wedding. I will ask him if he knows my true love."

"I think you shouldn't talk to these guys at all. Did Kurt okay this?"

"*Da*, of course. Special diplomatic dispensation."

That meant she'd bribed him with a can of the highly coveted Russian caviar she got mailed to her from back home. Reggie glanced behind them, where a tall, salt-and-pepper-haired man with a hangloose grin was leaning against the VIP tour van.

"You're a traitor to our country, Kurt!" Reggie called, knowing he was too far away to hear her. Kurt gave them a cheerful double thumbs-up.

Human-shaped silhouettes moved behind the dark windows as someone lowered a set of stairs. The first to deboard were a man and a woman in matching black hoodies—probably the film crew.

The man approached them. He was sandy haired, wore plain glasses, and had a complexion that suggested he didn't get outside often. Reggie immediately felt a kinship with him.

"Zach, sound tech," he said, offering Reggie a handshake.

She introduced herself in kind, then gestured to the demoness at her side. "And this is Katya Volkov from Roscosmos. She's a huge *Space Dude* fan."

She could feel Katya's eyes boring laser death holes into the side of her head.

Zach nodded. "That's Mimi over there on cameras—you'll meet her once we get the deplaning shots. We're going to film the first meeting for the media footage, if that's okay with you."

"Sure," she said, forcing a cheery smile. *Thirty days.* She could do this for thirty days, couldn't she?

Zach handed Reggie a wireless mic to clip to her shirt before jogging over to his colleague, a tall, generously built Latina woman with pigtailed braids who could be heard cursing at her video camera.

At least today would be easy, since Kurt was handling the tour. He'd even commandeered one of the vans they used for VIP tours, so they wouldn't have to cram onto the visitor tram. All Reggie had to do was tag along, listen to Kurt make small talk for two hours, and suffer through a "let's get acquainted" dinner with the crew, and then she could go home for the weekend. They didn't leave for Arizona until Monday morning.

"What is this *Space Dude*?" Katya asked.

Reggie snagged Katya's coffee and took a slow sip. Black, hot, and caustic—just the way she liked it. She handed it back. "The movie that Jon Leo is famous for."

The cosmonaut's top lip curled in exaggerated horror. "No."

"Yes. According to this guy's Wikipedia page, it's a 'satirical space opera with a cultlike following.'"

She hadn't been impressed by anything else on Jon Leo's sparse profile. Born in an LA suburb to an aspiring actress, Jon had attended the California Institute of the Arts for four years and then spent several years doing nothing notable until he'd been cast as a recurring character in the remake of the British comedy show *Business Place*. Then he'd done a few other straight-to-TV movies that Reggie had never heard of before getting his big break in *Space Dude*.

There was a photo of him on the page, and Reggie hadn't been blown away by that either. He looked like a classic pretty boy, with flawlessly tanned skin, high cheekbones, and eyelashes for days. His dark hair was short and coiffed in an expensive sort of way, and he had the kind of half-cocked, self-deprecating grin that attractive men seemed to have collectively weaponized to deceive naive love interests into believing they were blithely unaware of their own appeal (not her, of course, because she'd never had time to waste being *anyone's* naive love interest, but she'd observed the phenomenon often at local Navy watering holes, and it had made her supremely grateful about having the option to sleep with women instead).

The only piece of information that had caught Reggie's eye was that, at twenty-six, he'd finally been publicly acknowledged by his birth father and legally changed his last name from Stern to Leo—as in Brian Leo, the world-renowned actor and martial artist whom even *Reggie* had heard of. Shortly thereafter, his acting career had taken off.

A cynical part of her had wondered if Jon's acting success was merely a product of nepotism (and, in one particular photo, bedroom eyes so potent a single picture could melt a hole in one's computer screen—not *her* screen, because she'd immediately closed her browser and lowered the thermostat by two degrees, but it could happen to someone else's). Gushing reviews from fans, however, implied he could actually act.

Not that it mattered—especially not the part about his looks. In her experience, flashy packaging often disguised disappointing contents.

"Okay, we're rolling!" Zach called out.

Down the aircraft's steps came a man she recognized from her internet search as the movie's director, Rudy Ruffino. Rudy was a wiry man in his midfifties with a scruffy goatee and gray hair pulled back into a thin ponytail. He clamped one hand over his baseball hat to stop it from blowing away in the brisk wind and gave them a broad wave with his other hand as he approached.

"If it isn't the infamous Space Queen of Darkness herself," Rudy said when he was close enough to be heard. "Gotta say, I'm stoked about this collab. Loved you in that viral clip, by the way. You're a real firecracker, kid."

Reggie's cheeks ached from the effort it took to smile instead of scowl. "Regina Hayes," she said, extending her hand for him to shake. His fingers closed over hers, hot and clammy. She squeezed back firmly—though not as firmly as she'd have preferred. "Welcome to the Johnson Space Center. We're excited to have you here."

She began to introduce Katya, but Rudy had already turned on his heel, effectively dismissing them as he stalked toward the film crew to micromanage them. "Hey, guys, I want a wide-angle shot as Jon gets out of the bird . . ."

Katya raised a brow and took another sip. "Space Queen of Darkness? *Kid?*"

Reggie gave her a warning glance, then pointed at her mic. She'd already learned the hard way what happened when you said the wrong thing while cameras were rolling.

Then she looked up to see Jon Leo ducking out of the aircraft, the wind plastering his gray T-shirt against his muscled torso, and she was suddenly, briefly out of breath—because of a wind gust hitting her right as she inhaled. Nothing else.

She drew in a second breath, more carefully this time.

He'd grown his hair out since the picture she'd seen, and he wore the top half of it pulled back in an honest-to-goodness man bun. Inky strands whipped free around his face as he squinted into the sunlight. He'd grown facial hair, too, and it suited him. Gave him an edge that his clean-shaven face lacked.

He was better looking in person than in photos. Much better. So much better that it almost hurt to look at his impossibly muscled body as it flexed and moved beneath clinging cotton and designer denim; it was like staring directly into the sun.

In fact, she decided in that instant, Jon Leo was probably the most attractive man she'd ever seen in person.

You don't care about that kind of thing, remember?

"This Jon Leo has very impressive musculature," Katya said.

"Steroids," Reggie said dismissively. "Or he spends way too much time in the gym." *Worth it,* a devilish voice whispered.

"It is unfortunate about this"—she made a circling gesture around the back of her head—"man biscuit."

"Man bun?"

"Yes, this. Maybe you can cut it off before the wedding."

Reggie sort of liked how the hairstyle looked on him, but she'd never admit that to Katya.

Jon descended the steep staircase with ease, then waited at the bottom with an arm raised to assist a woman who wore dangerously high heels with her slim-fitting jeans and snowy blazer. He looked like some gallant knight assisting a princess, and Reggie hated herself for thinking it.

Under the guise of adjusting her mic, she muffled it with the collar of her shirt. Then she muttered to Katya, "He better have more than two brain cells bouncing around in that biscuit, or this is going to be a rough thirty days."

"Hmm," was all Katya had to say. The reflection in her sunglasses revealed an entirely below-the-belt view as Jon approached.

He shook Katya's hand first and exchanged pleasantries. His voice was deeper than she'd expected, which wasn't relevant to the training she'd be doing with him, and therefore she wasn't sure why she'd noted it, but now that she had, Reggie could see why people might pay money to see him in a theater with surround sound. His baritone was very . . . lush.

Katya—*thank God*—feigned professionalism and didn't ask about Zendaya.

Then, suddenly, he was in front of Reggie, his brown eyes looking down into hers. He was grinning, wide and lopsided, his expression open and eager, like a golden retriever who was excited just to exist. If he weren't so much larger than a puppy and the top of his head weren't so far away, she'd be tempted to ruffle his hair.

"Jon Leo," he said.

"Regina Hayes." She shook his hand. It was warm and dry and large enough to make her own work-calloused hand feel dainty. What were these things—bear paws? She resisted the urge to glance down. "Call me Reggie. We'll be spending a good deal of time together."

"Cool," he said.

"This should be fun," she lied, a bit pleased with herself for delivering her rehearsed small talk so smoothly. "You looking forward to the tour of the space center?"

He looked like he wanted to say something, but a beat passed. Then another. The cameras continued to roll. Her hand was still wrapped up in his, and she was instantly aware of the awkwardness of the empty seconds passing between them, stretching out like infinite, time-dilated monstrosities of social discomfort.

More than two cells. Please, let there be more than two.

"Cool," he said, finally. "Very cool."

Reggie's hopes withered. Jon Leo was an utter meatloaf. An attractive one, but a meatloaf nonetheless.

And she had to spend the next thirty days training him to be an astronaut *without* getting frustrated and losing her temper at his lack of competence.

Great. No problem.

CHAPTER 3

Cool? That was the best he could do?

He'd cued up a hundred witty things to say. He'd imagined he'd be confident and charming, teasing a smile from her with a wry observation or clever factoid. If she seemed game to be further delighted by his personality, he'd hoped an awful pun might seal the deal.

Instead, he'd looked into those arctic gray eyes and forgotten everything: his jokes, the space facts he'd memorized, his own name, how to operate his lungs—all of it.

Cool. Of all the options, that was the sole thing that he'd managed to force out of his mouth. Three instances of it, in fact.

Not very "cool" of you, brain. Not fucking cool at all.

Jon knew time travel wasn't really possible, but he still wanted to crawl into a black hole and reemerge in another time zone. Ideally, five minutes ago. Before he'd opened his mouth and biffed it extra hard in front of the hottest woman in the universe.

Her ice-gray eyes swept up and down the length of him, flat and bored beneath her signature smudged-charcoal eye makeup. He was nearly a head taller, and from his vantage point her blunt bangs cast her whole face in angled shadows. She was like some imperious witch queen, scouring him not with disdain but with disinterest. He'd fantasized all week about what it would be like to meet Reggie Hayes in person. His fantasies had never gone as sharply downhill the instant he'd opened his mouth.

Then again, in his fantasies, he'd mostly been doing different things with his mouth. (What? He'd never actually *do* anything inappropriate about it in real life . . . it was a perfectly innocent crush. Okay, an innocent crush with X-rated undertones, but he'd been super respectful about only jerking off to her educational NASA videos that one time, and he'd even watched the rest of the clip afterward!)

"Cut!" The photography director gave them a thumbs-up. "That was great!"

It was?

Rudy called out, "We're gonna skip the audio overlay on that one! Let's just get this show moving. Dinner resos are at six."

Jacqui looked up sharply and muttered under her breath, "You said seven on the phone this morning." She gave Jon a chagrined smile and tucked her Bluetooth earpiece in place. Like many of his brethren in Hollywood, Jacqui had also put in her fair share of hours in hospitality before she'd made a name for herself in publicity. "Excuse me a moment while I further inconvenience this poor restaurant on a Friday night."

As soon as Jacqui walked off, Reggie dropped his hand like holding it in the first place had been an excruciating experience. "You need anything else for filming, or can we get this tour over wi—started?"

He mutely shook his head.

Forget five minutes. He'd time travel to a day before humans had existed so no one else could witness his utter humiliation.

He had to fix this, but Reggie was already turning on her heel, gesturing for the cosmonaut to join her. He scrambled for something to say to her departing back and ended up blurting, "I really liked the videos you did on the ISS. The one about dyeing your hair in space was really cool."

"Cool" again? Really? Why couldn't he think of any other descriptors?

She glanced over her shoulder at him, then down at her watch. "Look, we're on a tight schedule for this tour, and I think Katya needs to get back to her duties."

"I do?" the cosmonaut asked. Reggie replied in Russian, and there was a brief exchange. Then Katya switched back to English. "My comrade reminded me of an appointment. It was very *cool* meeting you, Jon Leo."

He opened his mouth to make a witty retort, but all that came out was an awkwardly delayed "Same . . . too."

Without waiting to hear if Jon could muster anything more coherent, Reggie took off toward the parking lot, Katya following closely behind.

☆ 彗 ☆

Kurt, NASA's media liaison, introduced himself outside the van. Kurt had the relaxed energy of a favorite uncle who was always on the verge of giving you a high five, and Jon liked him immediately.

"You ever been to the Johnson Space Center before?" Kurt asked him as they all clambered into the air-conditioned vehicle. Jon said he hadn't, and Kurt's eyes crinkled at the corners, as if he was genuinely excited. "You're in for a treat. We're going to give you guys the VIP version of the tour, with a couple things Mr. Ruffino requested we visit that we don't normally show to the regular folks."

In the front seat, Reggie had strapped herself in and was currently glaring at the steering wheel, as if she could will it into motion with Sith-like telekinesis. So much for getting a seat next to her. Kurt hopped into the driver's seat and gave them a cheery overview of what they'd see on the tour, pointing out notable buildings as they meandered through the expansive campus.

Despite himself, Jon's pulse quickened. He *had* been genuinely looking forward to this. Inside him was that eight-year-old wannabe astronaut with thrift-store posters of the solar system taped to his wall, who was howling with delight. His mom had barely been able to afford a trip to the grocery store, much less a trip to Houston to take her son to see a bunch of nerdy space stuff. For the sake of that kid, he would try to enjoy this, and he'd try not to think of the dark-haired woman in the front seat, who launched herself out of the van the minute the doors opened.

At first it wasn't hard to focus on the tour, even though everything was staged for the film crew to capture it, which sometimes required Kurt to repeat things more than once, or Jon or Rudy to walk out of a room, turn around, and then pretend to be even more amazed by their surroundings when they reentered. But even though he tried his best to pay attention, Jon kept losing track of Kurt's voice as his focus drifted to the woman by his side.

Because Reggie was absolutely abysmal on camera, and it was the most fascinating thing he'd ever seen.

You know that saying *She made love to the camera*? Well, Reggie did whatever the opposite of that was. And the thing that really intrigued him was that she seemed to be trying. Like, really trying.

She made grimaces clearly intended to be smiles.

She attempted jokes that fell flat.

She held her petite body so stiffly that he worried pieces of it might snap off, but she kept trying to gesture at things in an animated manner, and it gave her the eerie, mechanical air of a windup doll.

Jon wasn't sure what to make of it. He thought *he'd* been awkward earlier, but nothing compared to this.

The DP—who he'd finally heard Rudy refer to as Mimi, so during a bathroom break he'd borrowed a pen and scribbled the name on his palm in order to remember it—kept cringing behind the camera, and Rudy looked progressively more inclined to write Reggie out of the metaphorical script with every tortured second. He wished there were some way to help her, but because Rudy was rushing them through every tour stop, Jon couldn't seem to snag a moment alone with her.

By the time they made it to CAPCOM—a.k.a. Mission Control, a.k.a. *Houston, we have a problem*—the *real* problem in Houston had become apparent to everyone.

As they stepped inside, Jon was enveloped in a steady hum of voices, clattering keyboards, and machine beeps and bloops. He gaped at the big screens at the front of the room, giddy with the reality of being in this place where sci-fi magic really happened. But it seemed he was the only one impressed by the view.

"I think we've seen enough for today. Let's move up dinner to five," Rudy said with a knowing glance at Jacqui. To the rest of the group, he made the "wrap it up" gesture and muttered under his breath, "The control room in *Armageddon* was better."

Reggie's shoulders sagged with apparent relief at the news they'd be done early, but Kurt clapped Rudy on the back and gave a hearty laugh. "All right, all right, I get it. You're done with the nerd stuff. But we've got to visit the underwater space station before we head out. I've saved the best for last!"

"The pool?" Jon couldn't disguise his eagerness. He'd watched a documentary about the enormous pool where astronauts suited up and trained underwater, and he knew they had a real, to-scale model of the International Space Station resting at the bottom. "Can I go diving in one of the spacesuits?"

Kurt's eyes twinkled. "Now, I'll get in a lot of trouble if we let a civilian splash around in there without clearance, but I'll tell you what—we'll get up real close."

"Sick!" Jon glanced at Rudy for approval, and he somehow got it.

Reggie did not look thrilled.

She looked even less thrilled when Kurt glanced at his phone and the twinkle disappeared from his eye. "Bad news, folks. I hate to do this, but I've got to head out, which means Reggie will have to take it from here."

Reggie grimace-smiled. Kurt continued in explanation, "I wouldn't miss the best part of this tour if it weren't an emergency. My teenager attempted to do his own laundry and just sent me a photo of a flooded basement."

Jon winced in sympathy. "Been there."

"You have kids?" Kurt asked.

"Oh, no, I mean . . ." Jon glanced around and realized that flooding one's own dwelling while attempting to use household appliances *wasn't* a common experience. "There was a flood at my place one time," he finished lamely.

Kurt excused himself to return his kid's call, and the rest of the group wandered in separate directions—Rudy to the bathroom, Mimi and the sound guy to film some building shots, and Jacqui to call the restaurant again.

"Rains a lot in LA, does it?" Reggie said under her breath as she passed by him on the way out the door.

His cheeks flamed. "It was an inside flood."

He watched her leave, momentarily fascinated by how someone so small managed to stomp so loudly, then realized that she was heading for the van, which meant he'd have a chance to talk to her alone.

He raced to catch up.

✦ 🌠 ✦

Reggie stormed toward the tour van. She was so ready for this tour to be over, and if it hadn't been for stupid Jon and his stupid puppylike enthusiasm, she'd be heading to her own car to go home and change for dinner instead of gearing up for another stop. One that *she'd* have to take the lead on, thanks to stupid teenagers and stupid Kurt and stupid—

Oh, who was she kidding? The person she was really mad at was herself, for volunteering for this damn assignment in the first place. She'd known how badly she performed on camera before she'd signed up. Now, everyone else knew it too.

Personal inadequacy made her want to puke. Having that inadequacy on display for others was even more repellent. If someone were to design a horror movie specifically to terrorize Reggie, all they'd have to do was make her watch clips of herself being bad at something.

Worse, she'd kept glimpsing Jon out of the corner of her eye, angling to get her alone like a kid determined to ask her to prom even though she'd clearly indicated that she'd rather slow dance with her graphing calculator in the library.

The thought spurred her to walk faster; she'd seen him perk up as she'd left and suspected he was only seconds behind her.

Maybe it was cowardly to avoid him, but she'd rather not have to entertain inane conversation right now. Wasn't the month they'd be spending alone together a steep enough price to pay?

She was halfway to the van when Jon managed to snag her sleeve.

"Hey, Reggie, hang on a sec."

Reggie didn't pull free of his grasp—that would be unprofessional. She simply looked at his hand, then back up at him.

His perfect cheekbones flushed, and he dropped his hold. "Sorry. I just wanted to talk to you before everyone else caught up. I thought maybe we could go over some stuff to talk about for this last recorded bit. Y'know, kind of bop some ideas around?"

"*Bop* some ideas around," she repeated.

"Yeah, like, pump it up a bit. Make it look a little more, uh . . . you know, more . . ."

Why did he look so adorably flustered? Absolutely infuriating. He had no business tugging at her heartstrings when everyone knew she didn't have any.

She stared at him. "More what?"

"Maybe . . . natural?" His lopsided smile looked more apologetic than anything else.

"Are you implying I'm unnatural on camera?"

"What? No!"

She raised a brow, and it made his tanned skin blanch to a sickly hue. Voice deliberately crisp, she told him, "Since we're going to be working together, I'm going to let you in on a little pro tip: I don't need anyone's help. With anything. But if you have a problem with my performance, say so instead of pussyfooting around it, and I'll take care of the issue. Don't bother trying to spare my feelings, because I don't have any. At least none that you should be concerned with. Understood?"

Without waiting for his reply, Reggie yanked the handle to the van's front door with gusto—

And nothing happened. The van door was locked.

Shit.

Reggie spun and leaned back against the van with her arms crossed, eyes straight ahead. There was really no way to salvage her pride on this one. "Door's locked," she mumbled.

Jon raised his hand, and the keys jingled in his palm. "Got these from Kurt—"

"Just open the fucking car."

He did, and she opened the door and slid into the driver's seat with as much dignity as she could muster. Jon slid into the first seating row behind her, and the van shuddered as he pulled the heavy side door shut. Closed into the stuffy silence with him, she felt the cabin shrink around them.

For several breaths, neither of them said anything.

He cleared his throat. "Just out of curiosity, why did you volunteer for this assignment?"

She tilted her head back against the headrest and stared up at the pilling gray felt on the van's ceiling. "Great question."

"Because . . . and correct me if I'm wrong, which I am sometimes. Maybe a lot of times. But it really doesn't seem like you're having fun, and I'm worried Rudy might be kinda pissy about it, so I thought I might try to help, but not because you *need* help, but because I want to. Unless you don't care if he replaces you with someone else because you're having a bad time, which is totally cool if that's what you want—" He made a frustrated noise, then said, "I do know other words besides *cool*, believe it or not."

"Such as?" Reggie tried to think of something else a himbo from Los Angeles would say. "Tubular?"

"Sorry, did you say *tubular*?"

Reggie turned around to look at him, indignant. "What? That's a thing people say!"

"If you're a superpowered turtle eating pizza in a sewer. Sure." He looked like he was trying not to laugh.

"Oh, so sorry I'm not hip to all the current slang. I didn't have time to watch Cartoon Network when I was learning to fly fighter jets faster than the speed of sound."

"That's hot." His puppy dog chocolate eyes twinkled with merriment. "And also very cool."

What was wrong with this guy? She was being a jerk, and he didn't seem ruffled by it in the slightest. It made holding on to self-righteous anger real damn hard. "Stop being so nice," she demanded.

"I don't think I can."

"Try."

He looked genuinely apologetic. "Fuck . . . you . . . ?" The words hung in the air. He seemed unsure what to do with his hands, and he thrust the left one through his hair. It got stuck on the hair elastic; he'd clearly forgotten about his man bun. His hand pulled free, leaving half his hair sticking out from his head in disheveled, looping arcs that reminded her of solar flares.

The last of her annoyance dissolved, but she suppressed the smile that tried to emerge in its wake. "You might want to . . ." Reggie gestured vaguely around her head.

He gave her a plaintive look, clearly desperate to win her over. "Jacqui thought this hairstyle would lend me an air of sophistication. Is it working?"

"No." Now guilt was seeping in. *Damn it.* "It's . . . fine."

It wasn't really Jon's fault she'd developed an aversion to nice people, with their soft feelings and fragile hearts, or that she'd been raised in a world where the worst possible thing you could be was unintelligent. Or that, for some reason, looking at his tree-trunk thighs flexing beneath very, *very* tight denim made her viscerally angry.

She watched him fiddle with his hair. His movements were unpracticed, as if he were trying to corral a handful of slippery eels, and Reggie had the irrational and totally inappropriate desire to slip her hands into that head of silky hair and do it for him. She gripped her chairback—firmly—and tried to focus on the important thing he'd said. "Do you really think he'd request a different astronaut?"

"Maybe. Rudy's known for being kind of . . . capricious."

He pronounced it wrong, as if he'd only seen it written, but it surprised her. Up until now, 50 percent of his vocabulary had been the word *cool*. Was he smarter than he let on?

Jon's hands settled at his sides, having finished their repair attempts. The bun hung from the back of his head, lopsided and dejected, but he grinned at her proudly.

Reggie exhaled. She wasn't the opening-up-to-strangers type, but something about Jon's earnestness made her want to spill her guts. "Look, I can't afford to lose this opportunity. I volunteered because I thought it would make me look good to the Astronaut Selection Board when they select for the upcoming mission to the moon. I know it's hard to believe, but I don't exactly have a reputation for being a people person."

Jon scrunched his nose. "Nah. I just think you're the type who doesn't suffer fools. You probably have way more important things you could be doing than pretending to schmooze with us on a tour."

For some reason, her chest tightened. Maybe because he was being far kinder to her than she deserved, and kindness made her want to squirm. "Anyway," she rushed out, "I'll try to be more *natural*, if that's what he's looking for."

Exactly how she was going to do that, Reggie had no clue.

"That's why I wanted to talk to you. I know how to work the cameras and get people to like me. It's pretty much all I'm good at, actually, and I can give you some tips if you want. Not that you need them. Totally for informational purposes only." His eyes flicked to the side again. "Looks like the group is headed back to the van."

Her fingers tightened on the fabric of the seat, pride warring with . . . also pride. Admit to Jon she needed his help? Or risk looking ridiculous in front of everyone and possibly getting kicked off the project before it even began?

"Is this because you feel sorry for me? Because if so—"

"No!" His brows drew together, jaw tightening. It was the first time Reggie had seen him look anything but wholesome and cheerful, and it was disturbing how much it appealed to her. She'd always been attracted to intelligence and success—never something as superficial as appearance—but the raw intensity in his glower made her skin hot.

She shifted in her seat. "Fine. Regale me with your expertise, but be warned that I probably won't use it. I'm just curious about what you have to say."

"Don't try to look at the camera," Jon said, speaking quickly. "In fact, pretend it's not even there. Look at whoever you're talking to, and trust Mimi to adjust the shot. And unlock your knees. I used to do that all the time when I first started acting because I was so nervous, but it makes your whole stance awkward, so try to channel someone with swagger. Quick, who's the most badass person you can think of?"

"Gordon Cooper," she answered automatically. "When the Mercury capsule's automatic landing system failed, he invented an entire manual landing procedure on the fly using only his pocket watch to time firing the fuel thrusters *by hand*. By hand! Then, after he somehow survived instead of crash-landing into Earth, he very calmly said he'd always wanted to do that anyway and the electrical failure just gave him an excuse to do it. Can you imagine the sheer fucking insanity of doing complex calculus while you plummet to your death, pulling several Gs of force, I might add, and meanwhile the cabin is filling with carbon dioxide? It's absolutely mind blowing. And the best part is he did it himself, without anyone's help in Mission Control."

"Okay, wow, that's . . . wow." Jon gave her a strange look. "You're really animated when you're passionate about something. Can you do whatever the heck that was, but on camera?"

They were almost at the car now. Mimi was saying something with exaggerated hand movements, and Rudy threw back his head. Muffled laughter filtered through the windows. No one was paying attention to her and Jon except for Jacqui, the publicist, who eyed them with an unreadable expression.

Reggie's throat squeezed. "I don't know."

"I'll set you up with softball questions. Follow my lead, okay?"

Jacqui slid the side door wide, bursting their quiet bubble open and filling it with chatter and noise. Zach, the sound tech, clambered into the back first, and the rest of the group followed.

"What time should I change the reservation to now?" Jacqui was asking Rudy with a somewhat exasperated air.

"Let's do five thirty." Rudy settled into the passenger seat and turned to look at Reggie and Jon. "This stop better be good. Have to call the ex-wife tonight, and she's on East Coast time."

She glanced at Jon. He gave her the smallest nod.

"Don't worry, we're going to get some great shots at the pool." Reggie beamed at Rudy, and for a moment, he seemed caught off guard by the force of her good cheer.

He recovered quickly. "As long as it's fast," he muttered.

Reggie faced forward and drove, heart thudding in her chest all the while. She'd never felt comfortable in a world so heavily reliant on social interaction, though she'd learned to fake it well enough to get this far. Space, though, that was where she really excelled. Alone in the silent, infinite expanse, looking down at Earth like the outsider she was . . . that was comfortable. She could be herself there and not worry what everyone thought of her.

But to get back to that magical place, she'd have to pretend to be someone she wasn't. Someone people actually wanted to be around for extended periods of time. Someone funny and exuberant and *likable*.

She really hoped Jon could help her pull this off.

CHAPTER 4

Reggie stalked into the giant, pool-filled room where the Neutral Buoyancy Lab (NBL, for short) lived, Jon following close behind her. Humidity coated her skin, a feeling as familiar to her as the pervasive smells of chlorine and the support crew's microwaved popcorn. She'd spent a lot of time training for her last space mission here, where a near-identical replica of the ISS lived beneath metric tons of water.

She stole a glance at Jon, whose gaze swept over the cavernous concrete room with wide-eyed wonder. For once, she couldn't blame him. This was one of the largest swimming pools in the world, filled with over six million gallons of water.

During a training exercise, the water's surface would be rippling from divers, equipment, and astronauts moving around in it, but it looked like most scheduled activities were over for the day. The surface of the Caribbean-blue water was glassy, the room relatively quiet aside from the sound of pumps and the echoes of a group of teenagers at the far end of the pool. Interns, probably.

"This is so c—" Jon caught himself. "Killer."

Reggie gave him a sideways glance. "Yes, it is. This is where we practice doing space walks and maintenance on the outside of the Space Station. The water lets us practice floating in zero-g."

"Wait, hold that thought." He waved Mimi over. "Let's get this all on camera."

A boulder took up residence in her gut, and she stiffened in response as the camera's blinking red light switched on. Rudy looked up from his phone with narrowed eyes. How was she supposed to look *natural* when nothing about this was natural at all?

"Repeat what you just told me," Jon said, redirecting her attention. "And maybe point at the pool. Can we get closer to the edge too?"

"Sure." Reggie dutifully walked him across the wet cement to where a painted yellow safety line marked a one-foot distance to the water. She placed them right on the line, nodding at the dive team leader on duty as she did so. Though during training exercises the divers provided skilled support for the astronauts, during off-hours they were primarily present for liability reasons. No one had ever been dumb enough to fall in (as far as Reggie knew, anyway), but with such expensive equipment lurking below the surface, you could never be too safe.

"Ready?" Jon asked. He leaned in closer and murmured, "Unlock your knees."

"They're not locked," she whispered back, even though they had been until that moment. "Do I have to smile?"

"Er—"

"That was a joke." Reggie pasted on her practiced smile. Katya always called it the "bear-killer" smile, though Reggie had never really gotten the joke. Reggie had never killed a bear; she'd punched one, and it was only that one time. The cosmonaut had a strange sense of humor.

"On second thought, maybe don't smile."

She scowled at him.

Jon gave a nervous laugh. "Never mind, *do* smile. Try thinking of something that makes you happy."

She imagined hurling the video camera into the pool and giving everyone the double middle-finger salute on her way out the door.

"Yes! Exactly like that."

Mimi gave her a signal, and Reggie mechanically repeated her spiel, adding a few bonus factoids for the sake of it.

It all sounded boring as shit to Reggie's ears, but Jon nodded encouragingly. "That's really *cool.*" From the twinkle in his eye, she suspected the verbiage was intentional.

Her lips quirked of their own volition.

"What's that platform thingy over there?" Jon asked. He moved closer so he could point at something behind her, and from a full foot away she could feel the heat radiating from his skin. Or was that just her imagination? He leaned in closer and whispered, "Stop looking at the camera."

"I'm not," she whispered back, tearing her eyes away from the red light. She glanced where Jon was pointing, and in a louder, camera-worthy voice she intoned, "Well, Jon, I am glad that you have asked this question! It is an interesting platform, this platform we are looking at. It is used to lower astronauts into the pool during training exercises."

He prompted her with a follow-up question, and before her eyes could stray back to the lens, she made herself focus on Jon's face and the way his big puppy eyes lit up and the creases at the corners of his mouth deepened as she spoke, and the tightness in her shoulders eased a fraction.

"We use the platform because when we're doing an exercise underwater, we practice in full spacesuits, and they're fairly heavy."

She gestured for Jon and the cameras to follow her over to where the top half of a spacesuit was suspended from metal supports. The entire contraption was attached to a crane designed to slowly lower its wearer into the water. "After all, these suits are the only things protecting us from the vacuum of space, including all the radiation from the sun. Imagine wearing a dentist's lead x-ray apron, but thicker, and around your whole body. Trust me when I say you'd rather get lowered into the water than accidentally belly flop while sporting an extra two hundred and eighty pounds."

Jon laughed—the first time today anyone had laughed at her attempts to joke—and confidence zinged through her. She was actually doing this. Crushing a publicity bit like she was some kind of late-night show host.

Jon inspected the headless and legless suit. "Where's the rest of it?"

"Probably in one of these rooms behind you. Astronauts get the pants on first, then wiggle into the torso from the bottom. You usually have several people helping you, because it's not easy."

"Like some kind of king." Jon's eyes crinkled at the corners. "Space King Jon . . . I like the sound of that."

Reggie rolled her eyes, forgetting for a moment they were on camera. "Of course you do."

Jon winked at her, and then his eyes snapped over to the side, as if his attention had been suddenly caught by something else. He'd done that often throughout the day. One second he'd be fully engrossed in whatever they were talking about, and the next he'd be wandering off, drawn to whatever had caught his eye. "What's this here in the water?"

The dive lead perked up as Jon approached the pool's edge, and Reggie hurried to catch up to him.

"Stay behind the line," she warned him.

Jon shuffled back one reluctant step. "Is that what I think it is?"

Reggie followed his line of sight and craned her neck to get a closer look. "Huh," she said, slowly. "I didn't realize they'd set it up already."

"Wow . . . the Apollo moon lander."

"No." Reggie grabbed his bicep, and answering heat swept up her forearm into her chest. She pulled her hand back, quickly, but not fast enough to stop the heat from spreading to her face. "That's the new Orion lander. Next year, that lander will ferry six astronauts from the Artemis III shuttle to the surface of a crater at the moon's south pole."

"Seriously?" Jon leaned forward again, and this time she didn't stop him. The radiant imprint from his skin was still hot on her palm.

"Seriously. It'll be the first time humans have set foot on the moon in over fifty years." She managed to keep her voice steady. Somehow.

"Cut!" Rudy called out. He smacked his hands together in applause, the sound amplified by the high-ceilinged room. "That was phenomenal, kiddo. Fucking phenomenal."

Her smile instantly withered.

"He calls everyone that," Jon said in a low voice.

That did not make it okay, but now was not the time to make a stink. Not with cameras nearby—even if they weren't rolling.

Keeping her teeth clamped together, she forced her smile back into place.

Suddenly, a screech rent the air, followed by a high-pitched "Oh my God, it's the Space Dude!" The shrill sound bounced off the water and concrete in a cacophony of unholy echoes, and everything that followed happened in slow motion.

Jon jumped, startled.

Reggie spun toward the source of the sound and saw one of the teenage interns barreling toward them, two of her cohorts close behind.

Jon's voice came from behind her. "Oh . . . shii—"

Reggie's stomach plummeted. She turned back around but was too late.

Jon hit the pool in a full flail, arms windmilling out to the sides, and Reggie barely had time to squeeze her eyes shut before water exploded all over her.

The dive lead blew his whistle and dived in, but he was at the other end of a pool two-thirds the size of a football field. Below her, Jon continued to thrash around, spraying water over the side in frantic abandon. Voices shouted behind her, calling out in alarm, and Reggie had the immediate, horrifying thought: *What if he can't swim?* And then a worse thought: *What if he damages some of that equipment?* Even the mock-up of the moon lander was worth millions of dollars, and Jon had fallen in on her watch.

Still . . .

Then one of the interns cried out from behind her, "Are you getting all this, Yasmin?"

"Oh, I'm *so* recording it!"

Great. The last thing she needed was yet another viral video with her name on it, especially if footage showed her standing by like an idiot while Jon inhaled pool water. (Headline: *Goth Astronaut Hates Men and Wants Them All to Drown—Literally!*)

Without a second thought, Reggie kicked off her sneakers and dived into the pool.

✦ ⭐ ✦

Jon knew how to swim, but it was one thing to take a casual dip in the pool at his apartment complex and another thing to slip and topple in butt first while your mouth was still open in surprise. He'd gulped water instead of air and panicked. By the time he'd righted and managed to surface, hacking up a cocktail of chlorine, spit, and bile, someone had already jumped in. Strong hands grabbed his shoulders, steadying him, and he felt the hot press of another body along his side. A *soft*, hot body.

He blinked, trying to clear the stinging water from his contacts. His vision was blocked by tentacles of his own hair, but he made out a blurry crowd huddled close to the pool's edge. Their shouts of concern were muffled, and he snorted to dislodge water from his ears.

He couldn't believe he'd fallen in. He was often forgetful and occasionally a little uncoordinated, but this wasn't him losing another one of Jacqui's binders or accidentally knocking over his water bottle all over a set piece. This was way worse. It was only day one of a shoot he was unbelievably lucky to even have gotten, and he'd already managed to screw up—big time. More important, he'd told Reggie he'd make them both look good on camera so she could impress her bosses, and this was definitely *not* an impressive look.

"I've got you." He recognized Reggie's voice in his ear. Felt her soft breasts pushed up against his left shoulder blade. Shame and adrenaline thrummed under his skin.

His dick getting hard was normal. A totally normal thing that happened when a man who liked tits was smooshed up against a banging rack—and holy shit, were her nipples hard? Either way, it was a reaction he didn't want to advertise. Especially on camera. *Especially* in front of a bunch of teenage fans. *Yikes.*

He tried wriggling out of her hold, and she only tightened her grip. "Jon, hold still."

Where she held herself against him, he burned. From his shoulder down through his rib cage and the left half of his butt. It was delicious. It was torturous. He felt like a horny sixteen-year-old again, lusting after his way-hot but way-adult physics teacher. Reggie was a woman so far removed from his sphere of possibility that it felt dirty to even consider her in a sexual way, but he did, and that only made the ache in his balls worse, and she was so, so soft—

He needed to get ahold of himself. Now.

He coughed and managed to choke out, "You can let go."

And then, finally, she did. "Can you get out on your own?"

"Yep." He doggy-paddled over to the side of the pool and slung an arm over the concrete lip. Half a dozen hands thrust in his face, and he waved them away. "Just need a sec. My, uh . . . my contacts."

He blinked rapidly, making a show of poking at his eyes. In fact, one of his contacts was gone completely, which explained why everything was still so blurry. Mostly, though, he was waiting for his erection to chill out.

It was in no hurry to comply. That part of his body was still extremely enthused about Reggie's *Baywatch*-style rescue, and the designer jeans his stylist had picked out were uncomfortably tight.

"Holy crapazoid. It really *is* him!" The not-so-discreet whisper came from one of the teenagers.

Jon squeezed his left eye shut so he could see better. Surrounding the pool, worried expressions on their faces, were the film crew, Jacqui, and Rudy. To their left was a pod of three teenagers in matching NASA T-shirts and one similarly dressed adult woman wearing a mortified expression.

Reggie pulled herself out of the water, her movements precise and graceful. Her khakis and polo shirt were soaked through, clinging to her compact frame like a wrinkly second skin, and her dark, shoulder-length hair lay plastered to her head. Ribbons of smudgy eye makeup trailed down her cheeks. She was still gorgeous—in his eyes, anyway—but even Jon recognized this wasn't her finest look.

"Did you get the whole thing, Yas?" whispered one of the other teenagers. A redheaded boy with glasses.

The leader of the pack, a girl with frizzy brown hair, held up her phone. "Sure did."

Jacqui's head snapped to the side, her catlike eyes narrowed as if sensing prey, a calculating smile already in place. "Oh, did you happen to record some footage?" She extended a hand to the pack's leader. "Jacqueline Shaw, publicist for WME talent agency in Los Angeles. I'd love to take a look . . . Yasmin, was it?"

His publicist was a freaking godsend. This was humiliating enough without the entire internet bearing witness, and Jacqui would do everything she could to get her hands on that recording.

The teenager eyed Jacqui's hand suspiciously and slid her phone into her back pocket. "You got 'take a look' money, Ms. Shaw?"

Their handler interjected with some hasty apologies.

Jacqui gave a dismissive wave, her bracelets tinkling. "No worries at all. Take my card . . . I'd love to circle back with you about working something out before that video goes live. Oh, and did I mention that Jon loves meeting fans? In fact, Jon would love to give out some autographs right now. Right, Jon?"

Squealing ensued.

"I'd love to," he wheezed. At least he'd delayed long enough he could get out of the pool without getting arrested for public indecency.

The sound guy extended a hand. "Let me help you outa there, dude."

As he clambered onto the concrete, gallons of water pooling beneath him, the guy who'd been lifeguarding in one of those full-body wet suits swam up behind them, his hand outstretched. In his palm was what looked like a lump of coal.

"Anyone lose this?"

Reggie made an odd sound and scurried over to snatch up the strange lump. "That's mine. Sorry." She curled her fingers over it protectively. "Must have come out of my pocket when I jumped in."

The diver folded his arms on the edge, shaking his head. "Glad y'all aren't too worse for the wear. Never actually seen anyone fall in before, and Lord knows what kind of paperwork I'd have to fill out if anything untoward had gone down."

Reggie narrowed her eyes. "I think it's best if this doesn't get mentioned to anyone, period."

"You know I have to let the head diver know so he can report to the chief astronaut . . ."

"Do you?" Reggie fixed her arctic glare on the diver.

"Uh . . ."

She continued to glare.

"Maybe not?"

"Fantastic." Reggie grimace-smiled. She marched away to snatch a towel from a nearby table and dried off with short, jerky movements, her expression tightly closed again.

Jon had sworn he'd been making progress in getting her to warm up to him. The way they'd been bantering back and forth on camera had been brilliant. They'd had the kind of natural chemistry you couldn't rehearse into existence no matter how hard you tried, and Rudy had been *loving* it.

. . . And then he'd gone and fallen into the pool, ruining everything.

Why did he always have to screw things up?

He stepped toward Reggie, wanting to apologize or at least resurrect the sliver of friendship they'd begun, but Jacqui laid a hand on his arm. "Autographs," she reminded him, producing a permanent marker from her bottomless Mary Poppins bag.

"Oh, sign my notebook!" the redheaded kid cried out, holding up a moisture-wrinkled spiral pad.

"Oooh, me too, me too! I looooooove *Space Dude*. You're the coolest actor ever."

Jon dutifully accepted the proffered pads. "Do you want me to sign a message or anything?"

"Do Space Dude's line! 'Surf the gravity wave, dude.'"

He did as asked, almost on autopilot. He didn't even internally cringe at the line—not like he'd used to, anyway. When the movie had first come out, it had been a huge financial flop. But when it had been released on streaming services months later, *Space Dude* had blasted into sudden word-of-mouth popularity online. Teenagers had (collectively, apparently) decided his dry delivery of the corny, borderline-nonsensical lines elevated *Space Dude* from a pulpy, throwaway action flick to a satirical sci-fi send-up dripping with edgy, ironic coolness.

Who knew what had possessed him to deliver his lines that way, but the director had let him, and it had worked. He'd become a pop culture sensation overnight. Not in the ways that really mattered, of course; his agent still fought to get him roles, and no one over the age of twenty-five had any clue who he was. But it had been enough to land him this coveted, award-bait role on *Escape Velocity*.

And here he was, torpedoing his one big shot. Already.

From the corner of his eye, he saw Reggie leaving. "I'm going home to change," she told Jacqui. "It'll take at least an hour round trip with Friday rush hour traffic, so don't wait for me."

Rudy smacked his forehead. "Great, we'll have to push back dinner. See if you can move it to seven, will ya, Jacqs? I'll just do my call before we eat." He shuffled off, muttering something that sounded a whole lot like *fucking disaster* as his thumbs flew across his phone screen.

Jacqui turned away from Rudy with a distinct glint in her eye that said the director's days on this earth were *numbered*, and that number would be zero if he changed the reservation one more damn time.

The door slammed behind Reggie. Every cell in Jon's body wanted to run after her, but he didn't. He had autographs to sign, and he had to be a good show pony. He'd already messed things up enough already.

He only hoped he could come back from this before Rudy kicked *him* off the movie.

CHAPTER 5

Reggie paused outside the door to her condo, mentally girding herself. Strains of familiar music filtering through the door indicated Katya was already home and watching something in the living room, which meant Reggie had zero chance of sneaking by unnoticed.

When Katya had announced her extended stay in Houston, Reggie had graciously offered up her spare bedroom, thinking it would be good to switch things up and have some steady social interaction outside of work or the occasional drink with Deb. For the most part, it had been. But there were times Reggie longed for the privacy to storm around her apartment in a petulant rage without having to explain herself to anyone, and this was one of those times.

As soon as Reggie's key wiggled into the lock, the movie sounds went quiet. She opened the door to find Katya cross-legged on the couch, casually flipping through one of Reggie's coffee-table books about rocks. "*Zdorovo*," Katya said, not looking up.

"Hey, yourself." Reggie kicked the door shut behind her. "Were you watching that movie with the ice sisters and the talking snowman again?"

Katya flipped a page. "You insult me. I am a cold Russian woman. I do not watch movies for children."

"Okay, okay. I'll . . . let it go."

Katya slammed the book shut and finally looked up. "You are such an Els—" She trailed off. "Your hair is wet. Why are you wearing gym clothes?"

They'd already worked out together this morning, so the fact Reggie was in her gym clothes was suspicious, but she hadn't wanted to drive home soaking wet. Reggie sighed. "Jon fell into the pool in the NBL."

Katya's eyebrows shot up. "No."

"Yes."

Reggie kicked off her shoes and headed upstairs. Katya followed, stopping at Reggie's bedroom door. She leaned against the doorframe with her arms crossed, waiting as Reggie undressed by violently flinging each item into the laundry bin. After spending six months together on the Space Station, where privacy was essentially nonexistent, neither of them bothered with modesty.

"It appears this tour did not go well," Katya observed.

Reggie stood in front of her open closet, flicking each hanger aside with impatience. What the hell was she supposed to wear for this dinner? She hadn't even thought to ask what kind of restaurant it was. "It was a complete clusterfuck. I tried to act fun and approachable on camera, and instead I came across like a cyborg pretending to be human."

"Eh." Katya shrugged. "This is not important. You are a very good astronaut. Not as good as me, but very good."

Reggie yanked a black shift dress off the hanger. This would be fine. Serviceable, boring, and black—Reggie's fashion prerequisites. "Thanks for your vote of confidence."

"Why do you need to do this? I do not care how friendly my comrades are in space. Friendly will not be useful in catastrophic system failure."

"Technically, nothing is really useful in a catastrophic system failure." Reggie dragged the dress over her head. It floated down her body, settling into a shapeless, knee-length column. "But you know that six weeks is a long time to spend on the lunar surface when the current record is seventy-four hours. Isolation in space is psychologically demanding, for one, and more importantly this mission is a big deal and they're doing a lot of press for it, so they're looking for a crew that's ready to suck up to the media to help generate hype."

Katya silently eyed Reggie's outfit with a cryptic yet somehow judgmental expression.

Reggie continued, "You know what sucks the most? Jon actually pulled me aside and said he was going to help make me look good on camera, and he almost did. At the NBL, he managed to ask all the right questions in just the right way . . . I can't explain it, but he somehow made me feel like we were just talking one on one, and I could tell we were killing it. Then he fell in the goddamn pool like some big, dumb puppy who can't walk without tripping over his big, dumb paws, and I jumped in because I thought he couldn't swim, and I looked like an *idiot*. And now I have to sit through an entire meal with these people, and it's only a matter of time before I get asked to step aside from this assignment. Then I can kiss my chances of landing on the moon next year goodbye."

Katya's face twisted with revulsion. "Step aside?" She shook her head. "*Net.* You go to the dinner; you tell this director he will choose you. Then it is done. This is how you have always done things. A bear comes to eat your friend? *No,* you say, *I will kill you instead.*"

"You know that's not what happened," Reggie reminded her. This was an old argument she might never win. "Anyway, I should be happy about getting reassigned. Can you imagine me having to puppy-sit Jon Leo for an entire month? He'd probably get thrown off balance by his own freakishly huge biceps and fall into a ravine before the end of the second day."

"Hmm."

Reggie marched into the adjoining bathroom and dug her hair dryer out of the cupboard, but she didn't turn it on. She poked her head back out of the bathroom. "What's *hmm* supposed to mean?"

"Nothing."

"It means something."

Katya strolled over to the bed and sat, toying with the end of her long ponytail. "This is what you are wearing to dinner?"

"What's wrong with it?"

"It is ugly." Katya never pulled any punches.

Reggie chuffed in outrage. "It's not ugly!"

"You look like you are going to a funeral service for a very religious uncle. Wear my purple jumpsuit."

"Oh, no. No. Noooooo. That's not my style. Thank you, but no."

"Your chest looks very good in this jumpsuit."

"I'm too short for it."

"So, you wear heels."

"Uh-uh." She ducked into the bathroom and turned on the hair dryer to tune out further discussion. There was no way she'd feel comfortable showing up to dinner in that formfitting eggplant . . . *thing*. Katya was confident in her own skin in a way Reggie could never be.

Once—one freaking time—she'd made the mistake of confessing this to Katya. They'd had too much vodka after a weekend playing tourist in downtown Houston. Somehow, they'd gone from shots in the kitchen to playing dress-up out of Katya's shopping bags, and Reggie had ended up in the jumpsuit. "I wish there was someone I'd feel brave enough to wear this for," she'd said.

Reggie finished drying her hair and plugged in her straightener. When she came out of the bathroom, the offending garment was laid out on her bed for her next to a pair of Katya's tallest heels. Curse that woman for being the same size.

She held the jumpsuit against her torso and stepped up to the full-length mirror. What would Jon think if he saw her in this? The second the thought entered her brain, she erased it. Never in her life had she dressed to please someone else, and she wasn't going to start for an airheaded *actor*, of all people.

This was the thing Reggie had learned about men—and most women, too—when it came to sex: no one turned down a no-strings-attached fuck because they didn't like your outfit.

Not that she was going to sleep with Jon. That was absolutely the last thing on her mind. In fact, she failed to envision a single scenario in which begging that man to fling her facedown over the hood of her sensible Honda Accord while caging her in with his thighs and mercilessly pounding her to orgasm before dinner had anything but disastrous repercussions.

Not that it mattered, because she wasn't thinking about it.

Reggie glowered at her wan reflection. She'd scrubbed off the dregs of her heavy-duty foundation, and the acne-scarred skin beneath looked especially pitted under her bedroom's unflattering overhead lighting. Reapplying her makeup would take at least fifteen minutes, and she was already going to be late to dinner. She didn't have time to indulge impractical fantasies.

"I'm not wearing this, Katya," she called out into the hallway. There was no reply.

*. ⭐.

Jon used his fork to prod at the balsamic blob swimming in his side dish of olive oil, only half listening to the conversation between Rudy and Jacqui across from him.

Reggie had sent Jacqui a text saying she'd be late; she lived in the suburbs and had to deal with the tail end of rush hour traffic. Still, Jon worried she might not come at all.

Jacqui had chosen the dinner venue with Rudy in mind: it was packed with a desperately trendy crowd, it blared incongruently loud and repetitive music, and everything on the menu cost about three times as much as it reasonably should—so it felt just like a regular LA restaurant. He hated it. He'd worked at a lot of restaurants exactly like this one before he'd gotten a role that paid well enough for him to afford to quit serving, and dining at them now unfailingly reminded him of how fast his star had risen—and how quickly it could plummet back down to earth.

Their server stopped by their table with a bread basket, fragrant steam still rising off its contents. Jon had never wanted anything more than to bury his entire face in that basket. "No, thank you," he said politely when it reached him.

Rudy gave him a teasing elbow nudge. "Watching that action figure, huh?"

"You know it." That yeasty-crisp smell of deliciousness made Jon's mouth water with longing, so he grinned to make sure it didn't show on his face. "My trainer has me on that Leading Man meal plan."

"Got you on enhancers too?" Rudy tore a hunk of bread off and crammed it in his mouth. He chewed with his mouth open. "The bigger the better these days."

The whole reason he was on such a strict diet and exercise regimen was so he *didn't* have to go on steroids to get the inhuman physique that superhero movies had popularized. Jacqui had always advised him to be evasive with the media on questions like that, but what was he supposed to say if the director himself was the one asking?

Jon flicked his publicist a look, and she jumped in. "We think the natural approach is working well for Jon, but we've always been open to the studio's input."

Natural approach. He poked at his balsamic art again. Ignored the crushing emptiness in the pit of his stomach. This is what he wanted. He *wanted* this. Someday soon, he was going to stand on that stage accepting his shiny gold Oscar and see his mom smiling with pride in the audience, and it was all going to be worth it.

"Good, good." Rudy scanned the table, found the bread basket at its center, and hauled it back to his plate for seconds. "You hear from that intern chick yet about the recording?"

Jacqui sighed. "Not yet. She seemed pretty interested in the walk-on cameo offer, but at the end of the day she's within her legal rights to post it."

"Listen, kid. A lot of people think any publicity is good publicity, but they don't know what the fuck they're talking about. We control the brand; we control the message. That's why we're doing this behind-the-scenes astronaut-training shit." Rudy pointed at Jacqui with a crust of bread. "So we get that vid. I don't want my lead astronaut falling in a pool like some numb-nuts on camera. He wants to get caught doing lines of coke off some hooker's rack, fine. He wants to get wasted and assault the door guy? Fine. Better than fine, it's *in character*. Numb-nuts? Not in character. Got it?"

"Got it." Jacqui's smile didn't falter, but her eyes sparked in warning. Rudy didn't seem to notice; from what Jon had observed thus far, this was how the man spoke to everyone. And no one did a damn thing to correct the habit because he was *Rudy Ruffino*, Oscar-winning director who turned every movie he touched into gold. The fact that he was a massive shithead—that he was insulting Jon, talking about him like he wasn't even there—didn't matter.

His stomach twisted, and he was suddenly sure he was about to puke. As if his body were acting of its own accord, he folded his napkin into a crisp tent and pushed back from the table. "Gotta step out for a quick phone call. Mom's on vacation in Europe, and you know how it is with time zones . . ."

Rudy chuffed in irritation, even though he'd used a very similar excuse earlier.

"It's so sweet how close he is with his mother," Jacqui added in his defense. Absolute legend. He really should pay her even more than he did. They'd cut him a decent check for this movie, but it wasn't the kind of life-altering windfall he'd dreamed it would be. Maybe when he had Oscar clout . . .

Yeah, maybe then.

He stepped out into the brisk evening air. Jacqui hadn't been lying to Rudy about how close he was to his mom—after all, it had just been the two of them for most of his life, and in his biased opinion, she was a pretty cool lady. But he'd already called her today, and right now, he simply needed a minute alone.

They're just words, dude. Get it together. Yeah, it sucked to feel like he was smarter than people gave him credit for, but as insults about his intelligence went, he'd heard way better than Rudy's lame jabs. Heck, *he'd* made harsher jokes about himself before, back when he'd dabbled in stand-up and perfected the self-deprecating routine he'd been working on since the third grade.

The restaurant was located on a downtown city block, so there was no parking lot to hide in, but a short walk down the block and around the corner took him to a quiet side street lined with cars. Someone was parallel parking, but the street was otherwise empty. Still, the last thing he wanted was to be recognized by fans right now. He ducked into the entry alcove of a closed shop.

The car's driver executed a flawless parallel parking job, turned off the car, and stepped out. She wore a skintight, dark-purple-colored thing that hugged her ass and waist like a glove before flaring out at her breasts, leaving her bare shoulders glowing in the bruised light of the streetlamps. A leather jacket dangled from the crook of her arm. It was something a vampire seductress would wear in an old movie, but more modern.

Hot. Then he blinked in recognition. "Reggie?"

"Jon?" She squinted into the shadows. "What are you doing out here? I thought the reservation was for seven."

"It is. Everyone's inside. Just needed to get some air."

Her heels clicked on the pavement as she crossed the sidewalk and joined him in the alcove. It wasn't a big doorway. Even though he stood with his back pressed to the concrete wall on one side and she stood against the other, there was barely two feet to spare in between.

She'd redone her makeup, but it was different than before; the shadow around her eyes was darker. Her lips were painted some deep shade that looked almost black in the poorly lit alcove. She could have been a witch. Had she asked for a pint of his blood to casually raise demons from hell before dinner, he'd have opened up his veins for her then and there.

Shadowed gray eyes swept over him, up and down. "What happened?"

He almost lied again. It was reflexive. You didn't go spilling your guts to people you'd just met. In Hollywood, you didn't even spill your guts to your closest friends. You went out and bought a potted fern or something, and then when no one else was around, you talked to your fern. You never had to worry about plants selling your secrets over to a gossip blog for a few thousand bucks. But something about Reggie made him want to be real with her.

"Rudy's being a prick."

"Shocking. He seems like such a nice guy. What's his problem?" Reggie's face lit up. "Did your publicist knee him in the balls for calling her 'kiddo'?"

"No, but I'm sure she wants to. Rudy's annoyed with me about the . . . pool thing."

"Hmm. Understandable."

He hid a wince. "I'm sorry about that, by the way. Really." He waited for her to say something. When she didn't, he hurried to stanch the awkward silence. "I should have been more careful. It's one hundred percent my fault, and after you left, I made sure everyone knew that. If it makes you feel better, I think Rudy was digging the segment up until that point."

Reggie looked away. "It's fine. Forget it."

"Seriously! You were doing so well before that happened. Listen—"

"I said, *forget it.*" She crossed her arms, which had the unfortunate side effect of boosting her killer breasts. So supremely unfortunate. He tried to look away. He really, really tried. So much so that he barely heard her continue. "Look, this little training thing might not be a big deal to you, but it is to me. I can't afford to look bad in any media that the selection board might see. So when we get to the Arizona base, I'm going to ask that you take this seriously and pay very close attention when I give you instructions. For example, *Don't get too close to the edge of the pool. Stay behind the line,* and so forth. Are you capable of committing to that?"

Was that a sliver of areola or merely a shadow?

"Jon?"

"Yes?"

"If you aren't up to this, say so now. I'd rather not waste a month fucking around when the mission I want is on the line. I'll let my colleague Wes take over, because I'm sure he'd *love* this bullshit. You two can stage a whole damn talent show."

"I don't want Wes, though. I want you." As soon as the words were out, he realized how they sounded, and his chest and face flooded with heat. She cocked her head, but it was too dark to read her expression. Was she upset? Insulted? He had to fix this. "Not like that—" His throat closed over the words. Oh, this was bad.

"Not like that?" she repeated in a monotone.

Panic buzzed through him. "I mean, yes, like that, but not like *that.* Professionally. Respectfully." He swallowed. "Very respectfully."

A single heeled click echoed in the tiny alcove as she stepped forward. There was only a foot between them now. Barely enough air to breathe.

Her voice was low. "I do appreciate respect."

"You do?" he croaked.

He was going to die here. Flames engulfing him, his heart beating so hard it exploded in his chest, his lungs struggling for air. Because it seemed—and he wasn't entirely sure, which was the problem, but it *seemed*—like Reggie was flirting with him. It *seemed* like she might step forward again, which would mean she'd be touching him again like she had earlier in the pool. Her whole body fitted against his, the outside of her thighs pressed against the inside of his thighs, her breasts—holy *hell*, those breasts . . . boxy polo shirts did not do her justice in any way, shape, or form, because those were the tits of a goddamn goddess—they'd be pressed against his rib cage, and all he'd have to do was reach out, and his hands could skim over the impossibly gorgeous expanse of bared skin at her shoulders, and then . . .

"Yes." She stepped back, and when the streetlight slid over her face, it revealed perfect composure. Had it all been his imagination? "That's why I'm asking for your cooperation in giving this project your full effort and attention in order to mitigate further 'accidents.' I *need* this assignment to go smoothly."

He nodded, not trusting himself to speak. It wasn't like he had a *thing* for authoritative women—at least, he didn't think so—but when Reggie spoke like this, it definitely got blood pumping straight to his dick.

Well, that and her—

"And stop looking at my tits."

He clapped a hand over his eyes. "Sorry!"

"So we have an agreement?" A pause. "I'm holding out my hand for you to shake."

He stuck out his other hand, feeling through the air. He finally found hers and clasped it, agreeing to . . . whatever it was he was agreeing to.

Her faint snort was barely audible. "You're being ridiculous. You know that, right? You can uncover your eyes."

"I can't. I'm very, very sorry."

A sigh. "I guess it's my fault. My tits *are* really excellent in this."

He carefully lowered his hand, staring resolutely at the wall behind her head. "You are a very accomplished and intelligent woman." His gaze flicked down, then back up again. "With extremely nice breasts."

Heeled footsteps approached, sure and determined. Reggie drew back until she was up against the opposite wall again, just as Jacqui came into view. "Jon? What's taking so long—" Jacqui caught sight of Reggie and came to a full stop. In a single glance, Jacqui read the room, and she read it well. "Reggie, I'm glad you could make it. How was traffic?"

Reggie cleared her throat. "Not too bad for a Friday. We were just headed in. Has everyone ordered?"

"Not at all. We started with drinks." Jacqui gave Reggie another once-over, like she'd done something to merit a second evaluation. "Nice jumpsuit. Zara?"

"Probably." Reggie shrugged and began walking alongside Jacqui toward the restaurant. She glanced at him over her shoulder. "Coming?"

Jesus. A few seconds more in that alcove, and he might have been.

CHAPTER 6

Her goal for the evening was to win Rudy's approval and dissuade him from any second thoughts he might be having after seeing her earlier on-camera failures, but dinner was nevertheless a torturous experience for Reggie—and Jon's proximity didn't help.

The semicircle booth seating was cramped and intimate, and the only place to sit was to Jon's left. Jon was left handed, which meant her right arm was constantly in danger of bumping into his left as she ate, and that meant she could barely breathe for fear of brushing against his stray hand or elbow. She sat stiffly in her seat, trying to create as much space between them as she could, but Jon's clumsiness made it impossible to avoid contact.

"Sorry," he mumbled every few minutes as his skin made inadvertent contact with hers.

If it were anyone else, she'd think he was doing it on purpose. But each time it happened, he froze and his cheeks flushed like some eighteenth-century schoolboy catching his first glimpse of bare ankle. It would have been oddly charming if she weren't already doing her damnedest to stifle her inappropriate attraction to him.

If only it were easy to concentrate on something else, but Rudy seemed determined to fill every conversational break with the sound of his own voice.

Between the entrées and dessert, Jacqui, who was sitting across from her, took out her phone and leaned forward. "You're a Capricorn according to your birth date on NASA's website, but do you happen to know your rising sign? Or maybe what time you were born?"

"No, I don't."

"Maybe your mother would know." Jacqui's tone was hopeful.

"I'm sure she does."

"Could you—"

"No." Reggie reached for her wineglass and drained it. She'd hoped to make the glass last the entire meal, but that clearly wasn't happening; she wasn't normally a heavy drinker, but sipping from her glass gave her something to do with her hands when conversation got awkward.

It was already very, very awkward.

She scrambled for something to say. Anything besides having to explain why she'd rather avoid calling her mother to ask for anything, even something as small as her time of birth. "I know I was born in the very early morning hours."

She had no idea if that was true, but it seemed to satisfy.

Jacqui's neatly penciled brows drew together, and she typed something in on her phone. "I can work with that."

From the corner of her eye, she could see Jon pushing his garnish around his plate with his fork like the conductor of a choo choo train. His elbow brushed against her, and he stopped. "Sorry."

"Do you want to switch spots?" Reggie whispered.

Jon wrinkled his nose, then leaned over to speak in her ear. "You don't want to sit next to Rudy, trust me. He sweats. A lot."

His breath tickled the spot right below her ear. Reggie swallowed. When he moved away again, her thighs unclenched.

Flirting with Jon outside had been a risky move. She regretted wearing the jumpsuit. The way he'd looked at her had made her feel far too bold, and the shadows of the alcove had made her feel far too confident.

No, not confident—*stupid*. The odd moment of sexual attraction they'd shared back there was a blip, and nothing could come of it. Until she clinched her spot on the Artemis III team, her laser focus would remain fixed solely on the moon, and if she had to pack her entire vibrator collection to hold out the full month with Jon, so help her, she'd do what needed to be done.

Speaking of dramatic sacrifices, it was time to suck up to Rudy to ensure there was no question about her aptitude for this assignment.

Bear-killer smile: activate. She leaned forward so she could see past Jon. "So, Rudy," she began, "I'd love to hear more about this film—"

"Whoa, kiddo! You're out of wine!" Rudy snapped his fingers in the air like he was calling for a cab.

Jon looked like he wanted to melt into his chair. The open bottle was in the middle of the table, and he grabbed it and began to pour for her. He filled her glass to a reasonable level, glanced at her face, then emptied the rest of the bottle into her glass.

Their server appeared at the table. "How may I—"

"Wine." Rudy snapped again and pointed at Reggie's glass, which was now generously full.

Jon visibly stifled a wince as he addressed the server. "Maybe another bottle, whenever you have a chance. No rush. Sorry. And thank you. And really sorry for the trouble."

"Jesus, kid, you sound like me in the confession booth." Rudy laughed. Big, thigh-slapping hee-haws. "Hah! Forgive me, waitress, for I have sinned!"

Jon laughed, too, but it sounded pained.

Rudy wasn't done. "Please, oh please, I didn't *mean* to drink all the wine, waitress. If you could find the kindness in your heart to, I don't know, *do your job*, surely the Lord will forgive me!"

Reggie could not believe her chances of walking on the moon came down to the whims of this piece of human garbage. "I'm surprised you can get through an entire confession without spontaneously combusting." Rudy froze midchew, his cheek bulging with bread like a lopsided hamster, and everyone else had fallen silent, so she clarified her joke. "Because of all the hot air. Inside you. It's a chemistry joke about how quickly oxygen reacts with flame, which is why on the Space Station, we use an atmosphere-like nitrogen blend . . ."

Jacqui, the publicist, was desperately trying to telepathically communicate something using only her eyes. Probably something along the lines of *Shut up*.

Reggie took a sip of wine. A long one.

So much for pretending to be a people person. Rudy's face had turned a fascinating crimson ombré, the hue starting at his neck and working its way up.

"Ha ha." Jon jumped in with a plainly forced diffusion attempt. "Science jokes! Love 'em."

She should probably apologize, shouldn't she? She opened her mouth, but the words wouldn't come. Apologizing had never been her forte. But then, neither was joking. Or talking to people at all.

Jon went on, "Hey, did you hear the one about the planets getting married?"

Frustrated gloom descended over her mood, and she took another big sip of wine to buffer herself against facing her own failure. Why couldn't she control her innate bitchiness for *one* fucking meal?

"How do they do it, you ask? I'm so glad you asked," Jon continued.

"No one asked," Reggie muttered.

"Yes, they did," he said out of the corner of his mouth. Raising his volume, he finished his joke with a flourishing "They *plan* it! Get it? Planet?"

Rudy finally gulped down his bread in a swallow that looked painful.

Jacqui issued a cheery "I'll get the check!"

Rudy guffawed and smacked the table with both hands, making the silverware and glasses shudder. "Yes! *Fuck* yes! *This* is what I like about you, Regina Hayes." He pointed at Jon. "You, kid, you gotta get to the cojones store and buy yourself a set like hers."

From her side vision, she could see Jon's grin falter before pulling a heroic recovery.

Reggie blinked. "You liked my joke?"

"Oh, no, the joke was fucking terrible." Rudy paused to wave a beleaguered busser over, hijacking a basket of bread that appeared to be on the way to a different table. He hauled the whole loaf out and tore it in half like a bear who'd just emerged, half-starved, from hibernation. "Can you believe the ex-wife was gluten intolerant? Now I eat all the bread I want. Hah! Anyway, forget your joke, it sucked, loved the attitude behind it, though."

"You did?"

"Abso-fuckin'-lutely. I saw that clip of you telling that reporter to, and I quote, eat shit and die, and I thought to myself: That's it. That's the energy I want Jon to emulate for *Escape Velocity*." He sat back in his chair, swirling his wine around his glass like some sort of comic book supervillain and cradling the bread basket in his lap like a pet.

"He wasn't a reporter," was all she could think to say. "Milton Fetzer is a Mars Truther. He thinks NASA is some glorified production studio and all our rover footage from Mars is fake. He runs a blog purporting that Earth is the sole planet in existence."

She *had* said those words to Milton—she just hadn't realized they were being recorded. He'd been hounding her for weeks; somehow he'd found her home address and had camped out on the street in a parked van, waiting for her to leave for work every morning. He'd kept demanding she "admit" that the International Space Station was an underwater movie set. She'd reported him to the police, and they'd issued a warning, so he'd gotten more creative, hunting her down at her favorite lunch spot and at the gym and even at the grocery store. He hadn't harassed any of her male colleagues. He'd targeted her.

Eventually, she'd snapped.

"You want an interview?" she'd said. "Let's do this, then. Ask your questions, and I'll tell you exactly what I think of your One Planet propaganda."

He hadn't told her his buddy was filming them. Nor had he mentioned that he was recording her words on his cell phone. According to NASA's lawyers, she'd agreed to an interview, so her expletive-ridden exchange was considered on record.

The interview was a juicy piece of trash; Milton had spliced the footage to hell and back so that he looked like an innocent reporter besieged by a scowling harridan. Then he'd sold it to a sensationalist online "news" site during a slow news week. Within twenty-four hours, "'Eat Shit And Die' Says Goth Astronaut In Expletive-Ridden Tirade" had been the number one trending video online.

Rudy's reminder was a bracing shock of cold reality. The interview had not been NASA's favorite publicity piece; she'd almost been asked to resign. Only her sterling record and Deb's good word had swayed sentiment in her favor.

"Point is, you really reamed that guy a new one, and that's the energy I want for Jon's character. I'll be real with you guys: I was even set on casting a chick for the lead role, but the studio wasn't crazy about having a girl astronaut doing all that sex and drug stuff. Said it wasn't believable. So I said, 'What, you don't think successful broads can be morally bankrupt? Clearly you haven't met my ex-wife.' Ha! Just kidding, we separated on great terms. Great woman."

It occurred to Reggie she had no clue what this movie was about, and suddenly that felt extremely relevant. What had she signed up for?

Rudy hadn't finished chewing, but that didn't stop him from continuing his tangent. "Then again, I'm not entirely sold on Pool Boy over here, either, so you're going to have your work cut out for you either way."

Was Rudy challenging himself to see how many different ways he could be offensive in one sitting? Reggie stole another glance at Jon, but he was staring down at the tablecloth, hands balled around the linen in his lap. He was still halfway smiling, but he was doing it with his jaw clenched so tightly his ears twitched. Despite having thought the same thing about Jon's capabilities—or lack thereof—only hours prior, she now had the irrational desire to defend him.

A strange calm settled over her. "Actually, I've been impressed by Jon's level of knowledge during today's tour. It's clear he's done his research." As she said it, she realized it was true. At least, he seemed to have memorized a surprisingly specific repertoire of obscure space facts.

Then, in a stroke of sublime timing, the dessert course arrived, and Jacqui expertly wrested conversation from Rudy's control, steering the table to the less controversial pastures of sports, food, and the merits of the Christmas holiday falling on a weekend this year. The latter fact meant they wouldn't have more than a three-day break in filming, which pleased Rudy, who was eager to wrap preproduction as soon as possible.

"Studio wants this out by September to qualify for awards season. We're going balls to the wall on this puppy," Rudy told them. "Especially since Mariana already has a competing movie in production. Shit, she even landed Zendaya for the lead."

Jacqui raised a brow at that. "Mariana del Reyes? As in, your former wife?"

"Look, I've said already, there's no bad blood. She's directed some great films, and I respect that." Rudy sawed at his chocolate cake with vigor. "But I do want *Escape Velocity* out in theaters before hers hits. Not like I have something to prove, though. Just a little . . . friendly competition."

Reggie participated as much as she was required to, but she barely paid attention to any of it.

She'd gotten lucky in Rudy's strange affinity for her lack of social graces. But if she slipped up and lost her patience on camera again, NASA would have zero tolerance, and the moon could be out of reach for a long, long time—maybe forever.

⋆ ⋆ ☆ ⋆

Jacqui was unusually quiet in the rideshare on the way back to the hotel. Jon watched the city lights go by in a blur, wondering if he should have accepted the invitation to join Rudy and the film crew on an impromptu adventure to discover the jewels of Houston's bar scene. Reggie had already departed without bothering to give any excuse at all.

Normally, Jon would have been down to party. He liked the social aspects of drinking, he loved exploring places he hadn't been before, and, most importantly, he needed to ingratiate himself with Rudy after today's fumbles. Especially since Rudy was scheduled to fly back to LA after scoping out the Arizona site on Monday and Jon wouldn't see him again until the table read in two weeks.

The thought of the script rolled up in his carry-on, waiting for him back at the hotel, spurred Jon to pull out his phone. It wasn't too late to meet up with the crew. He could even shower and change before heading back out. In the end, it came down to one simple fact: he was good with people, and he'd rather do something he was good at than struggle with something he was bad at.

He had the text app open when he realized he didn't have anyone's number. The spreadsheet Jacqui had made him was in the pocket of his pool-soaked jeans, which were currently being dry-cleaned by the hotel concierge.

"Hey, Jacqui? Could I bother you for Zach's number?"

Jacqui set her phone down against her thigh and gave him a weary look. "I thought you were calling it an early night."

Could she read his mind? Was this a side effect of all the woo-woo star sign stuff she was into? "I am. I mean, I was. But I was thinking, maybe it would be good to go out for a few drinks. Get on good terms with Rudy."

"I can't tell you what to do, Jon. But since you're paying me for my expertise, I can tell you I think that's a bad idea."

"Why?" It came out sounding more defensive than he'd meant it to.

"For one, you didn't get your workout in today, which means you'll need to make up for it this weekend." Her bracelets clattered as she ticked off items on her fingers. "Two, Rudy's temperamental and already having second thoughts about your casting, and with men like him it's wise to lay low until he cools down, because your presence is only going to keep today's incident top of mind. And three, I know you haven't finished memorizing your lines yet."

Then she raised her brows and looked at him like she could see into his soul. Damn, she was good.

"I'll learn my lines this weekend." Technically, he had to read the entire script first, but maybe he could memorize as he went. Yeah, that was a good plan.

"You have a lot of work to do, then, because you still need to familiarize yourself with the schedule for the upcoming month. In that binder I gave you, each day is broken out into sections with an overview of the experiments you'll be doing, the shots the film crew needs to get, and the content specs for your social media postings."

Ugh. He'd try to skim it, but he knew himself well enough to know he wouldn't get far before *something* more interesting popped into his head and lured his brain down a totally unrelated path. Last time he'd tried to read one of Jacqui's binders, he'd ended up on the internet for an hour learning how toothpaste factories worked. Luckily, he had an unofficial degree in the fine art of Winging It.

"Okay, okay," he said in what he hoped was a reassuring tone.

"Oh, and I did Reggie's star chart, and I'll warn you that you two aren't the best fit, romantically." The car came to a stop in front of the hotel, and Jacqui thanked the driver in a honey-sweet tone and gracefully exited, as if she hadn't just dropped a grenade into Jon's lap.

"What's a star chart?" he said, belatedly, as she closed the door behind her. He thanked the driver again and got out, racing to catch up with Jacqui. She'd nearly made it to the elevator bank when he reached her. "And why are you doing one for Reggie?"

Jacqui sighed and gave him an apologetic look. "As your publicist, it's none of my business, but as your friend . . . well, you wear your heart on your sleeve, and I don't want you to get hurt. Besides, you've got enough on your plate already with preparing for this role."

The elevator dinged, and he followed her inside. "I do *not* wear my heart on my sleeve." He pointed at the tiny brand logo on his T-shirt sleeve. "See? It's a . . . well, I don't know what it is. A symbol thingy. But it's not a heart. So we're all set."

Jacqui shook her head, but she was clearly stifling a smile.

"Listen, I'm going to be one hundred percent focused on training for the movie, I swear." He grinned and waved aside her concerns. "How am I going to find time to fall in love when I have a *binder* to read?"

"Jon."

"Yeah? Oh." The elevator was buzzing, waiting for him to select a floor.

He paused, finger hovering over the panel. His room number was probably written on his room card. Which he'd definitely remembered to take with him.

Jacqui reached past him to press the button. "Ninth floor," she reminded him. The elevator moved. "I'm just saying, it wouldn't be the first time you've let heartbreak distract you from work. Need I remind you of what happened with Fang Yin, that stuntwoman you dated?"

"First of all, I wasn't heartbroken. I was mildly disappointed that she didn't tell me she was married."

She raised a brow. "You missed your call time two days in a row, and I found you crying in a Taco Bell parking lot."

"She pretended to care about me, but she was just using me for sex!" Jon crossed his arms, glowering at his own reflection in the elevator doors. What did it matter, anyway, if he had a small, inconsequential crush on Reggie? Lust wasn't a two-way street. He couldn't even be sure she *liked* him, so the odds of anything happening were close to nil. But to appease his concerned publicist, Jon begrudgingly said, "I promise I'll be careful."

When the elevator spit them out, Jacqui indicated her room was to the left. His was in the opposite direction (probably). He paused at the split in the hallway, stalling.

Jacqui misinterpreted his hesitation. "You have nothing to be nervous about. Rudy's not going to be there, and the film crew will be operating out of the RV nearby, so they'll only drop in to film for a few hours each day. The base also has satellite Wi-Fi, so you can text or email me anytime. If you just follow my media outline and listen to Reggie's instructions, this will be the easiest movie prep you've ever done. Think of it as a nerdy vacation, even."

"I won't let you down," he assured her.

He gave Jacqui a hug and wished her good night, then walked slowly in the other direction. When he heard her room door clatter shut, he spun on his heel and headed back downstairs to get a new room key. He really needed to start remembering his key card.

Starting tonight, he was going to get his shit together.

Okay, it was already late, and he was going to have a hard time sleeping with the memory of how Reggie looked in that purple outfit seared into his eyeballs. But tomorrow he would get on top of the preparation, for sure.

Well, tomorrow he had to catch up on his workouts, and then he'd be pooped, so that day was probably shot.

Sunday, however . . . 100 percent, he was going to read that script and gear up for astronaut training.

CHAPTER 7

From the window of the studio's private jet, Reggie could admire the vast rust-and-sienna beauty of Mars—or its earthly cousin, at least.

NASA had intentionally built its mock moon base in the middle of nowhere. The rocky expanse of Arizona's high desert was a fitting analog for the lifeless landscapes of the moon and Mars, but Arizona still was a hell of a lot easier to get to than the similar bases they'd built in Greenland and Antarctica, so it was the Agency's preferred choice for hosting Hollywood guests—not that they often had many. These were valuable research bases, not movie sets. The studio had doubtless offered a sum with many zeros at the end to win exclusive access to one for an entire month.

Reggie spotted the habitat gleaming white and silver at the northern rim of a shallow volcanic maar crater. The futuristic oasis of curved architecture and shimmering metal appeared absurdly out of place, like it had been plunked down by an alien race who'd planned to come back and finish the rest of their colonization at a later date but then never bothered to return. About a quarter mile away from the base, the earth sloped up before flattening into a rocky mesa dotted with stunted, windblown trees. A concave array of solar panels perched on the rim of the crater next to a giant satellite.

She'd trained at the Greenland base, which was little more than a handful of modular tents, but never this one. The Arizona Habitat Analog Base—AHAB, for short—was the newest and sexiest of its ilk, in large part because NASA had contracted with a private corporation to test the materials they'd be using.

Rudy, who was sitting in the row of seats ahead of her, whistled when he saw it. "It's perfect. Exactly like the one we built in the studio. What do you think of that, eh, kid?"

A grunt came from the seats behind her as Jon sat up from his nap. He squinted over the top of his sunglasses at the view.

"Yep," he said.

Then he slid back down until he was lying with his back flat across two seats, his massive legs scrunched against the bulkhead.

There was no reason for Jon to be acting like he'd been dragged out of bed in the middle of the night; the call time for their party had been a reasonable 6:00 a.m.

Jacqui leaned over to Reggie and said, "He's not a morning person."

It was now half past ten. Reggie raised a brow but refrained from voicing her judgment aloud. Jon was probably the kind of guy who partied until sunup and slept in to fend off the resulting hangover. What else did actors do with their time—stay up until dawn conditioning their hair? Unfortunately for Jon, the daily schedule NASA and his publicist had concocted suggested a start time of seven in the morning, so he was going to have to adjust. Fast.

Unlike the man sprawled in the row behind them, Jacqui looked as if she'd been awake for hours before the call time, yet she still looked incredible. Although Reggie had done her own eyeliner-heavy makeup and even worn her nicest work boots, being around beautiful people like Jacqui and Jon made her feel like an insecure, acne-plagued teenager again—and she was irritated with herself for even caring; she was an *astronaut*, after all. She had far more important things to focus on than appearances.

Especially Jon's. And Jon's bulging thigh muscles, which probably required a separate berth to house their enormity.

Nope, nope, nope. Not an appropriate train of thought.

Reggie turned away and checked her phone. There was a new text from Deb, most likely sending her well-wishes. She opened it: **Call me when you have a minute.**

Her stomach flipped, and at the same time, the pilot took the aircraft into an aggressive descent. Reggie inhaled sharply, willing the contents of her stomach back into place.

She was fortunate in that she had a strong stomach—she'd only puked once when she'd first arrived at the Space Station, which was better than average—but Deb's ominous text put her on edge. Was she being pulled off the assignment already? No. A ridiculous thought. Even if Deb had found out about Friday's pool incident . . .

Jacqui turned and prodded Jon's knee. "We're landing. You might want to sit up."

With a tortured groan, Jon slapped his giant bear paw atop the back of Reggie's seat and hauled his lumbering torso vertical. His cheek was pink and creased from resting on his jacket sleeve, his inky hair mussed, and Reggie imagined one might find him adorable, if one were into eminently huggable men.

The aircraft came to a bumpy landing along the no-frills landing strip, and everyone clambered down the stairs. As she stepped into the cold desert air, Reggie zipped up her fleece jacket and thanked her past self for having left a tube of ChapStick in the pocket. Even though the sky was a spotless cerulean, the light wind had a biting edge to it, and she knew from her experience at the Greenland base that this kind of dry winter climate would suck moisture out of a body like it was a flesh-wrapped Capri Sun pouch.

From the corner of her eye, she could see Jon vigorously rubbing at his bare biceps. Surely he'd packed a jacket. The planning team had sent everyone involved a welcome email with a packing guide.

83

"Damn, it's cold," he said.

"You packed a coat, right?"

He grinned, displaying a row of white teeth and a single sheepish dimple. "Probably."

"Probably?" She couldn't hide her disbelief.

"Hey, don't worry about me. Just takes me a second to adjust." As if to prove his point, he unclasped his arms and spread them wide, taking a deep breath of air. "Ahhhh . . . perfect temperature. So refreshing."

"This isn't LA. The high desert gets down to single-digit temperatures overnight," she warned.

"I run hot once I get the blood flowing." He began swinging his arms from side to side, then bent over to touch his toes. Halfway down, he stopped with a pained grunt.

"Are you—" She realized her hand was reaching out to touch him, and she retracted it.

"Leg day," he wheezed, audibly stifling a groan as he drew back up to his full height. Then, as if to reassure her, he flashed what he likely thought was a charming grin, but it was so toothy and crooked with poorly masked agony that it made her cringe. "Already feeling warmer," he added with unconvincing cheer.

His muscled forearms were covered in goose bumps.

Reggie took a breath. It would be fine. There was a NASA support crew still on site that had arrived early to stock AHAB with all the supplies and test equipment they'd need for the next month, and one of them had to have an extra sweatshirt Jon could borrow. She eyed his broad shoulders, rippling under his tight black T-shirt as he returned to his arm-swinging calisthenics, and tried not to consider the unfavorable odds of anyone owning clothes remotely big enough.

A battered SUV rolled up to the runway, and a woman who introduced herself as AHAB's base manager helped them load their luggage into the back before shuttling their party to the base, which was a fifteen-minute drive from the landing strip down into the shallow crater.

As they descended by way of a narrow, rocky gravel road, Reggie got her first unobstructed view of her home for the next four weeks.

AHAB was actually a series of connected modular units, with six individual rooms laid out around a central hub in such a way that astronauts could navigate from one room to another as easily as possible, without ever having to leave the base. From above, it looked sort of like a flower. Two of those spokes were the living units, intended to house up to eight astronauts on the lunar surface. For now, she and Jon would each have their own unit—a fact she was more relieved about than she cared to analyze, given the close quarters she'd shared with her colleagues on the ISS.

With Jon, the idea of cohabitation felt . . . different.

The base manager explained that the base was approximately 80 percent operational, so they'd closely—but not completely—experience how AHAB would operate in an extraterrestrial atmosphere.

"That includes pressurized entrances," the base manager said. "The atmosphere inside AHAB operates independently of the outside atmosphere, so during your stay you'll get to experience our upgraded air-filtration units. I know you'll appreciate that, Reggie."

Reggie snorted. The filtration systems aboard the Space Station were a long-running source of headaches for astronauts aboard—literally. The decades-old relics were nightmares to maintain, and they often operated below optimal efficiency, which caused oxygen levels to fluctuate. Reggie had awoken far too many mornings with her head pounding, cursing the ancient monstrosities that kept them all alive.

Zach and Mimi were waiting for them when they pulled up to the base. The duo had driven out yesterday with the truck and trailer housing all the film equipment. They'd parked up at the rim of the crater, where they could plug into the solar panels' electricity with a converter especially designed for the purpose, but they'd be able to unhook the truck if they needed mobility.

"Welcome to the moon," Mimi said dryly once their party had disembarked. She wore a yellow beanie and the same studio-branded sweatshirt she'd worn on Friday. "The bar scene sucks, but at least we have satellite Wi-Fi."

Inside her pocket, Reggie's hand closed around her cell phone. She should call Deb—

Her thought was interrupted by Rudy clapping to get everyone's attention. "Let's get rolling! I want this wrapped up by noon. Got a five o'clock meeting in La-La Land, so let's all quit la-la-lollygagging and start filming the kids' first look at their new digs."

Not a big deal, she told herself. It would be better to call Deb later, anyway, after they'd settled in and Reggie had some privacy in her quarters. Thankfully, a beneficent soul somewhere high up in NASA's chain of command had nixed the studio's initial request for hidden cameras throughout the habitat; the film crew would be allowed to record them only while on site during the afternoons, allowing Reggie and Jon to spend the rest of the time focused on actual training. Unfortunately, they'd also have entire weekends off to do nothing of value, because apparently everyone except Reggie had interests beyond science, work, and finishing this charade as fast as fucking possible.

Mimi hoisted the camera onto her shoulder and began giving instructions in unintelligible Hollywood-speak. "Let's get you and Jon starting at the southernmost entrance. We're going to do this *House Hunters*–style, okay? We already did the GV shots of the interior, so we're just going to follow you into each room with tracking shots, then pause for reaction singles. The rooms are tight, so try to stick to the marks. Rudy asked for a couple OTFs, but we don't have a narrative yet, so we're going to play those by ear."

Reggie looked at Jon to see if he'd understood any of that jargon, but he was nodding along without a lick of confusion in his expression.

"Any questions before we start?" Mimi asked.

The camera's round eye was pointed directly at Reggie, and she could see her miniaturized, upside-down reflection in the lens. Insecurity slithered out of the recesses of her brain. The ligaments in her knees locked tight.

Someone cleared their throat, and Reggie felt the weight of Jon's gaze as he tried to catch her eye. He probably wanted to give her more of his pro tips, but she'd be damned if she'd reveal weakness in front of everyone else.

She shook her head. *I don't need anyone's help.*

"Okay. Picture's up. Rudy, we roll on your mark."

✩ 💫

The filming was an awkward mess, from start to finish. Jon had tried to reclaim whatever magic he and Reggie had managed to harness during the pool tour, but nothing had worked. She'd responded to all his questions and prompts with short, stilted answers. As filming stretched into the late afternoon hours, Jon almost wished there were a pool to jump into, just to put an end to the torture.

Rudy, Jacqui, and the NASA crew had long since departed by the time Mimi called a wrap on shooting, and now their remaining party members were gathered in a common room that served as the base's central hub. Even with midafternoon light streaming in through the portholes and cheery white uplighting along the ceiling's perimeter, the atmosphere in the room was grim.

On a fold-out table in front of them, rushes—raw footage from the last run-through—rolled by silently on Mimi's laptop. Even Zach, who had been the quietly patient one of the film duo, looked frustrated as they all watched another shot of Reggie marching into one of the living areas, her movements wooden and her face frozen into an uncomfortable half scowl.

"Gonna have to do retakes on, like, half this shit," Mimi said.

On the screen, Jon watched himself grimace as he knocked his head on a low-clearance doorway. He looked like a lumbering knucklehead trying to navigate the cramped habitat. It hadn't helped that he'd tried to cram all three of his prescribed workouts from the weekend into a single Sunday. He'd barely been able to walk without crying—much less *stoop down*—and he didn't even want to think about what agonies tonight's workout had in store.

Mimi paused the footage and sighed. "Reggie's angled away from the camera in so many shots."

Jon didn't dare glance at the woman standing stiffly beside him. He cleared his throat. "Guys, it's been a long day. What do you say we break here and start fresh in the morning?"

Zach and Mimi needed zero convincing. With barely concealed relief, they began packing up their equipment.

"Join us in the RV for grub?" Mimi offered. "We have beer and hot dogs."

"I still have a growler from that brewery we went to on Saturday. What was it called again?" Zach looked at Jon expectantly.

"Can't remember," he mumbled. He shoved a hand into his hair and winced as his fingers snagged on elastic.

Mimi laughed. "Dude, I don't remember anything after the third bar either. Your fans sure are generous. Can we bring you out with us all the time?"

"Yeah. Sure." He thought of the script, still rolled up in his bag like some cursed relic. "Pass on the hot dogs, though. I think it's time I got used to eating astronaut food."

The duo said their goodbyes and departed, but it was only after the pressurized door sealed shut behind them that Jon registered the enormity of what the film crew's departure meant.

They were alone. Together. Only an arm's length of space apart.

He couldn't help it. His thoughts immediately flashed back to the way she'd looked at him in that dark alcove, and his pulse skyrocketed.

Nothing's going to happen, the only working part of his brain insisted, but the rest of his mind—and body—begged to differ. Though he could hear the air filter humming low and steady in the background, the air between them felt too thin, and it suddenly required effort to keep his breathing steady.

The chemistry arcing between them was so abruptly intense that he'd be shocked if Reggie couldn't feel it too. Screw Jacqui's stupid star charts. This was the real deal.

Reggie turned to look at him, her lips parting the barest fraction, and he couldn't have looked away even if he'd wanted to. A mouth like hers begged to be studied in detail. The top lip was bigger than her bottom by just a hair, as if she had the slightest overbite, and they were petal pink. They held the softest sheen, too, as if they'd just been licked, and that image alone was enough to launch an entire night's worth of pornographic inspiration, even though he knew it was because she'd been applying some sort of sheer fruit-scented ChapStick to them all day. Cherry, maybe? He fought the urge to lean in closer, just to see if he was right.

She abruptly turned away. "I need to make a phone call."

Her curt words were like a slap upside the head. He nodded, not that it mattered—she'd already marched out of the room. The heavy clunk of the door to her living quarters sealed him off alone with his own shame and misplaced lust. Her tone and body language sent a crystal-clear message that any reciprocal interest on her part was either imagined by him or unwanted by her.

Of course she's not interested in you.

"I'll get dinner started," he said to the closed door. It was early for dinner, but they hadn't stopped filming to eat lunch, and his stomach was eating itself alive.

If she heard him, there was no reply.

Heat crept up the back of his neck until his ears flamed with humiliation. She probably thought he was some sort of creep, panting over her like a teenager who'd just discovered masturbation.

Feeling vaguely useless, he wandered over to the wall-mounted culinary unit and studied the labels on it. Reggie had given him a brief overview on all the basic equipment, but verbal instructions always seemed to fall right out of his head and into the ether. He needed to read things to really *get* them, but when he searched for an instruction booklet, he came up empty.

No worries. He wasn't a supersmart astronaut, but he'd worked in a restaurant for half a decade, and he'd been raised by a feminist who'd insisted her son grow up to be the kind of man who could both cook *and* wash the dishes afterward. He could figure out how to microwave a freaking pouch of food, couldn't he?

Beneath a circular slot on the unit, a label read: INSERT FOOD PACKET HERE.

Simple enough. The meals weren't hard to find; everything in this place was stored in tidy sliding drawers, leaving the fold-out tables and counters bare, and the options were organized by meal part: breakfast, lunch, dinner, and dessert. He flicked through the stiff silver pouches of shrink-wrapped food and pulled out two copies of spaghetti and meatballs.

He paused. What if she didn't like meat? At the restaurant on Friday she'd ordered the shrimp scampi.

He sifted until he found a shrimp stir-fry. An arrow at the top of the pouch pointed to a nozzle that looked like it would fit in the appropriate hole, and when he tentatively inserted it into the culinary unit, a green light lit up.

"Bam," he whispered, making an exploding motion with his hand. "Space Chef Jon, fuckin' flavor genius in da *house*."

He stepped back, admiring his handiwork. Green light. Pouch in hole. Done. It would take, what—three, maybe four minutes to cook?

That seemed about right, based on his extensive childhood Lean Cuisine training. His mom had always worked late when he was a kid, so she'd kept their freezer stocked.

With the hem of his shirt, he wiped off the table Mimi had been using for all the film equipment, then began hunting for plates and utensils. Maybe he couldn't impress Reggie with his sparkling wit—since that seemed to flee whenever she was around—and he definitely couldn't impress her with his intelligence, but he could at least prove he had basic life skills.

He'd opened nearly every cabinet and drawer he could find and was close to giving up when he smelled smoke.

✦ ⭐

Reggie's phone vibrated in her hands, but she hesitated before picking up. Her first call to Deb had gone to voice mail, which wasn't unusual; it was a workday, and Deb didn't answer her phone during meetings unless it was an emergency.

The fact that Deb was calling her back in under ten minutes was disconcerting.

Her pounding heart was solely due to dread at whatever bad news Deb had to deliver and had nothing to do with the searing intensity of an actor's heavy-lidded gaze.

Jesus, get ahold of yourself. They'd been alone for less than two minutes, and she was already hiding from him. What was wrong with her? She'd climbed on top of a rocket loaded with close to one million gallons of explosive fuel and her pulse had barely registered a change, but one look from Jon and she was trembling like some virginal maiden who'd never seen the outline of a guy's dick in his pants before.

Did he even realize—

Her breath caught. Before she could continue that line of thought, she swiped up on Deb's call. "This is Reggie."

"Reggie, glad I caught you. How's AHAB treating you folks so far?"

"Still has that new-car smell," Reggie returned, willing her voice to sound even.

"Good to hear. You know, I hadn't seen a social media post from you yet today, so I worried there were still problems with the base's satellite signal, but it sounds like that's been resolved if I'm talking to you now."

Deb *never* bothered with gift wrapping her threats in pleasantries. What was this about? "No problems so far. I'd have called sooner, but we only just wrapped filming for the day." Reggie paused, then bit the bullet. "What's up?"

"I wanted you to hear this from me, personally," Deb started, and Reggie's insides went into free fall. This was it. They were pulling her off filming. They'd seen the clip. Or worse, they'd released the short list for Artemis III weeks ahead of schedule. "Milton Fetzer posted a new video this morning on the Mars Truther website. It seems he's taken a particular interest in your visit to AHAB with a film crew. You can imagine how he's spinning it."

Her words took a full six seconds to sink in. "Oh." *That's all?*

"We don't expect this to be an issue, but I didn't want the news to catch you by surprise."

"I appreciate that," she said. And she did. Deb knew how much Milton had harassed her in the weeks leading up to her infamous interview, even if she didn't approve of the way Reggie had eventually handled it.

"I'm having Jon Leo's publicist send over some material from Friday's tour so we can generate some positive press . . ." Deb kept talking, but Reggie's focus waned. Something was wrong. She could feel it, like a prickle of static down her spine.

"Can I call you back?" Reggie blurted. She didn't wait for a reply before hanging up.

A fraction of a second later, the alarms went off.

CHAPTER 8

Jon yanked the food pouch out of the wall unit and cringed at the wisps of acrid smoke curling out of its spout. He turned in a frantic circle, searching for a trash can, but he knew in his gut it was too late to hide the evidence. Even if he could find a way to shut off the blaring alarms, the air reeked of melted plastic and burnt shrimp.

Shit, shit, shit.

Out of sheer desperation, he shoved the pouch into the back pocket of his jeans, its contents crunching into the tight space. God*damn*, these jeans were tight. He needed to talk to his stylist about going up a size—

Reggie burst out of her living quarters, assessing the situation in under three seconds flat. Her flinty eyes flicked to the still-smoking culinary unit and then over to him standing next to it, no doubt looking guilty as all hell, and he could almost see her sexy brain calculating the different things he could have done wrong.

The door behind Reggie started to buzz loudly. Seconds later, it slammed shut on its own, and a red light came on over the door. Probably some sort of fire-safety mechanism to seal off each compartment.

He waited for her to say something, but she merely shook her head, stormed over to a wall panel, and calmly pressed a sequence of three buttons. The alarms fell silent, the doors hissed and clunked as they unsealed, and the red lights blinked off.

"What did you do?" she asked as she approached the culinary unit for inspection. Her tone was calm, but not in a reassuring way. In a way that made him feel like he was very, very busted.

He reached up to swipe a hand through his hair before remembering that he couldn't do that anymore. "I thought I'd get dinner started, but I think there might be something wrong with the machine."

There had to be a chance it wasn't his fault, right? Maybe something had malfunctioned. These things happened.

She poked at the slot where he'd put the pouch. Her nose wrinkled. "I see," she said blandly. She inspected the unit, prodding at its buttons and switches. Then she glanced at the spaghetti pouches lingering on the countertop. "Everything appears to be in working order. Where is the meal bag you used?"

"Ah, it's . . ." He stalled, tugging the hem of his shirt lower as he scrambled to explain why he'd thought it would be a good idea to hide the evidence. He couldn't tell her, *I thought I could cling to a shred of dignity if I blamed the Space Microwave.* At best, she'd pity him, and that was even worse.

She opened a sliding compartment clearly labeled TRASH—if he hadn't panicked, he'd likely have found it and avoided this mess—and when she looked at him again, her brow furrowed. "Jon?"

"Yes?" He did like it when she said his name.

"Why is there smoke coming out of your backside?" She advanced, clearly intending to investigate.

He neatly sidestepped. "Squats," he said. "I'm on a rigorous exercise regimen."

"Squats. Really?" Her eyes narrowed. She attempted to skirt around his left flank, but he skipped out of reach. "In those jeans?"

So she *had* noticed. "Spandex blend. Very cutting-edge design."

"Spandex is flammable. Give me the pouch before you melt a hole in your pants." She feinted left again; she was a spry one, but he had endless fight-scene rehearsals on his side, preparing him for this very moment. If he weren't so sore, he'd be even faster.

"I have no idea what you're talking about," he said, angling his body out of reach.

"You're being childish." Her tone was laced with annoyance, but her eyes sparked in a way that told him she was enjoying this—he should have known she'd like a challenge. She planted her hands on her hips and sized him up. "Hand it over now, and I'll pretend this didn't happen."

He tried to suppress his smile and failed. "Are we negotiating?"

"Keep it up, and you'll be negotiating for your life."

"You can't kill me," he said cheerfully, dodging another swipe. "Astronaut's Code."

"Astronaut's—" Reggie paused in a moment of genuine confusion. He used the opportunity to back up against the wall. "That's not a thing."

"Oh, my bad. I'm thinking of pirates."

A little growl erupted from her throat as she lunged at him. This time, he let her, although *let* wasn't the precise word for it. He wouldn't have moved out of her way for all the money in the universe.

Her left hand shot out to snake around his lower back, bringing her torso flush with his side, and he froze. Just like in the pool, heat scalded him where her breasts brushed against his rib cage, and it spread out through his body, burning away the last of the desert chill.

Air felt heavy in his lungs, so he held his breath, terrified to move lest she notice what she was doing.

What she was doing to *him*.

Reggie, with that single-minded determination of hers, hadn't noticed his reaction. When her touch seared across the denim at the low, low base of his spine, he began to sweat. Profusely.

"Ha!" she crowed, ripping the pouch free. She pulled away and held her prize aloft like an Olympic medalist, an expression of pure triumph on her face. And then she realized how close she'd been. Exactly where she'd had her hands only seconds ago. He could see the minute realization dawned on her by the way her eyes rounded, her lips forming a little O of consternation. "I didn't mean to . . ."

"Grab my—" He cleared his throat, wishing he could get his mind out of the gutter. "Grab my ass, you mean."

Her face hardened. "That was unprofessional of me, and it won't happen again."

"If I'd minded, I wouldn't have let it happen," he said in a low voice. He stopped short of telling her she could do whatever she wanted to him, because *that* would have been unprofessional.

Her eyes slid away, as if she wanted to look anywhere but at him. She inspected the bag she'd fought so hard to retrieve. "You forgot to add water. It's dehydrated."

He groaned and smeared a hand down his face. Something so simple . . . "I'm an idiot."

"You're not," she said, far more sharply than he felt was necessary. "You just don't pay attention. I knew you weren't listening when I went over the instructions earlier."

He opened his mouth to argue but saw her expression and thought better of it. What was the point? She was right. He *didn't* pay attention. Unless it was something very, very interesting—then he couldn't tear his focus away.

Like Reggie's mouth, for instance. That was an endless source of fascination. Could he really be blamed for watching it move instead of listening to the sounds coming out of it?

Yes, you knucklehead, that's exactly what she should blame you for. He'd never been good at remembering verbal instructions, but being aware of his shortcomings didn't excuse him from trying to do better. He was lucky he'd only toasted some stir-fry; what would she have done if he'd set a whole moon base on fire?

"You're right, and I'm sorry," he said. "Will you please show me again? I promise I'll listen."

Reggie looked down at the toasted meal packet in her hand, then looked back up at Jon with a wary expression. "Why don't I handle cooking tonight, and we'll start your training again tomorrow morning? Clean slate. For now, you can get unpacked and settled in your quarters. The schedule has us eating dinner at eighteen hundred hours. That's six o'clock."

"Gotcha." He ignored the ping of disappointment skittering through him at her dismissal.

He slunk off to his quarters, feeling a little bit like he'd just been sent to detention, and flung himself down on one of the fold-out beds. The foam cushioning wasn't uncomfortable, though it gave off a plasticky smell, but the bed was short enough that when he lay flat on his back, his feet dangled off the end.

It was kind of nice to have a whole room to himself. Not that he was living in what most people would call the lap of luxury; the habitat pod was about half the size of an LA studio apartment (which was to say, small), with no decor unless you counted the single window over each bed and the ceiling-hung curtains he supposed were for subdividing the pod into four smaller rooms. Still, aside from the gently pulsing hum coming from the air vents along the rim of the ceiling, the room was blissfully quiet.

No distractions . . .

He scrubbed a hand down his face and let his head loll sideways so he could see the pile of luggage he'd chucked onto one of the other beds. The top of his rolled-up script peeked out of the side pouch of his laptop bag, its pages still crisp and pristine at the corners.

At the sight of it, the constant, circular berating in his own head started up again.

Who the hell agreed to act in a movie without reading the script first?

Counterpoint: Who said no to a chance to act in a movie directed by Rudy Ruffino, regardless of what said movie was about?

It wasn't that he didn't like reading; as a kid, he'd blasted through every sci-fi book and comic he could get his hands on through the library, and even as an adult with a busy filming schedule, he still managed to devour books on flights and listen to audiobooks during hair and makeup. The problem he had with the script was that the more he'd avoided reading it, the more daunting the task had become, and now it hovered over him like a metaphorical guillotine. And if he didn't familiarize himself with his lines before the table read exactly twelve days from now, his head *would* roll.

He groaned and dragged himself up to retrieve the offending tube of paper. There was still plenty of time left tonight to read the damn thing, and more importantly, he'd run out of excuses and distractions.

As long as he didn't think about Reggie, that was.

As his hand closed around the script, his eye snagged on the corner of Jacqui's binder peeking out of his bag. He should *skim* the schedule for tomorrow, at the very least. Maybe he could even look over the experiments they'd be doing so he wouldn't embarrass himself again. Or set anything else on fire.

His stomach growled, and he rummaged through his bag for a protein bar to hold him over until dinner. It was an unwelcome reminder of yet another obligation he'd been dreading: his daily workout. The mere thought of moving in any direction except down into a sprawl made his muscles throb in dismay, but of his current responsibilities, Kahlil's "Death by Squats" plan inspired the least amount of self-recrimination. Sure, he'd crammed three workouts into a single day yesterday, but at least he wasn't woefully behind schedule.

He changed into track pants and sneakers before heading out. Reggie was still in the central hub when he emerged from his room, with a thick and official-looking booklet in front of her. She looked up at him, a question in those big, round eyes of hers.

"Going for a quick jog," he explained. He paused, half expecting her to stop him, but she merely shrugged.

"Copy that."

"I'll be back in time for dinner."

"Okay."

He strode to the door that he remembered would lead him out to the pressurized entry node, where they also kept the spacesuits and hatch to the moon rover. As his hand fell on the door lever, he slowed. The desire to offer an olive branch, to somehow make her *like* him, was overwhelming. Mustering a casual air, he asked her, "Do you want to join me? I always appreciate a good workout buddy."

She blinked at him. "I work out in the morning. Probably before you're even awake."

"Right. Of course. Maybe some other time, then."

He stepped into the entry node and hit the button to close the door behind him, which would let the airlock's master computer know to start the simulated "pressurization" process. This make-believe space door had seemed super cool the first time he'd used it, but now he recognized one of the drawbacks of the lunar lifestyle was being unable to sulkily slam the door behind him. The door had almost fully sealed shut when Reggie called his name.

He mashed the button again until the door jolted to a stop, then kept pressing it until the LCD wall panel flashed a stern, all-caps warning that he dismissed without reading. Finally, the door hissed open again, and he poked his head back into the room. "What's up?"

She trotted over, a folded gray cloth in her hand. "The sun is setting soon. I couldn't find an extra sweatshirt big enough for you, so take this. Just in case."

He took the thin blanket from her, momentarily stunned by the gesture. It was the same color as her eyes.

She must have mistaken his silence for argument, because she hurried to add, "It's small and light enough you can tie it around your waist, but it's a high-quality wool blend, so it will keep you warmer than you'd think. I took this with me to the Greenland base. I bring it on long flights—"

"Thank you," he said gruffly.

He knotted the fabric around his waist, taking care not to stretch the delicate material. It draped down to his knees, and he knew he probably looked ridiculous, but it didn't impede his movement. Not that it would have mattered; he'd ensconce himself in a Stay Puft marshmallow suit if Reggie was the one gifting it to him.

He gestured to his new look for approval. "Look at that. Perfect fit."

Color tinged her cheeks as she looked him up and down, and for a second—the briefest second—he thought there might have been a flash of interest in her eyes. Like a flicker of lightning behind storm clouds. Then it was gone. Her expression went flat and her gaze slid away, fixed somewhere on the curved doorframe by his right shoulder. "Just don't overdo it out there. We have a zero seven hundred start time tomorrow, and I don't want to start training off behind schedule."

Seven in the morning? That's early as fuck.

He wasn't a morning person, but he could adjust to this. He'd managed to get to set before sunup countless times during filming for *Space Dude*, and only half those times had his arrival been preempted by a call from Jacqui asking where the hell he was.

He flashed her a reassuring grin. "Seven a.m.? No problem."

CHAPTER 9

Jon was not in AHAB's central hub at 0700 hours.

Reggie sipped from a thermos of weak instant coffee and stared at the closed door to his living quarters. She'd give him until fifteen after, and then she'd knock. A reasonable margin of error. It was his first day, after all, and she'd promised him a clean slate.

At 0706, she added a second packet of instant coffee to her hot water and stirred. Was it her imagination, or was NASA's coffee even less potent than she remembered?

At 0711, she busied herself reviewing the day's training schedule for the fourth time. It never hurt to be overprepared.

At exactly 0715, Reggie congratulated herself on her patience and rapped on Jon's door.

Silence was her only answer.

She pressed her ear against the smooth metal, listening in vain for sounds of movement. Nothing. Then again, each door was thick enough to serve as a vacuum barrier in the event of depressurization on the lunar surface, so there was a good chance Jon was awake and moving around and she simply couldn't hear it. That was why every one of AHAB's node connections sported upgraded versions of the ISS's intercom panels.

After a microsecond of completely irrational hesitation, she stabbed the white button below the speaker. "Jon?" she called. "Are you awake?"

No response.

She took a deep breath, counted to five, and let it out. "Fine," Reggie told the door. "I'll get started without you."

Three steps away and she stopped. How was she going to train Jon to be an astronaut without Jon present? Except for a mandatory social media post and the filming break they'd be doing with Zach and Mimi after lunch, every single item on the day's schedule had been designed with his education in mind.

Maybe if she knocked loudly enough . . .

She pounded at the door. "If you don't get up, I *will* come in there."

She waited, silently cursing Jon for putting her in this position in the first place, but only dreaded quiet met her pleas.

There was always the option to keep waiting—but for how long? Based on how easily Jon had slept through the entirety of the aircraft ride, he was a heavy sleeper. And sure, today's task list was intentionally light to allow them both time to settle in, but throughout Reggie's career as an astronaut, she'd made it a point of pride to never fall behind on mission assignments. Jon might think this was all a fun little publicity stunt, but Reggie intended to take this training as seriously as she did everything else.

She cracked open the door, and held her ear up to the gap. "Jon?" she murmured, but the only response was the whispering hum of the air-filtration system. She could feel that same air softly brushing her cheek through the crack, almost beckoning her into the room.

What if he slept naked? Her brain wasted no time providing a visual to accompany that thought.

Stop being a coward.

With a bracing inhale, she pushed open the door and marched into the dark lair. It was hard to see anything in the dim red glow of the recessed ceiling lights, but she managed to make out a large, man-shaped lump on the far-left bed. He was sprawled on his back with one arm flung over his face, and from beneath a tangle of sheets, a single bare, muscled leg jutted out and dangled onto the floor. Reggie ignored the illicit tightening in her stomach at the sight.

He hadn't even stirred when she'd entered. Was he dead? She glanced at her watch: 0719.

"Damn it, Jon," she whispered. She smacked the control panel on the wall twice to turn on the day lighting and raise the window panels, and glaring light flooded the room. Louder, she announced, "Time to get up."

"Mmmphhhh." His groan was guttural, pulled from deep in his chest, and her body reacted in a predictably favorable way, her skin heating and her breath quickening.

She was only human, after all, but right now her body's response was profoundly irritating.

His luggage was piled in disarray across the cot on the opposite wall, and Reggie grabbed the first thing she could find of appropriate weight—a rolled-up tube of papers—and flung it at him. It hit him square in his massive chest, the document unfurling to splay across his face.

"Hey!" Jon's heavy-lashed eyes blinked open, and his face twisted in disgruntled confusion. "Reggie?"

He batted the sheaf of papers off his chin and pushed up onto an elbow. The move dislodged his sheet, revealing his bare chest. His very large, very impressive bare chest—

Reggie locked her eyes on the wall above his head. "Up. Now."

"What time is it?"

"Zero seven twenty. You're late."

He let out another low groan, and Reggie fought the urge to flee. "Stop complaining," she snapped, more harshly than she'd intended. "We're already behind schedule, so get dressed and stop wasting my time."

"Okay, okay." Fabric and paper rustled, then stopped. "Uh, slight problem . . ."

Exasperated, she answered, "What now?"

He cleared his throat but didn't answer. When Reggie glanced at him again, he was sitting on the edge of the bed facing her, leaning forward with his elbows on his knees, face buried in his hands. The sheet bunched unnaturally across his lap and thighs, leaving the rest of his smooth, sun-bronzed skin uncovered.

He does *sleep naked.*

Her breath caught, and she swallowed it before she could make a noise.

Through his hands, his voice came out muffled. "If I could have a second. Alone."

Her pulse pounded low in her stomach. "You have five minutes," she managed before she all but bolted from the room.

✩ ⭐

Jon waited until Reggie left before dragging himself over to his suitcase and attempting to dress. After thirty seconds of blindly pawing through his duffel bag for his glasses, he gave up and dumped everything upside down on his bed. By the time he'd found them, he had a new bruise on his shin from the metal bed frame—the pain from which had the fortunate side effect of dulling his raging morning hard-on.

Not completely, though, and that early wake-up call from the object of his dreams had only made the affliction worse.

He fumbled for his cell phone and held it up to his face.

Fucking brilliant, Jon. The alarm is set for 6:45 p.m., not a.m. No wonder she'd had to retrieve him. What a way to start the day.

In the bathroom compartment of his living quarters, he pumped water into the sink with the foot pedal and managed to brush his teeth and handle the rest of his morning needs without running into anything else. Then, still barely lucid, he staggered into another pair of too-tight jeans, wincing as he buttoned the fly over his still-half-hard dick, and threw on a shirt and shoes.

Reggie was standing in the middle of the central hub when he arrived, forearm raised so he could see the time on her wristwatch. She cocked her head. "You're wearing glasses."

Reflexively, he reached up to confirm and nearly poked himself in the eye. "Didn't have time to put in contacts," he croaked. His voice hadn't gotten the memo it was time to be awake. (Though in his opinion, it really shouldn't be—in fact, he'd yet to find proof that anything before 9:00 a.m. really existed.)

"Hmm." She busied herself with something on the table. Then, as if it was an afterthought, she added, "They suit you."

He cleared his throat. "Is there any coffee?"

"I drank it all."

"Oh," he said. He supposed it was what he deserved for being late, but . . . it was *seven in the freaking morning*. Surely there were footnotes in the Geneva Conventions protecting him from such cruelty.

"I'm kidding. Don't cry."

"I wasn't going to cry."

Her lips quirked. "You looked as if it were a distinct possibility. Come here, and I'll show you how to use the hot-water dispenser."

She demonstrated the process and directed him to the stash of instant-coffee pouches, and for once, he had no problem paying attention. He didn't have issues focusing when it came to matters of great importance.

As he sipped the coffee she'd made, he watched Reggie hustling about with purpose, moving clear plastic baggies and markers and miniature hammer things into a soft-sided cooler. "Since we're behind on time, I'm going to explain everything in the rover. You can bring your coffee with you; just keep the lid on the tumbler." She narrowed her eyes at him, and he noted that she'd done her sexy raccoon eye shadow and makeup, even though it was just the two of them. "And don't touch anything unless I specifically instruct you to do so."

"Got it," he murmured, fascinated by how the material of her many-pocketed pants stretched over her ass as she bent down to throw away the coffee packets.

Hiking chic had never been on his personal fetish list, but Reggie had single-handedly launched it into a top-three slot. If she could make a sweatshirt look this sexy, what would she look like in a dress?

". . . Does that sound like a good plan?" Reggie asked him, slinging the cooler strap over her shoulder.

"Definitely."

"You have no idea what I just said, do you?"

"Well . . ." He drained the last of his coffee, buying time to search through a fog of short-term memory. All he came back with was a snapshot from the dream he'd been so rudely awakened from, in which he and Reggie were in a pool and neither of them was wearing clothes.

She let out a huff. "I asked if you thought you could pull the rover with a harness, like an Iditarod dog."

Deadpan, he replied, "Probably. How big is the rover?"

His reward was an exasperated headshake—and, if he wasn't mistaken, the tiniest hint of a smile. *Bingo*.

"Nothing gets to you, does it?" she asked as they made their way to the outer bay. She pressed a button, and a wall panel slid open, revealing a small squoval hatch that opened into the back of the moon rover.

"What do you mean?"

"When your director was being a total dick to you at dinner, you didn't seem fazed at all. Is that real, or are you just a good actor?" Reggie pushed the cooler through the porthole, then clambered through, gesturing for him to follow. "Even when I compare you to a dog, you don't get angry or annoyed."

He scraped a hand through his hair, grateful that he hadn't had time to pull it back. "Dogs are cool, though, so that's kind of a compliment," he said, eyeing the entrance warily. "I don't think I can fit through this."

Sterling eyes swept over him, measuring. If she'd noticed his clunky change of topic, she didn't let it show. "It'll be tight. Astronauts are usually . . . smaller."

"Remember the guy who did the first space walk? He couldn't fit back through the airlock afterward because his suit was all inflated. That's going to be me going through this door."

She paused before answering, an odd look on her face. "You're not wearing a suit, so unless your shoulders are full of pressurized air, I think you'll be fine," she finally said. "But if you're not comfortable with it, you can go around the outside. To keep things simple, we won't be walking through depressurization procedures every time we go in and out of the base, although we're scheduled to demo it for the cameras on Thursday."

He squeezed through the opening with a grunt, though it left him squatting uncomfortably in the back of the rover, his knees mere inches from Reggie's in a narrow space. She scooted backward, as if she thought avoiding all touch would negate the way the air charged with electricity whenever they closed distance between them.

Or maybe the spark he felt was his imagination working overtime, as it usually did. Maybe the way her eyes had dilated when she'd seen him nearly butt naked this morning had nothing to do with attraction at all.

Jon felt himself hardening again and forced himself to stop feeding this inconvenient, likely unrequited lust. He had to, or he'd never survive this month. He made a mental note to text Kahlil later and tell him this week's workouts were too easy.

"Welcome to the Artemis rover," Reggie said, drawing his attention back out of his pants.

As Jon surveyed the cramped interior, giddiness bubbled in his bloodstream. From the outside, the rover had looked like a glorified mail truck, and the inside was no more glamorous. Everything was purpose built for withstanding lunar terrain, so the seats were spring mounted, the floors were dull rubber, and the "back seat" cargo area was packed with mounted storage boxes and complicated machines sporting yellow warning labels. Still, it wasn't lost on him that he was in a freaking *moon rover*. For the first time, he felt like he was truly experiencing a childhood dream.

Possessed by an inexplicable desire to tease Reggie, he shuffled toward the driver's seat. "Dibs on driving first."

He gave her a sly glance, if only to ensure she was glaring at him with the appropriate amount of ferocity.

She was.

Withdrawing the keys from a pocket, Reggie dangled them in front of his nose. "Nice try. Into the passenger seat with you, Mr. Leo."

Mr. Leo. It still threw him for a loop when people addressed him with that last name, even though it was his legal one now. Despite the mixed emotions that came with it, his father's name had opened doors in Hollywood and given him opportunities like this one. He was grateful for that, if nothing else.

Once he'd clambered into his seat, Reggie helped him strap into the five-point seat belt harness, her hands coming dangerously close to brushing his abdomen as she did so. She tightened the buckle, and he carefully sucked air along the roof of his mouth, trying not to imagine her hands straying any lower.

"Now, I'll warn you," Reggie said when she'd finished torturing him. "I've flown some of the fastest jets in creation, and when I trained on this rover, I still wasn't prepared for the experience. Are you ready to gun it? Do you think you can handle this?" She revved the engine, and the rover vibrated roughly beneath them.

Excitement shot through him. "Fuck yeah, I am." He gripped the handlebar below the dash, bracing himself.

Reggie donned a pair of mirrored shades, closed both hands tight over the joystick-like control, and slammed the gas. Beneath a golden sunrise, they launched forward into the rust-hued desert.

Slowly.

Excruciatingly slowly.

Jon glanced at the mounted console. The speedometer read ten miles per hour.

"Come on," he groaned, falling back into his seat.

A smug smile spread across Reggie's face even as she kept her eyes locked straight ahead. "I told you. It's an experience."

He shook his head. "You are a cruel, cruel woman."

"And you were late," she returned primly. "But I think you've had enough punishment . . . for now."

From you? Never. He shifted uncomfortably in his seat. She was *not* flirting with him. Not possible. Not even remotely. "What's the top speed on this thing?"

"In zero-grav? Fifteen, maybe twenty miles per hour. Theoretically. Slower over rough terrain."

He nodded along as she continued to extol the merits of the new rover build, which she followed with a rousing summary of rock-sampling procedures for the morning's excursion. Exhaustion weighed his eyelids, but he was too wired from coffee, adrenaline, and Reggie's presence to drift off to sleep.

"Don't touch that," she warned as his hand wandered near the console.

"I only wanted to—"

"Don't. Touch. Anything."

Shame pricked at him, heating his ears. He wanted her to see him as a man, not some disobedient child.

He crossed his arms, stared out the side window at the landscape chugging by, and imagined himself as someone else. Someone like his fictional alter ego, Space Dude—a man who was so cool, capable, and confident he could *literally* surf the intangible output of two black holes colliding. Reggie would probably date a guy like Space Dude.

But a guy like Jon Leo? Not a chance in this galaxy.

☆ ⁎ 🌠 ⁎

Who was this man next to her?

Just when Reggie thought she had him pegged as an overstuffed himbo, Jon would do something like reference obscure space knowledge, such as Alexei Leonov's death-defying space walk.

Or deftly change the subject when she asked probing questions, making her wonder if there was far more beneath the surface than he let on.

Or look at her with so much banked heat in his dark eyes that her body threatened to melt through the rover's floor.

They arrived at their destination after an hour of bumpy driving. Reggie had reviewed the mission objectives during the drive, and for the sake of efficiency, she'd assigned all the simple tasks to Jon and given herself the difficult ones. It wasn't precisely how tasks had been divvied up in the mission manual, but Reggie had been given leeway to improvise as she saw fit.

She glanced at Jon, who'd nodded off halfway through the drive with his head propped against the side window. Strands of tousled dark hair lay over his face, fluttering against his cheek with each soft exhale. Her fingers itched with the temptation to reach out and brush the locks back from his face. To judge for herself if his hair was as silky as it looked.

No.

He looked good in glasses. Maybe because it gave him a professorial air, and Reggie had always had a thing for smart people.

An illusion, she reminded herself.

She parked the rover in the shade of a rocky outcropping. When she cut the engine, Jon came awake with a molar-flaunting yawn. He caught her staring and gave her a lazy smile that sent blood rushing straight to the apex between her thighs.

"Sorry," he said gruffly. He straightened and scanned his surroundings, like a house cat startling from a nap in an unfamiliar location. "I'll get used to the early mornings, I swear."

Guilt needled her. Had she been too hard on him this morning?

Just as she opened her mouth to apologize, Jon's hand strayed toward the console.

"What's this 'Activate Drone' button f—"

"Don't touch that." She shooed his hand away. "That feature is still in development for the Mars missions. We haven't been authorized to play with it."

Jon's eyes sparkled as if she'd told him pressing the button would make the sky rain candy. She keyed the rover off, shutting down the screen, and ignored Jon's crestfallen reaction.

Before getting out of the vehicle, she refreshed Jon on the morning's experiments. Specifically, that he would stay and babysit the rover, and she would pick up a smattering of substitute "moon rocks" for them to bring back to AHAB for analysis in the afternoon. This would be their primary task over the course of the first week, mimicking basic experiments lunar-stationed astronauts would undergo during a real mission.

Jon gazed out at the boulder-strewn area Reggie had chosen for the day's exploration. "It's because of the moon pirates, isn't it?"

"*What* now?"

"Me staying to guard the rover. You're worried about it getting commandeered." He gently patted the dashboard. Reggie managed to stifle a reflexive *Don't touch that* before he continued, "This girl is quite the trophy for an enterprising space scoundrel."

She'd wondered if he was going to make a fuss about not being assigned a task, and she'd already prepared her response. "Jon, you're guarding the rover because there is no atmosphere on the moon. Even with a protective spacesuit on, every second an astronaut is in the vacuum of space and thus away from the safety of the pressurized habitat, her life is in grave danger. Out here, the rover is our one and only lifeline, and we only have each other to count on. If I fall and puncture my spacesuit, you will have mere minutes to rescue me before the oxygen evaporates from my lungs, all the moisture in my body sublimates, and my cells become irreversibly irradiated."

Behind his glasses, Jon's eyes went wide with alarm.

She smiled serenely. "And of course, there's the moon pirates." Reggie extracted a set of handheld comms—glorified walkie-talkies, really—and handed him one. "Keep me in your line of sight at all times and check in every three minutes. Ready?"

He clutched the walkie-talkie like zombies were at the door and she'd just handed him a shotgun. He nodded to accept his role as her noble savior. Then he whipped out his phone. "Before we go, let's take a shot of the two of us in the rover."

"Hmm, let me think about that." *Take a selfie? I'd rather eat glass.*

Reggie pushed the driver's door open and hopped out, then slammed the door behind her. She busied herself by attaching her rock-hunting gear to her belt, knowing he'd follow.

The passenger door clunked open and shut, and footsteps approached, crunching in the gravel-strewn dust. His sneakers appeared in her line of sight. His left shoelace knot was on the verge of unraveling. "We're supposed to do one social media post a day."

Reggie didn't look up. She *had* promised Deb she'd do exactly that, but there were plenty of photogenic rocks out here in the desert that would suffice. "Take a picture of yourself, then."

"It would be better if we were both in the photo."

"Why?"

He shrugged. "Fans like to see behind the scenes."

"And why do you need me for that? Take a picture with the rover. NASA spent a lot of money on it."

He emitted some hybrid grunt-huff. "You really won't be in the photo?"

"Do you *need* me to be?"

"No, but—"

"Then take it without me." She zipped the cooler bag up and shoved it at him. "I'm heading out. I put bottles of water in there if you're thirsty. And don't touch anything."

His ever-present grin seemed to wilt before her eyes. "I know. You don't have to keep repeating it."

"Don't I? The last time you touched something, the fire alarms went off."

The muscles at the back of his jawbone flexed. "I was trying to help."

"You can *help* by doing what you do best." She pointed to a spot in the shade of the rover. "Stand there and look pretty."

He looked at the spot. He looked back at her, his expression unreadable. "So you think I'm pretty."

Her ears heated. "Pretty *annoying*, I meant."

"I'll take it," he said, rather smugly for her liking.

"That was an insult, you oaf."

His grin returned. "I know."

A thousand retorts flipped into her head, all of them unprofessional. Some of them downright lurid. Before one could slip out, she snatched her comm unit from the hood of the rover and stormed off.

Working with Jon's unique brand of chaotic charm was going to require a lot more patience—and personal willpower—than she'd thought.

CHAPTER 10

The rest of the week was a slog, in part because Reggie was doing the work of two people in an effort to reduce Jon's potential for screwing anything up, and in part because Jon still found creative ways to screw things up.

A few hours into Wednesday's fieldwork, Reggie was chipping away at some iron-oxide-threaded shale when she felt that same tingling sensation on the back of her neck as she'd felt on the phone with Deb, and her watch revealed it had been more than twenty minutes since Jon's last check-in. A glance back at the rover proved her instincts accurate.

Jon was gone.

She raised the hand comm. "Jon, where are you? Over."

Static.

With a curse, she marched back to the rover, glad she'd kept to a tight radius for their first few days, and found his comm unit abandoned on the cooler. She scanned the nearby area, tension tightening her shoulders when her charge's hulking form was nowhere to be seen. She thought of the snaking ravine they'd driven past—an ancient streambed that had run dry long ago, the hot sun sucking at the earth until the crumbling sandstone had cracked in two—and imagined Jon's lifeless form wedged between the canyon's narrow walls. Her palms began to sweat as future tabloid headlines paraded through her head:

Goth Astronaut Prime Murder Suspect in Actor's Death—Negligence, or a More Sinister Motive?

"Hey," came Jon's voice from behind her.

She whirled, but not before wiping all traces of worry from her expression. Jon crouched twenty feet above her on the slope of the maar crater, the midday sun casting long shadows beneath his eyelashes.

"Where were you?"

"Exploring." He pointed at a shadowed gap in the jagged rock wall behind him. It was a little triangle of space, only large enough for someone Reggie's size to fit through if she crawled on all fours. If there were a through tunnel, he could have easily gotten stuck, and she might not have found him until it was too late.

He continued blithely. "You think an animal lives in there?"

She scolded him for straying from the rover and leaving behind the comm unit, for putting himself in potential danger, and, most importantly, for making her wonder if her ass was about to get so fucking *unbelievably* fired.

When he rejoined her at the rover, she laid into him a second time, if only because she'd had to watch his magnum thighs flexing heroically as he'd clambered down the hill like some golden god descending Olympus. He had to know what he looked like in those jeans, and—worse yet—he had to have seen her looking. But what was she supposed to have done? *Not* look? She'd been concerned for his safety. Watching him was a moral obligation.

He even made a grand show of brushing the dust off his thighs right in front of her, feigned innocence plastered across his disgustingly perfect face.

"I was bored," he explained with a shrug.

Reggie tossed him a wad of plastic bags full of rock samples. "There's a marker in the cooler. Label these with the date and coordinates where we found them."

The task kept him busy the rest of the morning, which thankfully meant Reggie could focus on work without seeing the remains of her astronaut career flash before her eyes. She made a mental note: *Find more busywork to keep Jon distracted.*

After lunch, Mimi and Zach came by to film a short segment in which Reggie allowed Jon to sit in the driver's seat of the rover for exactly five minutes of supervised reenactment time, and Reggie successfully avoided being on camera for more than the absolute minimum required of her.

When the pair left, Reggie reviewed basic station maintenance procedures with Jon before setting him up with the thrilling duty of recording each rock sample in the sample log—a task that required so little brain power it could conceivably be conducted by a trained cabbage. To his credit, Jon grumbled only a little before hunching over the table with a pencil clutched in a boulder-size fist and determination set in his square jaw.

Reggie turned back to her work, hiding a satisfied smile. She'd unlocked the secret to keeping Jon from irritating her—occupying his every moment with mundane chores while she handled matters of importance. Maybe they could have a cooperative working relationship after all.

She made them dinner to eat while they worked, and Reggie was pleased to note that when they'd finished the afternoon's tasks, they'd been exactly four minutes ahead of schedule.

Jon merely shrugged when she told him the happy news. "I'm going for a run," he said, abruptly standing. Overtaken by a sudden magnanimity, Reggie waited for Jon to invite her to join him again so she could graciously accept.

When he didn't say anything, Reggie added, "I could use a run myself."

Jon still didn't respond right away. Instead, he thrust a hand through his hair and nodded. "Sure. Yeah, I'll wait up if you want to change."

Cold swept through her. A sudden, familiar certainty her presence was unwanted, not unlike the feeling she got when her colleagues made a conscious effort to invite her to after-work drinks. It wasn't a sense of *We enjoy Reggie's company* but rather *It would be rude not to invite Reggie.*

What had she expected? Jon probably resented her for assigning him grunt work instead of anything remotely interesting. But it wasn't like he could be trusted with anything valuable; he'd already proven he was easily distracted, and she wasn't willing to risk him screwing something else up before they'd even logged a full week of training. So what if she didn't trust anyone other than herself to do things? The risk of failure was lower that way. If the price she paid was Jon's dislike of her, then she'd have to live with it.

Standing stiffly, she headed for her living quarters. "Never mind. I think I'll call it an early night."

"Reg—"

She let the door suck itself closed with a thud behind her. It was a nice, solid sound. A righteous "I don't need your company" sound that she hoped would convey how infinitely comfortable she was alone.

Reggie lowered herself onto her bed, the Navy-trained folds of her sheets squeaking taut under her butt, and glared at the empty wall across from her. She'd awoken before dawn this morning and hadn't bothered to raise the window shades. If she concentrated, she could pretend the pitch black of the blind was a view of the empty lunar sky and that she was, in fact, stationed on the moon.

It was both a comforting and disconcerting thought: that this was what it would be like if she was chosen for the Artemis III mission.

She'd have every single task completed ahead of schedule, and the other five astronauts in her crew would rather fling themselves out the airlock before voluntarily spending time in her company.

Her phone was in her hand before she really knew what she was doing.

"*Allo*," Katya answered on the first ring. It was not phrased as a question, which meant her friend had checked caller ID before deigning to answer. A sultry pop song trilled in the background for three more bars before falling silent.

"Was that 'Genie in a Bottle'?"

"You are mistaken."

Reggie clucked her tongue in mock admonishment. "Don't lie to me, comrade. That's my Spotify account you're streaming from, and I have the means to change the password and revoke your poor taste at any time."

"Ah yes," Katya said. "Perhaps I will switch to this superior playlist I see you have played many times. What is this? *Reggie's Rad Jams?*"

Reggie hissed in a breath. "You bitch, stop snooping through my playlists."

"I will hold the phone to the speaker for you to hear."

Percussive keyboard from the opening chords to Bon Jovi's "Runaway" blared over the phone.

"Katya."

The volume increased.

"Katya!"

"Yes?" The music thankfully went quiet. "You have something you wish to say to me?"

Reggie sighed. "I'm just giving you shit. Christina Aguilera is a national treasure, and I don't know why the fuck I agreed to do this."

"Ah yes, I see," Katya said, as if she understood everything from Reggie's single sentence of a complaint. For a brief moment, Reggie's chest went tight with a keen sense of kinship and understanding. What would she do without Katya? She'd never had any close friends before.

The moment was ruined by Katya adding, "You have sexual frustration."

"What? That's not what I'm talking about!" Reggie jumped up and began to pace. "I'm talking about Jon screwing everything up. It's like

I'm sharing the base with fifteen baby raccoons in a trench coat pretending to be an adult man."

"But it is true."

"It's irrelevant. Katya, the first time I left him alone for more than five seconds, he stuck a food pouch in the irradiator without adding water first."

"So? These pouches are flame retardant, yes?"

Reggie pulled the phone away from her face, gave it the middle finger, and then smashed it back against her ear. "You're being deliberately obtuse. You *know* me. You know how hard it is for me to be patient with someone like that. I'm going to last a week before I either murder him or rage quit."

There was a pause as Katya seemed to consider this. "These are the only options?"

"No," Reggie said, even as she gritted her teeth at the admission. "I could be professional and power through. But . . ."

"But it is difficult for you, and you do not like to do things with a high risk of failure," Katya said, filling in the blanks with ease. Only half their friendship was due to a bear encounter; the rest was because they understood each other on a level that only two of the youngest women in their nations' space programs could. Katya was the one person Reggie had ever let breach the hull she'd built around her private life, and if they gave each other shit, it was because people like them didn't *do* displays of affection.

Or maybe because we don't know how.

"Look, I suck at people stuff, and I know it, you know it, the film crew knows it, and Jon *definitely* knows it. I can't magically become likable because I'm on camera, and when the board sees the footage, it's going to confirm what everyone already suspected. That Regina Hayes isn't 'the right fit' for Artemis III."

"Hmm. It is lucky, then, you have Jon Leo. I have watched his interviews. He is very good with people."

Katya had watched interviews with Jon? "How does that help me at all?"

"You will insist he gives you training in this. Inform him his life is at stake. He has no choice. He must train you as if you were a space orphan who has come to the Galactic Dude Dojo for guidance."

"Sorry, *what?*"

"I have now seen *Space Dude*. Jon Leo is a very talented actor. He does not wear a shirt for many scenes."

"You have too much free time. I'm emailing your bosses that you've expressed interest in refreshing your Arctic survival skills. I think there's a certain Siberian bear who misses you. In fact, I heard she has three ferocious cubs now. She's been training them since birth to recognize your face. *The One Who Got Away*, they call you."

Katya gave a dramatic gasp. "This sexual frustration has made you very cruel."

"I'm not sexually frustrated!" Reggie kicked the aluminum bed frame.

"I do not see the problem. You have made love with colleagues before."

It was true, but if it were just about scratching a metaphorical itch, she'd bark up Zach's or Mimi's trees. Although Zach was the nerdy type she normally went for, she'd overheard him cooing on the phone with someone yesterday, so that was a nonstarter. Mimi, however, was appealing in a grouchy, punk sort of way, and she had the no-nonsense air of a woman who would sort out your business before dawn but call you a rideshare before breakfast was served—perfect for Reggie's busy schedule. Well, usually.

Hard to take a shine to anyone else with Jon standing in the way, blocking the light.

Reggie plopped back on the bed and rubbed at the base of her neck, where a headache was beginning to form. Calling Katya had simultaneously improved and tanked her mood. A thousand excuses paraded through her mind: sleeping with Jon would be unprofessional; it would distract from her goals; none of this was Katya's business . . .

Instead, she mumbled, "I'm not sure he's even interested."

Though Reggie couldn't see her, Katya's "so what" shrug was nearly audible. "If you are sure, I will not argue. You seem very sure. Yes?"

"Yes." The image of Jon's heavy-lidded expression when she'd approached him in that purple jumpsuit flashed through her mind. It was the same way he'd looked at her earlier, in the rover. Or when she'd been bending over to load the cooler and he'd almost certainly scoped out her ass. "Okay, no. But . . . *why*? Aside from the fact that I'm the best astronaut—"

"The best who is not me," Katya interjected.

"You're a cosmonaut. I'm not competing with you, fortunately." Reggie rolled her eyes, even though Katya couldn't see it. "Anyway, Jon and I have nothing in common. And he's probably used to dating people with competent social skills."

"Ah yes. And your taste in music and clothing is poor. But you have a very nice chest. And with you, he will always be safe from bears."

"You flatter me," Reggie said dryly, even though these barest of compliments sparked warmth between her ribs.

"You must go. Offer your willing body in exchange for training."

"I'm hanging up now," she warned.

"Do it. Defile him for your country. For the galaxy—"

Reggie ended the call, though her reflection in the black screen of her phone betrayed the smile tugging at her lips. She forced her features back into a familiar glower. She was *not* going to proposition Jon. Definitely not in exchange for his help with her public image issue . . .

Even if it *would* save her pride to make a fair trade for his assistance instead of asking for it gratis. Besides, would he even help her after how she'd treated him?

No. What was she thinking? She'd always managed to solve challenges on her own—why should this be any different?

Kicking off her sneakers, she flung herself flat on the bed and squeezed her eyes shut to try and wipe the idea from her brain.

Stop thinking about it.

For the rest of the night, she thought of nothing else.

☆ 彡 ☆

Jon's Friday morning started the same way as every other morning had for the prior three days.

Every day, he met Reggie at the rover in some varying stage of lateness accompanied by varying excuses, he drank his coffee while Reggie drove and talked at him about important stuff (he assumed) while he watched the sunrise gild her cute doll-like nose, and then he sat on a hill for several hours watching Reggie poke at rocks while the untouched script at his side burned a hole in his conscience. After a brief break for lunch, it became routine for Jon to propose a social media post that Reggie would decline to participate in, followed by an afternoon of labeling plastic bags with increasingly inappropriate and elaborate descriptions to amuse himself, and finally, when he could no longer bear the excruciating boredom compounded by Reggie's ever-increasing outward irritation with him, he'd download Kahlil's suggested workout plans and do all of them. Twice.

Had someone designed a hell specifically to torment him, it would probably be just like this week. Except Reggie would be wearing clown pants or something. After all, watching her bend over in those worn yet close-fitting cargo pants had quickly become the only thing he looked forward to. She had a habit of tucking her hands into the front pockets when she was thinking, which had the pleasant effect of stretching the fabric tighter across the soft globes of her ass.

Reggie spent a lot of time thinking. He knew this, because he spent a lot of time watching her. For safety purposes.

This morning, however, watching her reminded him of the text he'd gotten from Jacqui last night. A text he really, *really* didn't want to bring up with Reggie, even though he had no choice but to do so.

Eventually.

As soon as he could find the right moment.

He lifted the walkie-talkie to his lips. "Moon Otter, this is Pirate King. Do you copy?"

"Copy." Static crackled, then: "I thought I told you to quit it with the code names." Reggie was far enough out into the field that he couldn't see the details of her expression, but it wasn't hard to guess. Her dark little brows were probably shooting down from beneath her row of bangs, her cherry lips cinching together into a frown.

"Acknowledged, Moon Otter. But how will I know it's you without the code names? This is an open channel. Over."

She'd been on all fours investigating a pile of rocks that looked like every other pile of rocks Jon could see, but now she sat back on her knees and looked in his direction. "We're alone in the middle of the fucking desert. Over."

"What about the aliens? Over."

More static, then a long, aggrieved sigh. "As you know, I'm not authorized to discuss the aliens with you, Jon. I'd have to kill you, and as tempting as that is, I wouldn't know what to do with your five-hundred-pound corpse. Over."

Jon's pulse sped up. Usually, she ignored his sad attempts at flirting. Or any conversation at all. "What if I bequeath my body to science? You could do experiments on me." *Sexy experiments,* he almost added.

"I'll keep that in mind. If I ever run out of rocks, I'll open up your thick skull and find the ones you're storing in place of a brain."

He tried not to let her words cut deep enough to strike actual feelings. But something about the sharpness of her tone, or maybe simply the fact it was Reggie who'd said it, made him want to curl up around his wounded ego to stanch the wound before he bled out in a pool of self-pity.

A reflexive smile stretched his face like an armored coating. *Sticks and stones . . .* something, something *. . . I'm too cool to give a shit.*

"Jon?" Her distant form was standing now, arms akimbo. She could see him. She knew he was still there.

He cleared his throat. "Sorry, Moon Otter. I thought I saw a scorpion."

"Stay calm. The only species out here that's worth worrying about is the bark scorpion, and they're usually nocturnal, though in the winter they might come out to warm up in the sun. Fortunately, they fluoresce, so there's a UV flashlight in the cooler if you want to do a quick once-over of the site."

Great, now she thought he was stupid *and* helpless. "I'll do that," he said. The next words fell out of his mouth before he could stop them. "Jacqui needs you to be in today's social media post. Rudy called her about it."

He saw Reggie stiffen. Imagined the fury flitting over her face. And he instantly felt bad. Not for delivering the news, because he hadn't been given a choice, but for taking a glimmer of pleasure in her distress.

"Heading back now. Over," she said.

Guess he did give a shit after all.

☆ ⭐ ☆

Reggie crouched next to Jon's outstretched phone, the UV flashlight clenched in her fist like a weapon. All the shots he'd taken looked exactly the same to her, but Jon kept insisting on retakes.

"Scowl more," he told her. "You're a ferocious scorpion hunter. Really sell it."

When she complied, he studied her pose for a moment longer before squatting down beside her and pretending to check under a rock. His bronzed movie-star grin beamed back at her from his phone screen, a dramatic contrast to her own pale, grim countenance.

He was close enough that she could smell the dust and sweat on his skin. A heavy weight settled on her shoulder blade, the heat of his palm fusing the worn fleece of her sweatshirt to her flesh.

"Ready? Three . . . two . . ."

Reggie swallowed and choked up on the flashlight, focusing all her efforts on not letting her hand tremble.

"One."

Jon retracted the hand holding his phone. The other stayed in place on her shoulder. There was absolutely nothing inappropriate about his hand placement. Of all the places he could touch her, it was one of the most innocuous. It shouldn't be making her legs feel like they couldn't hold her weight.

But it did.

She glanced at the photo they'd taken. It actually . . . wasn't bad. Jon was good at helping Reggie look "fun." Now that was a skill.

Katya's advice had been tumbling through her head, and after another abysmal day of filming, she'd resigned herself to asking for Jon's help—*without* the sex deal. But now that she'd insulted him, she'd be lucky if he helped her at all.

The exchange looped through her mind on tight orbit, determined to make her insides crawl from sheer cringe. Why was she such a colossal bitch? Why couldn't she manage to do teasing repartee like a normal human being?

Thing was, Jon obviously *wasn't* dumb, which made the "rocks for brains" jab such a cheap take. Was he clumsy and disorganized? Perpetually late? Impulsive? Definitely not paying attention to important instructions, ever? Yes, to all of the above. But his vocabulary betrayed a steady relationship with books, and he had no trouble grasping complex science concepts. More to the point: he had *social* intelligence, which Reggie did not. Her whole life she'd railed against her parents' narrow interpretation of what constituted success, and yet here she'd been since their first meeting, judging Jon by those same superficial metrics.

Jon had every right to be pissed, but instead he acted like it hadn't happened, which was worse. It meant she'd have to . . . *apologize*.

"I'm sorry for saying the thing about your brain rocks," she blurted.

The weight of his touch disappeared as Jon stood, groaning at the effort. He didn't look at her.

"*Oof.* Leg day." He stamped his feet a few times, shaking out the muscles, then added, "Ready to head back? I'm starving, and I think there's a pouch of beef-flavored Styrofoam with my name on it."

Oh, hell no. She'd spent all day working up the humility for this conversation; he wasn't going to dodge it so easily. "You know I don't really think you're stupid, right?"

He paused, then seemed to force a half smile. "Yeah, more like stupid *handsome*, am I right?"

"What? No!" she lied, then inwardly winced at how it sounded. Cheeks hot, she attempted to walk it back. "I don't—you look . . ."

He raised both brows, waiting.

"*Fine,*" she choked out.

His expression morphed into a blinding grin, and she sputtered an excuse about the sudden urgency of packing up their field equipment. It wasn't until she'd retreated to the vehicle that she realized how deftly he'd avoided addressing her apology.

Jon made no effort to aggravate her on the drive back to AHAB. If anything, he was even more cheerfully polite than usual. He didn't even tease her by pretending to reach for the drone button, as he did every time he got in the rover. She wondered if this was Jon's version of a bad mood.

He was good at conversationally outmaneuvering her, but she'd find a way to win him over. Somehow. Then she could broach the matter of obtaining what she'd started to think of as a charisma apprenticeship.

Without the sex, she reminded herself as her gaze began to stray to the corded forearm propped on his bent knee. It never hurt to be reminded.

CHAPTER 11

Reggie had no luck buttering Jon up on the drive back, and at the base, Mimi's mood was in equally poor form. Maybe there was something in the air.

Mimi had taken over the workspace in the central hub again, and Reggie found her hunched over her laptop with the hood of her sweatshirt up and cinched tight around her face, leaving her braid-waved hair spilling out the bottom of the face hole onto the keyboard. Her muffled voice leached through the neck of her sweatshirt. "There's no fucking narrative. It's just a fucking biopic about fucking rock collecting."

Unsure how to address that, Reggie stepped over Mimi's splayed feet and began unloading the cooler. Jon was still outside, ostensibly stretching, but something else was missing. "Where's Zach?"

"Pouting in the trailer. His headphones broke." Mimi stabbed the keyboard, freezing a frame on the screen. "See this shit? It's shit."

Reggie had initially wondered why Mimi and Zach, who seemed perfectly normal, would continue to work with someone like Rudy Ruffino. After five days in Mimi's company, Reggie was starting to catch on.

She peered at Mimi's screen. It was stuck on a tableau of Reggie standing over Jon as he pretended to use the spectrometer to analyze a sample of composite sandstone. Her face was pinched, arms crossed over her chest. Jon was smiling into the viewfinder, but his dimple was missing. It looked like a stock photo someone would use in a mediocre PowerPoint.

A headache was beginning to blossom in the back of her head. "This is what astronauts do, Mimi. This isn't Hollywood. We don't spend all our time prancing around with laser guns going, *Pew pew, I'm an astronaut!*"

Mimi yanked her hood down and gave her a narrow-eyed glare. "Anyone ever told you that you're a raging bitch?"

"Excuse me?"

"You heard me."

Reggie stared at the other woman, vaguely aware her mouth was open. What was she supposed to say to that? She wasn't even wearing earrings she could remove in indignation to signal preemptive combat.

As if she could read Reggie's mind, Mimi shrugged and said, "Look, I'll fight you if you want. This week's been boring as hell, and it might be fun. But personally, I don't give a shit about your attitude. I work with plenty of people I don't like. Hell, I work with Rudy, don't I? The difference between you and me is I don't make it a point to go around projecting my unresolved emotional bullshit on everyone I work with."

"I don't have—"

"Spare meeeeee," Mimi groaned, flopping back in her chair dramatically. "Of course you do. Everybody does. What's your thing? Only child? Parents who withheld affection while placing undue weight on outward symbols of success like academic performance and money? Were the popular girls mean to you in school, and now you're a bottomless well of bitterness, resentment, and loathing? Stop me if I'm getting warmer."

It *was* hot in here, wasn't it?

The entry door hissed open, and Jon ducked through the doorway. He took one step into the room and stopped, looking back and forth between Reggie and Mimi. "Everything okay in here?"

Mimi snapped her laptop shut and stood. "Forget filming today. It's Friday, and I think we all need a goddamn drink. There's a bottle of Jack in the trailer. Let's go."

Jon's brow furrowed. "Reggie?"

"I . . ." She pinched the back of her neck between her middle and pointer fingers in a last-ditch attempt to stem the throbbing in her skull, then let her hands drop to her sides in defeat. The alternative was spending the rest of the afternoon alone, wallowing in a slurry of irritation and—*fine,* she'd admit it—sexual frustration. Maybe she really did need a drink. "Yeah, whatever."

✰ ⭐ ✰

By six o'clock, Jon had given up trying to match the others drink for drink.

Not because he couldn't hold his own, he regretfully explained when the bottle of Jack made its way back to his side of the firepit, but because he'd already blown past Kahlil's recommended "A-Lister Diet Plan" calorie count. Though, while that was technically true, Jon regularly fudged the numbers in his tracking app anyway (he was a growing boy!). The truth was, Mimi and Zach—like many film crew veterans—were professional drinkers, Reggie was a stone-cold badass, and Jon was a total lightweight who'd end up as red as Clifford the Dog (and about as coherent) if he tried to keep up.

Zach, who had barely spoken all week, had become a world-class storyteller in the space of the afternoon. ". . . And so I turn around, and Denzel is standing right behind me!"

As everyone burst into guffaws, Jon stole a glance at Reggie. No way was she unaffected by the bourbon-spiked coffee in her thermos, but aside from the silvery sheen in her gaze and the way her normally stick-straight spine had melted into her camp chair, she barely showed it.

Still, seeing Reggie relaxed was an addictive treat. It teased his extraordinarily active imagination with forbidden ideas.

Like, *really* forbidden. The "rainy Sunday morning in bed, snuggling and watching cartoons" kind.

It wasn't like he hadn't tried to smother this kindling lust for her—he'd given it his best effort all week. Probably to the point that Reggie thought he was mad at her for giving him so much busywork. Which did somewhat annoy him, but whenever he began to get grumpy, all he had to do was claim he'd lost another pencil to get her to bend over and search under the table, and then his mood instantly brightened.

"Okay, okay," Mimi managed to get out through snorts. "Your turn, Reggie."

Mimi had passed around a joint earlier, though both Reggie and Jon had declined, and the chilled air smelled of weed and woodsmoke. The cloudless sky had dimmed to a vivid indigo, and Venus was a shimmering pinprick above a half moon. The trailer was parked up on the crater's edge near the solar panels, and sunset already cast AHAB in slate-hued shadows at the crater's base.

"Craziest thing to happen at work?" Reggie mused on the prompt, taking a sip from her thermos. After a moment, she shrugged. "Every single day I was in space, I guess."

Mimi booed. "That's a cop-out answer. Give us the real juice."

"Yeah," Zach chimed in. "Tell us about the aliens!"

Jon smirked, and Reggie caught it. She shook her head, exasperated. "There are no aliens, smart-asses."

He leaned forward and cupped a hand to the side of his mouth to whisper sotto voce to the film duo, "That's what they say when there are definitely aliens."

Zach nodded knowingly.

"Fine," Reggie conceded with a smile that she poorly camouflaged with another sip. "How about this . . . I fought a bear once."

Jon sat forward. "Hold up. In *space*?"

"No. During Arctic survival training. All astronauts headed to the Space Station used to launch from Baikonur, the Russian spaceport, and during reentry there's a chance of landing off target in the Siberian wilderness. So we're required to rehearse surviving out there with no supplies until the support teams can reach us, which could take up to three days. I trained with Katya Volkov, whom you met, and on the first night she went off to relieve herself behind a tree. Unfortunately, a bear had already claimed that spot for her own business."

Mimi whistled. "How big?"

"Like . . ." Reggie stood and slashed a hand in the air as far as she could reach. "This high."

Jon stood and ducked under her hand. "My height?"

When her fingertips brushed the top of his head, she snatched her hand back as if it were burned. She cleared her throat. "Yeah. About that high. We were lucky . . . it was an adolescent. If it were full grown, we'd probably be dead. Anyway, Katya called out for help, and I ran up and threw a flare. I think the bear was honestly as scared as we were, but at the time I saw it rearing back onto its hind legs and thought it was about to attack. So I ran up behind it and . . . I punched it."

Zach clapped a hand over his mouth and let out a muffled "No way. What did it do?"

"It ran away. Like I said, we were lucky."

Mimi saluted her with the empty booze bottle. "I take back what I said earlier, Regina Hayes. You're still a raging bitch, but I like you now."

"Whoa, what did you call her?" Jon said. He said it lightly, but he couldn't stop his muscles from tensing. He was *not* cool with casual misogyny, no matter the source; his mom had raised him right. And he made a point to cut that bullshit off at the pass if it ever came up on set.

"It's a compliment," Mimi argued.

"I don't care. Apologize."

"Jon—" Reggie placed a hand on his arm, and pure electricity snapped through his nerve endings and shot straight to his dick. His muscles tensed, bicep jumping beneath her touch, and when he glanced at her, their eyes locked. And he knew she felt it too.

Mimi narrowed her eyes at them, her gaze measuring. "A*ha*. That's it. That's the narrative. You see this, Zach?"

Zach looked up. "No?"

"Apologize," Jon repeated, calmly but without give.

"Okay, okay, *fuck*. Sorry about the 'bitch' thing. Good enough for you, Ser Jon?" When he gave a stiff nod, Mimi pointed the nearly empty bottle at them, neck first, and nudged Zach again. "Look, though. See that tension? They're going to Bone Town. One hundred percent. Have they been yet? No. Maybe? I can't tell. Shit, I'm high."

Zach pushed his glasses up his nose and squinted. "They don't seem to like being near each other, though."

"Yup," Mimi said smugly. "Like I said. Bone Town."

✩ 🌠 ✩

Bone Town echoed in the air like a misty prophecy falling over the land. Heat swept up and down Reggie's skin. It was the alcohol. No, the fire. She was standing too close to the fire.

Reggie backed up a step, but Jon's hand shot out and caught the curve of her back. It was like thudding into a bar of steel. "Careful," he said, and a glance over her shoulder revealed how close she'd been to tumbling backward over her camp chair, which she'd parked only a few feet away from the crater's downward slope. The irony of Jon doing the catching, rather than the other way around, was not lost on her.

Why hadn't Jon said anything to contradict Mimi? If he wouldn't do it, Reggie would have to.

The denial stuck in her throat. It occurred to her that naming the false claim, giving it undue weight, would somehow realize it. Maybe if she pretended she hadn't heard it . . .

"We should get back," Reggie said instead, pressing the cool back of her hand to her cheeks. It wasn't true. Tomorrow was Saturday, and they didn't have anything scheduled. Mimi and Zach had offered a ride if either she or Jon wanted to join them on a jaunt to the artsy city of Sedona to shop for Christmas gifts, but they'd both declined. Jon had claimed he had important reading to do, and Reggie straight up wanted to avoid being trapped in a vehicle with other human beings for hours.

"We're out of booze, anyway," Mimi said. "You two cutie-pies head on back, mkay? And don't get up to too much trouble this weekend while we're gone. That would make for *terrible* narrative." Mimi waggled her eyebrows.

It was cold away from the fire, and Reggie welcomed it as they made their way back to the winding dirt roadway that switchbacked its way down into the crater, Jon leading two paces ahead. He wore her gray blanket tucked around him like a shawl, with the longer end flipped back over his left shoulder. It should have made him look ridiculous, but on his hulking frame it gave him the air of a primordial warrior.

Whenever he looked back at her—which was more often than she felt was necessary—his breath clouded along the side of his face. "Are you cold?" she asked.

"Not even a little bit. Don't worry about me, Moon Otter; I'm snuggly warm in this lovely scarf."

Scarf? The blanket was large enough to wrap her entire body in like a burrito. "Why is Moon Otter my call sign? Do I look like an otter to you?"

"I thought it was obvious. You love collecting rocks. So do otters."

"Otters collect rocks?"

He flipped around to face her but kept walking. "Yeah, for cracking open shells. I watch a lot of science and nature documentaries."

Well, that explains his eclectic array of knowledge. "Turn around. You're going to trip."

"I won't trip. I'm a space dude." He executed a one-two punch. Surprisingly deft of him, given how much bourbon he'd consumed.

"Stupid name for a movie," she mumbled.

His feet scuffed over a shallow divot in the road, and he caught himself before stumbling. Flipping around, he fell into step beside her as if she hadn't noticed his little dance.

"I saw that."

"Saw what?" He sounded so innocent. Acting was the right profession for him. "Anyway, I happen to agree with you about *Space Dude*. It's a terrible name for a movie, and the script was even worse."

"But you still took the role."

"Yeah. Well. They paid me enough." He didn't elaborate. She desperately wanted to ask, but his tone of voice indicated he desperately wanted her not to.

They marched along in silence for several minutes. It was getting dark faster than they were walking, so Reggie withdrew her keys from a pocket in her pants and lit their way with her LED key chain.

"You're so prepared," he marveled. Like she'd just demonstrated a proficiency with magic instead of a very basic level of foresight.

"Unlike *some people*, I can't just coast through life on my good looks and charm. I have to rely on my brain." Her tongue was loose, and the words tumbled out. She suppressed a wince.

He stopped walking.

Three steps later, so did she. She swept the flashlight in his direction, the dot of light zigzagging over the elegant lines of his face. A sudden desire to replace the light with her touch made her fingers curl tighter around her palmed cluster of keys. "Why did you stop?"

"I think you could if you wanted to. Coast by on your looks. I think you're pretty." He thrust a hand into his hair, ignoring the resulting ping of his hair elastic as it shot off into the night. His man bun unraveled, the hair falling forward into his face.

She wanted to claw her hands into that hair. Twist it tight around her knuckles. Straddle his lap. Grind herself against his hard—

"Fuck off." Reggie resumed walking. Her shoulders knotted together so tightly the muscles around her right scapula twitched.

He jogged to catch up. "I'm serious!"

"Don't pull your smooth actory bullshit on me. It doesn't work."

"First of all, it does too work," Jon countered.

"I'm immune."

"Second, it's not bullshit. Why are you so mad? Did I do something to upset you?"

"I'm not mad." She wasn't. Not really. What she felt was . . .

Was . . .

Reggie shivered, even though beneath her air-frosted skin her muscles flushed with a buzzy sort of heat. Was she so bad at naming her own feelings now? She'd been trained to compartmentalize, but sometimes, she felt like her emotions had been in cold storage for too long and she'd lost the access codes.

She picked up her pace, but he followed suit, so she powered forward, her breath coming faster and faster. They were almost trotting now, but he was still following.

The trail flattened. AHAB was only a few steps away when Jon asked, "Do I really annoy you that much?"

"Yes."

"Why? Because I'm just a dum-dum?" He used a goofy voice, like he was making a joke of it. "Big, stupid Jon—can't even pick up rocks without supervision."

Now it was her turn to come to an abrupt stop. He followed suit, circling back until the lighter half of the twilight sky was behind him, casting his face in shadow.

"Don't do that."

"Do what?"

She poked at his chest with her flashlight. It was like hitting a steel boulder. "Call yourself dumb."

"But didn't you—"

"I apologized for the brain-rocks thing," she snapped. Didn't he realize how much that humility had cost her? "You're obviously not stupid, so don't let people talk to you like that."

"Even you?"

"*Especially* me."

He cocked his head at her, and it made him appear far too adorable. "But it doesn't bother me. I've always been kind of, you know . . . spacey. Being self-deprecating about it is part of my charm."

"Well, your charm pisses me off!" She poked him again, because it felt good to do it. He had no right to combine such compelling physical appeal with genuine humility. No right at all. If the world were fair, he'd be a complete asshole.

"*Ow*, you're so mean." He swayed backward, as if she'd wounded him, when she knew she hadn't. Moonlight reflected off his teeth as he grinned, a quicksilver slash in the dark. "If I didn't know better, I'd think you were flirting with me. But you're not. Obviously." A pause, then: "Are you?"

She barked a scornful laugh, even as blood sizzled in her veins. She felt bubbly. Light. Like gravity wasn't quite on its A game right now. "You wish."

His voice went gravelly. "You have no idea how much I do."

"I'm definitely not flirting with you."

"Don't worry, I know."

"I would *never* flirt with you," she repeated, because declarations of disinterest worked like naming Beetlejuice; if you said them three times, they became true. "That would be unprofessional."

He nodded. "You're right. And Mimi's so wrong. We're not going to Bone Town. No way."

But then he stepped in closer, and she could see the individual goose bumps on his skin above the collar of his T-shirt. A fascinating place. Lots of neck tendons and muscles and hollows. She could even see his pulse beating, the shadowed flesh jumping with each throb.

She thought, "Is this what it's like to be a vampire?"

"Uh, what?"

Oops. "Never mind. Just get it over with already." She squared her shoulders, drawing up as high as her earthbound bones would allow, and thrust out her chin.

"What are you talking about?" He cocked his head at her, and even though she *knew* he was being coy on purpose, she had the irrational urge to stamp her feet in frustration.

"This. Whatever you're . . ." She waved the flashlight back and forth between their chests. "Whatever you're going to do," she finished lamely.

"Do you—" He stopped, scraped a hand over his face, and let out a groan. When his hand came away, his expression was dark, his eyes hooded. And when he spoke, his voice was so deep it set off vibrations low in her belly. "Do you want me to kiss you?"

CHAPTER 12

Reggie couldn't catch her breath. She might as well have been staring out a yawning airlock, confronting the sheer gut-hollowing dread of letting go of the handrail. In fact, she'd rather be two hundred miles above the ground than be six inches away from Jon Leo's mouth, because he'd just asked if she wanted him to kiss her, and the proximity—the *possibility*—of that outcome made her head spin.

No, she opened her mouth to say, because she needed to cling to the solid metal of a human construct. But *no* wasn't what came out of her mouth. In a strangled voice, she answered, "Is that what you want?"

"God, yes."

Her pulse skipped erratically. She could barely see the details of his face in the darkness. It made him seem all the more mysterious. The circumstances more thrilling.

He didn't move, and she understood he was waiting for her to make the move. To jump first into the void.

Just a kiss. No one will know. Within her rib cage were the binary stars of fear and desire, whipped into tightly accelerating orbit and destined for an epic explosion.

Her hands found their way under the gray blanket to the iron planes of his pectorals, her chilled fingers stinging where they made contact with his heat. She splayed her touch wide, momentarily marveling. "Huh. You *do* run hot."

He groaned. *"Reggie."*

"Just one," she whispered, stepping in and coming up to her toes. One kiss was reasonable. Easy enough to dismiss as a momentary . . . lapse. "Agreed?"

"Is this negotiable?" His muscles twitched under her touch.

"That depends."

Their bodies were flush now, ever so lightly. Knees and breasts grazing, the tip of her nose brushing the wedge of stubble-roughened skin where his chin and neck joined. His mouth was still too high to reach, so she discreetly inhaled, like some feral animal scenting prey, filling her lungs with the earthy, sweaty smell of him. There was nothing poetic about it. No fancy cologne, no signature soap. Yet it triggered something deep within her core—something primal and even a little depraved.

His throat moved as he swallowed. "Depends on what?"

As if compelled, her tongue flicked over his skin. Salt. Alkalinity. Hints of ferrous dust. The delicate overlay of whatever chemical-based aftershave he used. If he were a rock, he'd be a feldspar silicate—her favorite class of mineral. Like the lump of anorthite in her pocket. Like all the brightest surfaces of the moon.

Her fingers curled, short nails digging into flesh through thin cotton. "Depends on if I like it."

He gave no warning. Massive hands closed around her waist, crushing her against him. Her feet left the earth, and she was spinning; then cold metal thudded against her back. *The door to the base,* came the dim thought, and then it was gone.

Air whooshed out of her lungs, and he shifted her higher against him, the buttons on his fly scraping against her stomach, dragging the hem of her sweatshirt up. Then his hands were lower, roughly cupping her ass, and she instinctively locked her legs around him, and finally—*finally*—they were eye level, her mouth so close to his she could suck in his exhaled breath.

Yes. She closed her eyes, waiting for his mouth to slam down, for the bite of his teeth and the bruising tangle of tongues . . .

His nose brushed against her jawbone, breath fluttering over her skin.

She blinked.

"I thought you were going to kiss me." Her voice shook. She sounded desperate. *Embarrassing.*

"I am." He mimicked how she'd sampled him with the slow, teasing press of his tongue over her carotid pulse.

She tried to measure her breathing. Make her voice steady. "That's not how you do it."

"Oh. What about this?" He pressed his lips over the same spot. A sweet kiss. Almost innocent in its purity. "Is this what you want?"

She crushed his T-shirt in her fists. "No."

"What about . . . ?"

The edge of his teeth scraped her flesh, and a sound unfurled from her lips. A shred of a moan, caught in a sudden inhale. Then she felt a sharp pinch and realized he'd nipped her. Electricity bolted straight to her core, and a breathless *"Yes"* tore from her lungs.

He hummed against her throat, and the buzz of it made her thigh muscles spasm, crushing him tighter against her. "Okay, I think I get it now," he murmured against her skin.

His mouth grazed a searing path up the underside of her jaw in a torturous exploration of every square inch of her flesh that didn't belong to her lips.

Was he going to make her beg? Because she wouldn't. She had to retain some dignity.

"Please," she moaned.

His lips met hers, and it was worth it.

Jon didn't bother with niceties—no more teasing, no chaste, close-mouthed presses. He forced her mouth open, tongue rasping against her teeth, sucking her lips into his mouth, and Reggie pushed back with the same fervor, returning every lick, every scrape of teeth, every sexy, guttural sound.

It went on and on. Time dilated, every second an agonizing push-pull against the need ballooning inside her and stealing oxygen from her lungs. It had to stop eventually, but she never wanted it to stop. Never wanted it to end.

He dragged her harder against the hard ridge in his jeans, and she moved with him, reveling in the escalating friction. She needed this. Needed *more*.

Head spinning and pulse pounding, she ripped away from the kiss and let her head fall back against the door. "Inside," she gasped.

"Hold on to me." He shifted her to one hand, as easily as if she were weightless, and her arms looped around his neck as he brought her inside, fumbling the first of the two pressurized door locks closed behind them.

As soon as the door slid shut, the blaring alarm and flashing red lights pierced through the fog of lust in her brain.

CHAPTER 13

The alarm was so startling he nearly dropped Reggie. Reflexively, he gripped her soft body tighter against him.

"Put me down," she snapped, struggling against his grip.

He lowered into a squat so she could jump off, and she launched toward a control panel on the wall. Her kiss-swollen lips tightened in consternation as she read the numbers flashing on the screen. "Oxygen levels are abnormally low inside the habitat."

Jon nodded dumbly, wishing there were something for him to do aside from stand in the middle of the airlock with the most insistent erection of his life about to bust a hole through the fly of his jeans.

She tapped at the digital display and swore. "It's the air unit."

"Can we just open the windows?" he tried. God, he hoped it would be that simple. The drive to get back to that mouth of hers was all-consuming.

"No, Jon, we cannot just open the windows." *You complete idiot,* she might as well have said. "AHAB is designed to be a closed system. The air unit is connected to the water recycler to extract moisture from the air, and that's connected to the—look, let's not get into it. We'd have to power down nearly everything and call for tech support, and then not only will that put us days behind schedule, but Lord forbid the problem is a result of user error. Deb will be *pissed.*"

Deb? His brain scrolled through Jacqui's list of names and matched it with Reggie's boss. "How could this be our fault?"

Reggie gave him a look.

"I didn't do anything!"

"I didn't say you did." She turned back to the panel, a hand coming up to rub at a spot between her neck and shoulder.

"You implied it," he countered sullenly. He wanted to punch something. Or rewind five minutes and never have opened this fucking door. Schrödinger's air filter: if he'd kept kissing Reggie, the alarm would have been both activated and not activated.

The alarm took nine minutes to deactivate. During that time, Jon managed to wrangle his raging hard-on into a less painful state of existence, though watching Reggie bending down to tinker with a low instrument hatch had him gritting his teeth in renewed agony.

As soon as possible, he was getting her ass in his hands again. It was his new obsession. They had the whole weekend with nothing to do, didn't they? (Technically, he had a script to read, but that wasn't nearly as important right now.)

Reggie closed up the panels and let them into the central hub. The air inside was stuffy and damp, but as the door sealed shut behind him, a mechanical thumping-and-humming duet kicked on somewhere in the walls, and currents of fresher air began blowing down from overhead.

"It's fixed?" Jon ventured, stepping in close. He ducked to capture her stern mouth—

Her hand came up to block his advance. "It's rerouted. For now, I shut down life-support systems in every unit except the central hub."

A challenge, but he could work with this. He strode to the table, gripped it by the sides, and jiggled to test its sturdiness. "This'll do for now." He hopped up on it and patted his thighs. "Where were we?"

Her brows disappeared into her thick bangs. "You can't be serious. Our air unit is operating at thirty-nine percent efficiency right now."

"I am. I am very, very serious."

"I need to manually close vents in every room we're not using so we don't suffocate in our sleep."

He tugged her wrist to draw her into the space between his thighs. She came willingly, and up close he could see her cheeks flush a rosy pink. He let a smirk slip through, and in a low voice he informed her, "I have no plans to sleep tonight."

The catch in her breath was audible. For a moment, triumph reigned. Then: "If I don't get this fixed, you definitely won't be. And not in a sexy way."

"Hmm." His hand snaked around her waist to nudge her closer. Maybe if he pretended he didn't hear her . . .

"Jon."

He leaned in. "I like kissing you, Reggie. Forget about the air unit. We'll fix it later. We have all weekend."

She stiffened in his hold. "We do not. I planned to use the weekend to get ahead on experiments and do some personal geological research."

"*Or* instead—"

"This was clearly a bad idea." Now she was shrugging out of his hold, crossing the room to widen the distance between them. She began pulling tools out of a wall cabinet. "I'm not looking to make this a thing, and you obviously are."

"What, exactly, do you mean by *a thing*?" A rare headache welled between his temples, and he centered a fist against his forehead, rubbing at the sharp ache.

Reggie didn't answer. Her movements were short and jerky, ripping tools out of their prong-set placeholders like they'd insulted her on a personal level.

Undaunted, he continued, "I like you, Reggie. I want to spend the weekend kissing you and maybe getting to know you better, and ideally, if you can spare the time between rock samples, I want you to sit on my goddamn face so I can eat your pussy until you pass out. Is that a thing? Is that inconvenient for you?"

A wrench clattered to the ground. Reggie snatched it up in a white-knuckled grip. "Yes, it is," she said, but he smugly noted her voice wavered. Then her voice rose an octave. "Don't you have a script to read? You don't need another distraction."

The fucking irony. How to explain to a woman like Reggie that to him, everything in the entire world was a distraction. She was the only thing that felt clear to him. When he kissed her, the cacophony in his brain went silent.

So what if he thought she was cute, he liked listening to her talk, and they had demonstrably excellent chemistry together?

Okay, maybe he did want a . . . thing. What was the problem with that? His mental voice of reason began to chirp in warning, but he stifled it. *Not now, buddy. This is a horny party, and you're not invited.*

An alarming idea arose. "Are you already seeing someone?"

"No. I don't see people." Reggie pulled up on the handle, and a giant flap in the wall folded down, revealing a loud, whirring mechanical unit the size of a car engine.

"At all?"

She examined the unit, fisted hands propped on her hips. "At all."

"Is it"—he tried to think of a polite way to phrase it—"a religious-type thing?"

She snorted. "I'm not celibate, if that's what you're asking. I'm thirty-five, Jon, not some blushing maiden. I get my needs taken care of."

"And that's it? No dating?" When she shook her head, he asked, "Not even sexy movie nights on the couch? Just . . . sex?"

"I'm going to be the first woman to walk on the moon. I don't have time for the other stuff."

He absorbed this, weighing his sinking heart against his unflaggingly optimistic libido. He'd never considered himself a romantic, per se, but he supposed he'd always wooed women with the intent of, well, *dating* them. Until now, he'd never considered a no-strings-attached fuck.

The concept felt . . . wrong. Selfish.

Or maybe he was just projecting, considering his own conception. At the height of his movie-star fame, Brian Leo had screwed his way through a swath of young, impressionable female fans, and Jon's mom had been one of them. All she'd gotten out of it was a kid, a stalled acting career, and a $10,000 check predicated on the promise she didn't tell Brian's wife about his illegitimate spawn.

But what if Reggie didn't want to be wooed? Was it still selfish if sex was all she wanted in the first place? In a way, wouldn't making Reggie scream in pleasure while he railed her with his hard cock be a *selfless* act?

Said cock throbbed in agreement.

Jon was a good guy. He wanted to do the right thing.

"I can take care of your needs," he said. Even though she was hunched over the machine with her back to him, he could see her shoulders draw together, and he raced to finish before she could interrupt with another dismissal. "I don't need a thing. At all. We can do it on your schedule, and when you're done with me, you can tell me to fuck off and go play with the Mars drone or something."

"You're never touching that drone. You know that, right?"

He groaned dramatically. "I don't know; I'm just so turned on right now with no outlet for this pent-up energy. And when I get like this, I just want to touch things I shouldn't . . ." He mimed poking buttons and was rewarded with a narrow-eyed glare.

"It's not a toy. It's a specialized surveying-device prototype comprised of highly sensitive, fragile, *expensive* components."

He pretended to stroke an invisible object, closing his eyes as if in bliss. "Sweet, sweet Mars drone toy. Only you can soothe my tormented soul."

He cracked his left eye open to sneak a glance at her. Her lips were twitching.

"Are you blackmailing me into sex?"

He pretended to consider his response. "Will that work?"

"Absolutely not."

"Hmm."

She came to her feet, kicking the panel shut. Then she gave him a measuring look. "Fine. I'll think about it. Wipe that grin off your face right now."

He tried. He really did. "I can wait."

"And don't bug me about it." A calculating expression stole over her face. "And it's an automatic no if you show up late, wander off, touch things you shouldn't, or otherwise misbehave."

He nodded sagely. "I respond very well to positive motivation. But if I'm expected to be awake before seven every morning, I demand double coffee portions."

She narrowed her eyes. "You're in no position to negotiate."

"Counterpoint: I can be in any position you want. In fact, I'm in the best shape of my life right now. According to my trainer, my lung capacity is in the top fifth percentile. That means, when you eventually agree to this, I can go down on you for *hours* without coming up for air." He was pleased to see her eyes widen. And was it his imagination, or was that wrench in her hand trembling too? He crossed his arms. "Double portions."

Instead of responding, she tossed him a flashlight. "Let's go. I need to get up on the roof to make sure the vents aren't leaking into the atmosphere."

✩ ⋆ 🌠 ⋆

Only Deb would call after 1800 hours on a Friday night, thinking it was a good time to have a casual chat to recap the workweek. Then again, weekend nights usually *were* a good time for Reggie to take a work call. Her industriousness—and relative lack of social life—was one of the many reasons Deb claimed to like Reggie so much.

If only she weren't balanced precariously on top of a lunar habitat in the dark, her legs hooked around a metal strut while her top half dangled into a disassembled air-intake hatch, as her phone buzzed insistently against her leg.

"Your phone's ringing," Jon pointed out, using the flashlight beam to paint a circle on her thigh pocket.

"You're a veritable rocket scientist," she said, reaching across the open hatch to hand him pliers. "Hold these and stay quiet. It's my boss, and I'd prefer she didn't know we broke AHAB already."

Jon's lips contracted into a silent whistle. *Someone's in trouble . . .*

The infuriating man still hadn't registered it was mostly *him* she was covering for. He was remarkably accident prone for someone so innately intelligent. They'd somehow gotten away with the pool incident, but if he'd broken the air filter, there'd be hell to pay. Then they'd *both* look bad.

"Hi, Deb," Reggie answered, holding a finger up for silence.

"Reggie. Is this a good time? Thought we could debrief week one before your weekend starts."

"Absolutely. I've actually just stepped outside to enjoy the lack of light pollution out here." It wasn't entirely a lie. The sky had darkened enough to reveal an unblemished starscape, and the Milky Way poured across the inky canvas like someone had given a bored toddler access to the glitter stash.

Deb gave a longing sigh. "Lord, it's been a while since I've had that privilege. I need to get back in the field. If I can offer you any advice in my advancing years, it's this: never take a desk job."

Small talk again. What had gotten into her mentor lately?

Reggie snorted. "Advancing years? Please. You're barely fifty and still on the active roster; they're not going to waste you on paperwork for much longer."

"We'll see about that," Deb demurred. "How's Hollywood life treating you?"

"Great!"

Jon raised a brow at her enthusiasm.

Deb's tone was equally skeptical. "Huh. Unexpected, but good to hear. How's it been operating out of AHAB? Run into any trouble?"

"None." A small twinge of remorse followed the lie, but she ignored it. Why cause Deb needless concern when Reggie was confident she could fix whatever was wrong with the air filter before it became imperative to escalate the issue? "We're completely on schedule to start soil sampling and testing the new surface drill next week."

"Good. And how's our astronaut trainee holding up?"

Reggie glanced at Jon, who had tucked the flashlight between his thighs to free both his hands and was now in the process of pretending the spread handles of the pliers he'd found were a pair of legs, his tongue hovering provocatively over the fulcrum. "Jon's loving it. I think he's found the experience integral for his upcoming role, though he did mention in passing that he's something of an early bird, and he'd prefer if the workdays started an hour or two earlier."

Jon froze in horror, tongue hanging from his mouth in a comical tableau.

"I can talk to his publicist—"

Reggie held full, deliberate eye contact with the man in question. *Behold my power and cross me at your peril, mortal.* "No, no, that won't be necessary. I think we've established a comfortable rhythm in the last few days."

"I did notice you've only been featured in one of his social media posts this week, and I don't see anything posted to your individual NASA handles either."

Shit. It wasn't phrased as a question, which from Deb counted as a level-two threat. She counted herself lucky; a level-one threat signaled bat'leths at dawn. Reggie gritted her teeth. "It's been a busy week—"

"We had an agreement, if you recall. And I imagine I don't need to remind you about the significant costs NASA and the studio have each incurred to green-light this project in the hopes the resulting media, and specifically the positive press response to that media, returns our investment tenfold. Are you suggesting your daily tasks need to be further adjusted to allow you a spare five minutes to post a photo once a day? Because if so, I'm curious to know why your trainee has managed to find the time when you have not."

Jon could surely hear Deb's side of the conversation through the receiver, because his expression was unbearably smug.

Reggie narrowed her eyes at him even as she forced deference into her voice for Deb. "I'll adjust accordingly starting Monday."

"Thank you," Deb said. "One more thing before I go . . ."

"Yes?"

Jon pretended to stroke the flashlight protruding from his crotch, biting his lip in exaggerated pleasure. It should have made him look beyond ridiculous—infantile, even—but somehow it made her want to laugh, which seemed to be his intent.

Stop it, she mouthed, clamping a hand to stifle an inconvenient guffaw.

"Everything okay, Reggie?" Deb asked.

She cleared her throat and managed, "Sorry about that. I thought I saw"—her imagination came up empty—"a cat."

"A cat."

"Yes. A cat. But it was just a rock, so. False alarm."

Now Jon was laughing, and she angrily waved him to be quiet. He stuffed his forearm against his mouth—and the pliers in his hand torpedoed off into the night.

He stilled, eyes going comically wide.

Deb sighed. "I spoke to your mother this morning, and she asked me to pass along a message—"

"Why?"

The two of them still spoke regularly ever since Dr. Hayes had served as Deb's adviser, but that didn't explain why her mother was

151

using NASA's chief astronaut as a glorified telephone when real telephones existed.

"Look, I'm doing this as a courtesy to the woman I owe my career to. You have a problem, take it up with her. This isn't my business. Hell, I have my own family bullshit. Phil wants a goddamn dog for Christmas."

"Don't you two already have three dogs?"

"Yes! And speaking of Christmas . . ."

"My mother requests my presence," Reggie finished flatly. No wonder the ever-tactical Dr. Hayes had gone through Deb—now Reggie wouldn't be able to use work as an excuse.

Reggie said her goodbyes and hung up before she did something impulsive, like hurl the phone off the roof so it could keep her missing pliers company.

Jon peered up at her with a sheepish expression. "The deal about misbehaving starts tomorrow, right?"

She clapped both hands over her face, closed her eyes, and let out a muffled roar of frustration.

"The tool thingy is probably really close by!"

"I'd make you get down and find them, but you'd somehow impale yourself on them in the dark!"

"I'll make it up to you. Just tell me how." He sounded genuinely remorseful. She considered telling him that thanks to NASA's devotion to redundancy there was already a second set of pliers in the tool kit, but that would have been too easy. Better to let him grovel a bit.

Especially since Deb's call was an unpleasant reminder that she needed his help. At least by asking for it this way, it wouldn't be contingent on sex.

As she resealed the hatch, she told him, "Fine. I need you to help me do more social media posts."

"That's all?"

"I'm not good at people stuff, and you are. I want you to help me look good on camera so my boss and the board think I'm, you know . . ." Reggie gestured to him to fill in the rest, but he only cocked his head at her.

"Uh . . ."

"You know. Like *you*."

"Handsome? Well endowed? Remarkably modest?"

Was he really going to make her spell it out? "Friendly," she bit out. "You know, the kind of person people want to spend time with. Specifically, the kind of astronaut you'd want to spend six weeks on the moon with."

"I'd spend six weeks on the moon with you, Reggie," he said in an earnest tone that made her want to bolt into the desert and not stop running until she was back in Houston. As if he knew his words made her panicky, his grin flashed white in the flashlight's glow, and he added, "But only for the moon sex. Duh."

"Forget I asked," she snapped. "Help me put away the rest of the tools."

"Please," he prompted.

She glared at him.

"If you want people to like you, it helps if you say *please* and *thank you*. And: *Yes, Jon, you can have double coffee portions.*"

She drew out the word in an exaggerated, saccharine tone: "*Pleeeasse?*"

Then she flipped him the bird—just to be petty.

And if she was being perfectly honest, the call with Deb had put her in a spiteful mood—as had the inevitable outcome of the air filter situation, which she'd yet to inform Jon about.

She waited until they'd packed up and moved back inside before breaking the news.

"Here's the deal," she told him as she irradiated a set of lasagna pouches for a late-night dinner. His growling stomach was starting to get on her nerves. "There's a problem with the exchange valve in your living quarters. There's no repair diagram in the handbook, but I can almost certainly figure it out. I'll need to get a better look in the daylight tomorrow."

"Okay," he said, watching her warily. "What does that mean?"

She could see the wheels turning behind Jon's melted-chocolate eyes, and she imagined him shuffling through a mental smorgasbord of things he could have done to cause this catastrophe.

Again, she weighed the compassionate option of admitting the rooftop inspection had revealed that—for once—this was an unfortunately frequent equipment malfunction (a curse, if you will, that had begun with the very first air-filtration unit aboard the ISS) and not a Jon malfunction, but watching him squirm a bit buoyed her mood.

He hadn't needed to look *so* smug when she'd asked for help.

"It means that after dinner we're going to move all your shit out of that unit and seal it off so that air from the contaminated part of the filter doesn't get cycled through the rest of the habitat. Have you noticed how when you're inside AHAB, you feel kind of headachy?"

He rubbed his forehead. "That's because of the air thing?"

"Yes. The unit isn't scrubbing the carbon dioxide properly. I should have recognized the signs earlier. Headaches, vision issues, irritability—don't you dare."

Jon pressed his lips together, though such restraint seemed to cost him dearly.

"I'm always this irritable," she snapped. "You're exacerbating my natural state."

He raised a brow. "I have a suggestion."

"Yes, you've already demonstrated how far you can accidentally fling an object off the roof of a building mid cunnilingus."

"Better hold on tight, then," he growled in that goddamn voice of his. The man had to know what that low pitch did to her. He clapped a hand on his shoulder to indicate where such holding on would be occurring. "We'll get those delicious thighs of yours firmly situated."

This conversation was rapidly deteriorating. Despite her best efforts to remain unmoved, his provocative teasing made her embarrassingly wet. Every time she thought she'd started to recover from that mind-blowing kiss, he'd do something like *look* at her, and her aching pussy would nearly careen off the edge into a full meltdown.

Reasoning for why they shouldn't spend the weekend screwing each other's brains out was starting to fall apart by the second.

And then there was the other thing. Highly inconvenient proof that odds were not in favor of scientific productivity.

Reggie squared her shoulders and delivered the news. "Until the air unit is fixed, you'll need to move into my living quarters."

CHAPTER 14

By the time Jon moved his mountain of clothes onto one of the spare cots in Reggie's unit, she'd already slid the flimsy partition across the room and closed the little curtain walling off her cot. The ceiling LEDs glowed night-light red, the window shades were drawn, and only the Tinker Bell glow of her bed lamp told him she was still awake. He glanced at his fitness watch: half past nine.

Jon tossed a stray sock from his bed onto the spare one and plopped down onto his back, a move that elicited squeals of distress from the metal frame.

"If you break it, you're sleeping on the floor," came Reggie's muffled admonishment.

He was tempted to bounce up and down just to get a reaction from her, but he couldn't be certain the bed *wouldn't* break. Jon was no Hollywood diva—he'd slept on a broken futon in his buddy's living room for three years after college—but that brushed-aluminum floor appeared mighty uncomfortable, and his overworked muscles ached merely looking at it.

The thought was an unpleasant reminder that he'd missed today's workout. He'd have to make up two of them tomorrow, or Kahlil would catch on that he hadn't uploaded his stats to the fitness cloud app.

He groaned. What he wouldn't give for a really, really long, hot shower.

Even better, a hot shower with Reggie.

His cock throbbed, reminding him he'd yet to satisfy that pressing need. It didn't help that the source of his discomfort was mere feet away yet completely untouchable. He pressed the heel of his hand against the swelling member and stifled a second groan.

"Keep it down. I'm trying to get some sleep."

He swallowed. He couldn't very well stroke himself off with her in the room. That would be rude. Unless she was into that sort of thing . . .

"Liar," he said roughly. "I saw your light on. You're not really going to sleep this early on a Friday night, are you?"

Her light audibly clicked off. "Yes, I am. Don't disturb me."

There was a sharpness to her tone that made him second-guess himself. Was she genuinely bothered by him? Or worse, had he mistaken tolerance for genuine interest? A part of him still marveled at the idea that an incredible, accomplished, smart-as-hell woman like Reggie was even giving an oaf like him the time of day. He knew he could make her laugh, but how far would that take him?

Reading people was usually one of the few things he was good at, but flirting with Reggie was like being thrown in a maze blindfolded. He was still afraid he'd wake up and realize Mimi had spiked her bourbon with acid and his explosive make-out session with Reggie had been a vivid hallucination.

Though his instincts suggested Reggie liked to be challenged, that kind of foreplay was a risky path to venture—if he pushed her too hard, she might close off completely.

"Good night, Reggie."

"Good night."

He stared at the dim scarlet glow of the domed ceiling, trying to will himself into tiredness. It was impossible. When he closed his eyes, all he saw was Reggie's arousal-flushed face, her lips parted on breathy moans as he ground between her splayed legs.

Fuck. He'd never get to sleep at this rate. And he'd already determined that sorting out his now-raging hard-on was out of the question, unless—

Where was he going to go? Outside? The bathroom was barely the size of an economy toilet on an airplane, and it was only separated from the rest of the room by the plastic walls that didn't go all the way up to the ceiling. When questioned about this lack of real privacy, Reggie had explained that with square footage in short supply aboard the Space Station, astronauts were simply used to it.

It still didn't explain how astronauts on the Space Station handled problems like *this*. They didn't go months without jerking off, did they?

Fuck, fuck, fuck. His brain always did this to him—got stuck on the one thing he was trying not to think about.

Desperation drove him to fetch the crumpled script from his bag. He'd brought it out to the field every day, but he'd never gotten past the cover page. The thing was a mess now, littered with rust-colored fingerprints and worn at the edges from where he'd worried it into a tight tube, over and over again.

The table read was next weekend. Impending doom.

He inhaled for courage and began to read.

Space. The camera closes in on a distant object—it's Earth, seen from far out in the solar system. As the title credits slip across the frame, the sun sets, casting an ominous red glow from behind the blackened globe.

Cut to the inside of a lunar habitat. White and silver, modern yet archaic, the habitat is both a relic of a long-defunct space program and testament to the New Era. Pan to our protagonist. Naked, covered in dust, bowing before a bloodstained altar—

"What the hell?" he muttered aloud.

"Shhhhh."

"Sorry." Jon flipped back to the script's cover page. *Escape Velocity*. Yup, this was the right script.

What had he gotten himself into?

With a sinking feeling, he kept reading.

✩ ⭐ ✩

Reggie lay awake for far too long after she'd turned out the light, listening to the sounds coming from the other side of the partition. From the quiet swish of papers and the occasional intelligible whisper to himself, she'd guess Jon was finally reading his script. The same one he'd carried out to the dig sites all week, though it had mostly been used as a pretend telescope and occasional flyswatter.

She wondered why he'd put off reading it for so long.

She wondered what he thought of it.

She wondered whether he was going to touch himself after he thought she'd fallen asleep, stroking his hard cock while he thought of her. Fantasizing about doing to her exactly what he'd said he'd do if she asked—hold her down and lick her aching pussy until she couldn't move.

If she'd accepted his offer, she wouldn't be awake right now, clinging to her sleeping bag for dear life, lest her hands stray between her legs. Or worse, lest they guide her to breach the flimsy barrier protecting Jon from her selfish needs.

Not that he wouldn't enjoy it—he'd made it clear he would enjoy sex with her very, very much. But Jon was the kind of man who wandered off to see if he could spot cute desert animals. The kind of man who snuck outside before a work dinner because he couldn't hide his hurt feelings when someone spoke poorly of him. Hell, Jon was the kind of man who probably called his mom once a week and only dated people who he genuinely wanted to be in a relationship with.

Sweet, puppy-eyed Jon wouldn't appreciate being used and discarded, no matter how much he claimed otherwise. He'd almost certainly catch feelings and end up moping around after her with a dejected air, making her feel like a heartless monster for prioritizing work.

But Reggie couldn't give him anything else. Even if her career ambitions weren't the single most important thing in her life, she really *was* a heartless monster. For one, she only spoke to her parents when morally obligated to do so. And two, aside from Katya, she couldn't even count anyone else in her life a friend.

And if she couldn't even figure out friendships, how was she ever supposed to navigate the complicated world of modern dating?

A long time passed as she mulled this thought over, until she finally drifted off, musing on a last ironic idea that she might be the only woman on Earth who thought it more feasible to walk on the surface of the moon than to embark upon a romantic relationship—even with someone as attractive, funny, and genuinely kind as Jon Leo.

☆ ⭐

Reggie started awake to the sounds of violent battle. Dissonant screaming, clashing metal, screeching guitar. The cacophony blared through the partition like an auditory nightmare come to life.

Instantly alert, she flung back her sheets and glanced at her watch. Zero six fifty-five. Jon had apparently set himself a musical alarm designed to rouse the souls of everything dead within a forty-mile radius. And the volume was relentlessly escalating, which meant he'd programmed some sort of app to torture himself into waking, and Jon was still somehow *sleeping through it.*

She marched across the room and smacked the control panel to activate daylight settings, illuminating Jon's naked body sprawled across his bunk facedown. Of course, he hadn't bothered to pull the privacy curtain, and Lord knew what that man did while he was sleeping, because his pillow had been flung across the room and his lone bed-sheet was tangled around his left ankle, leaving the rest of his bronzed body unadorned.

Part of her wanted to relish the view, particularly of his gloriously bare, rounded butt—like a Greek sculpture, really, no mortal man should have an ass that fine—but just as she tilted her head to freeze-frame the view, Jon's phone emitted a wailing crescendo so jarring that Reggie's brain nearly liquefied.

How was he so oblivious?

She rushed to his side and fumbled at his phone. Briefly, she registered the photo on his lock screen was a selfie of himself and an older blonde woman with the same fantastic cheekbones, because of course Jon had a great relationship with his mom (hadn't she guessed as much?), but when she swiped up to turn off the alarm, the screen went white and a prompt appeared:

GOOD MORNING! MATCH THE QUOTE TO THE MOVIE TO SHUT OFF ALARM:

"Sixty-nine, dudes!"

A) Jurassic Park

B) Bill & Ted's Excellent Adventure

C) Pirates of the Caribbean

D) Amadeus

Reggie cursed, grabbed the thick muscle of Jon's shoulder, and shook him as hard as she could manage. "Jon. Jon!"

"Huh?" His eyes blinked open, and as soon as he saw her, a languid grin curled his lips.

She froze. *I haven't put on makeup yet.* But his eyelids were already drooping, and her focus snapped back to the urgent need to keep Jon awake.

"Can you turn this off?" she shouted, thrusting the phone into his face. "What is *sixty-nine, dudes* from?"

"Sixty-nine?" He issued an approving grunt and pushed up onto an elbow. The move twisted his torso to face her, and Reggie kept her eyes fixed firmly on his face so she didn't catch a glimpse of whatever phallic weaponry he was packing. She didn't need that kind of temptation to start her day; based on what she'd felt through his pants last night, the sight of Jon fully naked would be impossible to wipe from her retinas.

"Your alarm! Off!" she clarified.

He gave her a sleepy wink and tapped the screen into beautiful silence before collapsing with a grunt. "Too early," he grumbled. He scooped an arm around her middle and tugged her down onto the mattress.

For a few seconds, she lay stiffly beside him, trapped beneath his meaty arm, wondering why she hadn't fought against this capture. He nuzzled the top of her head, then stilled, seemingly content. As his breathing slowed, her traitorous muscles began to melt into his hold. The heat of his body was a delicious contrast to the morning chill, especially since she wore only the tank top and cotton bike shorts she'd gone to bed in.

Guilt twisted in her stomach, but her limbs were growing heavier by the second as his warmth seeped into her skin. She shifted, careful not to disturb Jon's hold, until she was fully on the bed, her left side lying flush with his. She did have a no-cuddling rule, but since she was on her back and he lay on his stomach, this technically didn't count.

Plus, she hadn't slept well. And though she rarely lounged in bed past dawn, technically the December sun wouldn't rise for another twenty-two minutes, and it *was* a Saturday.

Maybe just a little bit longer . . .

☆ ⭐ ☆

She awoke with a start. A sensory scan found Jon's hand cupped possessively over one of her breasts and a hard appendage pressed against her hip. Her own legs had taken the liberty of tangling with one of his massive, hair-dappled calves.

Snuggling, her brain supplied. Reggie squeezed her eyes shut, mentally cursing her weakness.

A time check revealed an even more horrifying truth: she'd been in Jon's bed for over two hours.

Her only saving grace was Jon's apparent ability to sleep through anything, which allowed her to slither out of bed, dress, do her makeup, and exit the room without a trace.

Maybe, she mused as she drank her coffee and booted up her laptop, *he won't even remember I was there.*

Her hopes were vanquished the moment Jon thudded into the seat across from her with his hair adorably mussed, his cheeks sleep creased, and his chocolate eyes sparkling far too cheerily for a man who hated mornings.

At least he'd thrown on a pair of pants and a T-shirt. She wasn't strong enough to bear another second of his naked body in her line of sight.

"Good morning, Regina Hayes."

She narrowed her eyes at him over the rim of her thermos, then slid his coffee across the table to him. "If you know what's good for you, you won't say a word."

He lifted the lid and grinned. "Be still my heart. This appears to be a double portion."

"Don't make me regret it."

For the rest of the morning, she sequestered herself in AHAB's lab module under the guise of testing out the new x-ray diffraction machine they'd be using in the upcoming week. That was what she told herself, at least.

It had nothing at all to do with the kiss. Or the sex she'd promised to consider. Or the definitely-not-snuggling that might or might not have occurred.

And it definitely had nothing to do with the mounting sense that she'd gravely underestimated Jon—in more ways than one.

CHAPTER 15

Sensing Reggie needed space, Jon kept to himself most of the weekend. When she was outside tinkering with the air vents, Jon went inside and studied Jacqui's binder. When Reggie was cursing at the air machine from inside AHAB's walls, Jon went outside to work out. And when it was time for bed, he waited until long after she might have fallen asleep to slink into the room.

As far as his responsibilities went, Jon was a veritable gold star candidate. He couldn't remember the last time he'd been so productive.

As far as desire for Reggie went, he was completely screwed—and not in the way he wanted.

And so he was giving her space. Which was different than avoiding her and thus not cowardly at all.

Jon stepped back to admire the three-foot-tall rock person he'd constructed on his makeshift outside "set" between a stubby tree and the back side of his defunct living quarters.

"You'll do nicely," he told Rocky, his new rehearsal partner.

He flipped the script back to the beginning of the scene and began running lines again. "'I don't know where this blood came from, Corporal . . . it's not mine. It's not yours. Is it real? Are we real?'"

"What are you doing?" Reggie's voice came from behind him.

He turned, and the instant he saw her, heat flared all over his skin. She was in the tight running pants again, but this time she wore a spandex long-sleeved shirt that hugged her full breasts tight.

He cut his eyes to a scraggly brown plant by his toes. Another second looking at her, and he'd implode from horniness.

"Rehearsing," he said, and his voice cracked in the middle. He cleared his throat. "They're flying me out to Los Angeles for the first full-cast table read next weekend."

"I see," she said, peering over his shoulder at Rocky. She raised a brow. Then, because she'd apparently come to torment him, she popped her ChapStick from her pocket and swiped it on. He tore his eyes away from the sight, but not before his dick took notice and began to swell.

It was because of that kiss. If he hadn't kissed her, his fanboy crush would have been a mild inconvenience at most. Maybe he'd get a butterfly or two in his belly whenever she gave him one of those flinty looks, but he could manage that.

This, Jon couldn't manage. He was obsessed; brutally tortured by withdrawal symptoms. Whenever he saw Reggie now, his mind blanked, and on that empty screen his imagination projected vivid—and increasingly depraved—fantasies. Her riding him hard while he palmed her breasts. Him grinding against her from behind, her back arching as she came. On her knees. On *his* knees—

"I came to let you know I'm heading out for a run. I'll be back in a half hour, but I'll have the comm unit if you need to reach me."

Oh, thank fuck. A half hour of privacy was about six times longer than he'd need.

He casually lowered his script to shield the evidence of his arousal. Since she hadn't mentioned the sex and he'd promised he wouldn't pursue the topic, avoidance was his only remaining option. "Great, I'll just be here . . . rehearsing," he lied.

She shrugged and turned to leave, then paused. "Were those lines from this movie? It sounds weird."

You have no idea. "It's not very"—he searched for a diplomatic word—"accessible."

She held her hand out for the script. "May I?"

He let her take it, grateful she was focused more on the pages than on what was going on in his pants. As she flipped through, however, her eyebrows cinched tighter and tighter. He knew when she got to the climactic scene by the way her face went flat with horror.

Shame made him reach for the script, but she whisked it out of range.

"It's all metaphorical," he explained lamely. "Rudy is a very avant-garde director. He likes to push the envelope."

"It says here you're, and I quote, impregnating the alien queen with your engorged pe—"

"It's Oscar material," he rushed to assure her.

"*Ohhh*, I see what happened here." She handed the sheaf back to him and crossed her arms. "You didn't read it ahead of time."

He scoffed. "Who would sign on to a movie without reading the script?"

She gave him a look.

He held out for three full seconds before groaning, "Me. I would do that."

"Maybe you can get out of it."

He busied himself rolling up the script into its familiar little tube.

"Jon, come on. Even I can tell this movie is not exactly . . . *you*."

"Of course it is." He tugged at his stupid man bun as excuses began tumbling out. "This is my big break. I'll win tons of awards for this role. I mean, Rudy's an industry icon, and he's known for making edgy movies."

She raised a brow. "Edgy? Or just gross?"

"Look, I know it *reads* like art house tentacle porn, and yes, it doesn't take a genius to point out the alien queen's name is just Rudy's ex-wife's spelled backward, but I have to trust his vision if I want to be on the A-list. If I can pull this off, Hollywood will take me seriously as an actor. I won't just be that guy who does cheesy action comedies called *Space Dude*."

"I thought you said *Space Dude* paid well."

"It did."

"And apparently it's very popular with the 'cool kids.'" Reggie made air quotes.

"*Kids* is the key word. No one over the age of twenty-five has any clue who I am."

Reggie snorted. "And I doubt most of those *kids* know who I am, even though the future of our space program depends on them. NASA would love to have that target audience, but eighty percent of the comments on our social media feeds are from bots and wackos like Milton Fetzer and his pea-brained One Planet followers. Who gives a shit what critics think if you're already winning the most coveted demographic?"

"It's not just about the critics," he snapped. It was about living up to expectations. Living up to a last name it felt like he hadn't earned yet. "You wouldn't understand."

For a brief moment, Reggie's eyes flashed as if she was going to argue. Then, as quickly as the flash appeared, her eyes dimmed. She shrugged. "Whatever. It's none of my business what kind of garbage you star in. In three weeks, you'll be out of my hair anyway."

Jon absorbed the blow and did what he always did—he masked everything with a smile. Then he stepped in close and spoke low into her ear, deepening his pitch in the way that always seemed to make her breathe faster. "What I'm hearing is, you want me in your hair for the next three weeks."

When he pulled back, her cheeks were that pretty shade of pink again. She swallowed. "I'm still thinking about it."

She moved to leave.

"Wait," he heard himself saying. "Do you want company?"

What the hell am I doing? He finally had the opportunity to be alone and take the edge off his lustful torment, and instead he was volunteering to spend even more time with its source? He was an idiot.

A foolish, lovestruck, hopeless idiot.

✫ ⭐ ✫

"You're asking if I want to go on a run with you," she translated.

He shrugged. "Yeah. No big deal, though."

The way her heart tumbled over itself, like one hopeful little blip of joy, should have been enough warning to prompt her to say no. "All right, I'm game. But I'm not waiting for you if you fall behind, so you'd better keep up."

The uncertainty in his eyes disappeared, and his grin returned. "I'm going to leave you in the dust, Moon Otter."

She raised a brow. "You know I can pull three Gs without breaking a sweat, right?"

"We'll see."

With that, he lifted both arms over his head and stretched. The move caused the hem of his shirt to skim up and reveal an expanse of golden skin, and her gaze caught on the sight of it, helpless against the allure of the twin muscles ridging his hip bones before dipping down into his low-slung denim. Then he grabbed opposing elbows and stretched from side to side. When he was finally finished with his little floor show, he had the nerve to wink.

Reggie suddenly became aware her mouth was hanging open ever so slightly, and she snapped it shut. Heat suffused her skin.

In a low voice, he said, "I'm going to make you sweat so fucking hard."

Her breath caught in her throat. Desire twisted, fast and sharp, low in her abdomen. She backed up two steps, half-surprised she could manage even that much. Schooling her voice, she said evenly, "I'll meet you out front in five."

And then she fled.

✩ ⁂ 🌠 ⁎

Damn, she's fast.

Jon chased Reggie across the rocky desert, his heart pumping and his lungs glowing with a frosty sort of ache from the winter air. Though it had been sunny all week, the sky was a flat sheet of white glare today, and his skin itched where his hot sweat battled the brisk breeze for control of his body temperature.

Meanwhile, Reggie *wasn't* even breaking a sweat. She hadn't been kidding.

"Had enough yet?" Reggie's voice was only slightly raspy as she shifted gears to fall back to his side. They'd been running for nearly a half hour at top speed.

Well, Jon's top speed, anyway.

"Could . . . do this . . . all day," he lied between gasping breaths.

"Let's pick up the pace, then. Don't hold back on my account."

"Yeah . . . you go ahead . . . I'll keep up."

She darted ahead, faster than he could ever hope to match.

It was time to surrender. Slowing to a stop, he hunched forward, hands on his knees and his chest heaving mightily. A few breaths later, Reggie's running shoes appeared in his line of sight.

"I'm impressed."

He rolled his eyes upward to look at her through the web of hair that had freed itself from his twist tie. "You won . . . don't rub it in."

"No, really." She offered him a hand, and he took it. "It's rare a civilian can give me a run for my money like that."

"I have a very expensive trainer."

After several shameful minutes, Jon finally caught his breath, and they settled into an easy pace back to the base. They'd almost run all the way to the far edge of the crater on the trip out.

"Why do you need a trainer? Can't you just work out on your own?" she asked, then immediately followed with, "Never mind. That's none of my business."

"I don't mind." He didn't. He'd have answered anything she wanted to know about him, because it meant she *wanted to know about him*. And that meant she saw him as a man worth knowing—and not just biblically. That, too, though, if he played his cards right. "When I got the role for *Space Dude*, Jacqui recommended getting a trainer so I could keep up with training for the fight scenes. Ideally, she wanted me to get to the point where I could start doing more of my own choreography and stunt work instead of using a double, because that would be better for my image."

He glanced at her from the corner of his eye. Her brows were drawn together in thought.

"Because of my dad being a famous martial artist and all," he added, and her expression cleared.

"That's right. I can't believe your dad is Brian Leo—" She stopped herself. "Sorry."

"It's cool. It's not a sore subject." *Not anymore.* "The story is that my mom met my dad on set, they hooked up a few times, and *bam*, adorable Baby Jon enters the scene, and my dad was like, 'Oh no, this baby is *too* good looking to be mine!' Also, he happened to be married, and it wasn't like one of those cool, modern Hollywood open marriages. But mostly it was that I was too cute. So you can't really blame the guy for not publicly acknowledging my existence until his divorce about twenty-six years later."

Reggie's tone darkened. "Did he at least pay child support? He must be wealthy, given that he's famous enough that even I know who he is."

Now *that* was a sore spot. "We got some money," he said, casual-like. "The important thing is that when he came out to the press that I was his kid, it unlocked all kinds of doors for me in the industry."

"Doesn't that bother you? Having to attribute part of your success to someone else?" The way she said it implied that was the kind of thing that would bother *her*.

He sighed. "It used to. But I try to look at the big picture, and part of that is accepting the world isn't fair. Before that, I'd been trying to get my break in Hollywood for eight years, with shitty results."

"Why? I've heard you're a good actor."

Oh, had she now? He wondered exactly how much research she'd done on him ahead of time.

He thought of the "research" he'd done on Reggie and almost stumbled. Surely she hadn't . . .

Don't think about that.

Shit. Now he was thinking about it.

"Jon?"

He retraced his memory, trying to recall what they'd been talking about. "Right, acting stuff. Part of the problem was my look didn't really fit what Hollywood casting directors look for in their fresh-faced, twentysomething white-guy talent pool. My face wasn't interesting enough for character work, but I wasn't dreamboat leading man material either."

When she scoured him with side-eyed skepticism, he clarified, "I mean, *now* I am, even though I'm neither fresh faced nor twentysomething anymore. But I *used* to be a giant, clumsy nerd who thought twenty push-ups was a serious workout. Until I got Kahlil as my trainer, I ate cereal for, like, fifty percent of my meals and rocked a pretty bitchin' dad bod. I had a lot of, er . . . indoor hobbies. Reading. Watching nature documentaries. Napping."

"Napping isn't a hobby."

He scoffed. "If you do it right, it is."

"And what does 'doing it right' entail?"

"Yesterday morning, for example—"

She scowled. "Never mind."

"As I was saying," he continued merrily, "unless you have the right 'look,' it's almost impossible to make it in Hollywood if you don't have connections . . . unless you go the comedy route. And I'd always been good at making people laugh—mostly *at* me, but a laugh's a laugh—so I thought, Why not? I didn't realize how woefully outclassed I was auditioning against comedians who'd already been doing stand-up and improv for years while I racked up five-figure debt getting an arguably useless degree in theater. Aside from the full-time serving job I'd needed to afford living in LA, I'd spend about thirty hours a week learning lines, working on jokes for open mic nights at the clubs, and auditioning for roles. And still, nothing. Local commercials and bit parts. Then my dad made his postdivorce announcement that I was his kid, and two weeks later I got an offer of rep. A month after that, I booked my first substantial gig as a regular on *Business Place*, and a year later I booked *Space Dude*. Even my personal trainer, Kahlil, only took me on because my dad asked him to."

"What about Jacqui? She strikes me as too savvy to attach herself to some unknown actor just because he's got a famous dad."

The mention of Jacqui reminded him of his unmemorized lines. And that he'd promised he'd focus on the role and not the babe-a-licious astronaut he was training with.

"You're right. Jacqui's been with me from the start. We met in college, and she always insisted I had 'star potential.'" It sounded like he was bragging, so he tried laughing it off. "She also thinks you can tell everything about a person based on their star sign, so, you know. Take that with a grain of sand."

"Salt," Reggie corrected absently. "And I don't think you should entirely discount her opinion."

"On the star-power thing or the other star-power thing?"

Reggie seemed to consider it before answering. "Both, I suppose. I don't believe in astrology, but seeing Earth from space is humbling—there are a lot of things I used to be certain about that I now question. Regardless, having someone believe in you like Jacqui does is . . . enviable."

"I'm lucky to have her," he agreed. The mere thought of letting Jacqui down made his gut twist, but the reminder was necessary. He'd refocus. Spend the rest of the day working on lines.

They jogged in companionable silence for a while. They were nearly three-quarters of the way back to the base when Jon realized he'd been subconsciously slowing his steps because he didn't want this to end.

It has to, he reminded himself as they pulled up to the base. It was fortunate their kiss hadn't led to more; if they'd spent the whole weekend in horizontal heaven, he wouldn't have read the script. And if Reggie wasn't interested in dating, then sex was just another pointless distraction he didn't need (and he was already too good at finding pointless distractions).

As if the universe were conspiring against him, Reggie chose that moment to say, "I've been thinking about what we talked about . . ."

He jolted to a stop outside AHAB's entrance and bent into a hamstring stretch to avoid looking at her. "Uh, what thing?"

She paused. "The sex thing."

"Oh, that."

"Yes, *that*." A stolen glance revealed Reggie's glower. "You know what? Forget it."

He hid a wince. He was trying to be good, so why did it feel so bad? "You were right. It would be unprofessional for us to hook up."

In his brief experience, he'd learned it was very hard to slam a pressurized airlock door—but Reggie found a way.

☆ ⭐ ☆

This is why I don't let people get close. Let someone spoon you one damn time, and suddenly they think they have the upper hand.

Even after she'd showered and changed, anger still pounded through her veins when she entered AHAB's central hub. It burst free when she saw Jon shoveling food into his mouth.

Out of a steaming food pouch.

"I thought I told you not to touch anything," she snapped, rushing over to the appliance to check for smoke or a broken circuit or—who knew what else? Where Jon was concerned, any catastrophe was possible.

"I was hungry." Guileless brown eyes pleaded with her, but she was in no mood to show mercy.

"Do I look like I give a shit?"

"No. You look angry."

"What an astute observation. Congratulations." The words came out cold and condescending—a tone she was all too familiar with from her childhood—and Reggie hated herself for it.

She waited for him to get up and storm off or, even better, instigate the fight she wanted so badly. Instead, he calmly set the food pouch down. "I'm sorry for pretending like I didn't know what you were talking about back there. That was cowardly of me. The truth is, I really *do* want to have sex with you . . . like, *so*, so bad. You're basically my dream woman. I swear, if this role weren't such a big deal—"

Her hands curled into fists. "Stop. You're making it worse."

He groaned. "Normally I'm good at apologies, but when I'm around you, I can't seem to remember how words work. Will you please forgive me anyway?"

"No," she said. Great, now she sounded petulant. "Fine, whatever. I don't even give a shit about the sex, honestly."

"You don't?"

"Nope." She shrugged, hoping it looked casual, and a wicked impulse came over her. Cruel? Probably. But he deserved it. "I brought my vibrators. I'll be more than fine."

His mouth fell open.

"So you—" he choked out. "Now? Tonight?"

"Of course not. Not with you in the same room. How inappropriate. Once I get that air filter repaired and you move back into the other module, though . . ."

His eyes bugged, his cheeks flushed, and he looked a bit like he might die.

Reggie raised a brow. "Something wrong?"

He shook his head, stood up, and walked to the door. "I'm going to go work out."

"We just got back from a run," she reminded him.

He gave her a mournful glance over his shoulder. "I know."

CHAPTER 16

Reggie should have told him she'd fixed the air problem. Fixed it two hours ago, in fact. He'd have plenty of time to move his things back to the other living unit tonight.

I'll tell him after he comes back from his workout. She really meant it too.

But then Katya called, and Reggie was on the phone when Jon staggered back inside, muttering something about a shower, his sweat-soaked shirt already being tugged up over his head. It wasn't her fault her mouth went dry and her brain functions ceased when the rippling flats of his abdominals came gleaming into glorious, sinful view.

The daylight-simulating habitat lights spared no expense in high-lighting every curve of muscle, every sinew, every blood-fattened surface vein. Even his ribs had muscles. His torso was like a windswept desert of rippling gold flats and shadowy dunes. Her skin glowed hot; her lips felt parched.

She fumbled for her ChapStick, her hands oddly clumsy as she applied it. Good *fucking* Lord.

He winked at her as he stepped into the living unit and shut the door.

Oh, so that was how it was going to be, was it? He was trying to win the game of sexual torment she'd started earlier.

She'd underestimated him—again.

"You are dead, or no?" came Katya's dry voice.

"I'm alive, but I can't say for how long. Jon just took his shirt off," Reggie muttered, fanning herself with a stack of plastic sample bags. "Avenge me."

"Ah, it is unfortunate I cannot. Our blood debt has been repaid by the great sacrifice I have made for you today."

If it hadn't been for Katya, Reggie wouldn't have gotten instructions (on the down low) for repairing the air unit. She'd have had to call the base manager, who'd have reported to Deb, who'd have called Reggie to ask why she hadn't alerted them to the broken unit on Friday, and then Reggie would have had to explain why she was too stubborn to ask anyone for help, ever, for anything . . . and that was how quickly she'd kiss her Artemis III chances goodbye.

Still. "I fought a *bear* for you! All you did was spend five minutes talking to an engineering tech."

"Paul." Katya said his name the way someone would say *flesh-eating cockroach*. To be fair, Paul was a gregarious Texan who had a habit of talking about his kids. All the time. At length. To suggest Katya's conversation with him was merely five minutes undoubtedly failed to account for the twenty minutes of high-school-football-themed yarns she'd suffered through first.

"Well, no one asked you to. That's on you for covering my ass just so you'll have leverage in thermostat negotiations."

"You wound me. Out of great respect for my friend, I have not interfered with these cruel ice-palace settings."

"You know it's smart connected to the app on my phone, right? I can *see* you've turned my home into a sauna."

"Faulty sensor. It is a shame this technology is so fragile." Then Katya switched to Russian, as if Jon might somehow overhear her. "Is he still undressing? Take a photo."

Reggie rubbed at her aching shoulder, keeping one eye on the door in case Jon should reemerge while she was gossiping about his cut physique. "He's in the shower. But it's not right that any man should look like this. What am I supposed to do?"

"If you have come to me for pity, you have dialed the wrong number. I will transfer you." Katya made *beep-boop-beep* sounds. "*Allo?* You have reached the Sad American Problems Hotline; thank you for calling. Tell us your poor, sad story . . . what is this? You have sexual frustration? Have you tried inserting the penis into your—"

"Hey, Katya?"

"*Da?*"

"You still have that telescope I gave you for Christmas last year?"

"This line of questioning concerns me greatly."

"It should. Because when I get to the moon, I'm going to carve *KATYA SUCKS* into the lunar surface."

"It will be too small to see."

"I'll buy you a bigger lens attachment. Wow, what a sight that will be, huh? Just imagine. And without atmosphere, it'll just be there forever."

Her threat should have ended Katya's goading, but Roscosmos selected only the most doggedly persistent cosmonauts. She'd texted Reggie about the matter every day, and her abuse of eggplant emojis had, quite frankly, gotten completely out of hand. Katya could be on her deathbed, and her last words to Reggie would be, *Have his child, name her Elsa, insert eggplant emoji.* By the time the call ended, Reggie was ready to sleep with Jon just to shut the damn woman up.

Except the offer is off the table, remember?

Jon emerged from the habitat, still shirtless, but now with a pair of loose-fitting pajama pants clinging to his still-damp legs.

So he did own something to sleep in, did he? Funny that he always seemed to sleep naked anyway. So very inappropriate. Unprofessional too. She should set boundaries; this was an official NASA collaboration at a research base, not a sexy vacation resort. Clearly, Jon Leo did not take any of this seriously.

She squared her shoulders. "Jon, I'd like to address a few things." *There. Very authoritative and professional.*

"All right, hit me." Jon flipped one of the swivel chairs around and straddled it, settling his heavy frame into the seat and making the whole table and seating situation shudder. Reggie inwardly winced. The habitat's modular furniture was sturdy enough, but it was also constructed from light materials to reduce the expense of rocket fuel required to launch it into space in the first place—it was clearly not designed to withstand a man as exceedingly *built* as Jon Leo. Good thing Hollywood didn't have to worry about payload limitations when casting its astronauts, or Jon wouldn't have made the cut.

"We have a busy week coming up," she began. It wasn't where she should have started. *I fixed the air unit,* was what she'd meant to say, followed by, *You should wear proper attire to sleep. Per your wishes, our relationship going forward will be strictly professional.* "I would like for you to . . . well, I think it would be more appropriate if—"

"What's this?" Jon slapped an enormous paw onto the manual in front of her and dragged it across the table. His eyes went comically wide. "You've had an instruction manual the entire time?"

Confused, she sputtered, "It's not—these are AHAB's operating procedures, but I don't see why—"

A grin split his face wide open. He swiped through the thick booklet, his excitement palpable, and all Reggie could think was, *He's got three little birthmarks across his collarbone like Orion's Belt.* "Dude," he said.

"Dude?" she repeated inanely.

"Can I borrow this?"

This seemed highly suspicious. Her brain whirred into overdrive, trying to think of all the different ways he could manage to get in trouble with a binder full of NASA's dry technical specifications, but she came up blank. *Still . . . he's surprised you before.* "What do you plan to do with it?"

He leaned in close and in a conspiratorial tone told her, "Papier-mâché bird squadron."

Should she be relieved or exasperated by that response? Reggie let out the air she'd been hoarding and gave in to the absurdity. "You're not qualified to command a squadron, civilian."

He shrugged. "You could ordain me."

"That's not how military rank works."

"These are space birds, operating in intergalactic territory. They fall outside the standard jurisdiction." His demeanor was all heavy-lidded smugness. "I'll accept no further questions."

"You're incorrigible."

He cocked his head. "Huh. I always wondered how that word was pronounced."

"You do read a lot, don't you?" she observed.

"Rarely the things I'm supposed to be reading." His eyes locked on hers, and his voice went rough. "But when I have compelling motivation . . ."

Her breath skipped. He *hadn't* actually explained what he wanted the manual for, yet the wetness suddenly drenching her underwear suggested he'd explained perfectly. "Right. Well."

"So what did you want to talk to me about? Something about a busy week?"

Her mind was mysteriously blank. She licked her lips, mentally grasping for purchase on anything that sounded sensible and work related. "Yes. We have to do some . . . drilling."

He raised a brow. "I'm good at drilling. But I thought you said you had your vib—"

"It's a lunar surface drill for extracting rock samples from the ground. And you'll just be watching."

"I don't mind watching," he murmured. He was 100 percent not talking about geological equipment. "Any luck with the air thingy?"

A voice that couldn't possibly be her own answered, "No, unfortunately."

"Bummer." At first, he sounded anything but regretful, but then his expression turned worried. "You won't get in trouble with your boss, will you?"

She shook her head and forced a reassuring laugh. "Ha! No, I'll call the base manager in the morning. It's totally fine."

"Hmm."

"Seriously! Don't worry about it." She waved him off. "Have fun with the manual. And your birds, of course. Don't forget the birds, Captain . . . Pirate King . . . sir."

With one last, skeptical look over his shoulder, Jon finally retreated into the living quarters. Their *shared* living quarters.

Reggie slowly lowered her forehead to the table, raised it an inch, and let it fall. Then she did it again. "Idiot," she whispered. "Sexually frustrated . . . idiot."

✩ ⭐ ✩

She was lying.

He knew it. Not for certain, but he'd still have bet the Oscar he didn't have yet that Reggie had fixed the air in his old digs. He could *hear* it.

Usually he despised how attuned his brain was to background noise, but tonight he'd never been more grateful for his ability to recognize the subtle pitch change in the air filter's humming vibrations.

And why would she lie? (Of course, he knew the answer.)

Jon smoothed the pages of the precious handbook, illuminated under the spotlight of his reading lamp. Reggie had already slipped into bed behind that flimsy partition over an hour ago, her breathing long since transitioned to a slow and steady rhythm, but he was still wide awake.

Why had he turned down sex, again? He vaguely recalled something about distractions and responsibilities, but it seemed far less important than it had earlier.

Restless energy zinged through him now. Not even his extra-long workout had helped dispel the curse Reggie had laid upon him two nights ago in the dark, star-streaked twilight.

Though, if he was being perfectly honest with himself, his torment had begun at dinner the week prior, when his admiring crush had morphed into a sort of hungry obsession with a sultry, mysterious witch in purple. He constantly flashed back to that moment in the alcove at inappropriate times.

"I do appreciate respect," she'd said, her voice coiling around him like smoke, her shadowed eyes and dark hair and inky lips and pale skin and—God, her mounded breasts spilling up over the twin semicircles of the neckline (he tried not to think about that part, because that inevitably led to rude, pornographic thoughts that weren't respectful in the slightest).

Oh no.

His cock throbbed, insistent and increasingly urgent, against his thigh. An image flashed through his brain. He tried to block it out, guilt hammering him, but the harder he tried not to think about it, the more insistently the vision urged him to look. See what he'd do to her when he had her naked. On her knees. Pink-tipped globes dripping with glossy streaks where he'd spent himself all over her—

He squeezed his eyes shut as hard as he could, but he knew—he *knew*—it was too late.

As quietly as he could, he clicked off the lamp and lay back against his pillow, slipped inside his sweatpants, and took his dick in hand. He held his breath, listening to Reggie's side of the room.

Steady breathing. In. Out.

He squeezed the thick base, and a jolt of terrible, terrible pleasure spiked through him. At least it would be quick. Two minutes if he drew it out. Five seconds if he wrapped her gray blanket in his other fist, held it to his mouth to stifle the sound of his shuddering exhales, and sucked in her scent like a depraved pervert, which he absolutely would not do, because there had to be a line somewhere. A nonsensical part of his brain reminded him she was an astronaut, an accomplished scientist, a jet pilot, a woman out of his league by miles and miles, a goddamn American hero, so how dare he jerk off to fantasies about coming on her tits?

This isn't respectful. No, it wasn't. At all. He'd have to be so quiet, so careful. If Reggie heard him, she'd be outraged. Throw him out. Fuck, she could report him to the studio, get this whole project shut down. He was expendable; they'd replace him in a heartbeat, and he'd have to explain to Jacqui. To his agent. To his *mom*.

That alone should have dampened his desire. Should have. But then he thought about the way Reggie's pupils had dilated when he'd talked about drilling. The sharp cut of her inhale as he stripped off his shirt.

Reggie wanted him, and she was awful at hiding it.

He was a fool for throwing away his chance with her, no question. Heck, he still couldn't completely wrap his brain around the idea she'd asked him to kiss her in the first place. That experience had been so hot that it set him on fire whenever he thought about it; the least he could do was be grateful to have flown so close to the sun and landed unscathed.

But kissing her had made everything worse. So, so much worse now that he knew what her lips felt like against his. Now that he knew she wanted him, now that he could hear her breathing, now that the air in the room was charged with her presence or pheromones or whatever the fuck it was that made his skin feel too tight and hot.

He slung his left forearm over his mouth and clamped his teeth into his own skin, hard enough he could feel the rigidity of bone beneath the muscle, and with his right hand shaking with the thrill of doing this thing that was so very, very wrong, he began to stroke.

✧ ✰ ⭐ ✧

It took every last ounce of Reggie's willpower, training, and discipline to keep her breathing steady so he'd think she was sleeping.

He obviously thought he was being stealthy. But of course, he also thought she'd fallen asleep after she'd turned off her light an hour ago. How could he know that all this time she'd been wide awake, waging the same silent battle she'd fought for three nights straight? That she was so attuned to his every movement—every wavering hiss of breath, every whisper of shifting fabric, every glide of flesh on flesh—that she'd trapped herself in a personal hell where her heart slammed itself against its cage like a wild animal, her muscles burning yet forced to remain still so he wouldn't hear her move? Because if he heard her move, he'd stop for fear of waking her.

Or worse. He'd realize it was too late, that she knew what he was doing, that she'd let him continue anyway. And for all the self-deprecating comments he made about his own intelligence, that man was too shrewd to misinterpret what it meant for her to greedily revel in the subtle symphony of his self-pleasure.

A faint, muffled grunt reached her, and a lightning burst of need rammed down her spine. Lodged itself between her legs, where her clit pulsed so hard, so desperately, that even squeezing her thighs together threatened to send her over the edge.

She swallowed and reminded herself to breathe, in and out, slow and steady.

At least she wasn't touching herself too. That would have crossed a line. Instead, she dug her short nails into her palms until sweat stung the tiny crescent cuts. Bit her lip until she tasted blood. Squeezed her eyes shut and focused on breathing.

In. Out. Slow and steady.

The rhythmic zen of her prelaunch routine.

The measured intake of oxygen-rich air through her flight helmet as the jet beneath her thighs punched its way through the sound barrier.

Slow, steady, and in control of her lungs—if nothing else.

He knew she wanted him. He probably also knew that if he said he'd changed his mind, she'd resist for the sake of her pride—and how little effort it would take to overcome that resistance.

So very, very little.

But he wouldn't push if she said no, because Jon was a nice guy, and she owed his boundaries the same respect.

This torture was her own fault. She'd lied about the air filter, and now she was paying the price with her own unspent need.

His sounds were coming faster now. The harsh sips of air. The careful, near-inaudible wet slick of precum easing passage along his swollen shaft.

Her inhale caught. The pulse in her throat was so loud, the bands squeezing her rib cage wound so tight, a burst of dizziness struck her.

Breathe. Breathe, damn it!

Something in her snapped, as if her missed breath had taken a wrong turn and sliced through the fragile barrier she'd erected to stop herself from giving in.

Her right hand unfurled and snaked a path down her belly, gliding across soft skin damp with perspiration, her first two fingers skimming under the waistband of her cotton shorts and between her drenched folds.

Completely soaked and scorching hot. She shuddered at the first touch, and even without brushing her clit, her thighs spasmed helplessly. She was wound so tight, her need so keen, that she didn't trust herself to do more.

Fuck.

Her fingers hovered, paralyzed by the immensity of what lay beyond.

This wasn't what she'd hoped for. A controlled, tightly measured orgasm to take the edge off. Something manageable that would flow through her like water, that she could hide with a bit of jaw clenching and a long, focused exhale.

This was going to be a cataclysm. A torrent of pleasure as sharp as knives that would barrel into her with the force of a hurricane. She wouldn't be able to stop it.

Wouldn't be able to hide it.

This time, Jon's groan wasn't entirely stifled. It leaked out from behind whatever he was using to muffle his sounds, like he was helpless now, losing control.

Her pussy squeezed down hard at the thought, and a thrumming began to build, swelling behind her pubic bone in a way she recognized all too well.

No, no, not like this—

Panic clawed at her. She had to stop this. He'd hear her come; she wouldn't be able to hold back, wouldn't be able to steer it into something tame and discreet. Her back would bow up off the bed, every muscle in her body convulsing, her breath exploding through her gritted teeth—

With her last shred of willpower, she twisted and rolled out of the bed, swiping the curtains aside with a hushed screech of metal hooks on a track—in the illicit quiet, it was as loud as if she'd unsheathed a blade. Her feet slapped against the cold floor, carrying her to the bathroom as if she'd merely awoken from slumber and needed to use the facilities, even though her limbs felt like they were made of sand.

In the tiny compartment, she fell forward and gripped the sink like a lifeline, every cell in her body shaking. In the mirror, her eyes were wild, the irises huge and the pupils contracted against the sudden light. The place she'd bit her lip glistened a shocking crimson.

Look what you did, you bad, bad person.

Tomorrow. No, not just tomorrow—first thing in the morning. He had to move back into his living quarters.

She wasn't strong enough to last another night.

* ⭐ *

Jon stared at the twin shadows of her feet in the block of light leaking out of the gap between the floor and the compartment door, unspent desire still coursing painfully through his system.

He swallowed.

Had she heard?

Did she know?

Had she *liked* it?

He wasn't sure if he wanted answers to those questions, because the truth might ruin him for all other women, forever.

The only thing he did know was that he was in way over his head with desire for Reggie, and it was too late to back out now. He'd have to accept that this wasn't going away, and if falling in love with Reggie was inevitable, then he might as well wholly commit himself to his fate.

And that meant he had a new goal: to convince Reggie to fall for him too.

CHAPTER 17

Reggie had grown accustomed to having an extra half hour of personal time after her predawn jog and before Jon's 0700 call time. And as she kicked dust off her sneakers while the airlock sealed shut behind her, she decided she needed that time more than ever this Monday morning.

He'd wake late, obviously, which meant she'd have to go in and get him up, which meant she'd see him in whatever state of shameless repose he'd fallen asleep in, and then the memories from the night before would come rushing back, and God help her, but she was no longer capable of resisting if he dragged her into his bed again.

Not after the dreams she'd had. Dreams so shamelessly filthy that even *thinking* about them made her fan her cheeks with a shaky hand.

A glance at the control panel showed oxygen levels holding steady. Great. No reason Jon couldn't move back into his quarters immediately. Reggie pressed the button to open the second door to the central hub and—

She froze in the doorway and blinked.

Suddenly unsure of her own reality, she glanced at the time on her watch, then tapped the screen to make sure it hadn't frozen at some point the night prior. But no, it still read a time well before noon. A time well before 0700 hours.

Jon was awake. And dressed. And—well, not necessarily *ready to go*, but he was upright (mostly).

He hunched over a thermos of coffee as if his forearms were barricading it from predators, and when she entered, he gave her a bleary-eyed nod, apparently incapable of speech.

But he was *awake*.

"What's wrong?" she asked. Had his alarm exploded? Was he delirious from fever?

He cleared his throat before answering, and it sounded like a cat having a hair ball crisis. "Morning."

"Yes, it's morning. That's what I'm worried about. Are you sick?" She approached warily, scanning him for signs of illness. Her eyes snagged on the second thermos by his elbow.

He shook his head. "Fine. Made you coffee."

She sat, too astonished to do anything else, and tentatively sipped the beverage. He'd used two packets. Perhaps his mental faculties weren't completely shot, but this was still highly suspicious. "Dare I ask *why* you're awake so early?"

Sleepy chocolate eyes blinked at her. "'Cause. You said important stuff today. Now we can start early."

Reggie abruptly stood and busied herself preparing breakfast, giving herself time to process this development, because how else was she to interpret his statement other than in the most oddly endearing way possible? Though Jon was clearly suffering—she'd never seen misery written so clearly on anyone's face, and she'd survived a stomach flu outbreak on a Navy ship with only two functioning toilets—he'd gone out of his way to wake himself up early solely to demonstrate his commitment to training.

Yes, getting out of bed was a low bar to clear. But wasn't it the effort that mattered?

You are going soft, Katya would have said. But in the same breath, Katya would have also suggested immediately proposing to the man, so maybe Reggie shouldn't be accepting imaginary advice from her friend.

They ate breakfast in relative quiet, which seemed to suit Jon just fine, but by the time they'd arrived at the drill site in the rover, he'd already shed the last vestiges of grogginess. She knew this because he was back to annoying her again.

"Did you *know,*" he asked in an overly casual tone that immediately made hair prickle along her spine, "the instructions for the Mars drone are in the AHAB manual?"

"No."

"No, you didn't know, or—"

"*No,* you cannot play with it, not even once, not just to make sure it works. No, never, *net.*"

He sat back in his seat, smirking like a man who'd just gotten away with something. "That's right; you speak Russian. Say something else. Something sexy."

"*Nichego ne trogay,*" she told him. *Don't touch anything.*

He bit his lip and groaned. "Say it again."

His low emittance evoked memories. Inappropriate ones. Reggie clutched the steering wheel so hard her knuckles ached. "Get out and help me unload the drill from the back," she bit out. He opened his mouth, but before he could say anything else, she added, "Please."

"Thank you for asking so nicely! What a nice fellow astronaut you are. Why, it would be my *pleasure* to assist you." The smug pride in his expression almost made her want to take it back. "And what shall I be doing today while you're out drilling? Counting dust particles? Labeling cloud shapes?"

"You're coming with me into the field today. But if you so much as *breathe* on anything I haven't explicitly permitted you to breathe on . . ." She trailed off, leaving him to imagine whatever dire fate scared him the most.

Her threat was meaningless in the face of his wide-eyed excitement. Jon bounded out of the rover the minute she killed the engine, and Reggie finally released a shaky breath.

Four more days. Then he'd fly out for his script-reading thing, finally giving her a three-day break from the torment.

This was doable, she decided, vowing that he *would* move back into his quarters tonight. And during the day? She'd keep him occupied from dawn to dusk with fieldwork.

It was risky, of course, to give Jon actual duties. But she'd run out of things for him to label, and he was a liability when he was bored—and not only because of the way trouble and mischief hung around him like a special Jon Leo–branded cologne.

When he was bored, he watched her in a way that made her belly tighten and her nipples sensitive enough to chafe against her sports bra. And after last night's . . . incident . . . her self-discipline was hanging by a thread, and Reggie couldn't trust herself not to pounce on her trainee the next time he looked at her that way.

That was why it was time to depend on the one thing that never, ever let her down: science.

☆ ⭐ ☆

Jon had mentally girded himself for another week of excruciating tedium, so when Reggie directed him to a flat square of cracked earth and demonstrated how to use the hydraulic drill to extract soil samples, he hesitated.

He looked down at the T-shaped handle gripped in his hands and then back at Reggie. "Seriously?"

Reggie gave him a nod. "Remember, firm grip and level hold."

She wore a long-sleeved, zip-up stretchy top today in dark gray, with the zipper sealed up all the way to her neck, and today's leg wear was his favorite of her two "science Reggie" looks: the black version of her beige pants with all the pockets. He'd never seen an outfit so sexy in his life.

Thanks to this woman, he was forever doomed to getting hard the minute he walked into any sporting-goods store. This was his sad fate now.

He powered on the drill the way he'd been instructed to in the manual he'd read the night before and plunged the drill head into the soil, kicking up rocks, dust, and a whir of crunchy noise. Of course, Reggie had also given him instructions a few moments ago, but he'd been busy watching the way her breasts had bounced as the drill had vibrated beneath her. Thinking about the way she'd look riding him with such vigorous intensity.

Thinking about last night and the shadow of her feet and whether she'd been awake all along . . .

"Nice!" she shouted over the drill's low whine. After a few moments she indicated for him to stop drilling and stooped down to inspect his work. When she rose again, her voice had a note of wonderment to it. "Huh. This is actually a good sample. You paid attention when I told you not to extract it too quickly."

"Yup." He absolutely had not. But he *had* read the part of the manual about the drill until his eyes swam and he could recite the operating instructions line by line. A feat he'd only been able to accomplish because he'd been supremely motivated by the promise of something he wanted very, very badly.

Seeing Reggie look at him with begrudging respect was worth reading a million pages of the driest material on Earth.

Reggie showed him on her map where they'd be taking samples, just like astronauts would do on the lunar surface to unearth water ice that had been delivered to the moon via asteroid courier service. After two more test drills, she handed him the walkie-talkie and set him loose in a shallow area cordoned off by boulders.

At first, he was only drilling with the intent to impress. With Reggie side-eyeing his work like a chaperone at a high school dance, Jon made sure to grip the handle with as much unnecessary grunting, squatting, and bicep flexing as he could manage without breaking the damn thing. But as the sun inched across the cloudless sky and Jon still hadn't destroyed anything valuable, Reggie eventually branched out into the field ahead of him to mark new spots to sample, and Jon began to get lost in the simple pleasures of pummeling the earth like some sort of rugged construction man.

Hell, it wasn't a bad workout either. He'd have to tell Kahlil about drills when he got back to LA—surely, there had to be a SoulCycle-type market for people who wanted to hold powerful, phallic, vibrating things.

At a certain point, Jon got lost in the work, and his brain drifted to daydreams of strolling side by side with Reggie through various adventures. A trip to the hardware store, maybe, where she'd inspect power tools with a discerning eye and he'd buy her whatever she wanted, and then she'd roll her eyes when he tried to ghost ride the flatbed cart, but eventually she'd give in and race him down the lumber aisle—and she'd win, of course. As a prize, he'd lay her down in the back seat of their car (which, for the sake of his particular fantasy, came with tinted windows), and finger her until she shuddered under his hand.

It was only when he came to from that delicious reverie that he looked around and realized Reggie was gone.

Did he really have to flex so much while drilling?

Reggie snapped a photo of a patch of shale with moderate fossil potential with her Polaroid, then waited for the picture to spit out so she could label it with GPS coordinates. She tapped her foot. Had this camera always been so slow?

Geological fieldwork had a repetitive, detailed nature that usually soothed her, but today it grated on her nerves.

Out of habit, she glanced back at Jon—and immediately regretted it. Sweat glistened on his brow and turned his bare arms into lurid sculptures. He'd rolled up his sleeves so she could see the football-size swells of his shoulders too.

Her mouth watered with the urge to run her tongue over his skin. She wanted to slide his shirt up and follow the diagonals along his hip bones. Trace the sun's path along his abdomen and taste his strangely compelling cocktail of dust and sweat.

Shameless. Reggie wasn't sure if she was chastising Jon or herself.

Either way, she needed to stop letting herself get distracted by the view.

When a dull shimmer tugged at her peripheral vision, Reggie followed it. A trickle of groundwater, maybe. Or a mineral deposit. Even a stray candy wrapper would be worth investigating if it meant getting farther away from her personal gateway to Temptation Island.

Her foray lured her around a bend, out of sight but not out of comm range. That was how she justified it. *He'll be fine. How much trouble can he possibly get into in a few minutes?*

The mere thought made her shoulders twitch, but she forced herself to keep going. Her very sanity was at stake.

Crouching behind a low rock wall, she found her sparkling quarry: a divot where a spring of groundwater trickled into a bed of gravel. A dribble more than a stream, but enough to have carved a narrow niche into the earth. It extended the length of her arm before the narrow split widened into a crack broad enough to lodge a thick book into.

She snapped a photo just as a breeze swept in, and she tilted her head back to let air ruffle her damp bangs. Only then did she notice the odd, distant dark spot zigzagging along the horizon before dropping out of sight. Too small to be an aircraft and flying too irregularly to be a bird—she'd have written it off as a bug if it weren't so far away.

"Huh," she said aloud, squinting at the now-empty sky for another moment before scoffing at herself. This was how UFOs perpetuated the alien mythos when there were far more realistic explanations. AHAB was only a few miles south of the Navajo Nation land border and a short drive west from the Petrified Forest National Park—the object could be anything from a weather balloon to a tourist's far-off drone to a stray kite.

The wind tugged again, and Reggie heard a quiet plop as her photo dropped out of the camera's mouth and into the crevice. She swore as she reached for it. Fortunately, it hadn't fallen far, and she snatched the white square free with an easy tug.

Her instincts registered the sand-colored scorpion before her eyes did.

The photo fell from her hand and landed at her feet, but its hitchhiker deboarded midair and plopped onto her boot. Reggie threw herself back onto her butt so she could shake it off, but it was too late. The terrified scorpion, who'd been suddenly and rudely evacuated from her dark and cozy crevice only to be chucked into the cold daylight, scuttled up into the nearest safe place—Reggie's pant leg.

She remained calm, because she was an astronaut, and that was what she'd been trained to do in times of crisis.

The scorpion, on the other hand, was not calm at all. She was having an understandably terrible time in Reggie's pant leg, and when she stung, she stung with *fury*.

Reggie couldn't blame the scorpion for stinging; the vicious pinch was a fair price to pay for her own stupidity. Had she been less preoccupied with thoughts of rippling muscle and UFOs, she might have thought twice before sticking her hand into prime scorpion real estate.

Hissing at the pain shooting up her shinbone, she shook the hapless creature free and watched her scramble back to safety before rolling up the fabric to inspect the already swelling injury site. It didn't look good.

"Great. Just fucking . . . great," she muttered as a tingling numbness began to spread out from the puffy welt in waves. Her brain ran mental calculations for how hard it would be to get back to the rover on her own, limping on her swollen ankle, and concluded it would be painful but doable.

She staggered to her feet and took a halting step.

Maybe not so doable. Pain shot through her leg like an electric jolt, and she swore before reluctantly unhooking the comm unit from her belt. "Hey, Jon. How's it going over there?"

The drill's cacophony echoing off the boulders paused, and a second later his low-pitched voice came through, smooth and velveteen. "This is Pirate King; please identify yourself on this unsecured line. Over."

"I'm the only person in the vicinity, Jon." *I'm going to murder him.* She counted backward from three before adding, "Call sign Moon Otter."

"Moon Otter! What can I drill for you? I mean, do for you?"

She blew out a breath. "Whenever you have a free moment, I'm going to ask you to bring me the first aid kit from the rover."

CHAPTER 18

Jon almost dropped the drill. *Almost.*

Instead, he carefully laid it down before bringing the walkie-talkie back to his lips. "Where are you?"

"Head south past the boulders on your right. I'm around the bend."

Her voice was calm and steady, and that was what alarmed him most. This was the tone of voice people used when you had a wasp on your shoulder—a tone that specifically said, *Don't freak out, but . . .*

He took three swift strides toward her, compelled by some primitive instinct, then remembered the first aid kit. He hauled the drill onto his shoulder and sprinted to the rover and back in record time.

Images flashed through his mind as he ran: Reggie at the bottom of a ravine, Reggie with a broken leg, Reggie being eaten alive by a rabid desert mouse . . . but none of these calamities made sense. The idea of Regina Hayes being bested by any known threat seemed absurd, because in his mind, she was invincible. If anything tried to hurt her, she'd simply glare it into submission.

Still.

When he found her, hale and whole and leaning against a boulder with a scowl twisting her cherry lips, a wave of dizzying relief struck him, and he realized he'd been breathing through a throat so tight it was a wonder he'd been able to run at all.

He tossed the first aid kit on top of a nearby boulder and grabbed her shoulders, inspecting her for damage. "What happened?"

"I'm fine." Silver eyes slid away from his. Her voice was muted, and he noted her skin was a shade too pale. "Hand me the kit."

He caught the way she shifted, putting all her weight on her left foot, and he fell to his knees, reaching for her leg with a gentle hold. "What's wrong with your ankle?"

"Don't worry about it." She tried to wrest her leg free, but it elicited a hiss.

Gently, he used his free hand to lift the hem of her pants. Her ankle had ballooned to the width of her calf, and though Jon was no doctor (he hadn't even played one on TV), he was pretty sure its swelling was caused by the hideous pink blotch with a dime-size purple epicenter. He carefully lowered the fabric and looked up into a beautiful face pulled tight with suppressed pain. "Scorpion or snake?"

Reluctantly, she bit out, "Scorpion."

"Is it . . . ?" He tried to remember the one type she'd said was deadly, but his brain gears had locked up, stuck on the singular task of assuring himself that Reggie was alive and breathing.

"It doesn't matter. Even if it is a bark scorpion sting, we're too far away from medical resources for it to make a difference. Fortunately, deadly complications are rare. If I start to go into anaphylactic shock, I'll let you know. Otherwise, I just need supplies from the kit so I can clean the wound site."

She refused to let him help, batting his hands away from her leg and insisting the cotton pads and antiseptic be handed directly to her. When she was finished, he packed up the kit and helped her stand again.

There was no doubt in his mind she intended to walk. On her own. All the way back to the rover. Beneath her heavy bangs, her eyes narrowed, and her brows came down. Her lips flattened. Then she took one halting step, then another, shuffling forward with hands curled into fists.

It was so fucking cute it made him feel like something was clawing its way out of his chest, even though he'd never dare call her *cute* to her face. Even if she was so petite next to him. Perfectly pick-up-able.

"Don't even think about it," she said, eyes slitted, but he was already moving, scooping her up into his arms like the delicate damsel she wasn't. Her legs flailed as she squirmed, fists pummeling his chest, but he accepted the blows with a satisfied grunt. "Put me down!" she demanded.

"*Oof*, you're heavier than I expected," he lied, pretending to lose his grip. She gasped in outrage but, predictably, stopped squirming. "There we go. Nice and docile now."

He began marching back to the rover, ignoring the burning sensation beneath his chin, where her eyes were undoubtedly staring laser beams of vengeance through his flesh.

"I can walk on my own."

"I know," he said.

"Then why are you carrying me?"

He finally glanced down at her, and that strange band around his ribs tightened at the sight of her curled in his arms, her arms clasped tight to her chest like a little animal. How could one woman be so ferocious yet so huggable? "Because. Just because you *can* do something doesn't mean you have to. We're a team, right? You said it yourself—out here, we only have each other to count on. Since I'm not currently suffering from a scorpion bite—"

"Sting," she corrected.

"—I'm happy to carry you. And when I inevitably injure or maim myself . . . and I assure you, it could be any second now . . . I'll expect you to do the same for me. You would, wouldn't you?"

She huffed out a breath. "Only because I'm obligated to now."

He considered her words, and a glimmer of understanding flickered in his brain. "Are you worried about accepting help because you think it makes you obligated to people?"

"I don't need help. Ever. From anyone." Her chin jutted, but the words were delivered woodenly. Like she'd repeated this mantra to herself over and over again until she believed it.

Careful not to squish her, he adjusted her in his arms so she nestled more comfortably against him. He wanted to squeeze her tight. Say nice things to her about how she deserved kindness that she so obviously hadn't received much of in her life. But she'd probably close up again and lash out at him, so he let it be.

When they returned to the rover, he opened the passenger door to settle her onto the seat. It was a mistake.

"*Oh*, hell no!" She shoved herself out of his hold, tumbling awkwardly into the vinyl chair.

"You need to keep your leg elevated. I can drive the rover. I've read the manual."

He closed the door on her and sprinted to the driver's side, even as she scrambled to drag herself across the center console. He narrowly beat her to it, sliding into the seat and nudging her out of the way with his shoulder. With a strangled cry, Reggie dived for the steering wheel, but Jon responded by snaking his arm around her stomach and repositioning her in his lap. The feel of her soft bottom wiggling against his cock made him stifle a groan.

"Careful," he warned her, as he found the keys Reggie had left on the dash and powered on the vehicle. "I can't afford to be distracted while driving at such daring speed."

"You can't—"

"I totally can." He shifted into drive and levered his foot on the gas, letting the rover accelerate to a thrilling crawl, as Reggie continued to squirm in protest. The furious little gasps Reggie was making, combined with her movements, had him rock hard in seconds flat. He couldn't stifle the second groan. Then he gritted out, "You need to get back into your seat."

She ignored him. "Stop the rover, right fucking now."

"I'm warning you. If I have to hit the brakes, I'm going to kiss you again."

"Jon! I mean it!"

"So do I," he growled. He slammed the brakes. Jammed the lever into park. His hands came down to cradle her head, thumbs brushing her soft cheeks as his fingers tunneled into her midnight hair. Her gunmetal eyes went round with alarm, and she stilled. But instead of crushing her mouth to his, he merely lowered his lips to her forehead, gently blowing aside her bangs to press a soft kiss there. He pulled back and grinned. "Told you. Now, let's get you back into your seat before you hurt your ankle."

Emotions flickered across her face: surprise, confusion . . . disappointment.

Then, without further argument, she scooted off his lap and into the passenger seat. She propped her ankle up on the dashboard. With a shuddering breath, she said, "The parking brake is still on."

✦ ⭐ ✦

Her day was bad enough without pulling up to AHAB and seeing Mimi and Zach out front with their filming equipment set up. Mimi's wave turned into open-mouthed awe when it became apparent Jon was in the driver's seat.

"You will *not* carry me in front of the cameras," she warned Jon. Unfortunately, that meant backing up to the rover's airlock hatch so they could exit from the back of the vehicle directly into the habitat. It wasn't a difficult procedure, but it did require precision. "Switch spots with me."

His melted-chocolate eyes filled with hurt as he brought the rover to a halt, which was ridiculous, given that he'd already gotten to come out into the field with her, use the drill, *and* drive the rover. What more did he want from her? "I read the manual," he reminded her. "I can do this. Just coach me through it."

"I don't do coaching."

His jaw clenched. "Ignoring the fact that I'm here *specifically* to be coached by you . . . look. You're injured. Unless you can operate the gas with your ankle elevated like that, you don't have much of a choice."

Her traitorous ankle throbbed in agreement. At least it hadn't continued to swell.

Zach tapped on the window, indicating for her to roll it down—which, of course, it did not do, because one didn't roll down the windows on the moon. Behind him, Mimi angled the camera toward them like a grenade launcher.

Reggie hesitated, glancing back at Jon. Could she really trust him not to screw this up?

He raised a brow. "Think of how good this will look to the selection board. You asked for my help with that, remember? If you coach me through this, you can show them what a patient trainer you are. How easy you are to work with. Isn't this the whole reason you're here?"

No way to argue with that, as much as she wanted to on principle alone. "Fine. But if you don't follow my instructions, *to the letter*, you'll spend the rest of the month on rock-counting duty."

He tsked. "Pro tip number one: people respond better to positive motivation than threats."

"Follow my instructions or else . . . please?" she tried.

Zach tapped on the window again, and she moved to jerk open the door. Jon stopped her with a hand on her shoulder. "Wait. Mimi's already filming, so remember to smile, because our brains are wired to respond positively to a smiling face. And ask them how their trip was. People like it when you ask them questions, even if you don't actually care about the answer. Pretend you do. And finally, mention that it was your idea to let me drive, and compliment my progress." He chuckled at whatever he saw on her face. "Not for the sake of my ego, Reggie. Because it'll make you seem encouraging and generous."

Reggie nodded slowly. As much as it pained her to admit it, Jon's advice made sense; he'd framed social nuance in simple cause-and-effect terms. It was almost . . . logical. "Thanks," she offered.

He must have thought she was nervous, because he squeezed her shoulder and said, "You'll kick ass."

She wanted to snap that she wasn't nervous, but she didn't feel like explaining—not that someone like Jon would understand. How could an inherently lovable, happy-go-lucky human, with his good looks and natural charm and at least one parent who loved him unconditionally, ever relate to her social anxiety?

It was easier for Reggie to put up walls and hang up metaphorical **BEWARE!** signs all around her person than risk letting someone into her fortress of solitude, where they might irrevocably fuck things up. Make her feel shit she didn't feel like feeling. It was far better to be lonely than to lose control over her emotions like that.

But what if she could fake it? What if she could treat social interaction the way Jon described it—like a set of parameters designed to achieve desired results? Then she wouldn't risk anything. She could have her protective walls and make people like her!

Despite the pain thrumming its way up her calf, Reggie smiled.

☆ ⁎ 彗 ⁎

The problem with success, Reggie reflected as Mimi gushed over the afternoon's footage, was that people expected you to replicate it.

Mimi paused on a shot of Reggie and Jon, side by side next to the spectrometer they'd used to test the drill samples they'd procured. "This! This is the shit we want," she declared. "Look at the way you're smiling at him, Reggie. Like you're goddamn proud of him and maybe even a little horny about it? That's the narrative I think will resonate. Zach, what do you think?"

The ice pack fell from Reggie's fingers, and Jon, who was seated next to her, reached down and handed it back so she could reposition it on her ankle.

"Thanks," she mumbled, ignoring the heat in her cheeks. She wasn't going to respond to Mimi. The comment wasn't worth dignifying with argument, and it would probably only encourage her.

"Zach!" Mimi nudged her colleague, who appeared to be staring at the screen, lost in thought.

Zach blinked, then glanced at the group. "Sorry. What's up?"

Mimi rolled her eyes. "Did your doctor call you back yet?" When Zach shook his head, she turned to the group and explained, "He left his ADHD meds at a rest stop bathroom, so forgive him if he's a fuckin' space case for a few days until he can get a refill."

For some reason this made Jon's brows knit together, but Reggie only shrugged. Zach's problems were none of her business. At least he *had* an excuse for not paying attention.

Then again, Jon had surprised her by being on his best behavior all afternoon. He'd listened intently whenever she'd described something, and though he had accidentally knocked over several samples, Reggie had to admit he'd been far more useful than she'd expected—especially with her ankle temporarily out of commission, rendering her incapable of taking on the brunt of the work like usual.

Her bigger preoccupation was with the evening's sleeping arrangements. He had to move back—there was no way around it. Even glancing at the door to her living quarters brought back memories that made her skin go damp with sweat.

As Mimi packed up for the night, she turned the topic to an even less comfortable one. "Jon, I know you're heading back to LA with us this upcoming weekend, but what are you guys doing for the holiday the weekend after? I ask because I'm throwing a dope Festivus bash at my cousin's place in Santa Monica if you two don't have plans."

Jon grinned. "That could be fun. I figured I'd drop by my mom's for the weekend, but I don't have any solid plans." He glanced at Reggie, suddenly looking guilty. "Though I know Reggie's supposed to visit her parents."

"Yes," she bit out. Remembering his earlier advice, she forced a smile and added, "Thank you for the reminder that I need to book flights."

After the crew left, Jon helped her stand and let her hobble around. He didn't argue when she insisted on making dinner and storing the remaining equipment, probably because he knew she'd reached her limit as far as pretending went. When Mimi and Zach had learned about her scorpion encounter, they'd leaped at the opportunity to milk it for maximum drama. At least they'd accepted her refusal to reenact the experience.

She'd just taken the first bite of rehydrated beef stroganoff when Jon said, "You don't like visiting your parents, do you?"

"Why do you think that?" She swallowed, and the bite she'd taken went down like a lump of sand. She looked down at her pouch and stirred the brownish mush. Thoroughly.

"I can just tell. The way you reacted on the phone with your boss. And just now, when Mimi was talking to you."

"Huh," she managed to say with a noncommittal air. She stirred harder. "Oh, by the way, the air filter is fixed. You can move your mountain of junk back into the other habitat."

"I already know that," he said calmly. He crossed his arms. "Why don't you want to talk about your parents?"

"You *know*? How—"

"I could hear it last night. It sounds different. And stop changing the subject."

"Drop it, Jon." She threw down her spork and food pouch, ignoring the stew that splattered out the top. The bottom of her stomach felt hollowed out. If Jon had known the air filter was fixed last night . . .

"What if I go with you? To visit your parents?" He ran a hand through his hair, pulling his bun free as he did it. This time, he caught the elastic before it shot off. "Tell them I'm your lonely Jewish trainee who didn't have anywhere else to go for the holiday weekend."

"You're Jewish?" was all she could think to say. What else was she supposed to make of his insane suggestion? They'd met less than two weeks ago, and now he wanted to fly back to Boston with her for Christmas? *Meet her parents?*

"Guess so. My mom is, anyway. But she's kind of a free spirit . . . never put much stock in religious tradition when I was growing up, so even though Hanukkah falls around the same time as Christmas this year, I don't even know if she'll be home for the weekend. I think she's at a glassblowing retreat in Murano with her boyfriend right now." He gave that sheepish shrug of his, looking all melty eyed and adorable, and Reggie wanted to scream.

"But why would you want to come home with me instead? I barely know you!"

"Well, I've never been to Boston, for one. And I looked it up . . . it's snowing there right now. It would be kind of cool to have a white Christmas, since it never snows in LA. And more important, my presence might keep your parents distracted from whatever makes you so uncomfortable. It'll be fun for me, because I love meeting new people, and I can charm the pants off anyone." He considered, then added with a pointed look at her, "Well, almost everyone."

The idea of Jon charming her mother was laughable. Her father, though . . . maybe. He did have a distinct preference for cisgender males, so maybe Jon's presence would take the edge off his thirty-five-year-old grudge that Reggie hadn't been the son he'd wanted.

Maybe it was all the Tylenol she'd taken to dull the pain from her injury, but an odd sort of lightness began to settle over her. Maybe she would let Jon fly to Boston with her. Why the fuck not? There was no way that trip could be *more* unpleasant; at least with Jon there, she'd have something pretty to look at while she suffered.

"Fine. I'll book us tickets. But I want to be crystal clear that we're going as platonic colleagues. Don't get any ideas."

A lazy grin. Lowering his voice, he said, "Too late. I have a vivid imagination."

The way he said it . . .

Reggie sucked air in sharply through her nostrils. He knew. He had to. "You said no sex," she reminded him.

His warm hand closed over her trembling one, and his eyes locked on hers. Making sure she couldn't look away. "I might be persuaded if there was potential for more than sex . . . but you don't do relationships. Right?"

She blew out a wavering breath. "Right."

"I'm still going to think about it, though," he told her, voice gravelly. His index finger traced the back of her hand, trailing heat in its wake. Her nipples hardened. Her breath quickened. It was almost comical how swiftly her body responded to such an innocent touch.

"You shouldn't," she managed to say.

"But I can't help it. I'm sorry." He shook his head, but he didn't look sorry at all. He leaned forward as if he were revealing a deep, dark secret. "I'm going to think about that kiss before I fall asleep tonight, and it's going to make me hard. I'm going to think about what would have happened if we'd come in here and there was nothing wrong with the air filter. I'm going to think about what your pussy tastes like, and feeling your clit go swollen against my tongue, and how you'll be so wet when I put my fingers inside you that you'll melt all over my hand and drip down my wrist and . . . I mean, thinking about that will be torture if I don't stroke my dick while I'm doing it, pretending it's sinking into your hot cunt, imagining the little sounds you'll make while I shove the thick head in, stretching you out bit by bit, until you're crying. Begging me for it—"

Reggie gasped, her thighs clenching together in desperation. "I don't beg," she whispered, but Jon only leaned forward until his lips were next to her ear. Even that simple contact—the merest glancing brush of lips over the shell-like curl above her earlobe—made her shudder. God, she was wound so tight . . .

"If you don't, then I will," he murmured. "You'd like that even more, wouldn't you?"

Her hands spasmed, curling into fists. She opened her mouth to reply, but nothing came out.

To his credit, he didn't look smug when he sat back. His cheeks were flushed, his eyes a little glossy, and the prominent ridge straining his denim fly looked seriously uncomfortable. He looked just as shaken as she was.

He cleared his throat. "Anyway. I'm going to go move my stuff now. I'll see you in the morning . . . unless you change your mind about the dating thing."

She shook her head. Her voice couldn't be trusted right now, because she might tell him what he wanted to hear.

And that would be a mistake.

CHAPTER 19

Friday morning dawned, and Jon was no closer to getting Reggie to fall for him.

In fact, Reggie had kept him so busy all week he'd barely had time to *think* about romancing her (except at night, of course, when he thought about nothing else).

Though her ankle hadn't worsened, it did limit her mobility—which meant Jon had been promoted to doing real work.

Under Reggie's militant supervision, he'd been set loose on a wide variety of thrilling tasks, like drilling into rocks, looking at rocks under a microscope, putting rocks into machines, accepting responsibility for the rock samples he'd labeled with inappropriate names, relabeling inappropriately named rock samples with boring names, making Reggie groan with increasingly terrible rock-related puns, and so on. There was little time between tasks to plot Reggie's wooing, especially when her sultry gray stare followed his every movement (which he'd decided to pretend was a form of admiration and not a somewhat valid lack of trust in his haphazard, "this looks close enough" operational style).

It wasn't the kind of schedule he'd ever have considered exciting before he'd met Reggie, but everything was more interesting with her by his side. She made him *want* to pay attention, even to the lamest chores.

As promised, he'd done his best to coach her through his own areas of expertise: pretending to be cool on Instagram, pretending to have fun on camera, and pretending to be friendly to other humans in real life. Reggie was a fast learner—which made him wonder why she'd apparently gone so long pretending *not* to be likable. Maybe being intimidating made you smarter or something; he'd yet to determine his hypothesis for the Reggie Hayes Theory of Sociability, but he thought about her approximately 90 percent of the time, so he'd probably figure it out soon.

The week of playing astronaut had gone by so quickly that he'd almost managed to completely block out his conscience, which had grown increasingly concerned about the fact he hadn't unrolled the script again.

Not even once.

Which was why, when the time came for Jon to drive out to the airport with Mimi and Zach, he considered playing dead. Or sick. Or . . . anything that would excuse him from his real job.

Reggie found him outside well before their usual breakfast time, scanning the area with the UV flashlight. The sky was still indigo every-where except where the sun was coming up, and a thin layer of frost made all the brown trees, brush, and rocks look like they were made of fancy crystal.

"You're up extra early this morning. Had I known you were awake already, I'd have made you a coffee," she said, tugging her sleeves over her palms before cupping her hands tight around her thermos. "I thought you guys weren't leaving until eight."

"I couldn't sleep. Too excited about meeting the rest of the cast, doing that table read . . ." He flashed her a half-hearted grin before turning back to his hunt, sweeping the ultraviolet beam along the base of the habitat wall.

She saw right through it, like he'd known she would. "Let me guess. You're looking for a scorpion so you can get it to sting you, so you don't have to go to LA and confront Rudy about that ridiculous script."

"Uh, *no*. That's dumb. What am I, a character in a sitcom?"

"You're right, what was I thinking? Jon Leo, going to extreme lengths to avoid unpleasant responsibilities? You would never. Oh, look, there's one!"

"Where? *Where?*" He swung the flashlight frantically in the direction she was pointing.

She smirked. "Liar."

He clicked the beam off, dejection settling over him. It was damn cold out, it was *hella* damn early, and it was hard to fake his usual happy-go-lucky attitude under those conditions. "I'd rather stay here and do astronaut things with you," he grumbled.

She came to his side, and it pleased him to note her limp was almost imperceptible now. Then she silently held out her thermos to him. An offering.

As gestures went, it wasn't a contender for Romance's Greatest Hits, but Jon's overly hopeful heart perked up anyway. He accepted the coffee gratefully.

"You want to sit?" he asked. "Mimi says sunrises are metal as fuck."

"Nah."

But she didn't go back inside. She stayed by his side, silently watching the chilly sunrise with him (which was, in fact, just as metal as advertised) as they passed the thermos back and forth, until all the coffee was gone and the alarm on his watch went off, reminding him he needed to start packing.

He stopped the alarm and glanced at her from the corner of his eye, feeling oddly shy in her presence despite having spent so much time alone with her. She was still staring at the sky, but her face was relaxed—her steely guard lowered for this brief moment in time. If there was any time to confess his feelings, it was now—when he could run away to another city afterward.

He cleared his throat, reaching into his pocket to retrieve the tiny gift he'd found for her.

Be cool. Casual. Don't come on too strong. Remember, you're a future A-list Hollywood actor.

"I found this," he blurted, sticking out his closed fist. When she raised her brows in question, he spread his fingers, revealing the red rock he'd found Wednesday morning. It was a little lumpy but still fairly spherical as far as these things went (he should know; he was a bona fide rock expert these days), with dark red and black splotches drizzled across its surface.

"A rock," she correctly identified. "Impressive."

Flames edged up the back of his neck, but he soldiered on. "I know you're kind of a moon girl—uh, woman—but I thought it kinda looks like Mars, and I know you like to collect cool rocks like the one you have in your pocket all the time, so . . . here."

He thrust it out to her again, feeling foolish. Half expecting her to reject it. She eyed it with a furrowed brow—probably trying to decide if he or the rock had greater mental capacities. What had he been thinking?

But instead of laughing at him, Reggie accepted the rock with a simple "Thanks" before shoving it into her pocket. She looked down at her dirt-caked boots, her blunt-edged bob swinging forward to hide her face, and said quietly, "Good luck this weekend. I hope it's not as bad as you think it'll be."

✫ ˖ 💫 ˖

The table read wasn't as bad as Jon had dreaded—it was worse. Way, way worse.

Jon tried to catch Rudy's attention after the session ended, but Jacqui cut him off at the pass with a not-so-subtle look.

"Let's grab some coffee," Jacqui suggested. She'd told him she'd wanted to come to the reading to get a better feel for his chemistry with the other cast members so she could coordinate joint press opportunities. But as the other members of the primary cast mingled in the hallway, Jacqui made no effort to approach their agents or publicists.

None of his costars made eye contact with them as they left.

Jacqui picked a café near the studio, where drinks were served in chunky teacups delivered on flower-bedecked trays. She grabbed a sunlight-dappled table in the back garden and tucked her signature white blazer on the back of the chair, withdrew her notebook from her bag, uncapped a serious-looking pen, and leaned in with an accusatory look in her eyes. "What, pray tell, the *fuck* was that in there?"

To buy time to formulate a response, Jon gulped from the double-shot skim latte he'd paid almost ten dollars for and had a sudden, intense longing for shitty instant coffee in a dented thermos. When he set the cup down, liquid sloshed over the side and made a beige pool in the saucer. "I'm struggling to connect with the material?" he tried.

Jacqui handed him a stack of napkins to sop up his spill, shaking her head. "You read every single line sarcastically. What were you thinking? This isn't a comedy. You aren't Johnny Depp—you can't waltz onto every set doing the same schtick that worked for you the first time. What's gotten into you?"

He didn't know. That was the problem. He reached up to run a hand through his hair, caught Jacqui's eyes narrowing, and pretended to stretch instead. "Um, well. At the time it seemed . . . funny."

"Funny," she repeated flatly.

"Yeah. I mean, the script is . . . you know." He raised his brows, waiting for Jacqui to jump on the hint wagon, but she merely gave him an expectant look. He cleared his throat. "Terrible. It's terrible. You know it's terrible, right?"

Jacqui shook her head slowly. "You have to be kidding me, Jon. Didn't you read the script before signing up for this?"

He looked down at his coffee. The barista had drawn a little heart in the foam and told him she'd loved him in *Space Dude*, but now the heart was all deformed from being splashed about by his clumsy, awkward self.

"Oh, for the love of —" Jacqui threw down her pen. Closed her eyes and took a deep breath. Then she reopened her eyes and returned the pen to paper. "Okay, let's walk through the options."

"I'm sorry," he said, peeking at her through his lashes.

She gave him a curious glance. Still irritated but curious nonetheless. "Why are you sorry? You know *you* pay *me*, right?"

Guilt made his stomach sour. "But . . . you're my friend too. And I'm so difficult and flaky and irresponsible. I get excited and sign on for huge projects without reading the script, even though I know I should, because I go through life winging it and hoping for the best, and sometimes it works out, but this time it didn't. I completely understand if you don't want to work with me anymore. I'll release you from contract or whatever and still pay you for the full year."

For a second, Jacqui merely looked at him with that same bewildered expression. Then she laughed. "Oh, you sweet, sweet man. Do you really think you're the most difficult client I have? Jon, this is Hollywood. Until you ask me to color coordinate my outfits with your dog's manicure, I'm committed to working with you."

"You are?"

"Yes, you dork. I'm your friend, too, you know." She snorted. "And I still believe you have rare talent. I've seen you take roles and make them your own in a way that only the best actors can do, but I think your heart has to be in it in order for that to work. If your heart isn't in *Escape Velocity*, we can find you something else. What about an indie drama with a few rising stars? Or we can talk to the agency about finding you a show-stealing supporting role in a big-budget summer film.

Something to get your name out there without so much pressure. And of course, there's always—"

"No," Jon interrupted, shaking his head fervently. "I won't do *Space Dude 2*."

It wasn't the first time he'd said it, but it was the first time his words lacked conviction. It would be easy. Fun. *Lucrative.*

But he wasn't going to sell out like that. No way.

Jacqui sighed. "You don't have to decide right away. In the meantime, we can still get you out of *Escape Velocity* if you don't want to do this. After today, Rudy will likely be looking for an excuse to replace you, so if you've changed your mind, now is the time to say so."

The thought of losing this opportunity made his stomach roil. What had he done? What had he been thinking? Even if he didn't like this role, was he really going to give up his big break so easily? He'd promised his mom he'd take her to the Academy Awards next year. He'd promised *himself* he'd start landing roles he wasn't embarrassed about.

And then there was his dad, who would no doubt be watching his career closely. Wondering whether his son was worthy of the last name he'd deigned to give him. Did he really want his dad to think of him as the hokey Space Dude for the rest of his career?

"I want this role," he told her. He hoped it sounded convincing.

"Are you one hundred percent sure? Because it'll look far worse if you leave the movie after they start releasing promo footage from your astronaut training. If you pull shit like this again and Rudy replaces you, I won't be able to spin it like it was your decision to walk away."

It would be so easy to quit. A single word to Jacqui, and he could get out of this relatively unscathed.

But then he'd have no reason to go back and finish his training with Reggie. He might never see her again. Hell, he didn't even have her phone number.

"I'm sure," he told Jacqui. "I'll talk to Rudy and apologize for today."

She tapped her pen on her notepad, considering.

"Let me handle Rudy," Jacqui said after some thought. "Mimi sent me some of the raw footage she's gotten, and I have some ideas for how we can finesse this. You just fly back to Arizona and keep doing what you've been doing, and I'll work my magic to lock this role in for you."

He nodded. This was the right choice. The right thing for his career. The feeling of wrongness would go away eventually.

CHAPTER 20

It wasn't like Reggie had missed Jon while he'd been gone, but her pulse picked up awfully quickly the minute he returned to the base on Sunday night, proudly sporting a sweatshirt and a warehouse-size bag of instant-coffee packets.

"Reinforcements," he explained cheerfully.

She eyed the label. "Three hundred servings? We're only here for two more weeks."

He gave her a stricken look. "Do you think it's not going to be enough?" He managed three straight seconds before letting a grin take over. "Take the rest back to Houston with you. Consider it a bribe."

For what, he didn't say, but Reggie's imagination offered an unhelpfully graphic suggestion.

She'd hoped the weekend would clear the fog of lust clouding her brain, and that had been partially true. For nearly three days straight, she'd managed to convince herself the Jon thing was not only a bad idea but a bad idea born entirely out of loneliness and a sexual dry spell. With the entire place to herself, she'd made liberal use of her vibrators.

And when vigorous masturbation had inevitably failed to stanch the nightly dreams featuring Jon in the starring role, Reggie had scrolled through her digital Rolodex and lined up a booty call for the following weekend in Boston. Vince was an old Navy friend who'd recently weathered a divorce, and they'd had a good time when he'd had a stop-over in Houston last February. He bored her to tears conversationally, but he was a solid seven out of ten in bed, and most importantly, he looked nothing like Jon.

With that taken care of, Reggie had forced herself to stuff the Mars rock he'd given her into the deepest recesses of her duffel bag, along with all the silly ideas that had started to ferment in the cobweb-laden brain compartments where she'd stored all her excess feelings.

It wasn't like she'd ever *seriously* consider dating Jon. They had nothing in common. Her career goals required every iota of her time and energy. He lived in a different city, and Reggie had no interest in a long-distance relationship with someone she barely knew. Moreover, if she pulled this off and demonstrated her people skills to the selection board—and thanks to Jon's help, she might actually do it—she'd literally be *off planet* by this time next year. And that was a level of long distance no fledgling relationship should have to weather.

"How'd the table read go?" Reggie asked, following Jon as he dropped his weekend bag off in his living quarters. She stopped in the open doorway—an invisible barrier.

"It was, uh . . . cool."

"Cool?"

"You know. Tubular." Jon unzipped his bag and turned it upside down. The contents rained down on the larger, more impressive Clothing Mountain.

"Did you talk to Rudy about the script?" Not that she cared. She really didn't. All she was doing was asking questions to seem likable, just like Jon had told her to do.

But that script was a nonstop cringefest. Jon wasn't really going to let that fly, was he? He deserved better than a role like that, and the more she'd thought about it over the weekend, the more indignant she'd become on his behalf.

Jon shrugged. "Nah. Hey, you want to check out our social media stats from last week while we eat dinner? Jacqui showed me a summary, and spoiler alert, we're crushing it."

She'd already eaten but found herself agreeing anyway. Even though her ankle had returned to normal size, Jon insisted she sit while he irradiated food for them both. He handed her his phone to look at while he worked.

Jacqui had compiled all their media posts into a single pdf file, and Reggie scrolled through it begrudgingly.

"Look at all the engagements on the post from Thursday," he told her, but she ignored the graph. Instead, Reggie stared at one of the photos Mimi had taken. Reggie hadn't even really looked at it afterward; at the time, she'd thought it was another silly promo photo—they were all the same "let's pretend we're having fun" bullshit, weren't they? This one should have been no different. Jon was showing off the drill, flexing his left bicep like some sort of fitness model, and Reggie was supposed to have been kneeling by the hole with a thumbs-up and a smile directed at the camera.

But Mimi had captured Reggie between shots, laughing at some stupid thing Jon had said. And Jon was looking down at her with a mischievous twinkle in his eye and that adorable smirk of his, and the whole thing looked disturbingly domestic. An unbiased observer might think she and Jon had been having a really good time when that photo had been taken, not just a fake good time. They looked like they liked each other.

Like they really, *really* liked each other.

"We've got shippers," Jon announced with a cheerful grin. He plopped down across from her and handed over the dinner pouch.

That sounded ominous. "Shippers?"

"Don't worry, it's a good thing. Great PR. Boy, I can't tell you how stoked I am on this food. The whole time I was in LA eating all this award-winning, fifty-dollar-an-order takeout, I kept craving the taste of beef-flavored Styrofoam." He shoveled a heaping spoonful into his mouth, then immediately sucked in air. "Fuuuuuck, too hot. How's your ankle? Please say it's bad . . . I really like driving the rover. I'm ready to take it off some stunt jumps. I saw a plateau out by the western rim . . ."

"Perfectly healed. What are shippers, Jon?"

He took a long sip of water, watching her through low-lidded eyes. He released the straw with an exaggerated sigh of refreshment. "You know. Fans who think we're a good pairing. Romantically. Sometimes they write fan fiction, which is usually kinda bad and weird, but sometimes it's good. I guess it's something you get used to when you're in the public eye. Maybe they're on to something, though. We do look awfully smitten with each other in that picture."

Reggie shoved his phone away and stood. It was hard to breathe. The air felt hot. Stifling. "I think there's something wrong with the filter again. I'm going to go check it."

But with the airlock closed behind her, the dizziness only worsened. The panel showed the filter operating at a luxurious 86 percent efficiency. Practically mythical, it was running so well.

She wanted to crawl out of her skin and run away. So she did the next best thing and fled outside.

Somehow, he managed to find her, which shouldn't have surprised Reggie as much as it did. They were in a crater in the middle of the desert, after all—it wasn't like she had a vast variety of hiding spots.

Not that she was hiding, because she *wasn't*—she was merely stargazing. Behind an array of solar panels perched very high on the rim of a crater, accessed from the crater floor by scrambling up a steep, dangerously crumbly incline. This was a normal and reasonable place to stargaze.

His lumbering footsteps crunching along the cold earth were audible from miles away, but Reggie staunchly refused to give him the satisfaction of acknowledging his presence until he'd plunked down next to her.

"Hey," he said.

She clutched her knees tighter against her chest. "Go away." It came out sounding sullen, but she didn't care anymore. And he could probably tell she didn't mean it.

That was the problem.

To make matters worse, he simply sat there in silence, like a shadowy colossus in her peripheral vision, ostensibly looking at the star-studded sky. It wasn't like she could kick him back down into the crater, and asking him to leave *again* required sacrificing more pride than she could live with.

Only when she'd convinced herself that she could overlook his presence did he pipe up to ask, "What's that obnoxiously glowing star over there, next to the moon?"

She didn't need to look to know what he was referring to. "Mars."

"Why is it so bright?"

"Because it's very close right now." She hoped that would be the end of it.

It wasn't. "So how come you want to go to the moon and not Mars? There are probably way more cool rocks on Mars. I saw a documentary about it."

"I'll likely be in my midforties by the time NASA is realistically ready for a manned Martian mission," she snapped. What she didn't add was that she'd be the prime age to send an astronaut to Mars, because due to radiation limits such a long trip would likely be one's last before retirement. For that very reason, Reggie wouldn't get the opportunity to do both missions, and it was the moon she'd set her sights on long ago. "And I happen to like the moon just fine. It's barren and lifeless and blissfully free of cheerful actors who ask nosy questions."

"Sounds lonely."

"Exactly."

He sighed. "I fucked up the table read."

The sudden change of topic only threw her for a split second. "Intentionally?"

"I don't know."

She glanced at him and for the first time realized he wore her gray blanket even though he now had warm clothes to wear. He mimicked her hunched posture with his enormous arms wrapped around his shins and his chin resting on his knees. Loose strands of hair fell forward around his face. He was egregiously, darkly handsome yet managed to look vulnerable at the same time.

If only she could hate him. He made it so difficult.

"Why do you want to do this movie so badly?" she asked.

He tilted his head to look at her, and it made his cheek squish against his arms. "Everyone looks at me and sees a big doofus. I just want people to take me seriously."

"I'm sorry, but I'm never going to take you seriously if you say the line, 'Bequeath your accursed slime to me.'"

He retorted dryly, "You'll never take me seriously whether or not I say that line."

"What are you talking about?"

He looked away again, shoulders bunching up around his ears. "You know what I mean. You act terrified by the mere *concept* you might have feelings for me."

She reared back. "No, I don't."

Did she?

She shivered, suddenly aware of the way the cold air nipped at her exposed skin. Her teeth began to chatter, and a very guilty part of her fantasized about snuggling up between Jon's hot thighs and letting him wrap that blanket around them both.

If only.

"Maybe I do have"—she made her mouth form the word—"*feelings*. I don't know. But it doesn't matter."

"Why not?"

"Because I can't offer you a relationship." She had to make him understand. "Not only do I not have time for one, but I don't know how. I've never dated anyone, ever. So when you flirt with me and give me these thoughtful gifts and talk about people shipping us, I freak out."

"So you act like this because you like me?" A ghost of his usual smile appeared. How quickly he rebounded.

"As a friend," she lied.

"Do you get off while thinking about all your friends?"

Her cheeks flushed. It wasn't like he'd believe her if she denied it, so instead she said primly, "Fine. A friend I want to have sex with but won't. And for the record, I'd fuck all my friends if I felt like they could handle separating their emotions from the physical act."

He raised a brow. "Even Katya?"

Technically, Katya was her only friend, but she didn't tell Jon that. "Yes. Bisexuality makes logical sense, you know." When Jon appeared unfazed by that news, she continued, "But I wouldn't sleep with Katya either. She's a fairy-tale princess masquerading as a hardened cynic. Her YouTube history is exclusively compilations of unlikely animal friendships."

"Like cheetahs and dogs," Jon said gravely. She had no idea what he meant, but it seemed on-brand for him to be knowledgeable on the subject. Maybe she should set him and Katya up on a date.

The thought made her shoulder spasm, and she rubbed at the knotted muscle, trying to massage her scapula back into submission. An unhelpful reminder of her failed training exercise and how it had landed her here. She groaned at the memory.

She could feel Jon watching her, his gaze hot on her skin.

"Actors are excellent liars," he told her in an almost offhand manner. "I could tell you if we slept together I wouldn't get all sentimental afterward. I could probably sell it."

"You do realize you're foiling your own plan by telling me this."

"Sadly, yes. I'm my own worst enemy."

"Aren't we all," she muttered.

"It'll be ruined anyway when I wake up the morning after our marathon fuckfest and realize I'm hopelessly in love with you. I'll be crushed when you turn down my proposal." He let out an exaggerated sigh. "I guess I'll have to return the engagement ring too."

"Stop it. You're going to give me a heart attack."

"Will I get to give you mouth-to-mouth resuscitation?" He had the nerve to sound hopeful.

"No. Just let me die."

"So dramatic. You really are a goth, aren't you?" He leaned in like he had a secret to reveal. "That's so hot."

There was nothing left to do but laugh from sheer exasperation. "Do you ever give up?"

"Do you?"

"Of course not."

"See? We're so alike. That's why I'm willing to make you this one-time, very special offer. Hear me out. We have sex—"

She pushed off the ground, ready to make another break for it. "We've already been over this." She patted her pockets, searching for her mini flashlight.

He scrambled to his feet. "No, listen. We have sex, and no matter what—even if I fall madly in love with you—I promise you'll never hear from me again after this training ends."

She paused. *What if . . .*

"You're willing to say anything to get me in bed, aren't you?"

"Well, yeah. But I still mean every word. And it doesn't have to be a bed. We can start right here. I have a blanket!"

"We are not defiling my blanket," she sputtered. The word *yes* was far too close to falling out of her mouth, which meant this situation was getting rapidly out of control.

He clasped his hands. "Look, maybe you do end up breaking my heart. But it doesn't matter, because I swear to you, I will not bother you after this month ends. I don't even have your phone number, so you don't have to worry about me texting despondent poetry and dick pics."

"I shudder to imagine what a despondent dick pic entails."

He continued valiantly, "I vow upon the North Star"—he pointed in the opposite direction—"that I will disappear from your life and you'll never have to think of me again."

Her brain declared it the stupidest plan she'd ever heard.

Her lady parts, on the other hand, were fully on board. Hell, they'd already bought a first-class ticket and left the station on an earlier train.

"Fine," she heard herself say. "Two weeks and that's it."

He raised his palm like he was swearing into office. "Two weeks," he repeated somberly.

"And no mushy stuff while you're here. No more gifts. No more fan fiction–inspiring looks in front of the camera. This stays entirely between us. I prefer to keep my private life private."

"Private," he intoned.

It still felt too dangerous, so she added, "And no cuddling."

He frowned. "But cuddling is a crucial part of sex. *Some* would say the most crucial part. Not me, though, because I am a very manly man and girls have cooties."

"No. Cuddling."

"You really expect me to fall asleep without a comforting hand on your boob—"

"Jon!"

"Right, okay. No cuddling. Got it." He stuck out his hand. "Do we have a deal?"

She stared at his upturned palm, trepidation making her own movements sluggish. Moonlight cast blue shadows on his skin and made the surface of his hand look like a forbidden, dune-sculpted desert.

Her own hand settled into his grip and quickly became lost in it, swallowed up by his enormity. A dark sort of thrill coiled down her spine.

Sometimes, when Jon acted so goofy and chipper, she could focus her gaze elsewhere and think of him like an exasperating cartoon sidekick. But then she'd accidentally look at him—*really* look at him—and remember that Jon Leo was entirely and wholly a man. A huge one who looked at her with those dark-chocolate eyes of his like he wanted to devour her whole. It made her shiver.

"You're cold. We should head back."

She thought of AHAB's sterile surfaces, military cots, and bright LED lights, and it reminded her of work. But out here they had a view of the whole galaxy—most of it, anyway. And the moon was high in the sky, drenching them in the silvery light of the only star that really mattered. The desert wasn't quite the same as the lunar surface, but it was close enough.

"No," she said quietly. "You can keep me warm right here."

CHAPTER 21

Jon sucked in a breath. His skin buzzed with electric charge, his guts coiled tight in anticipation, and his dick throbbed so hard against tight denim he feared losing circulation in the whole area. His body was all in.

His brain, on the other hand, still hadn't caught on that this was really happening. Couldn't hurt to be sure.

"You want to do . . . this . . . out here?" he croaked. He'd been *joking* about that part. (Well, mostly.)

Silver eyes flickered, assessing him like a feral night creature eyeing her prey. "Yeah, I do. Is that a problem?"

"Nope," he wheezed. He cleared his throat, then tried again, more sternly. "No."

Her hand slipped free of his hold and trailed up the inside of his wrist, tracing the surface vein to the crook of his elbow, torching the flesh in its wake. She rose on her tiptoes and murmured close to his ear, "Tell me now if you'd prefer incense, wine, and candles."

"I—" He bit off a dismissal, torn between urgent need that had been building for weeks and the heart-shaped fantasy he'd built up in his mind.

He wanted to lay Reggie down on soft bedding and see her fully naked in the light. He wanted to trace every inch of her skin with his nose, mark her scent in his lungs, and then thoroughly retrace her with his tongue. He wanted to tease her, whisper sweet nothings into the folds of her wet, pink pussy. How was he supposed to worship her out here, on cold dust and gravel?

Maybe she didn't want to be worshipped.

"Huh." Reggie nibbled her lower lip, and the sight of it sucked the oxygen straight out of his chest.

He should have said yes. He could be inside her already if he weren't such a hopeless romantic. What the hell was wrong with him?

His dick throbbed in painful agreement.

Hurriedly, he added, "But I don't need the candles and stuff. I just wanted . . . I'd *hoped* . . . for our first time, that we could take it slow." Her face was unreadable, so he tucked a finger under her chin and gently tilted her face up to his so the moonlight shone on her pale skin. Beneath his touch, he felt her swallow. "Or we could just do what you want. That's fine too."

"What about both?" she whispered. "Fast first, then slow the second time."

"Now that's a compromise I can get behind." He paused. "Or under. Or on top of or . . . how do you like it? I just want to make you feel good. Should I—"

"Jon, stop thinking and kiss me."

He splayed the hand under her chin and slid his grip around the back of her neck, cradling the base of her skull. The blunt edges of her hair brushed the back of his hand, and he had the sudden urge to weave his fingers in and stroke through the short strands. Now that he could touch her freely, he didn't know where to start, and he wanted it all.

Then she tilted her chin up, offering her mouth to him, and he took it. He'd wanted to do it gently, despite her urging—she was so small, and he was this giant, clumsy beast—but at the first taste of her tongue in his mouth, desire slammed into his wall of constraint and shattered it.

A groan ripped from his chest, and the hand he'd buried in her hair curled into a fist, making her whimper.

He let go and gasped for air. "Did I hurt you?"

"Just enough." Her hands flattened on his chest as she pushed him backward.

"What are you—"

She urged him back farther, and his back hit a hard edge. The solar panels. Giant ones, curving up from the earth toward the sky at a near-horizontal incline, and still warm from the sun.

"Don't worry," she assured him. "These are designed to withstand the extremes of space. They won't break."

"We'll see about that." He grabbed her by the waist and hauled her up onto the heated surface.

☆ ⭐ ☆

Jon covered her with his large body, her bent knees parting for him as he held himself above her.

It wasn't enough.

She grasped his shirt in both her fists and jerked downward, arcing her pelvis up at the same time.

He slammed into her with a grunt. *"Fuck,"* he bit out as her calves locked behind his body.

Yes, yes . . . the heavy weight of him. His hard cock aligned between her legs. His control unraveling. This was what she wanted.

She clawed under his shirt, shoving it up so she could feel the muscled planes of his chest. Her nails curled into the flesh, claiming it, and she followed with her mouth. Laving his skin, teeth dragging across the dark points of his nipples.

He shuddered, trying to pull away, but she squeezed her thighs tighter and dragged her clit against his steely length. Even through fabric, it sent sparks down her spine.

"I'm going to lose it," he warned in a strained voice. When he pulled away this time, he succeeded.

She whimpered. "Don't tease me."

"I want you to come fir—" He choked on the words as she tugged her shirt free from her waistband and dragged it up to her collarbone, snagging her sports bra along the way. Cold air swirled around her breasts, the sensitive tips pinching tight at the chill. "Jesus, Reggie."

His mouth closed over her left breast, his right hand claiming the other, rolling the hardened peaks against his tongue and between his fingers. Spears of pleasure jolted through her, building fast but not fast enough.

"More," she urged, her hand pressing his head down to get what she wanted.

His hips jerked against her. One lone thrust at first, like he couldn't help it, but when it made her hum in approval, he did it again, slower and more deliberately, driving them both harder into a spiral of aching need.

Until she couldn't take it anymore.

"Please," she begged, fumbling at the clasp of her pants. Her fingers grazed against wet fabric. Her desire or his? Both, she realized.

She'd barely gotten the cloth past her knees when, with a deep growl, Jon rose up and shoved her farther back on the slanted panel beneath them. His free hand worked her pants down to her ankles, where they jammed up at the tops of her hiking boots.

She started to sit up to finish the job and free her ankles, but he flattened a palm against her rib cage and forced her down.

"Need to take care of something first," he murmured, easing his torso into the shallow diamond-shaped cradle between her legs. As he held her down with his left, his right hand trailed a blazing path down her stomach until it closed over her pussy. The heel of his palm pressed firm against her clit, and his middle finger parted her folds, stroking at her swollen, wet tissue. Jon groaned at the contact, his exhalation pouring his hot breath against her belly. "So good . . ."

Sharp pleasure arced from wherever his fingers touched, but he only grazed her, featherlight and careful. As if she were some skittish doe and not a woman taut on the edge of orgasm.

Forget this teasing—she knew what she needed.

She covered his hand with her own, lacing her fingers with his, and pushed him harder against her. "Like this," she bit out, as spots of lightning shot down her spine and began to gather. Her thighs tightened, her pleasure twisting deeper, as she ground his palm down and her hips worked in rhythm.

Her eyes squeezed shut. She was close, so close . . .

And that was when he tore his hand away.

Before she could complain, he moved. Shifting his weight lower. A second later, his scalding mouth replaced his hand, devouring her with his tongue like a starving creature at a feast. His moan vibrated against her wetness, and her eyes flew open, her abdomen spasming at the acute, near-painful intensity of it all.

He really is good at thi—

Her eyes flew open as the orgasm punched into her so quickly, so *brutally*, she couldn't move. Her breath flew out of her chest, the cry stuck in her throat, as her entire being seized in one overwhelming wave of agonized ecstasy.

And still, he kept going, driving her deeper into the sensation. Spots danced in front of her eyes, sweat breaking out across her flesh. She clawed helplessly at the surface of the solar panels, her nails slipping uselessly on the surface, but he simply kept going, building her up to another, higher peak. One she wasn't ready for.

Her heels drummed a frantic, desperate rhythm. Finally, she managed to inhale long enough to wheeze, *"Jon!"*

He broke away, rearing back onto his knees with a dazed look in his eyes, mouth swollen and glistening in the moonlight, and she finally collapsed. Limp and gasping for air in shuddering heaves, she stared helplessly at the stars.

The Milky Way spilled across the sky, and she was so delirious that she felt like she might fall into it.

"I'm dead," she breathed reverently.

When Jon didn't answer, she somehow gathered the will to lift her head up and saw him still on his knees but with his shoulders bowed inward and chest heaving. His body gleamed with perspiration, his corded forearms bulging from the twin fists propped on his thighs. He looked as if he were in pain, and when Reggie sat up farther, she could see why.

His erection jutted up over the edge of his denim, a half inch of the glistening crimson head visible against the flat of his abdomen. A delicate trail of precum threaded between the tip and that golden expanse of stomach.

He saw her looking and managed a shaky laugh. "I—I really, *really* love eating your pussy."

She licked her lips, a fresh pulse of desire throbbing between her legs. "I can tell." When she reached for him, however, he caught her wrist in an iron grip.

"If you touch me right now, I'm going to come."

"Really?" she whimpered, her thighs clenching. The thought spurred her to twist her wrist free, but he simply caught it with his other hand and levered himself over her. Pinning her down.

He gritted out, "Just give me a sec."

A challenge. She liked that.

Wriggling beneath him, she managed to distract him enough to free a hand and close it over the button at his fly.

He hissed as her pinkie finger intentionally brushed against the slick head of his cock. "Don't," he warned.

But he didn't stop her when she eased the button free and undid his zipper. Nor did he move when she roughly tugged the front of his pants down. When she freed his heavy dick and it fell against the back of her wrist with a smack, he only groaned in surrender.

Her grip closed around it, her thumb reverently sweeping along the smooth underside, and it pulsed in her hand.

"Now or never," he growled.

"Now." She bit her lip. "Condom?"

He gave a terse nod.

Then he fell forward, caging her in with his palms. His weighted length pressed into her soft belly, but the angle wasn't right; she was still trapped by the pants looped around her ankles, and she needed to spread her legs wider. Needed to take him deep.

She whimpered, trying to kick off her boots without his help, but it was no use.

"I need my boots off," she pleaded.

Jon swore, and his hips jolted, grinding his dick against her in a jagged rhythm. "No time."

He grabbed her by the waist and flipped her over, her bare chest lying flush against the panel, and time seemed to pause for that fraction of a second. Her cheek pressed down, absorbing the warmth the sun had left behind. She scented dust, hot metal, and the barest hint of ozone. Cool air prickled as it closed over her heated bottom. Distantly, she understood sounds of a condom packet being torn open, probably with his teeth, and another pained groan came, indicating he'd equipped it.

Yes . . . She closed her eyes, suspended in this near-perfect moment.

Then, with the dull thud of his hand slamming down inches from her nose, time restarted. And he was snaking an arm around her middle and moving her from behind, dragging her hips up until she was on her knees, her back arching for him. A denim-clad thigh roughly shoved her stance wider, and she felt him push the thick head of his cock against her drenched opening.

She'd never been timid. Never. But at that moment, she froze, uncertain. He was so big, and from this angle—

His fingers found her clit and circled, and she cried out as pleasure shot through her and she opened, her pussy melting around the slow but relentless slide of his cock as he filled her. He was big. Maybe too big. If she took his entirety . . .

Could she?

She gasped, overwhelmed, her sheath tightening in sudden hesitation.

He made a strangled sound. "Reg, I'm—"

"It's too much. Too big like this." She squeezed again, as if that would stop him from thrusting further.

"Fuck." His fingers moved faster, and suddenly, another orgasm was building under her pubic bone, sharp and decadent. "Do you want me to stop?"

She answered by pushing back against him, shallowing the arch of her back to take him deeper. Yes, this was what she needed. Now she could control the pace, timing each glide of his cock to nudge against her G-spot when she squeezed her inner muscles. *Perfection.*

He groaned again, and suddenly his body seized, every muscle going tense against her. A single drop of sweat splashed on her back. He trembled against her, frozen, as if in a desperate bid for control. "*Fuck* . . . I'm sorry, I—"

It didn't matter. She was already coming, her body riding a tidal wave of pleasure until it broke, shattering her. He was behind her, his body shaking violently, yet he held himself still until the last moment, ensuring she had control until the end. Protecting her.

Even though she was Regina Hayes, the fearless astronaut, and she didn't need anyone's protection.

They collapsed together, and Jon carefully withdrew from her before rolling onto his back. As steam curled off their bodies, Reggie let her head loll to the side to meet his eyes.

"That was . . ." She bit her lip, fighting against the irrational urge to giggle.

Giggle? Really?

Jon let out a low whistle, his face still flushed from exertion. "I think the word you're looking for is *tubular*."

She swiped a hand over her face, trying to erase her smile, but the expression stubbornly stayed put. At least the next two weeks were starting to look astoundingly pleasant.

Jon pushed up to his elbows, his expression turning serious. "Are you ready, or do you need a few minutes?"

"Ready?"

"Yeah." He leaned down to place a languid kiss on the underside of her left breast. "This time, we do it my way. Nice and slow."

CHAPTER 22

For three days, everything was fine.

Better than fine.

Jon was the consummate actor during the day when the film crew was around, and if Reggie hadn't personally experienced the myriad ways Jon had helped her defile the lunar habitat after each sunset, she'd never suspect a thing was different between them.

Moreover, the astronaut-training business was going splendidly. This week's subject was space botany—a change of pace that brought them out of the field and inside the experimental greenhouse unit that had previously been maintained by the base manager. As it happened, Jon had a green thumb, and he handled himself well in matters of tomato planting and water pH sampling and leaf analyzing. In a total of seventy-two hours, he only murdered four plants, which was a promising success rate for a man who was so large his man bun brushed the roof and his shoulders continually bonked into the low-hanging LED lights.

The cherry on top of Reggie's three-day sundae was Mimi's effusive praise about the quality of the footage they were capturing—delivered via email directly to Deb.

Reggie received a text from the chief astronaut on Wednesday that read simply: **On the right track. Keep up the work.**

Not *keep up the* great *work*, but Deb didn't do superlatives, and it still sent a dizzying rush of adrenaline through Reggie's bloodstream. *I might actually make the Artemis III mission.* She tried quashing the thought, because hope was a dangerously double-edged sword and she preferred to expect the worst in order to avoid disappointment, but Jon's influence had already tainted her mood irrevocably. At one point, she'd caught herself humming under her breath. In front of other people, no less.

"Is that Bon Jovi?" Zach asked, having popped into the central hub for a snack between takes.

She cut the song short. "No."

Zach frowned but thankfully dropped the subject. Jon caught her eye from across the room and winked.

I'm becoming Wes, she realized in soul-shriveling horror.

But even her new musical affliction failed to dampen her spirits. After all, this was assuredly temporary. When the month ended, the mind-numbing oral sex and the earth-shattering regular sex and the soul-rending orgasms delivered via other creative avenues . . . all of it would end abruptly. And so would her unusual good cheer and positive attitude. For now, she could live with it.

The other shoe dropped Thursday morning.

She woke with her back pressed against the surface of a heavily muscled wall that was approximately four degrees cooler than the surface of the sun, an enormous hand splayed across her breast, and her phone indicator light flashing that she'd missed a call while it was on Do Not Disturb mode. Her alarm hadn't even gone off yet.

It was strange to get a call so early in the morning, so Reggie reluctantly untangled herself from Jon's scorching body parts and unlocked the screen.

The first thing she saw was the text from Deb: Call me.

The second was a missed call from Katya.

Her stomach plummeted through the earth and left her hollow. The last time she'd gotten messages like this, it was because a fellow test pilot had died in a crash.

On numb legs, she padded out to the central hub, closing the door behind her—not that she was in danger of waking Jon up. It was the illusion of privacy she was after.

Katya picked up on the first ring and cut directly to the point. "You are famous. Ah, no, that is not the correct word. I am looking for *infamous.*"

✦ ☄ ✦

Jon woke from a deliciously pleasant dream involving a warm breast in his hand and a soft ass nestled against his cock and realized he was in a terrible alternate reality without breasts and asses—at least, not in the immediate vicinity. After all, he could not fathom any other reason Reggie would have gotten out of bed before he'd had a chance to deliver his now-standard morning coffee-and-orgasm combo.

You're getting attached, some sensible voice warned, but Jon dismissed it, because it couldn't be his conscience speaking. He'd banished that thing. It was a nuisance. It reminded him that months of despondent moping were in his future and that he was aggravating Future Jon's inevitable torment by allowing himself to fall in love with someone he couldn't have.

He didn't see a point in putting on clothes, so he was stark naked when he found her in the central hub. Something on her laptop transfixed her attention so utterly that she didn't even comment on his magnificent morning wood.

"Morning," he prompted, strutting to her side to see what she was looking at with the kind of murderous intent that made him a little scared and a lot horny. At least this time, it (probably) wasn't something he'd done. He realized he'd forgotten his glasses when he glanced at the screen and saw a glaring blur, forcing him to ask, "Uh, what are you looking at?"

"Someone leaked pictures of us to the press."

It took a moment, but Jon's mind clicked onto the answer soon enough. "Probably Jacqui," he assured her. "She said something about wanting to lock the role in. Maybe she wanted to get some buzz going."

Reggie made a strangled noise. "Are you kidding me?"

"What's the problem?" Jon squinted, but the screen refused to magically focus for him. "We didn't accidentally reveal NASA secrets or anything, did we? I told her not to mention the aliens."

"Look at the headline! *Out-of-This-World Romance: Space Dude Dating Hot Goth Astronaut*. What's going on here? They took all these shots that make it look like we're *romantic*. They even got a photo of us in the NBL pool that makes it look like I'm humping you!"

"Hold on." He darted back to the room and returned with his glasses. "Oh, wow. That's . . ."

It *did* look like Reggie was humping him.

"Are you smirking?"

He fixed his expression into a concerned frown. "No."

"That conniving brat," Reggie muttered, clicking on another link. Now there was another version of the article on her screen, but with the same zoomed-in photos. Someone had added clip art hearts to this one. He made a mental note to save some of the photos to his phone. Memories and so forth.

"You mean Jacqui?" He frowned. "Don't call her that."

"I meant Yasmin, the NASA intern who sold this photo to the highest bidder. But Jacqui too. This is completely out of line. I signed up to train you as a professional astronaut, not be a prop for a publicity stunt!"

Now was not the time to remind Reggie that this entire training charade was, in fact, a publicity stunt. And based on the number of retweets the first article appeared to have gotten, Jacqui had single-handedly generated enough press to render the final two weeks' worth of footage moot. Rudy was probably pissing himself with joy.

Hell, had he known the public was so stoked on him and Reggie dating, he'd have suggested the fake-relationship angle himself. It always worked in romantic comedies, didn't it? Then they'd "accidentally" fall in real love and—

Reggie's gunmetal glare suggested none of these thoughts were fit for print, so he gave her a solemn nod. "I'll talk to Jacqui and see what she can do about this."

"Thanks," she said. Her phone blinked and she glanced at it, then sucked in air through her teeth. "I'm so screwed. Deb's asked me twice to call her."

He winced. "I'll take responsibility—"

"You can't. That's like asking the kid to take responsibility for the babysitter getting caught messing around on the job."

"Jeez. That's kinda harsh, don't you think?" Jon instantly felt naked. Metaphorically and literally, he supposed. And there was an unfamiliar surge of something that seemed a lot like anger running beneath his skin. But that couldn't be—he never let himself get angry.

Reggie had the grace to look regretful. "Not the best choice of words. I don't think of you as a child. Merely . . . a little clumsy and forgetful. Maybe a little unfocused at times. And not very punctual. Or proactive. And—"

"I don't need to hear the whole list. I'm aware."

"Right. Sorry. I'm still working on this." She scrunched her nose in a way he found adorable, despite the fact she'd just cataloged his flaws like a goddamn soil sample. (Oh yeah, he had it bad.) "I do think you're a lot smarter than people give you credit for, though."

"People meaning . . . you?" he found himself asking, and he wanted to kick himself for it. He wasn't trying to start a fight.

Was he?

"Are you trying to start a fight?"

"Nope." He paused. "Actually, I don't know. Look, it's way too early for this, so I'm just going to . . ." He pointed vaguely in the direction of the bedroom.

She didn't respond, so he walked as calmly as he could into his own living quarters and got dressed. When he came out, Reggie had vanished. Or more likely, she'd stepped outside to return her boss's phone call.

He made himself coffee and stirred it, watching the chunky crystals dissolve with undue interest and thinking about Reggie's assessment of him. There was an idea he'd had poking around in his brain for a while, and now here it was again, waving its hand from the back of the classroom. Except every time he'd considered calling on it, something stopped him. Embarrassment, maybe, or fear—he wasn't sure.

But maybe now was the time to stop being a coward and consider it.

☆ ⋆ 彗 ⋆

He didn't know what the film crew did before their afternoon filming sessions, but Zach didn't hesitate to respond to Jon's text by inviting him to the RV for breakfast.

They sat in camp chairs under the RV's fold-out awning, watching the sunrise desert glow up, eating microwaved breakfast burritos, and shooting the shit for a solid half hour before Jon mustered the courage to pop the question.

"You don't have to answer this if you don't want to," Jon prefaced by saying. The egg wrap sat like lead in his stomach, but he'd given up hope he'd start digesting it until he got past this next part.

"Nah, man. I'm an open book. Hit me," Zach said with a shrug.

"How did you know you had ADHD? Like, did you take a test, or . . ."

Zach blinked at him from behind his thick glasses. "Hold up. You have it too, right?"

"What?" His heart started to race, and he blurted, "No, I don't."

"Oh. *Oh*. I thought for sure . . ." Zach's whole face colored. "Shit, super-duper apologies, my good man. Usually we kinda recognize our own, like a sort of kindred spirit thing."

Jon shook his head. *He's wrong,* his twisting gut insisted. Egg-flavored acid welled in the back of his throat, but he forced it down with a swallow. He would not upchuck his breakfast. (Not here, anyway.)

"Hey, I feel really bad. Sometimes I just say things without thinking about them first." Zach frowned. "But to answer your question, I got diagnosed at thirteen. I guess my parents got sick of report cards saying how smart I was, if only I'd try harder and, y'know, actually do my homework. So they took me to this special doctor, who asked me a bunch of questions, and then they put me on Ritalin. Man, that stuff is *wild*. It was way too much for me, so they kept trying different things, and eventually I got medication that worked."

"And?" Jon asked, but he wasn't sure exactly what he was asking.

Somehow, Zach seemed to know. "That first day I took the right meds was probably the best day of my life. I straight up bawled. It was like . . ." His hands pawed at the air, searching for description. "You know how sometimes everything feels so *loud*?"

Boy, did he. Jon nodded.

"For the first time in my life, it all went quiet, and I could hear myself think. And you know what? I was a little pissed about it too. I was like, Is this really how it is for everyone else? All the time? Damn, that's super unfair. It's like everyone else has all the loot box upgrades in a video game and I don't. Sure, it sucks taking meds all the time, but they're like my loot box. They make the game more fair." He gave Jon a sideways glance. "But lots of people with ADHD don't take anything for it. Everyone finds what works for them. My sister has it, and she just does a ton of yoga and meditates and stuff. That's cool too."

"Yeah, that's cool," he repeated lamely.

Autopilot ensured Jon responded with the appropriate pleasantries and "I should get going" excuses before returning to AHAB for one last day of experiments before the holiday weekend, but the conversation lingered in Jon's mind.

Fortunately, Reggie was too preoccupied by the morning's media bombshell to notice his own distraction. Apparently, Deb had scolded her for a lack of professionalism and issued a stern warning about the pool incident, but she'd stopped short of further discipline because the positive press had driven so many views to NASA's own social media accounts—and because Reggie had insisted there was "absolutely nothing going on" between them.

The call had undoubtedly tanked Reggie's mood even further. If he hadn't been able to tell by the way she stomped around like a hellishly sexy human thunderstorm, her displeasure was further evidenced by the fact that she didn't notice when Jon dropped his elbow into a petri dish, forcing him to hustle the evidence into the trash can when she wasn't looking.

In front of Mimi and Zach, Reggie was professional and distant, albeit far more polite than she'd been at the start of the month, and Mimi—undoubtedly sensing the tension in the air—wisely avoided the topic of their miniature scandal (particularly since it was quite obvious she and Jacqui were coconspirators).

As he'd promised Reggie, Jon left a voice mail for Jacqui, but his workaholic publicist had chosen *now* to respect weekends and holidays, and her response was a short text explaining she was hopping on an earlier flight to visit her parents for Christmas in Miami and that she'd call him after the weekend. When he conveyed this to Reggie, she muttered something about "intentional" and "mastermind," which seemed like an accurate assessment of the situation, though he knew better than to voice such an unpopular conclusion.

Before he knew it, the sun had set, and neither of them had brought up the elephant in the room.

Was there still anything between them?

✧ ⭐ ✦

Reggie was in danger. Not from a physical threat—that, she could handle. No, this was worse.

Jon was ruining her defensive perimeter, melting her icy walls and leaving her with a giant, messy puddle of discombobulated emotions. And the sex had only made things worse.

She'd thought she could compartmentalize Jon, just like everything else, by quite literally containing their relationship within AHAB's walls. But the leaked photos reminded her that life didn't work that way.

And tomorrow morning, he was coming with her to see her parents. What had she been thinking, agreeing to that?

She had to stanch this—whatever *this* was becoming—before Jon spilled over into any more of her real life.

But there was a problem with having sex with someone you were temporarily living with: you couldn't avoid them by refusing to answer their calls and texts.

When she came out of the bathroom in the bike shorts, tank top, and socks she'd worn to bed every night (except the last three), Jon was sitting on her cot in only his loose pajama pants, a hopeful twinkle in his big brown eyes.

Shit. She stopped in front of him and squared her shoulders, prepared to give him the Talk.

"Hey," he offered in a low voice. "Nice socks. You got those in . . . nude?"

"Oh, for fuck's sake." How could he disarm her so thoroughly and so efficiently? The man had some sort of superpower.

He winked at her. "Exactly what I was thinking."

"Jon . . ."

"Nope. Don't say it. Don't you dare say it. If you say this was all a huge mistake, it becomes canon. But if you don't say it, we can go on having moon-rocking sex like nothing ever happened." His hand slid around the back of her thigh and nudged her closer, and her traitorous body went pliant. The velvet-soft tip of his nose brushed back and forth along the strip of bare skin between her shorts and top. Goose bumps bloomed in its wake.

"We really shouldn't," she whispered, very unconvincingly. "We have an early-morning flight to Boston."

Her hands came to rest on his broad shoulders.

"You're probably right," he surprised her by saying, but he followed it with, "Counterpoint: let's do it anyway."

His breath burned a trail of fire down to the apex of her thighs and pressed a reverent kiss over her clit through her underwear, making her breath rush out from a sudden punch of desire. What a cheater. "Do you want me to stop?" he rasped.

Never. That was the problem.

Hours afterward, Reggie lay in Jon's arms, unable to sleep.

She should have sent Jon back to his own quarters, but his skin was warm, and with AHAB's air temperature set to an energy-efficient sixty-six degrees, it felt like a guilty treat to wallow in such a decadent heat source.

Nevertheless, every muscle in her body was wound tight, poised to flee from impending threat. It was always like this before a trip home.

Her sore shoulder twitched, and she reflexively went to massage it. The motion caused Jon to stir, his arm banding tighter around her stomach.

"Hey," he murmured against her nape. "You know I've got your back, right? Tomorrow. With your parents. Whatever you're worried about, just know I'm there."

Then his hand skimmed up her side and replaced hers, gently kneading the stubborn knot that had plagued her for weeks. It began to melt under his touch.

An automatic *I don't need anyone's help* formed in her mouth. Instead, she swallowed the words and whispered, "Thank you."

CHAPTER 23

There really was snow on the ground in Boston!

Sure, it had last snowed days ago, which meant the roads themselves were clear and the snowbanks on the side of the highway weren't exactly white. More of a . . . smoggy slush. But it was still authentic frozen water, and he was 100 percent going to make a snow angel later. Not right now, because he was driving and Reggie was glaring at him in a way that suggested there was a distinct possibility he wouldn't live to see Christmas morning. But if he was destined to die at the hands of a beautiful woman, he'd do it while rolling around in filthy gray snow like a true American man.

"Take this exit," she shouted over the wind.

The GPS lady expressed concern about their sudden course change, but Reggie turned off the navigation and directed him to a sprawling shopping mall. It was Christmas Eve, so the nearest parking spot he could find was on another planet, and when he tried to stop to allow a woman to cross in front of the car, she flipped him off for no discernible reason, but he was still having an incredible time. What a true Boston experience this was shaping up to be!

He killed the engine and grinned at Reggie over the top of his Ray-Ban knockoffs. "See? If we weren't in a convertible, we wouldn't get to hear the locals swearing at us."

"You're a lunatic. And you know I don't buy your story about this being the only car left." Her eye shadow was extra smoky today, and Jon suspected it was her form of war paint.

He cast her an affronted look. "I begged them for a sensible sedan. Do you think I *want* to roll up to your parents' place in a totally bitchin' Camaro convertible?"

The car was bitchin', indeed. And candy-apple red. And it would have been a very expensive rental if Bonnie at the Hertz counter hadn't been a huge *Space Dude* fan and offered him a complimentary upgrade to any of their choicest sports models. What did Reggie want him to do? *Not* drive around Boston in the most obnoxious and seasonally inappropriate vehicle available?

As they headed into the mall, a gaggle of teenagers in puffy coats caught sight of him and began doing that whisper-squeal thing he was all too familiar with. He slowed, reluctantly prepared to be besieged by fans, but Reggie pushed him forward like a no-nonsense prison warden.

"Not today," Reggie snapped as they swept by.

Sorry, he mouthed to the crestfallen teens. Several of the girls glared daggers at Reggie, and Jon entertained a brief, dazzling fantasy of going everywhere with Reggie and her forbidding aura, thus never having to sign *Surf the gravity wave, dude* on the back of anyone's Forever 21 receipt ever again.

"Let's make this quick. I need to buy something to wear to dinner tonight, and you probably do too."

He looked down at his standard denim-and-T-shirt combo. This shirt had a dolphin over the pocket, and he was rather fond of it. "What's wrong with what I'm wearing?"

As she led them to a store with a striped awning and fake shutters on the display windows, Reggie explained, "The Hayes family is very traditional, and Christmas Eve dinner is a somewhat formal affair."

She held up a chunky beige sweater to his chest, sharp brows slashing down below her bangs.

"You want me to dress like the captain of a fishing boat?" he asked, maybe a little too eagerly. Reggie hooked the sweater back on the rack, but he'd seen this coming and was already flagging down a store employee.

A lovely man named Hardley in a navy knit blazer thing bounded to Jon's side and offered his assistance, to which Jon replied in his finest Bostonian accent, "Yeah, uh, look, buddy, I'm tryin' to look wicked nice for this fancy broad's parents—*oof!*"

Reggie's elbow knocked the wind right out of him. With a blinding smile, she interjected, "Let's get him some plain black slacks and a white button-up, shall we?"

"And a plaid bow tie," Jon wheezed to Hardley's departing back.

Boy, was he having the best time. Most importantly, Reggie looked like she wanted to feed him his own liver, which meant his plan to redirect Reggie's obvious anxiety about their upcoming visit was going splendidly.

☆ ⭐

Reggie made Jon park the Camaro on the street, which meant they had to walk up the hill to the gated entrance to the long hedge-and-oak-lined driveway leading to the Hayeses' historic estate.

Which suited Reggie fine.

She entered the gate code, but nothing happened.

"Great. They've changed the code again," she muttered, punching the call button and waiting as it dialed the main house. The odds her mother had simply forgotten to inform Reggie about the updated code were zilch—though Dr. Victoria Hayes was closing in on three-quarters of a century, the former child prodigy still had a near-perfect photographic memory.

Reggie hadn't even gotten to the front door, and already the pointed jabs had begun.

"I just want to say—" Jon began.

The speaker began to ring, and Reggie held up a hand.

He said sotto voce, "You look smokin' hot in that dress. I'd love to bend you over that shrub—"

She hushed him again just in time for her mother's impeccably crisp voice to answer, "You have reached the Hayes residence."

"It's me. Regina." She waited a beat, just to be petty, then added, "Your one and only progeny."

"We expected you earlier."

A brisk wind swept up Reggie's stocking-clad legs. "Can you buzz us in, please?"

"Pardon, but who is 'us'?"

Ha. A spiteful ember glowed in her chest as she replied primly, "I've brought a guest. A colleague of mine." Her mother despised unexpected guests, but societal norms required she welcome Jon with all the bells and whistles. Furthermore, it would torment the woman to wonder whether her daughter was fucking a man who wore plastic sunglasses in December. Even though she and Jon would comport themselves with the utmost propriety, there'd still be a hint of uncertainty about their relationship, and the concept of uncertainty drove her mother absolutely batshit insane.

"I'll have Cecilia prepare him a room."

"No need! The Best Western had several cancellations. Isn't that wonderful?"

The speaker clicked off abruptly, and a buzz preceded the automatic gate reeling open. She glanced at Jon, who was looking at her with a sort of wide-eyed sympathy. "Shall we?" she prompted.

"That's really how your mom talks to you?"

"Actually, I think she's in a sentimental mood today," Reggie said dryly. "She called their house manager by her name instead of 'the house manager.'"

"House manager?" Jon's brown eyes were the size of ornament balls now.

"Cecilia's been with them a whole two years. I think it's a record. When I was growing up, they usually lasted months at best."

They started up the drive. Despite the flawless coating of ivory snow all over the rest of the manicured garden, the cobblestone driveway was clear. It was a quarter of a mile long, and all of it was retrofitted with underground heated pipes.

Not even the elements could best Admiral and Dr. Hayes in their stronghold.

Jon, meanwhile, was looking around at the colonial estate like it was his first time at Disney World. "You grew up here? Are you descended from Paul Revere or something?"

"Is that the only Bostonian historical figure you could think of?"

"Uh, *no*. I paid lots of attention in my US history class. Lots."

"Name another one."

"Easy." He gave her a sly glance. "Mr. Boston."

"Who—"

"He's related to Mr. Dunkin' Donuts. Surely you've heard of him?"

Reggie sighed and decided to surrender before he went off naming every coffee brand he could think of merely to be annoying. "No, I'm not related to Paul Revere. But I am descended from an unsullied line of elitist assholes, should you wish for my autograph later."

He looked over both shoulders, then swiped a hand under her jacket and trailed it ever so saucily along the top of her thigh. "I'd love to sully your elitist asshole."

She batted his hand away. "Paws off, perv," she chided him, but she had to bite the inside of her lip to contain her smile.

When they got to the front door, Cecilia was waiting for them. The house manager was a stocky white woman of indeterminate middle age and nondescript features with brown hair pulled back in a low bun, but Reggie could tell the woman was one of her father's hires by her military-stiff posture and the precise way she hung their coats in the entryway. No wonder she'd lasted so long—the Navy had a way of getting one used to meeting impossible expectations.

"Admiral and Dr. Hayes are in the drawing room," Cecilia told them, gesturing down the long, wood-paneled hallway to a set of closed doors. "May I offer refreshments?"

"No, thank you," Reggie replied, at the same time as Jon said, "Oooh, what are my options?"

Cecilia's impassive mask didn't slip an inch. "Might I offer you Pellegrino, Perrier, Evian—"

Reggie placed a hand on Jon's arm and gave him an apologetic look. "The Hayeses do not consume alcohol. It clouds the intellect."

"But you—"

She squeezed his bicep. Hard. "Let's just get this over with, okay?" When Cecilia withdrew, Reggie gave Jon a final once-over. "Is it too late to convince you to change your mind about the vest?"

He looked down at his black velvet vest with a skiing penguin in a red Santa hat emblazoned over the breast pocket. "It's festive! Besides, it matches your dress."

She looked down at her wool sheath. The sleeves went to her wrists, the hem touched her knees, and the high collar scraped her chin, but she'd chosen it—and the matching clutch—specifically for its vicious bloodred hue. Next to each other, with Jon's all-black ensemble and his dark hair pulled back, they looked like a pair of eclectic yet chic vampires. Her mother would *despise* it.

"Fine," she relented. He started forward, but something provoked her to squeeze his arm a final time (other than the fact it felt deliciously warm and huge beneath her fingers). "Wait. I need you to understand something before we go in. My parents can be . . . blunt. Just promise me that no matter what they say, you won't try to argue with them."

He narrowed his eyes. "Define *argue*."

"Jon. Promise me," she pleaded. "I'm used to the way they are, but it can be a jarring experience for those who aren't."

"You're worried about *me*?" He gave her an odd look before shrugging in apparent acquiescence. "Relax. I'll be on my best behavior."

The knots in her shoulders were so tight they threatened to suck her entire head into her torso, but she didn't dare keep her mother waiting any longer. She gave Jon a hesitant nod and forged forward, but he stayed put.

He cleared his throat and glanced pointedly down at where her hand still clutched his arm in a white-knuckled grip. "Didn't you say you were going to introduce me as just a friend?"

"Oh, right." She released him, wishing it didn't feel like she was jettisoning her only flotation device.

I'm thirty-five years old, she reminded herself. *An accomplished naval aviator and test pilot. A fucking astronaut—*

The drawing room doors swung open, revealing her mother's forbidding silhouette. The paltry courage Reggie had collected instantly slipped away.

"Regina. Do you intend to keep us waiting all evening?"

✧ ⭐ ✦

They were only five minutes into dinner, and Jon wanted to punch both of Reggie's condescending, sour-faced parents into the stratosphere. Problem was, he'd never punched anyone in real life—only in rehearsed fight scenes—and he wasn't sure he could pull it off.

Jon sipped a spoonful of the bland broth-type liquid in front of him and eyed Admiral Hayes surreptitiously. The ancient man at the head of the table looked like he might still put up a serious fight, especially in his formal Navy dinner suit decked out with so many badges and pins he could open up a hardware shop out of his left breast pocket. Though Reggie's dad looked like he'd once cut an imposing figure, time had withered away his fat and muscle, leaving his shoulders stooped, his fingers clawed, and his square jaw sucked into the hollows of his cheeks. Icy gray eyes glared at the world from sunken sockets, and he hadn't smiled once (maybe ever?). Jon thought he'd make an excellent Bond villain.

As if sensing Jon's regard, the admiral asked in a voice as cold and dry as the desert wind, "You ever served, boy?"

"No, sir," he replied, rather proud of himself for throwing the *sir* in there.

"Of course not. Haven't got the discipline or the spine for it, from the looks of you."

Ooookay. Across from him, Reggie stiffened, so Jon made sure his voice had as much flippant cheer as possible. "You're probably right. That's why I'm an actor!"

"Millennials," Admiral Hayes concluded with vitriolic gusto, stabbing his spoon into his soup.

"Theater, I assume?" Reggie's mother asked. Unlike her husband, Dr. Hayes looked as if she ate the concept of aging for breakfast and washed it down with the blood of her conquered foes. Her gunmetal hair was pulled back into a bun so tight it gave her emotionless face a terrifying face-lift, and her posture was impeccable. She wore pearls and a matching skirt-and-cardigan thing and an invisible cloak of superiority.

He took another sip of his soup. What was this stuff? Low-sodium vegetable stock?

"Nah, mostly Hollywood action flicks and comedies. The feel-good, trashy stuff."

"I see." Dr. Hayes set her spoon down next to her nearly untouched broth. With a practiced, elegant gesture, she motioned for a servant to clear the course.

When the server (whose name Jon had already forgotten) appeared at Jon's side, he made a point to smile and loudly thank her. She did not smile back. Moments of awkward silence later, the next dish appeared: a small plate of undressed romaine lettuce. That was all. No tomatoes or croutons or anything else.

He felt a nudge on his shin and stole a glance at Reggie, who gave an infinitesimal nod toward a silver pitcher in the center of the table. Salad dressing. *Thank fuck.*

What was wrong with rich people? If he had this kind of money, he'd be eating like a king every damn meal. And he wouldn't have servants either. It was super uncomfortable having someone stand and watch you eat. Especially since they didn't have any music playing in the background—only the stilted clink of silverware on porcelain.

Reggie poked at her salad, and Jon had the sudden revelation that this was how she'd grown up. Eating unseasoned food in the creepy silence of an ancient house while strangers hovered nearby and your own parents stared at you like a feral animal they'd invited inside out of obligation. The thought spurred a pang of sadness so sharp he nearly choked on his lettuce.

"Regina, Deborah tells me the Agency has not yet selected candidates for the Artemis mission," Dr. Hayes said after several long minutes of silence. "When will you be informed of your selection?"

Reggie took her time swallowing her bite, forcing her mother to wait. *That's my girl.* "Astronauts are usually given a year's notice to prepare for a mission."

"You are deliberately evading the question," her mother said calmly, but her piercing blue eyes flashed with warning. "I wish to know when *you* will be selected."

Reggie's jaw hardened. "I don't know."

"Don't know? Or perhaps you do know, and you don't wish to share with us. I cannot imagine the selection board overlooking your . . . interview."

"It wasn't an interview. And Milton Fetzer isn't a reporter."

Her mother shook her head and bulldozed forward, undaunted. "Your career may not recover from such a misstep. I must say, I was extremely disappointed in your lack of self-control. Your response to that man was highly inappropriate."

"I'd prefer if we didn't talk about this right now," Reggie replied, but it was like her words were made of smoke and they dissipated before they reached her mother's ears.

"And to discover your gaffe through a colleague, rather than from the source? Humiliating."

Reggie's fork trembled in her grip, but her voice was steady when she answered, "You're right. It was a mistake. However, I have since conducted myself with the utmost integrity, and my record is otherwise flawless—"

"Ha!" barked Admiral Hayes. He sneered at his daughter like he'd stepped in dog shit and found her attached to his shoe instead. Jon waited, expecting the man to explain his outburst, but nothing more came. The admiral continued eating as if the whole conversation wasn't worth his time.

But Dr. Hayes wasn't finished making her point. "You leave one to assume you hope to intentionally disappoint us and your heritage out of spite. Is that what you intend?"

"No, of course not," Reggie said quietly.

"Then I strongly recommend you *ensure* you will be selected for the Artemis III mission, Regina. We do not entertain mediocrity in this household."

What's wrong with these people?

"They'd have to be crazy not to pick Reggie for the moon mission," Jon said. "She's the smartest person I've ever met."

"Doubtless," replied Dr. Hayes with an unsubtle sneer.

He forged on. "Not only is she smart, but she's really determined and hardworking and organized and super good at handling pressure and . . . basically everything. I've been doing a simulated moon mission with Reggie for the past three weeks, and I can say for a fact that if I was a real astronaut, there's no one else I'd rather go to the moon with. But even if she doesn't get picked, I think you should still be really proud of her because she's a total badass babe." He paused, then hurried to add, "Respectfully, of course."

Both parents were glaring at him like he'd stripped naked and farted his way through "Jingle Bells," while Reggie stared, pale and stone faced, at the patterned tablecloth as if she'd plotted an escape into its folds.

It seemed dinner was already beyond repair. Oh well, what a bummer.

Jon stretched and pushed back from the table. "Time to pee!" he announced, pleased to see the Hayeses react with dual expressions of horror. "Reggie, can you show me where the bathroom is?"

Reggie stood like a wooden doll. "All right."

As the door closed behind them, Reggie's father scoffed again, "*Millennials.*"

☆ 🌠 ☆

Reggie started to show Jon to the downstairs bathroom, but he held a finger to his lips and nodded at the grand stairwell. He wanted to go upstairs?

She glanced back at the doors to the dining room, but she couldn't hear a sound. Had this house always had such heavy, stale air? It made her nostalgic for broken filter machines.

Feeling like a burglar in her childhood home, she led the way to the second floor. Everything in this sprawling house felt staged, from its careful carnation arrangements on doilies to the authentic oil paintings displayed under museum lighting to the austere wooden benches at the end of each hallway polished to a sickening gleam.

"No pictures?" he whispered, peeking into one of the guest bedrooms.

Reggie silently pointed at the giant painting hovering over the grand stairwell: a portrait commissioned of her and her parents. She'd been eight, and they'd curled her hair and dressed her like an old-fashioned doll. Her father was in his Navy dress uniform, her mother wore a high-necked blouse and pearls, and no one was smiling. Along the wall down to the entryway was a series of near-identical portraits: evidence of every miserable Hayes family unit since the dawn of "the colonies." Aside from those hideous testaments to tradition, the entire house could have been a museum—her mother disdained personal touches nearly as much as she hated people. And touching.

"Whoa. Creepy." Jon pulled out his phone and snapped a picture before she could stop him. A floorboard creaked as he stepped back, and his gaze snapped to her. "Haunted?"

She rolled her eyes and led him up to the third floor, where her old childhood room was, unsure why she was doing it. Jon clearly didn't have to go to the bathroom, and if they were gone for much longer, she'd have to come up with some excuse to give her parents. But something compelled her to open the door at the end of the hall and flick on the lights.

"This was my way of rebelling," she offered in explanation.

As Jon wandered into the high-ceilinged attic room and turned in a wondering circle, Reggie hung back in the doorway.

See? she wanted to say aloud. *This is who I am—not what you saw back there.* She wasn't sure why it should matter that Jon understood that, but it did.

She'd painted the walls black and splattered them with stars. Everything else, from the bedsheets to the blackout curtains, was a deep navy blue, like the ocean at night. Next to the room's only window was her dust-covered Celestron telescope and a topographical map of the moon. And just to the right of it was her pride and joy: a 2001 Bon Jovi tour poster that was simply a grainy picture of a radio telescope.

"Astrogothic," Jon declared with a slow-spreading grin. "I guess it's exactly what I expected."

Reggie joined him in the room's center. "I'm always surprised to find this room hasn't been redecorated."

"You're a Bon Jovi fan?"

"Oh, no. I just thought the picture was cool."

"Huh." He approached the poster, narrowing his eyes. "It's signed."

"Really? Interesting," she murmured. "I had no idea."

"'To Reggie: It's your life . . . don't bend, don't break, don't back down.'" He gaped at her. "Are you serious? This is legit! You met Jon Bon Jovi?"

She sighed. "No. I won second place in a contest, and the prize was a personalized signed poster. First-place prize was backstage concert tickets, which I did not win. Even though I tried. Really, really hard."

One minute, she was standing still in the middle of her childhood bedroom. The next, she was in Jon's arms, swallowed in a breathtaking hug.

"What's this for?" Her voice came out like a squeak.

His reply came, muffled, from somewhere in her hair. "I felt like it. And I feel bad for you."

She stiffened. "Don't."

She'd grown up with every privilege imaginable—how many other little girls could dream of becoming astronauts and understand that absolutely nothing stood in her way? His pity was misplaced.

"But you wanted those concert tickets so much . . ." He squeezed her tighter, and no matter how hard she wriggled, she couldn't get free. Surrendering was easier.

That was what she told herself, anyway, as she sank into his warmth.

"Why are they like that?" he asked after a few moments.

Reggie closed her eyes. "A therapist could spend years unpacking the answer to that question. But the short answer is that my mother had me at forty because she felt it was her duty to procreate and pass on her exemplary intelligence to another generation of ruthless scientists, and my father wanted a boy to continue the Hayeses' Navy legacy, and neither of them actually wanted to raise a child. Then again, neither of them really got what they wanted either."

"Good." He infused the word with the perfect amount of spite, and it pleased her soul. On the surface, she'd moved past her teenage resentment, but deep down . . .

Fuck 'em.

"We should probably go back down," she said, reluctantly breaking away after what felt like far too long (or maybe just long enough to feel guilty about wanting it to continue). "We only have to get through one more course and then dessert."

Jon cast her a doubtful look. "*Do* we, though?"

"Yes, Jon. We flew all the way out here. You can't just quit thirty minutes into the encounter because it's unpleasant."

"*Can't* we, though?"

She grimaced. "I assure you, as far as awkward Christmas meals go, this is on the tame end. You should have been there when I announced I was applying to become an astronaut instead of continuing my naval career. My father walked out midmeal and didn't speak to me until my grandmother's funeral four years later."

He gaped at her. "Isn't being an astronaut considered, like, the tippy-top tier of excellence?"

"Admiral Hayes thinks the world is his personal Risk board and that American tax dollars are better allocated to blowing up shit here on Earth instead of in orbit. Men like him are why we keep looking for a backup planet." She sighed. "I think his dying regret will be that I'll never lead the charge in World War Three, and I'm starting to realize there's nothing I can accomplish that will make up for that."

"That's horrible. *They're* horrible. Why do you keep coming here?"

"Great question," she said. It really was. "You have no idea how much I've dreamed of storming out of one of these annual dinners in dramatic fashion."

He raised a brow. "And you haven't, because . . . ?"

"It's just not something I could . . . do," she finished lamely.

Had he not met her parents? No one stood up to Admiral and Dr. Hayes—no one would dare. At the height of Admiral Hayes's career, he'd possessed the codes to the national nuclear arsenal. And legend had it that her mother had once made a grad student faint in the middle of defending his thesis by merely *looking* at him (naturally, Deb—being the Klingon enthusiast she was—worshipped the ground Dr. Hayes walked on). Her parents were terrifying and formidable in every way; the most she'd ever had the courage to do was mildly inconvenience and profoundly disappoint them.

Jon's shoulders slumped. "At least take the poster, Reggie. Come on. You can't leave that thing here. It's priceless!"

She hesitated. It *was* priceless, wasn't it? And though it technically belonged to her, it felt oddly like stealing to remove it from her childhood home. She didn't even have the gate code to this place.

Which made the "theft" all the more appealing.

When she finished excavating the ancient thumbtacks, she rolled the poster and tucked it neatly under her arm. Easy enough to hide it in the umbrella stand in the entryway and then snag it on their way out.

"Ready?" she prompted Jon, who'd already managed to get distracted by something on his phone.

"Yeah . . ."

Her neck hairs went on alert. "What are you doing?"

He peeked up at her through his lush eyelashes. "I may or may not have booked us a late-night flight to LA. You want to blow this hot dog stand or what?"

She stared at him, frozen in a flood of panic. "You what? No. *No.* Cancel the tickets. We can't—"

From the second floor came a muffled "Regina?" in her mother's voice.

Jon's eyes widened, but so did his grin. He strode to the window and eyed the slanted roof that it looked out onto. As with most older, colonial-style homes, the attic-level windows were set back from the rest of the roof. "You ever climb out this thing?"

"Yes, but—"

Her mother's voice came again, closer this time. "Regina? We are waiting to serve the main course. Where are you?"

Jon unhooked the lock and swung the window wide. She'd removed the screen at some point in her high school rebellion years, and apparently no one had seen fit to replace it, because Jon was able to squeeze his whole frame out the square hole without obstacle. She also knew from experience that from the third-floor rooftop it was a short drop to one of the decorative balconies on the second floor, then another easy shimmy down onto the shallow-sloped wooden awning that covered the back porch.

From the smug way Jon glanced back at her through the opening, he'd figured that out too.

Was he really trying to convince her to sneak out of her parents' house on Christmas Eve? Was this really happening?

"I don't run from fights. It's cowardly," she told him.

He held out his hand. "Come on, Reg. Don't think of it as running. Think of it as choosing your battles wisely. It's *strategy*."

Adrenaline bubbled through her system. The thrill of danger that had fueled her every time her jet had lifted off the tarmac. Every time she'd suited up and leaped into the vacuum of space.

Footsteps sounded on the stairs to the third floor. *Now or never . . .*

Reggie raced to the window. Hissed, "Move!" and scrambled out onto the snowy rooftop. Jon was right there ahead of her, clambering with surprising agility across the low-sloping shingles. She pointed out the path, and Jon took the lead. When he landed on the balcony, he reached up, ready to catch her if need be. As she shucked up her skirt and hooked her booted heels into the gutter for purchase, he let out a low whistle.

"Are those garters?"

"*Shh!*" She handed him her poster and her clutch for safekeeping, glanced over her shoulder to ensure her aim was true, and let go. Jon caught her like she weighed nothing, carefully sliding her down his body until her shoes crunched into wet snow. She supposed it would have been romantic if they weren't on the lam and all.

"Bad, bad girl," Jon whispered against her ear, and she shivered.

"We left our coats inside."

He glanced behind him, as if he was considering the prospect of going back for them. "Were you really attached to that coat?"

"Not particularly," she admitted. Her phone and credit cards were in her clutch, and the rest of her luggage was in the car.

"Well then." He nudged her forward and helped her climb over the railing onto the porch awning. There was only a foot-wide gap between the two surfaces, and they both made it over without issue. "It's sixty-eight degrees in Los Angeles right now."

She'd never been to Los Angeles beyond a layover at LAX. Lord knew what they'd do there for the weekend, but she supposed it wasn't the worst place to spend the holiday. After all, they were currently escaping from the *worst* place like fugitives in the night.

Jon hopped down from the awning and helped her down in the same way. Then, when he was sure she'd landed safely, he returned her belongings and inexplicably plopped onto his back in the middle of the snow-covered lawn.

"What are you doing?" Reggie asked, glancing at the nearest set of ground-floor windows, where she could see Cecilia and two of the temporary waitstaff bustling around the kitchen. Fortunately for her and Jon, it was dark, and no one was looking out the window—if they had, they'd only have seen their own reflections staring back at them.

Jon's arms and legs swept back and forth in wide arcs. "What does it look like I'm doing?" He hopped up and admired his artwork. "Snow angel, duh."

His entire back side was soaked through, and when he shook his head, his hair sprayed icy droplets all over her. She chided in a hushed voice, "Great, now I'm wet too."

Before Jon could issue a predictably lewd reply, the sound of a sliding door opening had them both freezing in alarm. "Regina? Are you out there?"

Reggie locked eyes with Jon, nodded toward the driveway, and mouthed, *Run.*

CHAPTER 24

Growing up without much money, Jon had become accustomed to discounted everything. Getting a sweet deal was a point of pride, and if you could get designer goods on the down low, that was even better; if you were asked about your new sneakers, you leaned in close and whispered, "Knockoffs. Forty bucks on eBay!" Hell, half the appeal of serving at an LA restaurant was eating the misordered dishes sent back from the dining room (those who might judge had never experienced the thrill of cramming an entire filet mignon down their gullet in a freezing walk-in after working a ten-hour shift on an empty stomach).

So when he got to the ticket counter at Logan Airport and threw down his credit card, a primal, deeply ingrained part of his soul howled in agony. He ignored it. "I'd like to upgrade us to first class, please."

Sure, it was probably close to a thousand bucks, but it wasn't like he didn't have good credit. He'd pay it off when he got the next royalty check from *Space Dude*. No big deal.

"Jon, you don't have to do this," Reggie whispered, looking up at him with that same shell-shocked expression she'd had since he'd convinced her to climb out the window of her childhood bedroom. She still wore her sexy Christmas dress, but cold and exhaustion had turned her nose a matching rosy red.

A convertible hadn't, in fact, been the best choice.

"Babe. I got this. What's the point of being a minor celebrity and a major astronaut if you can't travel in style on Christmas? Consider it my gift to you, from Santa."

"If you're paying, then Santa has nothing to do with it."

"Reggie, I'm *Jewish*. I don't know how Santa works," he reminded her.

Reggie rolled her eyes but didn't argue further.

The ticket agent, who was well into her finest years (and thus had absolutely no fucking clue what a Space Dude was) clicked something on her screen and gave a sympathetic wince. "For this flight, you're looking at sixty-two hundred."

Oof. "Total?" he managed to say calmly.

"Per seat. Sorry, hon, but it's nearly sold out." *And it's Christmas Eve, and you booked this flight two hours ago, idiot,* was the unspoken subtext.

"Oh." He cleared his throat. How awkward. He'd already spent most of the check he'd gotten up front for *Escape Velocity*, and after agent fees, publicist fees, stylist fees, and all the stuff that had seemed necessary to further his Hollywood career, he wasn't exactly rolling in celebrity levels of cash from *Space Dude*—which, during its initial run in theaters, had failed so spectacularly that someone at the studio had probably gotten fired for having green-lit its production at all.

"Are you Mileage Club members? You can always get on the wait list for an upgrade at the gate," the agent suggested, looking so pained on Jon's behalf that he briefly considered faking his own death just to get out of the whole thing with a shred of dignity remaining.

Reggie laid a hand on his shoulder and smiled—*smiled!*—at the gate agent. "Thank you, we'll do that. Happy holidays!"

Then she, thankfully, dragged him through security before he could humiliate himself further by getting his credit card declined in front of the woman of his dreams.

"At least we got seats next to each other this time. We can take turns napping on each other's shoulders," she reassured him as she hauled both their bags off the security belt as if they weighed nothing.

"You can have the window," he offered, cringing a bit inside at how pathetic it sounded, but she only gave him a grateful smile.

"Thanks." Then, out of nowhere, she rose up on her tiptoes and landed a peck on his cheek. "For everything."

Well, *now* he could die a happy man. He didn't even care that he was grinning like a fool as they rolled up to the gate, high on Reggie's freely offered affection.

"Reggie, is that you?" called a man's voice.

He and Reggie turned in unison to see a short, redheaded man in a pilot's uniform break off from his airline posse and beeline toward them in that eager run-walk that people did while dragging a rolling suitcase.

Reggie stepped away from Jon. "Vince. Good to see you . . . here."

Vince grinned. "Did you just land?" As if suddenly noticing Jon's existence, the man thrust out a hand. "Vince Favell. Old friend of Reggie's from our early flying days."

The wink he threw Reggie's way seemed awfully chummy for "old friends," but who was Jon to judge? He was on friendly terms with nearly all his ex-girlfriends (except Clarissa, who'd joined a multilevel marketing scheme, eventually leaving Jon no choice but to block her so he'd stop buying hundreds of dollars' worth of candles out of pity).

Jon introduced himself, then added the diplomatic half truth, "I'm playing an astronaut in a movie, and Reggie's been patient enough to spend a few weeks teaching me how it's done."

Reggie told Vince, "Actually, we landed this morning, but there's been a change and we have to fly back to Los Angeles tonight." Then she cleared her throat and tucked her hair behind her ear—something Jon had never seen her do before. "I was going to text you . . . unfortunately, I have to cancel our plans."

Plans?

Vince's grin wilted. "Sorry to hear that. I was really looking forward to catching up. Y'know, now that things are finalized on my end with Steph, I thought maybe . . ." He trailed off. Seemed to take in Reggie's stiff smile and whatever Jon's own face looked like. Recalibrated. "You know what? No worries. Totally misunderstood signals from the control tower, so to speak."

"No, no, it's my fault," Reggie argued half-heartedly.

Vince's smile didn't falter, but his eyes ping-ponged between Jon and Reggie with something bordering on horrified regret. "No, really, *completely* my bad take. Seriously, I—"

"Vince, honestly—"

Jon couldn't take any more of this. He reached out and clapped a reassuring hand on Vince's shoulder. "Our flight doesn't leave for about forty-five minutes. How about we buy you a beer?"

But if anything, Vince looked even more despondent. "I appreciate the offer; however, I don't think my next set of passengers will. Still have one more flight out and back to JFK tonight before I hole up alone for the holiday weekend, so . . ."

Now it was Jon's turn to inwardly cringe.

In that moment, he couldn't determine who felt the *most* uncomfortable in their absurdly polite love triangle.

Vince scratched the back of his head and nodded at the gate they were standing near. "You're on this flight?" When Reggie nodded, the pilot breathed a sigh of pure relief. "Let me talk to my colleagues over there about getting you on the upgrade list."

When Reggie started to protest, Jon jumped in to spare the poor man. "That would be incredible, my good dude."

Less than an hour later, he and Reggie took off for Los Angeles in fully reclining seats with hot towels steaming against their eyelids. Gratis.

When the towel cooled, Jon swiped it down his face and found Reggie looking at him, nibbling on her lower lip like she had something to say. "About Vince . . ."

"He's a very generous man."

"But I should explain—"

Jon held up a hand and said, gently but firmly, "Don't."

"You don't care? At all?" She blinked at him like he'd announced he planned to parachute out the side door.

He sighed. "That you've had sex before? No. Okay, *yes*, but only because I'm glad you've at least had some fun when you aren't working, which I'm guessing is what you do every other waking minute."

While Reggie absorbed this, the flight attendant stopped by and offered them glasses of champagne. Reggie politely declined.

"I'll have her glass," Jon said cheerily, plucking two plastic flutes from the tray. He waggled his eyebrows. "Did *you* know all the drinks are free in first? I had no idea. Almost makes me want to accept that *Space Dude 2* offer. Then I can have unlimited sky drinks!"

Reggie gave him well-deserved side-eye but didn't dignify the declaration with a response. He'd finished both glasses and flagged the attendant down for a refill when Reggie said, "I was going to sleep with him, you know."

The attendant stopped by, and Jon handed her his empty cups. "Another round, sir?"

Jon apologized. He'd changed his mind.

When the attendant departed, Reggie continued, "Do you not care about that either?"

"The champagne? Technically, it's prosecco. Which the French would have you believe is inferior, but—"

"*Jon.*"

"Fine," he gritted out. The cabin lights dimmed, and he lowered his voice. "Yeah, I care. But you told me I'm not supposed to."

Her brow furrowed. "You're right."

"So. I'm pretending like I don't care. Which is a problem, because I obviously do. And like most problems in life, including but not limited to the very temporary state of this thing going on between us, it would be much easier if we stop talking about it and pretend it doesn't exist."

With that, he tugged his (complimentary!) sleep mask down and pretended to go to sleep. Reggie made a sound that implied she thought he was being rude to so abruptly cut off the conversation, and she was probably right.

But it was better than letting her see the self-pitying tears welling behind his eyelids.

Thanks to the time zone change, they landed at LAX just before midnight, feeling remarkably refreshed—on Reggie's part, anyway. Jon, who looked like he was mere breaths away from death despite ostensibly sleeping the whole flight, passed out in the rideshare and spent the nearly hour-long drive drooling on the back seat window.

Reggie had assumed they were going to his place, but when the driver pulled up in front of a petal-pink, one-story house with a lawn chock full of giant ceramic animals, she had to shake him awake to ensure they hadn't been kidnapped and taken to some gingerbread witch's home to be baked into cookies.

"Is this your house?"

Jon swiped at his drool and squinted at her. He'd taken out his contacts at some point during the flight and had mumbled something earlier about forgetting his glasses. "Kind of?" he replied in a raspy voice.

He stumbled his way out of the car, grunted thanks to the driver, and somehow managed to carry all their luggage from the trunk to the front door without tipping over. Reggie followed, hesitant and suddenly aware of her smeared makeup, wrinkled dress, and sweaty armpits.

Please tell me we're not at his mom's place. Please, please, please . . .

An all-too-recognizable blonde woman in a floor-length silk robe swung open the door and swept out onto the front step, her arms and her smile miles wide. "Pooh Bear!"

"Hey, Mom."

Of *course*. This was the price she paid for trying to be fun and impulsive. Reggie glanced longingly at the departing car.

"Mom, this is Reggie," Jon said, having already chucked their luggage through the doorway. He held his arm out, as if Reggie was supposed to duck beneath it for an embrace. She stayed anchored to the walkway.

"Hello," Reggie offered with a stiff wave.

Jon's mother gave her son's shoulder a playful smack. "You heathen. Let the poor creature come inside and get washed up before you force her to interact with your mother. For fuck's sake, it's the middle of the night." She rolled her eyes and gestured Reggie forward. "I'm so sorry about my son. He was raised by wolves, so I'm not responsible for this. Excellent day care rates, though."

Reggie expected to be shown to a guest room, but Jon guided her out to a tiny one-bedroom cottage in the backyard. He flicked on the lights and told her, "This place is where my mom and I lived when I was a kid. Now that she owns the main house, I kinda just crash here on weekends and holidays. I promise I don't actually live with my mom. I rent an apartment closer to Hollywood."

The living room and kitchen area was well maintained and cozy, even if the decor was outdated and the kitchen wallpaper a bit yellowed. Then he showed her the bedroom, with its wrinkled movie posters, laminated constellation maps, and stick-on, glow-in-the-dark stars, and the space behind her breastbone glowed with a sort of aching recognition. The faded bedspread was even the same navy blue.

"It's just like mine," Reggie murmured, gingerly sitting on the bed.

"The trashy, low-budget version . . . sure."

She glanced over her shoulder at Jon's too-casual posture as he leaned against the doorframe, hands stuffed into his pockets, and fought the odd urge to reciprocate the hug he'd given her back at her parents' place.

A thought struck her: if this was his childhood bedroom, his mom had likely slept on the couch in the living room. That kind of selfless, motherly love was a foreign concept to Reggie. How could Jon feel ashamed of how he'd grown up when he'd had *that*?

"Didn't you say your father paid child support?"

Jon's gaze slid away. "We got by."

"I assure you," Reggie said quietly, "the only judgment behind that question was directed at the man who wouldn't take care of his kid as much as he could have. Your mom seems like a lovely, kind, funny person."

"She has what she deserves now," Jon replied with firmness. The topic was clearly closed. He kicked the door shut behind him and threw himself down on the bed behind her, kicking off his shoes as he went. His arm snaked around her midsection and dragged her into the little-spoon position. "Enough talk. Bedtime now."

Strangely, Reggie didn't feel like struggling out of his embrace. Though she wasn't at all tired, something about the way his big body folded around hers felt right. Her spine melted into the curve of his chest, her hips sinking into the shallow well between his hip bones, and even though he was visibly exhausted—had he not slept on the flight at all?—his cock was semihard against her bottom.

A wicked urge possessed her. She'd already made so many ill-advised, uncharacteristically wild decisions in the last twenty-four hours. If she was throwing caution to the wind for this brief window in time, why not go all in? In seven days, their training would wrap and Jon Leo would disappear from her life without a trace. *Shouldn't I indulge while I can, just to see what it's like to be fully bad?*

When she nestled in closer, his giant hand closed over her thigh and squeezed. "Stop that," he growled into the back of her neck.

She wiggled in encouragement. "Why?"

His hand slid up past the hem of her dress, his forefinger tucking under one of the garter clips and drawing a slow circle on the skin of her inner thigh. The hard length along her ass pulsed, and Jon breathed in, long and slow, before answering, "You make a compelling argument."

The garter clip snapped free.

✩ ⭐ ✩

By the time they slunk back into the main house the next morning, it was close to 0900 hours. Reggie had changed into a baggy tee and a pair of Jon's old sweatpants, cinched as tight as they'd go and the hems rolled up ten inches. She'd shoved her hair into a stubby ponytail, though every last strand in her bangs pointed in a different direction. A lazy swipe of her mascara brush was the only makeup she could be bothered to apply.

Several scathing texts from her mother had materialized on her phone since their grand escape, proving that Dr. Hayes did, in fact, know Reggie's phone number.

Reggie texted back: **We're in LA. Merry Christmas!**

Then she temporarily blocked the number.

She was a new woman: No-Fucks Reggie. Except she had most certainly fucked this morning—repeatedly, and with enthusiasm. Her skin buzzed with carryover energy. Her soul weighed nothing. Her stomach growled, and Reggie announced to Jon that she was *starving*.

"I hope you're ready for a Stern Christmas Day classic," he told her as they came into the kitchen. "Every year, we celebrate this most sacred of holidays with a breakfast buffet and a nature-documentary marathon."

His mother greeted them as they entered from where she sat on the kitchen counter in a white sweatshirt with kittens on the front. On the Formica table next to her was a spread of no fewer than twenty cereal boxes.

"Merry Christmas, you two lovebirds!" boomed a man's voice. An older Black man with a luxurious mustache and a ponytail waved at them from the recliner in the living room. He raised his bowl. "The *Raptor Road Trip* special is just getting started, so go ahead and help yourself to some cereal and kick back. The Froot Loops are in season."

"Oh, Reggie, I haven't introduced you to Tom yet," his mother said, giving her son an affectionate hair ruffle. "I'm still on vacation brain, you see. We just got back from the most *incredible* time in Greece."

Jon patted down his hair and waved at Tom. "Weren't you two in Italy?"

"Oh, we *were*. But we met this wonderful couple at a party, and they invited us to tour the Mediterranean on their boat, and when we landed in Greece, we met *another* couple who invited us to stay at their vacation home to celebrate their elopement, and you know how these things go." His mother winked at Tom, who gave a rumbly laugh. "What were their names again? Mary and Rufio?"

"What your mother is trying to say is, we took quite a bit of acid and weren't sure what country we were in for most of the trip."

His mother sighed dreamily. "Quite a bit."

Jon, who didn't appear at all shocked, merely gave his mother an indulgent smile. "I'm glad you had a good time."

"Thanks to you, my handsome baby boy!" She threw her arms wide for a hug, and Jon obediently let her smother him. Over the top of his head, Jon's mother said to Reggie, "First he buys me a house, then my own ceramics studio, then a trip to Europe? I must say, my diabolical plan is unfolding precisely how I'd imagined it thirty-two years ago. I'm telling you, Reggie, lock this one in soon, or he'll be stuck playing mama's boy the rest of his life. Did he tell you he's going to win an Oscar soon?"

"Uh . . . ," was all Reggie could come up with. How to diplomatically tell his mother that Reggie was only using her son for sex?

The tops of Jon's cheekbones flushed. "Mom. Reggie's just a friend."

"Oh! Mazel tov. Good for you. Marriage is a patriarchal scam designed to rob women of money and power," his mother said with undaunted cheer. From somewhere behind her, a ceramic bong materialized. "Would you like some holiday spirit?"

Reggie reluctantly declined, for the first time regretting NASA's stringent drug-testing policy. She felt like a boring stick person among Jon's free-loving flower people.

As she poured herself a bowl of Raisin Bran and settled onto the couch with Jon, Reggie tried to imagine what it would be like to come home to this every Christmas. A quirky, loving, *warm* family. Lazy mornings. Silly traditions. Curling up on the sofa with her feet tucked under Jon's warm thighs, enthusiastically cheering on an eagle with a GoPro strapped to its back as it dived for its prey.

It was . . . nice. Really nice.

Jon finished his cereal, then stretched his left arm along the back of the couch and slid his right arm over Reggie's back. His fingers curled over her right shoulder and began absently massaging it again. At some point, he leaned over and whispered in her ear, "I know it's wrong, but I always root for the mouse to escape the eagle's clutches."

Reggie rolled her eyes. "You would." But her chest felt warm and fuzzy, and her real-world obligations seemed to be some blurry, faraway dream, and though she'd never give him the satisfaction of admitting it aloud, she found Jon's sympathy for the underdog rather sweet.

Maybe, Reggie decided after the first hour, dating Jon wouldn't be so bad after all. But no, that was a ridiculous thought. Where had that come from?

Two hours of nature appreciation later, Reggie expressed interest in going for a jog, and Jon joined her. After their separate showers and a round of languorous oral sex, they returned to the main house for round two of cereal and documentary-sponsored cuddling.

As they settled back onto the couch, that earlier, ridiculous thought popped up again. She mentally batted it away. *No.*

This was a fling. A weekend adventure. Nothing more.

On the TV, the camera went to split screen on a pair of penguins as the narrator remarked, "The male penguin woos his potential mate with a very special gift: a perfectly smooth pebble, selected just for her from among the thousands of similar rocks on this beach. To us humans, this pebble looks the same as any other, but to the female penguin, it is a priceless treasure representing her mate's attention and devotion."

Reggie thought of the Mars-like rock in her makeup bag and snuck a sideways glance at Jon—and found his cocoa eyes already on her. His eyes darted back to the screen, but not fast enough.

Her stomach flipped. She'd tried not to think about what he'd said to her on the flight about *caring.* For the sake of her sanity, she'd stuffed the knowledge that he had feelings for her into a tidy storage box, but her brain kept tugging at the packaging.

And unfortunately for Reggie, her brain was relentless. It worried away at the box all afternoon and all the way through their take-out dinner feast. It fretted at the problem until long after she and Jon had tucked under the navy-blue comforter and kissed good night—an act that quickly devolved into Reggie vigorously grinding against Jon's thigh while he paid fervent worship to her nipples. Events then followed a natural progression that concluded as one might expect: with Jon coming on her breasts while she trembled from her third and final orgasm of the hour.

But even three orgasms couldn't quell her tumult. Long after Jon's breathing slowed and his limbs went heavy on top of her, she lay awake staring at the glowing stars on the ceiling.

It would never work between them . . . would it?

Long-distance relationships were for suckers . . . weren't they?

Would a man like Jon really be comfortable with a girlfriend who was always working—sometimes off planet? Wouldn't he expect more of her than she could comfortably give?

And what about her? How would she feel about Jon as his star inevitably rose in Hollywood? Would she be comfortable seeing photos of him—photos of *them together*—on the cover of tabloids, or turning on the TV and seeing beautiful women with flawless skin simpering over him on the red carpet?

Reggie squeezed her eyes shut and willed the tightness in her chest to release, but it wouldn't. Probably because, deep down, she knew the answers to all these questions.

And none of them were the answers her heart wanted to hear.

CHAPTER 25

The next morning, Jon stepped out into the back garden while Reggie showered and found his mom sipping coffee on the porch, her patterned silk robe spread around her like that of the movie star she could have been.

She patted the spot beside her. "Come sit. I've made friends with a blue jay, and he stops by to say hello in the mornings."

Jon obeyed, then awaited the inevitable.

"Your Reggie is a lovely human."

"I know," he said. "But she's also out of my league. There's a good chance she'll get picked for a mission to the moon next year, and I think that's her focus right now. She's made it clear she's not interested in a relationship."

She hummed in understanding. As dorky as it sounded, his mom had always been his go-to romantic adviser; her advice was unfailingly solid, and it came without a lick of negative judgment. "So that's the problem. She's worried you'll hold her back if you two get serious."

"I don't even know if she likes me enough to consider something like that."

His mother snorted. "Oh, she likes you. Women like her don't have a single fuck to spare for men who haven't earned it. If she's spending the weekend here with you instead of using it as an opportunity to catch up on work, she's got it bad."

Got it bad? Yeah, right. He had no illusions about what Reggie wanted from him: he was her temporary fuckboy. And since he'd interviewed aggressively for the position despite Reggie's repeated warnings there would be no opportunity for advancement, he had no right to complain. What was heartbreak but a small price to pay for a taste of your wildest dreams?

Not that he could say any of that aloud. There were some things you didn't share with even the coolest of mothers.

A mother suspiciously in the know about his love life.

"Hold up." He narrowed his eyes. "How do you know all that about Reggie? You met her yesterday."

She sipped her coffee with wide-eyed innocence. "I know how to use Google, Jon. I'm fifty-two, not stupid. Besides, I set up an alert for your name, and I saw the cute little scandal your publicist undoubtedly orchestrated. That Jacqueline is a brilliant strategist."

Sometimes, Jon wished he had a sibling to share his mother's attention. "Okay, topic change before you reveal you've discovered *Space Dude* fan fiction and I have no choice but to go into witness protection to salvage what's left of my ego. I need to ask you something."

A cerulean bird with a mohawk landed on the fence post and cocked its head at them. His mother smiled in greeting. "There he is. Hi, Steve!"

". . . ," said Steve.

"Mom, do you think I could have ADHD?"

His mother considered this, then shrugged. "I don't see why not. You know, I think it was your third-grade teacher who suggested the possibility."

"What?" He drew back. "Why didn't you get me tested?"

Confusion twisted her expression. "I'm not sure. I suppose it's because we didn't have insurance to pay for it, and besides, you always seemed so happy. I didn't want them to put you in some special class or put you on so many drugs you became a zombie."

His gut clenched. Happy? He'd once dreamed of being an astronaut like Reggie, but instead he'd set a school record for hours spent in detention. He'd flunked algebra *twice*. His classmates had mercilessly teased him for being "dumb" or a "spaz." If he'd seemed happy, it was because he'd learned at a young age that being cheerful, funny, and vaguely self-deprecating was the fastest way to make people like him; after all, insults lost power if he insulted himself first. Even better if he could make people laugh while doing it.

Maybe that was why he excelled so much at acting and comedy—he'd been practicing for a long time.

His mother searched his face, and her blue eyes went liquid. "I'm sorry, baby. I didn't realize."

"It's not your fault," he said.

How could he blame his mom? She'd had him at twenty, and even though she'd had no earthly idea what she was doing with a kid, she'd done the best she could by him. That was really all he could ask for. Seeing the way Reggie's parents treated her made it starkly clear his childhood could have been a million times worse. "When this training stuff is over, I'll go get tested. Although I don't know what I'll do with that information if it turns out I have it."

"Are you unhappy with your acting career?" his mother asked.

"Of course not." The response was reflexive, but even as he said it, Jon realized it was true. Knowing what he knew now, would he still choose Hollywood over becoming an astronaut? Yeah, he probably would. "Acting is fun, and I *do* like making people laugh. I mean, I'm being paid to dress up in costume and make people happy."

"And paid well, might I add." His mother swiped at her cheeks, but she was smiling. "I'm begging you to save some of your next check for yourself, though. You've spoiled me enough, and it's time you're cut off, kiddo. You don't want Reggie to think you're a scrub, do you?"

He pretended to cringe. "Mom, no one says *scrub* anymore."

"Well, I do. And Steve does." She nodded at the bird. "Isn't that right, Stevie-boy? Chicks don't want no scrubs, hanging out the passenger wing of your birdhouse ride—"

"*Mom.*"

She wrinkled her nose. "I know, not my finest remix."

Thankfully, Reggie chose that moment to emerge, her ebony hair freshly dried and flattened. He could smell her shampoo from across the garden, and that—and the brilliant smile she directed his way—made his heart balloon to a concerning size. You couldn't *die* from liking someone so much it hurt, could you?

Probably not. But every time he smelled that shampoo, it reminded him another day had gone by, which meant he was another day closer to never seeing Reggie in person again. He still didn't have her *number*.

His mother introduced Reggie to Steve. Reggie gave the bird a polite nod. "Morning, handsome sir."

Was it his imagination, or did Steve nod back? Jon gave the bird a stern look to convey the gravity of his personal claim on Reggie.

Steve puffed up his wings as if to say, *Good luck with that, buddy.* Even the bird knew the score, apparently.

If Jon were a brave man, he'd find an excuse to get her digits. If he were more confident in himself, he'd spend the rest of the week trying to convince Reggie to date him for real. Heck, if his career were in a better place—if he already had that promised Oscar under his belt—he'd move to Houston to be near her and leverage his star power to make Hollywood studios pay for his commute to and from movie sets.

None of those three things were currently true . . . but maybe the first two could be.

He had a week left to find out.

∗ ⭐ ∗

Reggie felt oddly light as she and Jon strolled along the beach beneath the pink sunset. Maybe it was the glass of wine she'd had with dinner or the way the Pacific Ocean frothed up around her bare feet . . . or maybe this was what it felt like to be happy.

No wonder it felt so unfamiliar.

"I can't believe it's December and I'm walking around barefoot on the beach," she marveled.

"The weather here does not suck." Jon flashed her a wry grin. "I mean, everything else here sucks, and you pay extra for the privilege of experiencing that suckage, but that's part of LA's unique charm."

Her hiking boots—the only pair of shoes she'd brought besides the heels she'd worn Christmas Eve—dangled in Jon's grip. Her toes were cold against the wet sand, but it felt wrong to stomp around on the beach in boots, even though that would have been the practical solution. For this weekend (and this weekend only) she was throwing practicality to the wind and embracing Jon's enthusiastic "fuck it—why not?" approach to life.

Trying to, anyway.

Her subconscious was rebelling against it every step of the way, convinced that with every laugh and sigh of pleasure, she was losing an integral part of herself. *What in fresh galactic shit are you doing?* her brain screamed in the background. *You can't relax! You have work you could be getting ahead on. Every hour you fritter away pretending to be a Normal Person is an hour further away from walking on the moon!*

It would be fine, she reassured her subconscious. They flew back to Arizona early tomorrow morning. In exactly six days, training would wrap and her life would be back to normal.

She snuck a glance at Jon's profile, and not for the first time that day. It was hard not to—the man was hot as fuck, and every time she looked at him, her brain went fizzy and her chest glowed brighter and her blood pulsed harder. He'd let his beard grow in thicker over the weekend, and with his loose hair waving in the breeze, he looked like a romantic knight of old.

Maybe . . .

Nope. Shut it down. The moon is all that matters.

Reggie let out a quiet sigh. At least they had this next week. They'd make the most of every free moment and generate enough memories to tide her over for those endless nights in space.

Funny—she'd never thought of them as endless before. The perma-darkness beyond Earth's atmosphere had always been a feature, not a bug.

They meandered down the beach until they reached the end of a pier, where several locals had set up fishing poles. She slung her arms over the wooden railing and gazed out onto the ocean.

Jon sidled up on her left, his big hands gripping the wood so hard she thought she could hear it creak. He cleared his throat. "Sooo . . . Reggie."

Static electricity crackled beneath her nape. "What did you do, Jon?" She glanced down. No, he hadn't dropped her boots into the ocean. As other possibilities careened through her skull, she wished it had been the boots. "Tell me you didn't book flights back to Arizona for the wrong day."

"What? No!" He paused. Took out his phone and swiped through until his shoulders loosened. He beamed up at her. "No, I did not, and how dare you suggest such a thing."

A smile wormed its way to her lips. "My deepest apologies. I was thinking of someone else."

"Forgiven. As I was saying," Jon continued, kneading the wood rail, "I've had a great time with you this weekend. Really great. You're a cool girl, Reggie."

"Where are you going with this?" Her wrist buzzed and she glanced at it, then wished she hadn't. Her smart watch was complimenting her on meeting her target heart rate for a workout she wasn't doing.

"I think it's time we take the next step in our relationship—"

She straightened in alarm. "We agreed—"

"We should exchange phone numbers."

She blinked at him, still trying to convince her racing heartbeat this was a false alarm. He wasn't proposing they begin dating.

She was *not* disappointed. She wasn't.

"Doesn't your publicist have it?"

"Oh. Yeah." His shoulders slumped. "Jacqui probably put it on the spreadsheet she gave me."

"There we go. Solved!"

"Solved."

"That's all you wanted to ask?" Reggie confirmed, nudging him with her shoulder. Why wasn't he smiling anymore? Jon's unsmiling face was like a night sky during a new moon—far less interesting and a bit eerie.

He began to absently trace something on the wood—something that looked suspiciously like a heart. "Reggie . . ."

"Yes?" She forced her spine to soften. Smoothed her face. He might as well say it. She'd say no, obviously. *Obviously.* It wasn't like she'd recently developed a habit of throwing caution to the wind or anything ridiculous like that to preclude her making the sane, logical choice of avoiding romantic entanglements until the heat death of the universe.

His phone, which was still clutched in his fist, began to ring.

"It's Jacqui."

The words *Don't answer it* were on the tip of her tongue, but she swallowed them. Whatever he had to say could be said after the call, so Reggie shrugged. "Go for it. You did say she owed you a callback about the footage leak."

It was a matter Reggie did want closure on, regardless of how much it had boosted publicity for both their causes. After Milton's so-called interview, she had zero tolerance for media bullshit that she wasn't a willing participant in.

Jon answered the phone and barely got out a cheery "Merry Christmas—" before his expression blanked. Then he turned his back to Reggie so she couldn't see his face.

All she could hear were his next words: "The movie's canceled?"

CHAPTER 26

A Christmas Miracle—but Not for Hollywood Studios

Love may be in the air, but in Hollywood studio boardrooms, the air is anything but lovely. News broke late Sunday night that two of the upcoming year's most anticipated summer blockbusters are dead in the water after their respective directors were secretly married on a boat in the Mediterranean—remarried, that is. Yes, we're talking about none other than visionary director Rudy Ruffino (of the upcoming space-set drama *Escape Velocity*) and ex-wife/wife Mariana del Reyes (of the upcoming underwater epic *Static Equilibrium*), the infamously on-again-off-again Hollywood power couple.

Rumors swirled when the estranged pair were spotted leaving a tattoo shop together Tuesday morning, but gossip blogs went into a tizzy when they posted on their recently created joint Twitter account Sunday afternoon:

Love finds a way, but it's our responsibility to chart the course. Taking a one-year sabbatical to journey to the center of our souls. #remarried #yachtlife #spiritualjourney #sorryfans

Respective studio representatives confirmed the news Monday morning. There is no word yet from *Static*'s lead star, Zendaya, but we received the following statement from the publicist for *Escape Velocity*'s Jon Leo (*Space Dude*): "Though Jon is disappointed he won't have the opportunity to immediately apply the astronaut skills he learned while training with NASA astronaut Regina Hayes, he's excited for opportunities this opens in his filming schedule. We're still finalizing details, but keep your eyes peeled for a big announcement soon!"

Dare we hope this means we're getting a *Space Dude* sequel? With current events as they are (you all know what we're talking about!), maybe a campy, satirical action-comedy is exactly what the world needs . . .

CHAPTER 27

The drive to AHAB from the Phoenix airport was approximately three hours long, but to Jon it felt like three seconds. Which sucked, because he was desperately trying to stretch every last moment in Reggie's presence.

"Look at that!" Jon pointed to a brown road sign. "Petrified Forest National Park. You want to see some scary trees? Or maybe it's the trees that are scared. Huh. Only one way to find out!"

Reggie stared straight ahead. "The trees are fossilized."

"They're rocks too? Even better." Jon flicked the right blinker on so that the cactus they'd passed miles back would know what their deal was. They hadn't seen another actual car for almost an hour. It seemed the week after Christmas wasn't exactly peak tourist season around these parts.

"No, Jon. Let's just get our shit and go home."

"When else will we get the chance—"

"Whenever you want. The park is open year round. You can go inflict your preternatural enthusiasm for nature on one of the poor park rangers on your own time."

The exit swished by.

It made him angry, and he didn't know why. "It's not like you had other plans for the week."

From the corner of his eye, he saw Reggie rub at her shoulder. So maybe he was stressing her out. Fine. He was stressed too. He'd thought they had a whole week left together, and now that everything was coming to an abrupt end, Reggie was acting like things between them were over too.

"I haven't been home in three weeks," Reggie said finally. "Has it occurred to you I have a life to get back to? A real job that doesn't involve wasting time on a project that ended up having net-zero impact on my odds of being selected for the Artemis team. Since the movie is canceled, the studio has no reason to air our behind-the-scenes footage, which means the selection board will never see any of the work we did here. This was entirely pointless."

"So sorry you had to suffer through this experience with me. I guess anything that doesn't help your career must be worthless, right?"

"Right," she snapped. "You wouldn't understand, because you're not going to miss your only shot to get an Oscar. You can still star in some *other* artsy, existential tentacle bullshit. I'm sure there are plenty of 'visionary' Hollywood directors who would be happy to take advantage of your willingness to play any role that you think will impress your deadbeat dad, especially if you haven't read the script ahead of time."

His chest squeezed tight, but he made himself breathe. Everything she'd said was true. He knew it. But why'd she have to say it at all?

Smile, damn it. Make a joke. Do something.

He focused on the way the car sucked the gray road under its hood as he drove.

Reggie's jaw set. "I shouldn't have said that. I'm sorry."

Reflex made him say, "It's all right," even when it wasn't. It wasn't all right at all.

"Stop it!" She let out a little roar. "Stop being so nice. Stop letting me get away with being cold to you. You don't deserve that. You act like you're so dumb, but you're not. You're innately smart and funny and intuitive, and you're probably the kindest person I've ever met. If it hadn't been for you, I'd be flying back from a miserable weekend in Boston right now. But instead, I probably had the best two days of my life. I don't know when I'll ever have that much fun again, and I owe you more than this . . . except this is all I know how to do."

Was his heart dying or merely breaking?

He slowed the car, pulled off the road to a gravel turnout, and shifted in his seat to face her. Like a slow-motion stunt gone wrong, he heard himself say, "I want to keep seeing you after this."

She froze, and her storm cloud eyes stared straight through the dashboard.

Before she even began to speak, Jon knew what she was going to say, but it still hurt. It still fucking *hurt* to hear the voice that had called his name in the throes of passion—over and over and over again—reply in such a brutally flat tone, "Before we started this, we agreed it would be temporary."

"I know what we fucking agreed!"

She reared back, stunned. At least she was looking at him now. "Then why are you asking?"

"Because I fell in love with you, okay?" He closed his eyes and let his head fall forward until it rested on the steering wheel. "Shit."

"Double shit." She swallowed audibly but didn't say anything else.

What had he expected? A sudden one-eighty on her lifelong no-dating policy simply because he'd made her come a few times?

He sat up and scraped a hand through his hair, dismantling his man bun, but he didn't care. Hell, he could go home and shave his head if he wanted to. Jacqui would kill him, of course. But then she'd revive him, because Hollywood publicists were omnipotent, and then she'd lecture him about how being dumped was no excuse for bad hair.

Not that he'd been dumped, exactly. More like his brief showing in the theater of Reggie's life had come to an end. She'd been solidly entertained while it had lasted, but now she was moving on.

If he'd made it awkward, that was his own fault. Only way through it was forward, full speed ahead.

In a deadpan tone he told her, "We can make it to Vegas by nightfall if you want to get hitched, abandon your career, and move to LA to raise a horde of sad shelter animals with me. Or kids, if that's your thing. I'm flexible."

She gaped at him. "Are you trying to joke your way out of this?"

"I'm playing to my strengths," he said with a shrug. "And I figured it never hurts to ask. Oh well! Better luck next time. Now that this travesty of a conversation is over, I'd appreciate it if you wiped all traces of it from your memory. Do you have one of those *Men in Black* forgetting pens? Don't lie; I already know about the aliens."

"I can't just pretend you didn't say . . . what you said."

"You're NASA astronaut Regina Hayes, woman wonder. You can do anything."

He reached for the gearshift, but Reggie's hand closed over his. "Look. I like you. A lot." She let out a shaky breath. "Maybe if—"

A flying shadow rolled over the car, and Reggie's attention fixed on it, her brow furrowing. "What's a drone doing out here? It's circling over us."

He craned his neck to see up through the windshield. The spindly drone hovered above them, adjusting position, and Jon got a better look at the camera mounted on its belly. It was pointed directly at them. "Huh. I thought Mimi and Zach said they weren't planning on coming back to the base."

"I'm getting out. I want a better look," Reggie said, but as she opened the passenger door, the drone's high-pitched whir zipped up an octave, and it flitted to a higher altitude. Then, with a halting dive, it banked to the north and zoomed off.

Toward the base.

Reggie shut the door and glanced at the rental car's mounted GPS screen. "We're only fifteen minutes away from AHAB. Let's get back. My neck hairs are tingling, and I've learned not to ignore that."

"I knew you were secretly a witch."

Reggie didn't laugh. "Yeah." Then, under her breath: "That motherfucker. I should have known he'd pull something like this."

He pulled onto the road. "Who?"

"Milton Fetzer."

A camo-painted ATV lurked in front of AHAB's front door, but Milton needn't have bothered with camouflage.

The conspiracy blogger and two of his cronies were right there beside the base. While he played drone operator, the prize individuals he'd brought with him were attempting to break the pressurized door open with a pair of goddamn crowbars.

Amateurs. Reggie was glad she'd locked the base via the keypad on the outer door—they'd need a whole truckload of crowbars to force open a sealed hatch designed to withstand the vacuum of space.

Milton's drone had followed their progress from a safe distance, but as they neared the base, it drew closer. Reggie fought the urge to roll down the passenger window and give Milton the finger. That was exactly what he would want: more footage of the "goth astronaut" throwing a tantrum.

"What's this guy's deal?" Jon asked.

"A great fucking question," she murmured. Why hunt her down here? Why would he have gone through the effort of finding AHAB in the first place—a location NASA didn't advertise to the public? Something sketchy was afoot, and it made her blood boil.

"Maybe we shouldn't go down there. If this guy really believes Earth is the only planet in the solar system and stalked you just to get a quote about it, he's probably not very stable."

"And do what? Call for help?" Reggie held up her phone. "No signal out here. To save electricity, I powered down the satellite before we left, and I can only reactivate it from inside the base. No, I'm going down there. I won't let these assholes damage the base or the rover for an infantile publicity stunt. The science is too important. Future lunar missions depend on it."

Jon gave her adoring puppy eyes. "You're so hot when you get fired up about science."

She laughed. Being angry tended to imbue her with a false sense of invincibility. Good thing Jon was into that kind of thing, because she was thriving on it right now.

Time for a rematch, Mr. Fetzer. I'll make you regret fucking me over last time. This round, she'd make sure he went straight to jail.

"Park the Jeep at the edge of the crater and hang on to the keys," Reggie instructed Jon as they approached. "When you get out of the car, duck down so the drone can't see you and hide the keys in the wheel well."

He did as he was told without question. "Do you really think he'd try to steal the car?"

"Probably not, but it's a long walk if we get stranded out here." She gave him a wry smile.

When they arrived at the base twenty minutes later, Reggie could see that Milton's henchmen had made zero progress on the door. One of them had given up entirely and was enjoying a cigarette break.

Reggie gave Milton a cheery wave, but to Jon she said in a low voice, "Stay behind me."

Milton sneered at her as she came closer. He'd always been a moist man, and even in the desert's dry heat, his graying curls clung to his forehead. His nose was peeling from the sunburn that covered nearly every part of his flesh except for a triangular strip across his eyes where a pair of sporty sunglasses might go.

"Regina! Welcome. How was your little trip?" He toggled the drone's control pad to make it swoop low enough that she risked bashing into it if she kept walking. The camera's red light glared into her face.

Reggie tried to sidestep.

The drone moved with her.

"Milton, turn it off." Reggie thought of Jon's advice and added, "Please?"

He snickered. *Snickered!* Like a little boy. She was going to force-feed him his own bone marrow. "Why? I have a right to film here. This is publicly owned land, and since we pay our taxes, we're within our rights to reappropriate it. NASA has no right to build their multiplanet propaganda movie set on *our* land."

Jon drew up alongside her and crossed his arms over his chest like a bodyguard who meant business. "Turn it off, or I'll turn it off for you."

"The drone is my private property. If you damage it, I can sue you for—"

Jon snatched the drone out of the air, flipped it over as its motors squealed in protest, and hit the power switch. When the red light faded, he stooped and gently set the machine on the ground, like King Kong showing mercy to a helicopter.

"There," he said, standing. "Now it's off."

Milton looked like he was going to hyperventilate, but he wasn't quite brave enough to challenge Jon's bulk. His face twisted. "You're just another brainwashed government tool. You don't scare me. I know you're out here filming some secret deepfake to fool the public. How much did they pay you to spread their lies?"

Jon feigned surprise. "You can get paid for that?" He turned to Reggie. "Why aren't you paying me?"

"Check's in the mail." She narrowed her eyes at Milton. "Let's talk. Can you ask your friends over there to stop damaging NASA property?"

The cigarette-smoking man tossed the butt on the ground and smashed it with his cowboy boot. "It's ours! We the people paid for that door with our—"

Reggie sighed. "Taxpayer dollars. I know. What exactly is it that you want, Milton? You've obviously gone through a lot of trouble to follow me out here."

"It was worth it. You're going to help us get the proof we need to wake up the sheeple about your little anti-Earth conspiracy. You can start by telling us the door code."

She couldn't help it—a laugh tore out of her. "You've got to be joking."

"Are you mocking me?" Milton's voice went up an octave.

It was enough to make Jon step forward, fists clenched. She laid a hand on his arm and gave him a look that said, *I've got this.* The last thing she needed was Jon starting a fight with this scumbag to protect her honor; Milton was probably salivating at the opportunity to play victim for the media—and the courts.

"I'm not letting you in there," she told Milton. "There's expensive equipment inside, and I know you'll mess with it, if not outright destroy it out of spite. And as much as I'd love to see you in jail for destroying federal property, I'd rather you not impede the advancement of scientific research along the way."

The third man set down his crowbar and strolled closer. He was blocky, buzz cut, equally sunburned, and the proud owner of a faded American flag neck tattoo. Of the three men, Reggie worried about him the most, and not because of the tattoo.

Because of the gun holstered at his hip.

Arizona had relaxed firearm laws, so she wasn't surprised to see it. But there was a certain glint in this man's eye that said he'd been waiting his whole life to whip that gun out and playact his imaginary alter ego, Mr. Vigilante Big-Dicked Patriot Man.

Even now, he let his right hand rest on the gun's butt in silent threat. "You need backup, boss?"

Milton seemed to consider it. "Yeah, you know what, Duane? I think we need to separate these two so they're more encouraged to cooperate. You have those zip ties, Ry?"

The cigarette guy reached down behind the rock he sat on and pulled out a hunting rifle. He wiggled a plastic baggie of zip ties out of his back pocket and tossed it at Milton. "Sure do," he said. Then he propped the gun on his shoulder and trained it at Jon. "Now, none of you move."

Reggie went still.

She had miscalculated. Big time.

✦ ☆ ✰

She let Milton zip-tie her wrists. As far as ill-advised bravado was concerned, she'd peaked during the infamous showdown at the Siberian Bear Corral.

Milton had always been harmless. When had he fallen in with the casual domestic-terrorist crowd? Reggie had hoped to reason with him; she'd have to get him talking to discover whether or not that was still possible.

They thought Jon was the bigger threat, so they zip-tied both his wrists and his ankles. "He's the guy from that space-cowboy movie," Duane with the buzz cut said knowingly. "Ain't about to get gravity punched."

Ry looked at Jon warily. "Maybe we should knock him out."

"No," Milton said, irritation tingeing his tone. "If we instigate, we look like the bad guys. Think about how this is going to play out in the press. We have to handle this delicately."

It seemed late to be concerned about public image, but Milton had a knack for justifying nonsensical things.

"What should we do with him, then?" Ry asked. They had Jon on his knees, trussed up like a sausage.

Milton nodded at the rover. "Duane, you get his phone and keys off him, then put him in the fake moon truck and drive it back to camp. He's a civilian, so I don't want him involved in this next part, but we need him out of the way."

Though they hadn't made a dent in the front door, they *had* managed to get into the rover and dump the contents of its storage trunk in a scattered perimeter. The mess did not bode well for what they had in store for AHAB.

"We keeping the truck, boss?"

"We're confiscating it on behalf of taxpayers. Use the right terminology." Milton narrowed his eyes. "I'll bet testing proves this thing hadn't even left the atmosphere. It's just a normal car with fancy plating."

Duane nodded sagely. "Yeah, you're right, man."

It took both Duane and Ry to drag Jon to his makeshift prison and haul him inside, and they had to drag him on the ground to do it.

Jon grinned up at his kidnappers. "You guys need to meet my trainer, Kahlil. He'll have you deadlifting my body weight in no time."

"Don't need a fancy city boy to tell me how to be a man," Duane grunted, pausing to wipe sweat off his reddened brow.

Reggie gritted her teeth as they dragged Jon over a football-size rock, causing him to grunt in pain.

"You know this is kidnapping, right?" she told Milton. "Let us go before you get in any deeper. This probably isn't going to end the way you think it is, and it's not too late to back out."

His darting eyes betrayed uncertainty, but Milton recovered fast. "You're the ones trespassing. The Constitution protects our right to defend American territory from occupying forces, like your fake-space-agency overlords."

It seemed she and Jon had stumbled on Baby's First Militia career day. What a delight. Had Milton even *read* the Constitution?

When Jon was safely ensconced in the rover, Milton poked Reggie between the shoulder blades. "Get over there and open the door."

"Okay." She slowly walked to the door and stared at the control panel, willing her anger to subside. She'd managed to compartmentalize everything else except that—and her fear for Jon's safety. "Strange. My telekinesis isn't working. You'll have to untie me."

She thought she heard Milton utter the words *fucking* and *bitch* under his breath, but surely she'd misheard. *Surely* he wasn't asking to have his balls relocated to his throat.

Meanwhile, Duane and Jon were peeling out in the rover at full speed, which, from the way Duane kept smashing at the dashboard, wasn't quite up to expectations.

Jon caught her gaze through the windshield. He looked worried for her, and Reggie wasn't sure how to tell him his worry was misplaced. It was him she was concerned about—being moved to a secondary, unknown location was considered Not Good when it came to irrational men with guns.

"Tell me the code," Milton demanded.

"Now you're thinking." She gave him what he wanted, and he unlocked the door. "While you're at it, consider the idea that if Earth were really the only planet in the galaxy, there's no reasonable motive for convincing the entire world that seven other planets exist."

"False hope," Milton spat. "They don't want us to know we're alone. That there's nothing out there."

"There *isn't* anything on those other seven planets! They're completely inhospitable to human life in their current states."

"The state of being a government lie, you mean. Big Pharma's in on it too." Milton glanced over his shoulder at Ry, who followed them into the habitat and shut the door behind them. He held a small camcorder, but his hunting rifle was still present and accounted for—he had it tucked under his arm like a newspaper. Reggie hoped it wasn't actually loaded, because Ry was flirting with taking a bullet in his own cowboy-booted foot.

Ry added, "They already cured our dependence on oxygen, but the antidote is only available to their elite ruling class."

"Yes, save us from the tyranny of oxygen," Reggie said dryly. "The heroin of the periodic table."

"That's right. They've got us all hooked. But we've seen through their lies, and now we're gonna fight back with the T-R-U-H-T." Ry paused, mouthed the letters back to himself, then gave it another shot. "T-R-U-T-H."

So much for reasoning with them. "Where are you taking my friend?"

Milton ignored her. The pair opened the second airlock, and she felt a damp hand settle between her shoulder blades, steering her forward into the central hub. The door sealed behind her.

"Sit," he ordered, pointing at a chair. When she did, Milton nodded in satisfaction. His beady gaze swept around the room. "We'll film your confession here. You're going to tell the world everything you know, starting with how NASA faked the moon landing, how they took the Mars rover photos on Devon Island in Canada, and how Space Station footage of floating astronauts is filmed on high-altitude planes. Then you're going to reveal what you and that cowboy actor are doing out here."

While Milton delivered his manifesto, his partner in crime began opening every drawer and wall panel and chucking the contents into the center of the room. When he found the cooler with the rock samples and supplies from their last field outing, he dumped it upside down and crowed in exultation.

"Look at that! It's one of their so-called moon rocks." Ry held up a plastic-bagged lump of gray shale. The bag was labeled in permanent marker: *Turd Nugget #69 Test Sample #42*.

Milton snatched the bag, eyes glittering as he held it up to the light. "This is it," he whispered reverently. "Collect all the evidence. Search the whole place."

"On it, boss."

Milton glanced at her and curled his lip. "You stay right there. Don't try anything, or I'll radio my compatriot and tell him to ditch your *friend* in the middle of the Navajo wasteland without any water." He patted the comm unit on his belt in warning. "NASA's got no power in the territories."

Reggie couldn't bite her tongue. "Where do you come up with this stuff?"

"The internet!" he snarled.

"Right."

Nearly an hour passed as they methodically trashed the place. She watched them stomp in and out of each of AHAB's units, smashing test vials and ripping lettuce seedlings free from delicate hydroponic tubes, but her thoughts were fixed on Milton's comm unit.

She needed to find a way to send for help. She didn't trust gung-ho Duane not to get trigger happy with Jon, and if Jon got shot out in the middle of the desert, he might bleed to death before help could arrive.

And if Duane had a comm unit in the rover, that meant there was a way to reach Jon. But that left her with a bigger problem.

The range on any of their comms was too short to radio for outside assistance, which meant she needed to either get back to the Jeep or steal the ATV, but that would be difficult with her hands tied behind her back.

She tested the zip tie for the thousandth time, twisting her wrists apart with all her strength, but the plastic only bit harder into her skin. When the pulse points at the base of her palms began to throb painfully, she gave up.

This wasn't good. The longer this went on, the further away Jon was getting from help.

Milton and Ry shoved their way into Reggie's living quarters and tore through her bags. If she craned her head, she was able to watch them as they pawed through her clothes and toiletries. A buzzing sound started, and Ry jumped in alarm.

"What's this?" He held up a slender black vibrator, his expression twisted in horror.

Milton grabbed the toy and held it up at eye level. His eyes narrowed in suspicion. "A homing beacon."

"A what?" Ry shook his head and shoved a cigarette in his mouth. "Goddamn. This is the jackpot, ain't it?"

He fished for a lighter.

Reggie's automatic response at seeing a fire-starting device kicked in, and she blurted, "You can't—"

Wait.

Both Duane and Ry were in a different compartment than she was.

"What? No one ever tell you secondhand smoke is a hoax?" Ry lit the cigarette, took a long drag, then tipped his head back and exhaled a cloud of particulate-laden air—directly into the air filter's sensors.

The alarm pealed. Lights began to flash. In Reggie's head, a silent countdown began: *Five . . . four . . . three . . .*

"The fuck?" Milton cried. He batted the cigarette out of Ry's hand, but it was too late.

. . . two . . . one . . .

Every door in AHAB swung shut and sealed its compartment off from the central hub.

Reggie hopped to her feet, ignoring the frantic banging and shouts coming from behind the door to her living unit. "You'll be all right!" she called. "It's just a safety protocol. Fire is very dangerous in space!"

She moved to the upturned field cooler, found the walkie-talkie, and toed it closer with her foot.

There were two options for rescue, as far as she'd determined.

She could deactivate the fire alarm (a struggle with her hands bound, but not impossible), unlock the front access doors so she could escape, find a way to cut the zip ties, and then drive the ATV or the Jeep to the ranger station at the Petrified Forest. It wasn't the worst idea, but that could take nearly an hour via main roads, and all it would take was one call from Milton for something very bad to happen to Jon.

The thought made her stomach flip. She tried to reason herself out of it—compartmentalize the panic—but it was no use. Her brain supplied a helpful image of Jon's lifeless body crumpled in the dirt, and a wave of nausea hit her. It wasn't *likely* that Duane would resort to violence, but it wasn't out of the question. And if Jon was hurt . . .

No. Traveling by car was too slow, and then there was still no guarantee they'd even be able to find Jon and the rover, wherever Duane had taken it.

There was one thing that was faster.

One thing that could use the powerful satellite mounted atop it to release an SOS with the rover's coordinates—just like it was designed to do for a future Mars mission.

She hesitated. The Mars drone was a multimillion-dollar piece of equipment. She wasn't authorized to test it, much less direct anyone else to operate it, and she'd sure as hell be answering to the higher-ups for the ensuing consequences, so she might as well kiss her lunar aspirations goodbye for the foreseeable future.

Furthermore, Jon didn't have the *best* track record with following instructions.

He'd also have to deal with Duane.

If you want something done right, you have to do it yourself. That had always been her philosophy. Always.

But she'd trusted Jon to drive the rover when she'd been stung by a scorpion. She'd trusted him to operate the drill. And she'd trusted him when she'd climbed out the third-story window of her childhood bedroom and agreed to fly across the country with him instead of spending another Christmas Eve trapped in a prison of filial duty and misery. All those times, she *could* have managed on her own, but because she'd accepted Jon's help and trusted him not to let her down, he'd made her life easier. Better. Happier.

Maybe relying solely on herself wasn't always the optimal solution.

She flipped the walkie-talkie on its side so she could kneel on the talk button and thought about what to say that would get her message to Jon but wouldn't tip Duane off . . .

"Pirate King, this is Moon Otter. If you can hear me, I'm authorizing you to touch anything you want."

☆ ⭐

"No shit, you really met Kid Rock?" Duane asked from where he stood behind the boulder where Jon was ostensibly taking a leak (he wasn't).

Jon also hadn't met Kid Rock, but winning Duane over was turning out to be a cakewalk. The zip ties had already come off ten minutes into the drive. "Yep. I've even got his phone number. Here, let me . . ." He paused for effect. "Oh, right. You have my phone."

"Can't give it back to you," Duane said, but was it Jon's imagination, or did he sound a tad apologetic about it? A few beats passed. "You done yet?"

"Performance anxiety. Sorry."

Jon glanced over his shoulder, eyeing the distance to the rover. Jon wasn't as fast as Reggie, but he might have a decent chance against Duane—if there weren't a gun involved. But even if he could outrun a bullet, what then? He needed to call for help, and Duane had his phone.

They'd been driving for almost an hour. His imagination ran wild, posing increasingly horrific scenarios that might be happening to Reggie back at the base. His peace-loving mother had raised him to consider violence a last resort, but if any of these dudes laid a hand on Reggie— or even *thought* about Reggie in a way that wasn't so fucking respectful you could bless water with the sentiment—he'd gravity punch their punk asses all the way to the stars. For real.

Duane grunted. "Yeah, well, get on back in the truck, then. We're close enough to camp anyway, and you can go there. I need a goddamn beer."

Jon had stalled as long as he could. He came around the boulder and gave Duane a sheepish shrug. The gun still gleamed dully from its holster, but Duane had a habit of absently stroking the handle the way a teenage boy might fondle his junk. This guy was looking for an excuse to shoot something.

Ideally, not me.

But if Jon could give him another target . . .

Jon glanced at the rover. The door on the driver side had been left open.

"You like watching nature documentaries?" Jon asked as they began walking back to the rover.

Duane chuckled. "I seen them before. I like watching them killer whales rip up baby seals. You know, like where they're thrashin' them around, whippin' them back and forth . . . heh heh. That's some funny shit."

"Wow, spicy take. What I'm really worried about are scorpions, though. You know about murder scorpions, right? *One bite, one kill . . .* those murder scorpions?"

Duane grunted. "Yeah, course I know about them."

No, you don't, because I made them up. "Good," Jon said, slowing his pace. When the rover was only a few feet away, he held up a hand, then stopped walking, which caused Duane to do the same. "Because I think I just saw one crawl under the driver's seat."

"Shit!" Duane yanked his gun free and pointed it at the floor mat.

"Shoot it!" Jon cried. "Don't let it get away!"

Duane didn't need to be told twice.

Bang! Bang! Bang!

Boy, were real guns louder than prop guns. Jon clapped his hands over his ringing ears and shouted, "It's still alive! I can see it moving under the seat!"

Bang! Bang! Bang! Click.

Duane let out a sound suspiciously close to a whimper. "Shit, out of bullets! Do you see it moving?"

Jon held his finger to his lips and slowly crept toward the rover. He got his hands on the driver's seat and pretended to sneak a peek underneath. Five bullet holes were still smoking on the floorboards, and a sixth had lodged in the seat. "It's still there," Jon whispered, shaking his head.

With slow movements, he climbed up onto the seat in a squat— and slammed the door behind him.

Duane yelped, "What the—"

Jon punched the lock button. Then he gave Duane a little wave through the window.

It was in that very moment that the walkie-talkie Duane had left atop the center console crackled, and then Jon heard a familiar voice utter the most beautiful words he could imagine:

"Pirate King, this is Moon Otter. If you can hear me, I'm authorizing you to touch anything you want."

CHAPTER 28

Reggie learned that park rangers were not to be underestimated. They rolled up to AHAB followed by a police helicopter and multiple squad cars, and not long after their arrival, matters were settled with a winning combination of handcuffs and three very sad men crammed in the back of an Arizona state trooper's car.

It didn't help that Milton and his cohorts had rather checkered pasts. Duane was wanted for multiple incidents of shooting the video lottery machine at his local bar, and Ry had been involved with multiple trespassing incidents at Area 51, several of which (according to a very exasperated state trooper who'd transferred from that jurisdiction in New Mexico) involved driving up to the front gate in different disguises.

And Milton? Weeks later, they'd learn Milton hadn't paid his taxes in over three years. For now, he was being charged with trespassing and destruction of federal property.

By the time they'd given their statements and everyone but she and Jon had departed, the moon was already rising in the periwinkle dome overhead. It had been a long, grueling afternoon, and Reggie had an even longer evening to look forward to (and that didn't even include a follow-up call to Deb, who was still on vacation). AHAB's base manager wasn't able to return until Wednesday, so even though she'd originally planned to fly back to Houston tonight, Reggie had instead volunteered to stay at the base to begin the thrilling process of cleaning up and inventorying damage.

The only problem was that Jon seemed to think he was staying too.

Reggie had dropped several hints that it was best he get on the road sooner rather than later, but using subtlety with Jon was like throwing sand into the wind.

As he followed her into the central hub, she tried using a heavier hand. "Do you want me to make you a coffee to go? It's a long drive back to the airport."

He paused in the entry and seemed to take in the destruction Milton had wrought. A muscle in his jaw worked.

"Jon?" she prompted. He'd already seen this, though they'd given most of their statements outside. Why was he acting so perturbed?

He stepped over a pile of electrical equipment to close the distance between them. Reggie stood stock still as his hug engulfed her, willing her muscles to relax. But they wouldn't.

"I'm really glad you're okay," he mumbled into her hair.

Her nose squished against his right pectoral, making it impossible to avoid inhaling his earthy smell, and that alone made her bones soften. Her spine curved forward to let her weight shift into him. Like an addict getting one last hit.

Feeling his solidity against her seemed necessary. How else could she prove to her brain that nothing had happened to him, either, and that this wasn't a dream and he wasn't dead?

It would be so easy to sink in all the way and slide her arms around his back . . .

Except this morning he'd said he'd fallen in love with her.

And she'd almost said something really, *really* stupid in return. If it hadn't been for that drone, she would have.

Panic fluttered through her. If she hugged him back, he'd never let her go. He'd smother her with demands for her time and her energy. Expect things from her, like outward displays of affection, sympathy for him after bad workdays, and patience for all his forgetful little errors. Would he want her to support his career by humoring the paparazzi and attending movie-premiere-type events with him? Yes, he probably would, wouldn't he? He'd want the whole package. The authentic girl-friend experience.

And it wasn't that she couldn't try to do all those things for him, but she'd inevitably fail because she still didn't know how to handle expressing her feelings and she certainly didn't have experience balancing romance and her career, and he'd be disappointed and unhappy, but he'd be too *nice* to break up with her, so she'd have to do it, and—

Reggie pushed back, but his arms only tightened around her. "What's wrong?" he asked in a roughened voice.

"Let me go," she said, shoving harder.

He drew back in alarm and searched her face. "Are you hurt?"

She broke free and retreated two full steps, crunching something under her heels as she went. Who cared—everything here was fucked. *Everything.*

And Jon had the nerve to look at her with those melted-chocolate eyes, chock full of love and concern. Goddamn him.

"I can't be with you! Don't you get that? I need you to go."

His expression hardened, but he didn't look surprised by the vehemence of her response. Well, good for him. Maybe he'd picked up on some of her subtlety after all.

"You don't get to tell me what to do anymore, Reggie," he said, voice quiet but firm. "I'm staying to help you clean up, and then we're going to talk."

"You don't get it," she bit out. She gestured at their surroundings, just in case he'd missed the memo. "All of this shit happened because of me. If I hadn't antagonized Milton . . . if I'd just humored him or ignored him in the first place, he wouldn't have gotten so fixated on me. He tried to interview several of my other colleagues, but he wasn't interested because he couldn't get a rise out of them. He saw me as the weak link. The one who would lose her cool if he just pressed me enough, and that's exactly what he wanted. I'm responsible for this catastrophe."

"That's not—" He shook his head. "Okay, I'm not going to invalidate you by arguing. There might even be some truth there. But I think *mostly* this happened because those guys have serious issues that have nothing to do with you. And none of that has anything to do with why I can't stay."

"Because I have the emotional maturity of a gnat!"

"Reggie—"

She threw up her hands. "That's why I can't be with you. I can't be with *anyone*, but especially you, because once the gloss of sexual attraction wears off—"

"It won't," he said with conviction.

"—We'll annoy the hell out of each other. I'll get sick of your clumsiness and your lack of focus and your forgetfulness. I'll end up blowing up at you and treating you like shit when you don't deserve it. And I'll know that I'm hurting you, but I won't know how to stop, because deep down, I'm an inherently cold, loveless person. You've met my parents, so you've seen what my DNA has in store for my future personality."

"You are *nothing* like your parents."

He wasn't listening.

Reggie stormed into his living quarters, the only area that Milton hadn't gotten to—though from the state of disarray no one would believe that—and began stuffing armfuls of his clothing into the first bag she could find.

"You're leaving tonight," she told him. "It's better to have a clean break so our lives can reset properly. After everything that happened here, I need to focus on work if I have a chance in hell of making the Artemis mission. And the sooner you're away from me, the sooner you can move on. Go make another movie. Fuck some pretty extras. Do whatever you need to do."

Jon tried to step in closer—probably to do some touchy-feely soothing shit that Reggie had no defenses against and therefore wanted absolutely nothing to do with. She shoved his duffel bag at his chest, forcing him to fumble for it.

"What if I love you despite all that stuff you think is wrong with you? No one is perfect. We can go to therapy. Everyone in LA is doing it." He managed a wry ghost of a smile. "Jacqui says that self-help is on trend."

Her throat felt like it was stuffed full of marbles, and her view was going blurry, and that was alarming enough on its own without Jon reiterating the forbidden L-word. She hadn't cried in . . . well, she didn't remember. However long it was, it wasn't long enough. How dare tears threaten to break her record after the day she'd had? The audacity.

"Pack up and leave, Jon."

"Are you asking me? Or ordering?" he asked.

"Asking. But don't make me do it again." She wouldn't be able to. The urge to give in to the hope he was offering was like rising water, threatening to drown her.

He clutched his duffel bag like a lifeline, even as its contents slowly spilled out the top. "At least give me your phone number. I can't go the rest of my life never talking to you again."

Indecision tore at her. "Your publicist has it," she forced herself to remind him. To give him nothing he might misconstrue as a chance. "And only if you need to contact me for business-related reasons."

"Right. Business reasons," he echoed.

He broke eye contact and let the now-empty duffel bag fall back onto the bed. His gaze seemed to take in the sheer chaos of his scattered belongings like it was a metaphor for something deeper and not merely an unimportant quirk of personality. Jon didn't care about keeping his things tidy because he wasn't a neurotic queen of darkness like Reggie— he was a human ray of fucking sunshine who couldn't be bothered, because life was too short to give a damn about the little things.

Jon Leo was far too good for her. If he was the sun, then she was the lifeless moon. He deserved someone who thrived in his light instead of casting it back down to Earth as if it were worthless.

"Goodbye, Jon," she said quietly. Then she turned around and left him to pack, terrified that if she waited a moment longer, she'd change her mind.

CHAPTER 29

Late February

Reggie was knee deep in shit when Deb walked in. Fortunately for everyone involved, the shit wasn't real—it was a custom slurry of doughnuts and apple juice that NASA's enterprising team of engineers had whipped up from the cafeteria.

"And that's why we always like to joke on the ISS that the toilet is easy to miss," Reggie was saying. She was rewarded with snickers and groans from the batch of ASCANs—their newest astronaut candidates—kneeling beside the disassembled toilet she'd splattered with the slurry.

Sure, it looked gross. But it was better these wide-eyed trainees learned how to repair the Space Station's new toilet in the presence of Earth's gravity, since everything floated in space.

Everything.

Deb took in the befouled toilet in front of Reggie and raised a brow. "I wondered why there were no chocolate doughnuts left when I had lunch. You have a minute, Reggie?"

She nodded and handed a wrench to Mi-jeong and her partner, Liam, who'd already volunteered to give the repair puzzle a first crack. "Good luck. Remember, this is a two-person job, so one of you handles the suction, the other one handles the wrench, but make sure you're communicating. I'm going to step out for a few minutes, but if you have any questions, that man over there is your master of toilet ceremonies."

Reggie pointed at Wes, who gave a good-natured wave. He stood next to the whiteboard, where he'd drawn a detailed, *Magic School Bus*–inspired diagram of a single poop's journey through NASA's new $23 million space toilet. Unlike the one that Reggie had used during her stints on the ISS, this one was actually designed for women to use too. It had only taken two decades to determine the necessity of that upgrade—not bad, all things considered.

Deb led her out of the building and into the courtyard. "Let's take a walk. I could use some fresh air after a morning of endless meetings," she said.

They'd finally been given a break from the relentless rain, and snippets of sun peeking through the clouds made everything sparkle. It wasn't quite spring yet, but little brown birds were out in force, getting a head start on the season. A particularly chubby one landed on a fence and looked at Reggie with its head cocked in curiosity.

Jon would think he's cute.

Reggie squashed the thought. She'd had a lot of those over the last seven weeks, and time didn't seem to be curing her like she'd hoped.

Deb asked about Reggie's day and how the ASCANs she and Wes had been assigned were coming along, and Reggie responded easily. She'd stopped questioning Deb's efforts to make small talk; though they seemed to be happening more and more these days, Reggie didn't mind it as much as she'd used to. Maybe she'd thought of Deb only as an intimidating mentor for so long—despite the mere fifteen-year age gap—because of Deb's relationship with her mother. But the more she got to know Deb as a human being, the more she realized Deb could be a friend too.

Well, if Deb weren't chief astronaut, anyway. That part *was* still intimidating.

"Any update on the Artemis selections?" Reggie asked, because she couldn't help it. There'd been no update for almost two months now.

Deb smiled. "That's actually what I wanted to talk to you about."

Reggie stopped walking, her gut knotting into a ball of anticipation—and hope. Her hand found its way to her pocket and closed around her little red sphere of rock. "Did I—"

"Nope."

An invisible hand plunged into Reggie's chest, plucked out her heart, and hurled it into the parking lot.

Her voice faltered. "Wh-what?"

Deb sighed and encouraged Reggie to sit next to her on the steps of a nearby building. "This shouldn't come as a surprise, Reggie. But it also shouldn't be such a disappointment."

"Who's the mission commander?" Reggie demanded woodenly. The MC always had a say in backup astronauts. Maybe there was still a chance—

"I am."

"You?" Reggie realized how it sounded and quickly added, "Of course, you're the most qualified of all of us. And you've earned it a thousand times over. I just . . ."

"Thought I'd pick you for my team?" Deb gave her a wry look. "Oh, don't look so betrayed. Do you have any idea how much I wanted to? Aside from me, you're one of the best active-duty astronauts in the program. Sure, you have some work left to do in improving your interpersonal skills, but you've already improved in leaps and bounds since your stint in Arizona, and if there's anyone who can accomplish such a daunting feat, it's you."

Reggie felt tears brewing again, but that had happened more frequently since Arizona, and even more since she'd started talking to a therapist recommended by NASA's chief flight surgeon, so she knew what to do now. She let the hurt sweep through her instead of fighting against it.

Reggie might walk on the moon someday, but she'd never be the first woman to do so. Deb would.

Deb would.

"Fuck, I'm an idiot." Reggie swiped at a rogue tear. "Congratulations! You're going to be the first woman to walk on the moon."

"Goddamn right I am." Deb grinned, then lightly nudged Reggie's side with her elbow—though "lightly" for Deb meant Reggie had to stifle a wince. "And you, my intrepid protégé, are on track to be the first human to set foot on Mars."

Reggie sat back, stunned. "How can . . . that's not for another decade. I'll be—"

"Forty-five?" Deb raised a brow, daring Reggie to deem the age too old. "You're the best candidate to command that mission, so don't blow it by wasting what's left of your radiation limit on the moon. Start training for Mars now. Prepare yourself so that when the time comes, you're so beyond ready that the selection board won't even bother to pretend there's choice involved. And for the love of God, live your life. Go find your handsome space dude and try to be happy so you have something worth coming back to Earth for."

"*Jon?*" Her cheeks heated. "I told you things between us were strictly professional."

"Huh. That's not what Katya said when she and I went shopping last weekend."

Deb went shopping *with Katya?* Even Reggie didn't have the stamina for that endeavor anymore—a relentless gauntlet of excess alcohol and excess spending. And now, apparently, excess gossip.

It was time she and her bear-loving friend had a talk.

✩ ⭐ ✩

Reggie found Katya suntanning in the backyard, even though it was in the low sixties and her lawn chairs were drenched in the morning's rainwater. A boy band sang about booty and devotion on her portable speaker. Something fizzed in a flute by her side, but it wasn't champagne if the empty cans of White Claw in the recycling bin had anything to do with it.

"When do you go back to the motherland, again?" Reggie said in greeting.

"Never. Look how pale I am. Is it not obvious I am a ghost sent to haunt you?" Katya eyed Reggie over the top of her oversize shades. "You do not look sad today. What happened?"

"I had a chat with Deb."

Katya sat up. "And?"

"When did you two go shopping?" Reggie accused, taking a swig from the flute. She cringed at the saccharine residue it left in her mouth.

"Last Saturday." Katya shrugged. "You said you did not want to leave the house. You said you were tired. You said you wanted to watch the *Space Dude* movie again and masturbate and cry."

"I did *not*."

Katya raised a brow.

Reggie raised her chin. Like hell would she cop to watching Jon's feature film for the purpose of either activity. It just happened to be a good movie. It made her laugh. It managed to ward off the ever-present clouds plaguing her mood lately. And she would absolutely not apologize for staying in on a Saturday afternoon to watch it. Again.

Reggie changed the topic. "I'm sure you've heard the good news?" Katya claimed to have no connection to any spy agency, past or present, but somehow she always knew about all the hottest news and gossip before Reggie did. (When questioned about this uncanny talent, Katya would look at her dead in the eye and say in a sinister tone, "I have one of those faces you can trust.")

"Of course." Katya snatched her drink back, then handed Reggie the tablet she'd been reading from. "But I think you are speaking of Mars, and I am speaking of *this*."

The tablet screen had an article from the *Hollywood Reporter* open, and her eyes locked immediately on the headline.

Space Dude *Star Jon Leo Gravity Surfs His Way to a $1.5 Million Deal with Netflix.*

Reggie couldn't stifle her gasp. Her eyes flew to Katya's, who was watching her with a smug expression.

"Two sequels and a rerelease in theaters next month," Katya said. "Oh, and he will be costarring with Zendaya. But this is not important. My only concern is the happiness of my dear friend Reggie."

Now that she'd seen his movie, she felt confident this was incredible news for Jon. It was obvious to anyone watching that he'd had fun filming *Space Dude*. And having fun was where Jon seemed to thrive. Instead of trying to fit himself in a box to impress other people with awards and obscure prestige, he would be playing to his strengths. And with a deal that lucrative, Jon wouldn't have to worry for a long time about accepting roles he didn't want.

"I should call to congratulate him," Reggie murmured. After Arizona, she'd planned to never think about Jon again. She'd lasted a week before she'd emailed his publicist to get his contact information.

But then she'd written his number down on a sticky note and folded it into her wallet and hadn't looked at it.

More than a few times, anyway.

The important thing was, he hadn't called her either. Which was exactly what she'd wanted—for him to move on.

"If you require a dress for the premiere, I have conveniently acquired several new options."

"Don't be ridiculous. This is a courtesy call. From a friend to a friend." Reggie pulled her phone out and typed in his number from memory. For some reason, her pulse sped up.

Katya made a show of standing up, stretching, and gathering her things. "I am in need of a shower. I will not be listening from the window upstairs. Your privacy is very important to me."

Under normal circumstances, she'd have a sardonic reply, but in that moment, Reggie was too keyed up to care. The universe had provided the ideal excuse to call Jon, and she was doing it. Right now.

Merely out of professional respect for a friend, of course.

Nothing more.

The phone rang. And rang. And rang.

And then it went to a voice mail recording. "Hey, it's Jon! Leave a message and surf that gravity wave, dudes!"

The beep sounded, but words bottlenecked in her throat at the sound of his voice.

What could she say? What *should* she say? Merely that she was happy for his success, or that she wanted to speak to him again, or that she missed him and wasn't sure she'd ever stop feeling that way? That she felt some strong emotion for him? Except she didn't know what it was—she only knew that it felt like the weight of a thousand Jupiters was pressing down on her chest cavity whenever she thought about something that would make him laugh only to realize he wasn't there.

Hands shaking, she hung up.

Katya's voice sounded from the second-story window. "Do not be discouraged. We will go to the premiere. I have chosen a dress."

Reggie fell back in the lounge chair so she could look up at Katya's upside-down face and said morosely, "You just want to meet Zendaya. Also, we're not invited, and I have no reason to go. It's not like I'm going to show up out of the blue after two months of no contact and confess my love for him, right there in front of everyone on the red carpet."

"Ah. I see."

Reggie narrowed her eyes. "We're *not* going."

"Mmm."

"Say it. Say, *Reggie, we are not going to the premiere.*"

Katya merely smiled.

CHAPTER 30

The last time *Space Dude* had premiered, Jon had taken a rideshare and worn an off-the-rack suit he'd bought earlier in the afternoon at the mall. Now he sat in a limo (still rented, but with leather seats, complimentary Veuve and Twizzlers, and remote-controlled colored lighting!), wearing a burgundy Tom Ford suit and paisley bow tie that Jacqui insisted was "playful, yet edgy, with a dash of whimsy"—whatever that meant. Netflix had also shelled out for a theater twice the size of the original location for this rerelease, and there would be a fog machine *and* a bubble machine at the after-party, per his request.

Plus, they'd stopped for pizza on the drive over, so this time around his growling stomach wouldn't drown out all the on-screen explosions. There were definite perks to bypassing the so-called A-list, even if his enthusiastic appetite meant Jacqui was constantly waving her Tide pen at him like a weapon. Kahlil still made him cry sometimes, but his new workouts were focused more on applicable martial arts skills and less on morphing into an overinflated balloon man—his movies were for teens, after all, and he wanted them to know you could still be a Space Dude with a soft bod.

He should have been happy.

"We've got a few minutes before we arrive; do you want to run through your speech?" Jacqui asked him. She sat across from him with her laptop propped open on her knees. Her opalescent white suit shimmered beneath the slow-changing rainbow light.

He flipped his phone upside down so he wouldn't be tempted anymore. "No, I've been rehearsing."

"Do you have note cards? Because I made a backup set just in case . . ." Jacqui started to reach into her bag.

"I appreciate it, but I actually brought mine with me." He opened the lapel of his suit jacket to show her the proof.

Jacqui sat back, suitably impressed. She gave a little laugh. "This new you is going to take some getting used to. I guess I should stop making backup copies of everything."

"No!" he blurted in alarm. Then, in a more measured tone, "Uh, I mean, let's not get hasty here . . . it's still a process getting used to these meds, and some days I'm a little more distractible than others. But it *is* kind of nice being able to hear myself think."

Well, mostly. Unless he had *too* much room to think, which inevitably led to thinking about Reggie.

He wasn't supposed to think about that.

Or stare at his phone screen, where it showed his missed call from her three weeks ago. (Her voice mail message had been seven seconds of empty static; probably a butt dial. If he called back, it would be awkward, and maybe he'd look desperate. But what if it hadn't been a butt dial? What if she was waiting for him to make the move?)

He was supposed to be moving on.

Besides, he had more important things to think about. Like the email he'd gotten from his dad this morning.

Jon (a.k.a. "Son"),

This email is long overdue. I know I have not been the best Paternal Figure in your life, and I can't make up for that. Truth is, there's a lot

321

I have to make up for. As I get on in my years, I've started to reflect on the Sins of My Past, as one does, and Lord, the list is long enough to pave my road to Hell and back.

I'd blame The Way Things Used To Be in the industry, but I've been enough of a coward for too long. In a way, it is a Blessing I didn't have a hand in raising you, because you are already a far better man than I ever was. And the Legacy you are building will do the Leo name prouder than I ever did.

I don't expect your Forgiveness, and I sure don't deserve it, but that doesn't stop me from wanting it. If you can spare it for an Old Man with nothing to offer but Regret.

The reason I am reaching out to you now is because my people have received an Opportunity from the good folks at Netflix. They want me to star as the Villain in *Space Dude 3*. A good role for an Aging and Tarnished Star like me. But I told them I couldn't accept until I had spoken to you. I will respect if you have no interest in making a movie with an Old Devil like me. However, if you would be interested, I would look forward to "surfing the gravity" with a handsome Young Buck like yourself!

Regards,
Brian Leo (a.k.a. "Dad")

It wasn't much of an apology. If anything, it was a thinly veiled invitation to his dad's own pity party, designed to leverage Jon's sympathy into saying yes to working together on a movie (his father had to suspect that Jon had veto power on casting choices written into his contract—after all, they had the same agent).

Nevertheless, Jon would probably give him the go-ahead. He'd spent all of three seconds considering whether to reject him out of spite, and then he remembered that he'd spent his whole life wanting to kick his dad's ass—and letting him sign on as Space Dude's nemesis was the perfect opportunity to do it. Over and over.

Besides, his dad was an acting and martial arts legend. What kind of shortsighted idiot would he be to turn down an opportunity to work with Brian Leo?

"I decided I'm going to green-light the thing with my dad," he told Jacqui. There, now it was out there, and he couldn't chicken out.

"Good. The publicity from that will be the perfect postpremiere bump." She narrowed her eyes, her fingers tap-tapping on her keyboard. "I'm taking the lead on the social media announcement, though. That man does his own Twitter posts, and I cannot stand all the arbitrarily capitalized words."

Jon shrugged. "I just thought it was an old-guy thing."

"What, you turn sixty and suddenly start writing everything like the Declaration of Independence? No. I won't let it happen to you."

"That's the Virgo I know and love. Glad to have you on my side, Jacqui."

She flashed her canines. "Don't worry. I might be a Virgo, but you're paying me Aries rates. Did you see the updated contract I emailed you?"

"I did. You're a cutthroat mercenary who's taking blatant advantage of my newfound wealth."

She beamed at him. "Thank you."

"I signed it yesterday and forwarded it to Peng to do whatever financial managers do with that stuff."

"Excellent. Oh! One more thing." Jacqui's tone went deceptively casual. "I gave out a few extra VIP tickets to some superfans. Make sure to stop by those seats before everything gets started to sign autographs."

He frowned at her. "Duh. That's where my mom and her boyfriend are sitting. I told her I'd stop by afterward."

"Go beforehand." Jacqui raised a brow. "Trust me."

He opened his mouth to question her further, but the limo slowed to a stop. A muffled cacophony of voices and music filtered into the vehicle. Bursts of camera flashes came through the tinted windows. Noise and brightness and chaos: this was where he'd always thrived—but he'd never been at the center of the storm before, only a bit player at its edges. What if he couldn't handle the fame? What if it sucked him up and launched him into the atmosphere without a parachute?

What if he ended up like his dad?

He took a deep breath.

A thought came out of nowhere: *I wish Reggie were here.* She'd be his rock, anchoring him to the earth. She'd never let his head get too big when studio execs and fans blew hot air at him all day long. He could let her be the star; he'd use his excess energy to keep her rocketing skyward.

Jon tucked his cell phone into his breast pocket. He'd call her back tomorrow, even if it was awkward, because he loved her, and he had to stop being a coward.

He had to try.

Someone swung the door open from the outside, and the maelstrom swallowed him.

⋆ ⋆ 🌠 ⋆

The movie premiere was nothing like Reggie had thought it would be.

"Keep it moving, thank you!" A black-clad woman with a headset waved Reggie and Katya through the stanchions set up beneath check-in tents for non-red-carpet guests. Someone had handed them name tags on red VIP-labeled lanyards, but then they were herded into an interminable line. It was like being in line at airport security, except everyone was glamorously dressed.

They could barely see the A-list entrance at the front of the theater because vinyl "walls" with *Space Dude*'s logo patterned across the surface had been set up along the red carpet to serve as a backdrop, and the guest entrance was cordoned off behind it. Even when she'd craned her neck and peeked through the gaps in the wall, Reggie could only see the backs of heads from the throng of press-type people and fans crowding the walkway. The only notice that someone important had arrived was a sudden burst of frenzied calls and camera flashes.

"Can you see Zendaya?" Katya whispered. She wore a vivid fuchsia dress that hugged her curves with a matching cape affixed to her hip by a giant bow. Katya had named a designer Reggie had never heard of and a price tag that no one in their right mind should hear of, but she looked like she belonged, unlike Reggie.

Reggie tugged at the low neckline of her silver dress and longed for something formless and black.

"Keep it moving! Thank you!"

"Go," Reggie replied, nudging Katya's back. They'd already gotten the evil eye from two separate staff members who didn't appreciate Katya's lackadaisical pace and unsubtle peeks through the wall gaps.

Katya, bouncing on her tiptoes to see over the crowd, went wide eyed. "Look, it's—"

"Excuse me! You two!" Another headset-wearing woman appeared in front of them.

Reggie winced and grabbed for Katya's arm, but she clutched only air. "Sorry. We're moving. Katya, let's go."

Her companion whirled on the poor staff member, planted her hands on her hips, and said to Reggie in Russian, "This goat is getting on my last nerve." Then, switching to English with her accent laid on like chunky peanut butter, Katya declared, "Do you have any idea who we are? This entrance is for peasants. Take us to the red carpet immediately."

The staff member was not amused. "Ms. Volkov and Ms. Hayes? I have instructions to escort you directly to your seats."

"Ah yes. Excellent." Katya gave a regal nod.

Reggie wanted to melt into the floor, but as the employee pulled them out of line and guided them directly to the entrance, it became clear their special treatment was unrelated to their collective misbehavior.

"Sorry about the wait," the staff member said before ushering them through an emergency exit hallway, up a set of concrete stairs, and into the dim theater. She showed them to a pair of seats on the second-level balcony, directly to the left of the stage. There were only eight seats in this section of theater, and all were empty but for two people Reggie recognized.

"Reggie!" Jon's mother cried, leaping to her feet. "I'm so glad you came."

Reggie let the hug engulf her, and when it was over, she introduced Katya to Jon's mother and Tom.

"Have you spoken to Jon yet?" his mother asked once they'd settled into their seats. "He promised he'd stop by after the showing."

"Not yet." *Not at all, actually.* Her stomach drummed a nervous pattern, and it echoed through her veins. Maybe she should have texted Jon to let him know. Katya's insistence on keeping their appearance a dramatic surprise suddenly seemed childish.

It wasn't too late. She could shoot him a quick one-liner right now, before the movie started. Something like, *Hey, just came by to show my support!* Nothing overly sentimental. That way, if he'd already moved on, she could slink away with minimal collateral damage to her ego.

Reggie cleared her throat and stood. "I'm going to use the restroom before everything starts."

She ducked into the back hallway and, with a surreptitious glance over her shoulder, stole into the emergency stairwell. It was quiet in here with the orchestral music and crowd muffled by the door, and in the plain fluorescent lighting she felt more like herself. Even in her glaringly shiny dress.

With a slow breath for courage, she pulled out her phone and started a text.

"'Jon,'" she murmured aloud as she typed. "'Just wanted to say . . .' No. Delete, delete, delete. 'Just a heads-up that I'm here . . . at the premiere . . .'"

She closed her eyes. *This is stupid.*

Everything she could think to type sounded wrong.

"Reggie?" came a deep voice, straight out of her clandestine dreams.

She jumped, her phone jetting out of her hand and clattering onto the cement. "Jon?"

"Oops, I didn't mean to startle you." Jon jogged up the remaining steps separating them and reached for her phone, just as Reggie recovered enough to do the same.

Their heads collided.

"Sorry!" they said in unison.

Even as she rubbed at her forehead, her whole body buzzed with instant, giddy energy.

Jon was here. In the flesh. As big and solid and disgustingly attractive as he'd been when he'd stepped off the aircraft the first time she'd seen him. His chocolate-brown eyes still made her chest feel like her lungs were overinflated. The dimple at the corner of his lopsided grin still made her pussy clench in longing. But the lines of his face seemed more relaxed and his cheeks weren't as hollow, which meant he was happier and healthier, and that alone was enough to make her want to fling herself into his arms and drown in the earthy scent she'd missed more than space.

Her skin was on fire. She knew she was staring, but just like when she'd called him and left that empty voice mail, everything she wanted to say was stuck behind some wall. A crumbling, decrepit wall, but a wall nonetheless. "Hey," was all she could manage to say.

"Hey, yourself." He shoved his hands in his pockets—or tried to. He looked down. "Huh. Fake pockets. What do you know. I guess fancy people don't need real pockets. Though it has a breast pocket on the inside. For phones, I guess. Not breasts. Though that wouldn't make any sense. Why would you put breasts in a pocket when they should be out there for the world to see?"

"I don't know. Yes, I guess . . . breasts should be out there."

"Cool. I'm glad you agree."

She nodded slowly. "Cool."

He smoothed his not-pockets and cleared his throat. "So I guess you saw my . . . thing."

"Your big deal. Yes, it's a really . . ."

"Big deal?"

"Yes! Congratulations."

"Thank you."

From beyond the metal exit door, a man's voice could be heard announcing over loudspeaker that the premiere would begin shortly and that the main cast members should join him onstage for speeches.

Alarm zipped through her. He would have to go, and she'd lose this moment.

"Jon, I came to . . ." Her throat closed.

Why, *why*, was it so hard to say? What was wrong with her? Had she really come all the way here, dressed up like space Barbie, to choke at the pivotal moment? She was doing *better* at expressing emotion. She'd been to therapy, for fuck's sake. After six whole sessions, she should be completely fixed already. (Well, *technically*, her therapist had said not to expect immediate results, but that warning was obviously for other people and not Reggie fucking Hayes, because she was the best at everything.)

She squared her shoulders and tried again. "What I'm trying to say, Jon, is that—"

"You're desperately in love with me and can't live a moment without me? You want me to rent an apartment in Houston so I can live there part time and we can try dating and take it slow, and if it doesn't work out, that's okay, but if it does work out, that's amazing?" He lowered his voice to something gravel-rough with emotion. "Because that's what I want."

"Oh."

She couldn't say more, because something was happening. Maybe something significant. It felt like that wall was finally collapsing, and everything was threatening to pour out, and that definitely couldn't happen *here*, in an emergency stairwell, right before Jon was about to go onstage. And definitely not when she was wearing enough eyeliner to paint the entire stairwell black and still have enough left over to blot out the sun.

Jon closed the distance. They were toe to toe. "Is that a yes?"

She nodded. His face went blurry. *Fuck.* "Yeah," she croaked. Her fingers delved into her strapless bra, desperate for something to do that didn't involve letting her tears fall. "I want to give you this."

"Here?" Jon raised his brows. Glanced behind him. Returned his gaze to her tits. "I mean, I won't say no—"

She withdrew her old good-luck anorthite. The pseudo–moon rock that she'd kept in her pocket for years—until Jon had given her a bigger and better dream to hold on to. *I love you,* she tried to say, but what came out instead was, "I know it's kind of ugly and the edges are kind of sharp, so it's a little uncomfortable to keep in your pocket if you're wearing tight pants, which I know you do, so be careful. But you gave me a special rock, so I wanted to give you a rock that was special to me. Like penguins do. It's not a real moon rock, obviously; it's actually a rare compositional variety of plagioclase that occurs in mafic igneous rock—"

His mouth closed over hers, swallowing the rest of her geology lecture. Her arms came up to loop around his neck so she could kiss him back with as much eager pressure as he was showing her, but even with her sensible three-inch heels, she was still too short, so he backed her up against the wall and lifted her so she sat on the railing, and they kissed properly.

His hand was sliding up her calf, looping her right leg over his hip, and then halfway up her thigh when the sound of a door opening below startled them enough to come up for air.

"Jon?" Jacqui's voice called. "You're wanted onstage for speeches, remember?"

Jon didn't break eye contact, but his eyes went wide. "Busted," he whispered. Louder, he called, "Coming!"

Jacqui's heels clicked up five steps. Stopped. "I see you're busy." She chuckled. "Good. I'll buy you a few minutes." Her footsteps retreated, and the door closed behind her.

Reggie gave him a slow, hesitant smile. "You should probably go."

His head fell forward to rest against hers. "But it was just getting good," he groaned.

"Maybe after the show we could—"

"Get a drink?" he offered quickly. "There's an after-party we could go to, if you're up to it. I want to introduce you to people. Nothing official, just . . . you know. Unless you want it to be official. I mean, I'd like it to be official. But only if you want. And then afterward, we can definitely go back to my place. My real place, not my mom's guest-house. And we're one hundred percent fucking. Because I really, *really* like your tits in this dress, and honestly? I don't think they need me to give a speech, and I've already seen this movie, so maybe we could find a closet somewhere . . ."

She laughed. Gravity didn't exist; she was light as air and just about as solid. "I'd love to go to the after-party with you. Can Katya come too? She's really excited to meet some of your costars. Well, one costar in particular. Actually, maybe it's best if we leave Katya behind."

"Whatever you want. I mean that," he said earnestly. "I want you to feel comfortable. I know this is your first time doing this relationship thing, and I don't want to screw this up like I've screwed up so many things before."

She shrugged. "You won't."

"You sound really confident about that."

"Of course. You're with me now, and I'm the best. We're going to be a fucking badass team. And I won't let anyone on my team fail. Ever." She gave his shoulder a light punch. "Now go out there and . . . what's the phrase?"

He leaned in until his lips touched her ear. "You know very well what it is."

"I do," she confessed. "I watched your movie so many times. Especially that scene where you punch the pulsar waterfall and radiation makes your shirt melt off. I watched it over and over again."

His whole body pressed against her, and she reveled in the hardness of him.

"You're such a creep," he growled into her ear.

"I know," she breathed.

"You rubbed one out to that scene, didn't you?"

"How dare you. I am one of NASA's most accomplished astronauts, a role model to our nation's youth, and a goddamn feminist inspiration." She licked his perfect jawline.

He groaned. "You *did*."

She pushed him away and slid off the rail, standing on trembling legs. "Go, before someone has to escort you onstage with your dick looking like it's going to rip a hole in the fabric of space-time," she said.

He looked down at the hard-on in question and grimaced. "I need to talk to my stylist about going up a pant size."

"Don't you dare."

"You promise you'll be here when I get back?"

"I promise. Now, get out there and . . . y'know."

"Say it. Just once, I want to hear you say it." He gave her puppy dog eyes, and she swayed toward him, compelled by his adorableness. He had to know she was helpless against such unspeakable power.

There was probably a goofy grin on her face, and she didn't care. At all. She blew him a kiss, and then, looking deep into his eyes so he knew her words came from the purest depths of her heart, she said softly, "Surf my gravity wave, Space Pirate."

AUTHOR'S NOTE

Dear reader,

I wrote this book for other people like me, who love space and science but who also want to read about two people falling in love. But when it comes to space science, I'm merely a casual fan and by no means an expert. So in order to do Reggie's character justice, I did my best to research what it's really like to be a NASA astronaut preparing for the Artemis lunar base mission (which, at the time of this book's publication, hasn't happened yet). The majority of the science in this book is accurate, but I did take some liberties in the name of furthering the romantic plot—since it's for a good cause, I don't think science will mind.

For example, the fire-safety system on the ISS doesn't slam all the doors shut with only a five-second warning; in the event of a fire, astronauts will manually close doors and shut off airflow to the affected area (the lack of convection and fresh oxygen starves the fire until it dies out). But hey, they haven't built the lunar base yet—maybe they'll implement my absurdly impractical version instead! Also, while the lunar solar panels *will* likely be strong enough to support two individuals . . . lying down . . . on the surface, they'd probably find all the sharp edges rather uncomfortable. And the Mars drone that Jon loves so much doesn't exist (as far as I know)—but it *is* loosely based on *Ingenuity*, the helicopter that hitched a ride to Mars aboard the *Perseverance* rover. There are several smaller science cheats I finagled into this book, but I won't bore you by listing every last one here. Of course, if you have specific questions or want to talk about anything space related (or just want to share cat pictures), I would love to hear from you on social media or through email.

If you're interested in learning more about what our real-life astronauts do to prepare for space, I highly recommend *Endurance* by Scott Kelly, which informed much of my background on Reggie's character. For a cool look at what a NASA analog base is like, check out the documentary *Mars on Earth: A Visit to Devon Island*. And if you simply want to know what our current off-planet humans are up to, most NASA, ESA, and Roscosmos space farers have better Instagram accounts than Reggie does, and they share fun insights and photos of what they're working on up there.

On a different but equally important note: I based Jon's story on my personal experiences with ADHD. If his story resonated with you but you haven't been diagnosed, it's something I urge you to explore. While everyone's experience with ADHD is different, many people who aren't diagnosed until later in life share a host of *feelings* about it, both good and bad. There's sometimes a bitterness or sense of loss in wondering what your life might have been like if you'd had earlier access to the tools that could help you manage your ADHD, but there may also be some joy or relief in confirming that you aren't actually lazy or stupid—nor any of the other negative labels you've spent your life hearing from others or inside your own head. Fortunately, the online ADHD community is incredibly supportive, and sometimes it simply matters to know that you're not alone. The fact you made it this far means you're already awesome.

Thank you for reading my book. May you all surf that metaphorical gravity wave, and live long and prosper.

XOXO,

Jen Comfort

www.jencomfort.com

ACKNOWLEDGMENTS

When astronauts go to space and actors accept their Oscars, they're only able to do so because of the teams of talented humans who've spent months working behind the scenes to ensure their success. The same is true for authors when they write a book.

Not me, though—I did everything on my own!

Just kidding. Seriously. I had no clue how to write a book when I first started, and I'm still not sure I do now. Fortunately, I had a wealth of talented humans who helped me fake it well enough to get this book published. Starting at the beginning of my writing journey with Elias Flynn, who helped me refine my first-ever pitch at ECWC, and Tera Cuskaden, who heard that first-ever pitch and became my #RevPit editor the following year. Along the way, I was fortunate enough to befriend Kate Maybury, who was my first-ever beta reader and has helped me with every single pitch rehearsal, manuscript draft, and "I know this chapter sucks, but I don't know why; help me!" email ever since. Then I somehow got lucky enough to meet Alexis De Girolami and Jo Segur, my other two main beta readers, whose feedback and enthusiastic emojis made this book funnier and sexier, and the rest of the Pony crew—Elle Beauregard, Lin Lustig, Jasmine Silviera, Kelly Blake, Chris Henderson-Bauer, and Mel Francois—whose friendship, manuscript notes, industry advice, moral support, and Discord chats kept me motivated to write through all of . . . well, you know.

In a literal (and literary) sense, this book wouldn't exist if my tirelessly badass agent, Eva Scalzo, hadn't taken a second chance on me, my writing, and my bonkers story ideas—I'm so grateful to have her in my corner. Nor would it exist if my editor, Alison Dasho, hadn't been a kindred space nerd who passionately championed this manuscript under the (so very correct) belief the romance world needed an astronaut romance like this one. Bonus thanks to Krista Stroever, my inordinately patient and eagle-eyed developmental editor, whose Virgo energy ensured (most of) my words made actual sense. And to Riam Griswold, my copyeditor, who undertook the level of superhuman detailing that I could never in a million years attempt to match without my brain imploding, and to my proofreader, Susan Stokes, who polished this book until I could see my reflection upon its grammatically correct surface. And extra credit to the whole team at Montlake who played a role in bringing this idea to life, including but not limited to Cheryl Weisman (the absolute rock star who put all the puzzle pieces together to make this finished product into an Actual Book), Jillian Cline, and Anh Schluep.

Most important of all: the people in my personal life who made my dream possible. Beginning with Mark Gill, who picked up that one shift for me that time I desperately needed a writing day, in exchange for the promise I'd include him in the acknowledgments of my first book. (See? I didn't forget! A romance writer always pays her debts!) My parents, who've been enthusiastic about my writing career even though I quit my full-time job to pursue it, which surely made them a bit nervous, since I've got two cats and a dog to support. My lifelong friends, Anchi Howitz and Anna Kim, who've seen me through my worst fashion mistakes and been a phone call away through all my existential crises. Virginia Fellows, my fellow restaurant manager turned friend, who went on so many outdoor doggy adventures with me during the Unspeakable Year and whose pragmatic advice also kept me from losing my mind through it all. To my Dungeons & Dragons guys: Ryan Stadler, Kyle Smith, Dave Newell, and Justin Churchill . . . thanks for giving me something to look forward to every week, even if it involves cleaning up imaginary crimes too egregious to put into print. My aforementioned two cats, Leo and Zero, and my husky-malamute pup, Taiga . . . I know you can't read this, but please sense this message I'm sending into the ether: you're the goodest pets to ever have existed.

Finally, to Ben, who unquestionably believed in my dream and did everything in his power to make sure I attained it—*you're my hero.*

ABOUT THE AUTHOR

Jen Comfort is a Portland, Oregon, native who dabbled in astrophysics before spending a decade working in restaurants in New York City and Portland. Now, she writes romantic comedies about hot nerds with very cool jobs. She spends her free time growing plants destined to die before their time, playing video games, and encouraging her two cats and malamute-husky dog to become internet famous with zero success.